Published in the United States of America.

First Publishing Date November, 2010.

ISBN: 978-0-9832556-1-1

The characters and events portrayed in this book are fictitious. Any similarity to real persons, living or dead, is coincidental and not intended by the author.

# Thine Enemy's Eyes

## A Fantasy Romance By

## Tonya Adolfson

Book 1 of the Souls of the Saintlands series

* * *

*Dedicated to Alison. Don't ever be afraid to try for what you want, but be careful what you wish for…you may get it.*

**In loving memory of my mom, Rosemary Virginia Manley, who always taught me to be true to my own self. Thanks Mom.**

* * *

Thanks for coming in & joining us in our visions! I hope you enjoy walking through my mind!

## _Acknowledgments:_

_First and foremost, I'd like to thank all the people who were inspirations for this book:_

_Gwen, for Gwen; Erik, for Dom; Brady for Markus; Cris E and Joe R.for Nicolai; and my daughter, Artemisia Marie, for Marie-Elizabeth and son Morgan for Alan. Without each of them, these characters could never have the depth they do._

_I'd also like to thank Rowena, Diana, Emma, Shauna, BG, Brady, John and Tenaya for their feedback. I especially would like to thank Larry Baker, the best Communications professor a student could have, a great editor and a good friend._

_I'd also like to thank Gwen J. and John F. for endless hours of editing and consultation. Thank you guys!_

_Thanks especially go to the artist Sting, for Soul Cages, and Counting Crows for August and Everything After, which were played incessantly during this writing. You're amazing._

_And finally, to my wonderful family: Morgan and Misha, for being so tolerant of Mommy's work; to my Daddy, Ray Lamar Manley, for inspiring me to tell stories for the sheer pleasure of my audience; to my Mom, Rosemary Virginia Manley, for reading historical romances; and to my wonderful loving husband, Todd, for being everything a Prince needs to be._

# *<u>Book One</u>*

*"All the ways of a man are clean in his own eyes, but the Lord weigheth the spirits."*
*~ Proverbs 16:2*

*"Your enemy is never a villain in his own eyes…."*
*~ Robert Heinlein*

**Chapter One:**
**"He that is despised, and hath a servant, is better than he**
**that honoureth himself, and lacketh bread."**
**~ Proverbs 12:9**

"I want you to assassinate the king."

His Lordship Myrgen the Grey, Chancellor to Charles and Elizabeth, King and Queen of Mervolingia, stood before the cage which protected him from the deadly woman within. Myrgen kept a distance of about five feet, his grey woolen unisex robes full and loose around him like fog. He knew better than to get near her, despite the woven fetters binding her hands and ankles in front of her. He had not given explicit instructions for her hands to be bound behind her and this meant she could still kill him if he was careless. He was fully aware of her abilities and had no intention of getting anywhere near her reach. Should the woman in the cage free herself from her bonds and get her thanatoid hands on him, he was uncertain his Nubian guard, Michael, would be able to stop her before she killed him.

"I have already told you my answer. Did your agent not convey my negative response, or did I need to remove digits instead of just breaking them?" Her voice was silken poison, the Caratian accent barely noticeable beneath the perceptible threat she exuded to Myrgen; an assurance his body would never be found, out of mercy to his next of kin.

"I wasn't asking a question," he tossed something at the base of the cage, metal clinking against the iron base, "and I think you'll find my previous offer is no longer on the table."

The once-ivory background subtly embroidered with tulips in beige silk, overwhelmed by the purple lioness stretching to the base of the cloth, now sported a new trait, that of blood. Fresh blood. The favor was the mark of Lady Tanglwyst de Holloway, owner of The Tanglwyst Trading Company, and Catriona's secret partner. More importantly, attached to the favor, there was a small necklace with a Caratian family crest on it. The necklace was a gift of a very helpful couple, to her son.

Her ebony hair hung along her toned olive-skinned shoulders and her viridian gaze stumbled about the gloom of the dusty air around her, barely aiding her in the forbidding light. She had the ability to invade a person's soul and strip it of his or her secrets, and thus, no one had ever seen anyone lie successfully to Catriona Morganosa. This fact alone made her the most deadly weapon against Myrgen in Mervolingia and he had insured the agent within her blood at present had a long duration and a very specific purpose: To impair her access to her special ability and nothing else. He needed her sharp and aware of what he was saying, but he couldn't risk a single secret he possessed getting into her hands any more than he could afford his person suffering that fate. The drug had been made with that purpose in mind by his own hands and he was very pleased to see it working. He would not need to get his hands dirty at all. If things went that direction, he had Michael.

Catriona studied Myrgen, trying to view his soul and discovering the purpose in the drug he had made. Since she would undoubtedly remember everything about this encounter later, he gave up nothing more. They had never met so she would know him more by reputation than anything. His ability to cover his tracks made him legendary in the Back Streets, Mervolingia's seedier side where lives had bags of gold attached to them, either as backers, or bounties. Myrgen always paid up when he said he would, and never threatened idly.

"Don't take too much time." He turned away from her as her eyes closed in defeat and left the chamber without another thought.

* * *

"Do you think she'll do it?" Michael sealed the door to the catacombs carefully, removing all traces of passage to the bulk of the maze in the absent-minded gesture of habit. Myrgen insisted on this because the catacombs of the Mervol Royal Palace where Myrgen lived were treacherous and confusing, and he refused to risk the life of a curious servant due to his lack of foresight.

"I'm certain," said Myrgen. "We have her son. As much as I despise involving children in something like this, it's done now, and she knows it." They stood outside the secret entrance to Myrgen's chambers; the paths navigated as much by feel as sight in the glow of the single candle lantern. The palace had suffered three fires since it was originally built and as wings were destroyed, they were buried or simply abandoned, and a maze of corridors was the result. There were several passages for the servants to bring food from the outlying kitchen buildings into the palace, but none of these connected to the two which housed escape routes for the king and queen. Myrgen's own room wouldn't have a passage behind it except that it was Charles' room when he was a young king under Catherine's regency. Myrgen turned to Michael, the small light casting insidious shadows across the conspirators' faces in the dingy corridor.

"What about the Queen-Mother, Catherine?" Michael asked. "Have you heard back from your sources as to her scheduled return?"

"Apparently she's due to return here within the month for a visit. I know she's not scheduled to stay long. Charles refuses to be alone with her and can barely stand her being in the same room. She's been assigned to the Papal City as an Ambassador of Mervolingia. My sources say she's still dealing with her 'victory' on Saint Michael's Day." Myrgen's disgust was blatant, an unusual thing for this secretive man. "The new Pope has the documentation of Plantyn's assassination and is contemplating the justified excommunication of the Royal Family."

Michael cocked his head. "I wasn't aware you were so offended by the incident."

"More than you know."

"Are you not Augustinian, Myrgen?"

"Wholesale slaughter should never be condoned, my friend, regardless of one's faith. That massacre was an embarrassment, not a victory. The vigorous pat on the back the king was receiving from the Bishops and most of the Augustinian Church is sickening enough to make me switch my faith."

Michael nodded. His own Nubian homelands had been invaded by a vicious man claiming to be bringing the faith of the Saints to the heathen masses, but his mission he had also been bloodshed and had resulted in few converts.

"Don't leave that woman alone too long," Myrgen said as he triggered the catch which would allow him into his room. "We need her to be put on her way, not to escape. If she navigates these tunnels and finds her way out, we're undone. Do you have the drug?"

"Right here," Michael replied, patting a pouch in his hip.

"Good. Get on it then, before the one that dulls her senses

fades from her system. It's the only reason we have her in this position to make our request. I just hope our source was right about her."

"As do I," Michael said with a glance over his shoulder. "Are you certain of the source?"

"It allegedly came from Dominic D'Medici. That family, if any, would know about assassins. Now go. The sooner she's on the task, the sooner the kingdom is no longer inflicted with the king's cruelty and weakness."

Myrgen entered the concealed chamber attached to his quarters, closing the door behind him, and took a moment to relight two candles which had blown out, the other twenty-two flames dancing with the shadows on the wall. He gazed up at the huge portrait of an elegant, ruby-haired woman resplendent in emerald silk and pearls. Her beautiful doe-brown eyes glittered from a hint of gold in the rims of the iris, and these subtle tricks of the artist made them seem to come alive and dance with graceful abandon in the firelight. The portrait had been done in secret by Myrgen himself, an amazing talent few knew he possessed, and was lit by a candle for every year of her life. He touched the painted woman's gloved hand, neatly life-sized, and whispered, "And the less time you must endure the prison of your marriage, my Queen."

* * *

Michael slipped quietly into the catacombs, leaving Myrgen to his homage. The trek was well known to him, but took a while to get from the entrance to Myrgen's chambers down to the ancient torture chamber, left over from the Inquisition. It always gave him time to think, and he liked it for that reason. The woman in the cells below intrigued Michael. He found her features to be painfully beautiful and terribly familiar to him, as if she descended from a royalty possessed by those of his own culture. Michael was Nubian, his dark flesh common among the jungles and deserts that distinguished that distant continent. He was an oddity here in Mervolingia, since most Nubians were sold in Mande, but Myrgen never treated him like a slave. He had not expected that when he was first brought to this kingdom.

*Michael had been out to slay a lion as his rite of passage.*

He had studied his feline quarry before killing him and claimed the heart as proof he had succeeded. He was returning home when he was hit with a net and captured. He was thrown into a slave ship and taken to Mande. A man bought him and went into a tavern with Michael in tow. The man was an obnoxious drunk and ended up in a fight. Michael was still bound in irons when the first attacker turned on him. As a strong young man raised to be a warrior, he used the chain on the first man who came after him, slapping the man across the face with it.

This repelled the first man well, but it angered one of his friends, who came after Michael, intent on teaching him his place in polite society. Michael, most impolitely, shattered his jaw with an upper cut with his double fists. The man hit the door to the tavern, flying out of it with sufficient force to knock the wind out of him, simultaneously alerting the townsfolk to fetch the city guard.

Myrgen was in the city at that time, on business for the Mervol crown and spending his new salary, when he saw the first of the tavern patrons hitting the cobblestones outside the pub. He moved over to the man and barely missed being hit by the next patron who attacked Michael. Myrgen, uncontrollably curious at this point, went to the tavern and opened the door wide while being sure to stay out of the path of catapulting bar patrons. It turned out he chose the correct side to stand on because Michael put another patron through part of the doorjamb opposite Myrgen.

Myrgen and Michael got their first looks at each other then. Michael ate up much of the doorway with his huge frame and was utilizing items at hand, or foot, in his defense. The man he was fighting at the time was trying to bite him, so he popped his elbow into the man's jaw, causing a few teeth to disintegrate. By Nubian standards, Michael was a true vision of strength and determination, his long bones and impressive muscles perfectly offsetting the youthful good looks which were actually becoming less attractive as the fight wore on and some of his attackers got in successful shots.

By the time the City Watch arrived, there were four more men on the streets and Michael was on the floor with six men holding him down with great effort. Myrgen watched the entire scene from the doorway. Michael's owner had been crushed beneath the heavy table Michael's captors were using to secure him. Michael fully expected to be executed for his crimes and

*Myrgen took great interest when Michael was taken away and locked up.*

*At the jail, Michael was sentenced to death for slaying fifteen men single-handedly in a tavern brawl. This impressed Myrgen, and he used his money and influence to take possession of Michael, switching the paperwork in the jail, and thereby sentencing another man to death while sending Michael to the auction block. Michael figured he did both men a favor.*

*The virulent circumstances surrounding their first meeting caused Myrgen to name this new acquisition "Michael" after the Archangel who led the battle against Lucifer's minions, as a reminder to Myrgen of how deadly this man could be, and Michael accepted this. After that, Myrgen treated him with the respect of a trusted ally instead of a possession, much to Michael's surprise, and a loyalty was forged in the bonds of that trust. It took a year for Michael to learn enough Mervolingian to understand more than hand gestures, but Myrgen had been ever patient with the process and now Michael was proficient.*

Myrgen had trusted Michael with everything from his life to his secrets, either of which Michael could have destroyed at will, but Myrgen actually intrigued Michael. One thing was certain: Life with Myrgen was never boring.

* * *

The Nubian opened the door to the chamber where Catriona's cage was housed and went over to stand in front of her prison, looking at the captive woman before him. Long waves of ebony hair, which she usually bound in a braid for convenience, announced their freedom across her toned shoulders and back. Her mocha skin, darker in the scant illumination of the large room, held her customized scent from a special oil, its suppleness arguing against her known profession of captaining a ship. She was decorated in doeskin leather gloves and boots, unencumbered by the societal feminine trappings of veils and hoops which emphasized the gender differences to an extreme. However, the leather-trimmed trews and high-necked bodice lined in battle-ready silk, which she wore without a corset, refused to deny her status amongst the fairer sex, and even without her special gift of insight, she could see that the young Nubian feared his admiration of her would interfere with his mission should he linger overlong in contemplation.

He took out a bottle and darts from his pouch and tainted the tips of the weapons with the drug. She caught the sheen of the poison on the darts and recognized the treatment. It was a rather insistent sleeping agent, about as virulent as the drug used to dull her senses. *That* drug was starting to wear off and she could move like normal but deeper brain functions were evading her. He loaded the dart into the blowgun and stood before the cage facing her. Catriona lifted her head, leveling her gaze at the man. His eyes widened as he recognized the signs of the drug impairing her wearing off, and his movements took on an urgency as he blew the first dart, aiming for her shoulder. Catriona moved imperceptibly left and the dart passed through the cage, harmlessly. Puzzled, he loaded another dart and blew.

He missed.

He moved closer, to give the dart less time to be avoided, and executed.

The dart slid across the floor behind the cage to lie next to the other two.

He moved in.

This dart hit one of the bars as it passed her, the pinging noise loud in the darkened room.

He moved in. Again.

She dodged. Again.

Frustrated and angry, the young man took the last two darts out of the case and threw them to either side of her, determined to hit her.

When these last two darts came at her, she dodged the left one but jerked her head as if caught by the right one, grazing the metal edge of her shackles across her own cheek, drawing a thin weal of blood. Concealing the dart, she slowly raised her head, looking again at the Nubian, turning her cut cheek slightly more to her aggressor, expertly showing but not showing him the damage.

He saw it, and relaxed, satisfied. He puttered around the table, resealing the bottle and straightening his doublet. She wavered and then collapsed into a heap near the back of the cell, falling so her hands would end up near one of the errant darts. She was hoping to grab one and conceal it as he waited for the sleeping agent to fuller affect her. As she lay there, her face closer the dart,

Catriona noticed the substance on the tip was changing color, blurring into a shade and substance which was deadly instead of sleep inducing as she'd first surmised. The subtle scent of a jungle paralytic she had seen before had seeped into the wood containing the dart tip. The two agents were reacting and had she actually let the dart graze her skin, well, she realized her "playing dead" act would be considerably more convincing. It made no sense for Myrgen to capture her, coerce her into this act with kidnapping, and then kill her before the job was done. The Nubian, while young, had clearly used a blowgun before today and was expecting her to be knocked out, not dead. He also knew nothing of this interaction.

That changed her plan completely. If she poked the Nubian with the dart as she had planned, he would die instead of falling asleep, telling her nothing. The drug in her system was taking its time wearing off, a trait for which it was undoubtedly engineered, but it *was* wearing off. She just needed this man still around when it did. If she could read him, she would know what was really going on. She closed her eyes, waiting for him to do whatever he had planned.

The door to the cell screeched open, echoing off the stone walls. There was something important about the stone walls, but her addled brain could not remember the significance. All deeper thought and memory was caught in a muddy matrix, blending together. Her survival skill was all she seemed to be able to access. Her muscles responded as she expected, for the most part, meaning if she could stall enough, she would be able to shake the drug's influence. She hoped to be able to do it in time.

She felt the man disengage the rope from around her waist, freeing her from the attachment to the cell. He picked her up, careful and gentle, which confused her. He was obviously here to maintain her capture, yet he was not treating her with the disregard of a man accustomed to this line of work. He was also not handling her like a rapist, a behavior with which she was all too familiar. His hand placement, his positioning on his shoulder: This was respect, and its presence disarmed her. She was accustomed to receiving respect from her crew, her people, her family, but from a kidnapper and ruffian? The conduct confused her and she forgot herself for a moment.

She swallowed.

The Nubian stopped, dropping her to the floor. She opened her eyes just in time to see his large fist hurtling towards her jaw, then she was fading into blackness.

*Chapter Two:*

*"Let not thine heart decline to her ways, go not astray in her paths. For she hath cast down many wounded: yea, many strong men have been slain by her. Her house is the way to hell, going down to the chambers of death."*
*~ Proverbs 7:25-27*

Myrgen walked into his bedroom and sealed the queen's portrait in the secret room behind him with a habitual flick of a stone trigger. He moved over to the hearth and stoked the fire, brightening the room and making it a bit more comfortable. He poured himself some raspberry brandy and sat staring into the fire. The scintillating dance of flames seemed to enrapture him, but it was actually his thoughts which held him in their arms.

Myrgen had come to the palace in 1572 to replace the Royal Castellan who had died the winter before. He had been trained in Bordeaux to handle finances and never believed he would rise to such a position. Apparently his connections, both at court and in the Patras Back Streets, had worked to place him in the palace so he would have more leverage to serve them. He had managed to return quite a few favors during his two-year role. He had also successfully garnered several more favors in return. He sipped his brandy and recalled Charles and Elizabeth's wedding, which was the first time he had laid eyes upon the royal family.

The Queen-Mother Catherine D'Medici had worn matronly black, her age beginning to show heavily in her face. Not exactly a pretty woman to begin with, her face seemed to settle in a frown naturally which served only to emphasize the less attractive aspects of her features. While serving in the palace, Myrgen had seen portraits of her as Henry's Queen. She had once been beautiful, her voice dulcet and her hands delicate. Sometimes, Myrgen still saw those qualities, but not very often. Most often, Catherine's appearance perfectly reflected her internal ugliness.

The king's brother, Alexander Edward Angloume, the Duke of Anjou, was resplendent, ocean blue velvet trimmed in gold and glass beads the color of a stormy sky, and many ladies of the court jockeyed for his attention, eager to become the concubine or possibly the beloved wife of such a fine gentleman. Alexander did not seem fooled by the waves of fancy tossed his way. Myrgen knew now that Alexander never courted any of the ladies, and never had a woman warmed his bed. For this reason, many believed he preferred men, but Myrgen had noticed that the man did seem to occasionally desire women. Alexander was just very put off by the currying of favor that dominated courtly life, much as Catherine dominated Charles.

Charles was dressed in a rich gold and royal blue velvet doublet and Mandian breeches, the immense Cloak of State draped elegantly behind him. His golden-brown hair was starting to harvest touches of grey from the burden of the Crown, and he sported the small beard and mustache of the times which, on him, actually looked attractive. His attire was appropriately regal and distinguished, befitting a King on his wedding day.

Myrgen had been observing the royal family for several minutes when his sister tapped him on the shoulder and whispered, "Here she comes." In walked an amazing vision of a woman, auburn hair loose and flowing. A gown of gold and green velvet cast itself around her, shimmering like sunshine on a perfect lake. The choir was singing, but to Myrgen, it seemed like the saints themselves were announcing Elizabeth's way into his heart. As she walked past Myrgen in the church, she glanced over at his sister and graced her with an incredible smile whose light washed over him like a long-awaited dawn.

Myrgen sighed deeply at the memory of watching her dance that night at the Grand Ball after the feast and that he had been allowed to ask for a dance from the queen, which she had accepted. They danced to Belle Qui, a rich and stately dance favored by Mervol royalty and it had ended far too soon for Myrgen.

Myrgen got up and poured himself some more brandy, surprised at how quickly the first glass had gone. He cast his thoughts back to the catacombs and Michael at his task, and hoped his friend was an appropriate match for the dark captive. She was a woman, to be sure, but a terribly dangerous one according to his sources, and an adept assassin. He entertained the thought of having her do away with Catherine after she got rid of Charles. By that point, the blood spilt would be more than warranted.

Charles had been ten when he assumed the throne of Mervolingia. Catherine had been his regent until he had come of age six years later. She had, however, gotten used to being in charge of the kingdom, something wholeheartedly and apparently wisely denied her during her reign as queen, and she dominated every aspect of Charles' life, from choosing his wife to choosing his friends and faith. There was talk of Catherine standing at the end of her son's bed during the consummation of his marriage, coaching him on how to take his wife.

But more than this, Catherine loved to play the eternal judge. She swung easily between supporting the Holy Augustinian Church, the dominant religion which believed that the role of the Saints was to speak to Heaven on the behalf of Men, and Emilianites, who believed all men were Heaven's Children and could speak directly to Heaven. A dangerous game in most cases, but Catherine claimed to be attempting to maintain balance between the two. It was Myrgen's opinion such matters should be left in the hands of The Almighty, but Catherine would have just assumed he was referring to her regardless. At present, she was visiting her daughter Margaret and son-in-law Henry, whose wedding day on the twenty-fourth of September almost two years ago was blessed by the blood sacrifice of three thousand Emilianites six days later as the Emilianites celebrated the princess's wedding, thanks to Catherine's pressure.

Count Gabriel Plantyn, a border town General in the Mervol army, had become a trusted advisor and friend of the king's, displacing his mother from his side. But Plantyn was also an Emilianite and having one church over the other controlling her son was a dangerous thing. She saw Plantyn as a monster, someone who needed to be eradicated from the world. Catherine tried to convince Charles to rid the world of this man, but he refused, steadfastly supporting the man despite her criticisms and complaints.

So Catherine stewed and steamed until an opportunity presented itself. On the twenty-fourth of September, 1572, she was to marry her daughter Margaret off to Henry of Vitus of the powerful house of Guise. This event was to gather all the Emilianite nobility together as this act could seal the political breach. Catherine had reason to believe a civil war was brewing because of enemies she had at court, so she took matters into her own hands to destroy the Count Plantyn. The opportunity arose on the twenty-fourth of September.

An assassin, intent on killing the aging Count who led the Emilianite forces, missed his mark and instead killed a lieutenant.

Plantyn had been wounded slightly in the right shoulder, but definitely not killed. Myrgen had been in attendance when the news was delivered of Count Plantyn's wounding on the twenty-second of September. Charles had rushed to Plantyn's side as he was brought into Patras, reassuring his friend as he walked with him to the tower in which he was to rest. Catherine had snarled in anger at His Majesty's support of this fiend, but was more irritated that the attempt to assassinate him had failed. Alexander had seemed annoyed as well, and when Charles had returned from his visit with the Count, the two of them had spent an hour and a half working diligently to persuade Charles to sign the man's death warrant. Myrgen had never before seen Alexander so passionate about anything and this passion seemed to fuel his mother as they wore away at Charles forbidden friendship.

Finally, around one o'clock in the morning, after the utterly exhausting day, Charles cried out loudly enough to be heard clearly in Myrgen's chamber, "By the Saints! Since you deem it well to kill the Count, I agree, but all the Emilianites in Mervolingia must likewise perish, so that not one be left later to abrade me." Alexander had left the room, scattering servants in his wake. Myrgen was frightened by this blanket statement and knew his sister was staying with some Emilianite sympathizers. He left to get her to the safety of the Augustinian church and as they were a block away from its front door, he had seen the Grand Guard Marcel's forces crashing down the door of a house with which he was very familiar. He left Tanglwyst to get the rest of the way on her own and ran into a nightmare that would haunt his dreams forever.

The blood of over three thousand Emilianites coated the streets of Patras in a single night and Myrgen himself was witness to several feats of atrocity. Images from that night would remind him frequently of the ability of men to destroy at the slightest provocation or opportunity. Catherine had written an account of the start of the night, and what had happened and something she had said, allegedly that Plantyn tried to kill Charles, had garnered the support of the Pope himself. It was a decision that would get that man assassinated and a new Pope, one Myrgen knew well, put in his place. It was unacceptable that Heaven's representative on Earth could be duped into wholesale slaughter.

The next few months brought news of the deaths of

thousands of Emilianites across the face of Mervolingia, from every province. Each place heard in turn of the Pope's praise of the killings and took it upon themselves to follow suit. By mid-November, there were reports of as many as seventy thousand dead. He marveled some days that he still found himself willing to claim membership as an Augustinian, but he had not practiced since that night.

Catherine had spread the word the king had managed to vanquish an assassination attempt upon His Royal Personage, much to Myrgen's repulsion. Alexander had disappeared but Catherine assured nobility and commoner alike that he was searching for those guilty parties who had tried to murder their king. The Pope's return missives originally congratulated them on successfully escaping such cruelty. Myrgen had seen the reports from the Papacy and read the letters with increasing abhorrence, knowing it was Charles' weakness which had brought the kingdom to this end. Had he not bent to his mother's whims, the kingdom would not have had this horror imbrue its national soul.

However, the Archbishop of Patras himself had smelled falsehood and when the previous Pope had sent a missive to Catherine to complete the job she started, that missive somehow found its way, with Myrgen's help, into the hands of the Bishop and several church officials. The Pope died (assassinated Myrgen was certain) several months later and the new Pope had come out against the killings in Mervolingia. Catherine was in the Papal City most of the time now, unable to get a private audience with Charles any more, sent there to "renew her faith" and try to clean up the mess she had made. He didn't know how many people suspected she was behind the Massacre, but Myrgen felt absolutely certain those deaths were on her shoulders.

Her only saving grace was that before, and after, the Massacre, she had always been loyal to Mervolingia. This was at the heart of everything she did. He could even understand her reason for wanting Plantyn out of the public eye as being the King's best friend and suspected Charles' defiance in the face of her desires and awareness of the revolts that could occur were just him standing up for himself for once. It was this childish foot-stamping that had led to the more drastic measures Catherine had taken to rid her son of this influence. There were hundreds of ways to hide a friendship, especially if one were king.

Myrgen placed his goblet upon the small table next to his hearth chair and went to his bed, removing his robes as he did so. The brandy was soothing, but he didn't want to overindulge at this time. He had gotten drunk often after the Massacre, exorcizing his own personal demons left over from the incident. The nightmare had come almost nightly ever since and it was a rare night when he actually got up *after* dawn. About twice a month, he would be tired enough to sleep all night and the nightmare be damned. Tonight marked a different reason for him to stay alert. The deadly woman in the catacombs below had a mission to do and he sincerely hoped she could do it. Whether he loved the queen or not, Myrgen wanted Charles dead. If this woman assassin could be counted on, he would be dead in very short order.

*Chapter Three:*
*"They are all plain to him that understandeth, and right to them that find knowledge."*
*~ Proverbs 8:9*

When Catriona opened her eyes and saw the huge, old church before her, she knew at once she was unconscious, not dead, and she exhaled, finally. A low fog scampered around the edges of the churchyard which faded into darkness despite the always full moon. She had never gone to where the darkness began, knowing somehow the edge of the world lay there. The church was one which was destroyed six years ago in a fire, yet here, it always looked freshly built.

The ornately carved white wood doors were standing open, as usual, and she walked in. She knew she would find a priest in here named Father Benjamin, and that the priest had given his life protecting her infant son, Alan, just after he was born, ten years ago. The recollection of the incident which changed her life, her world, her entire perspective, returned unbidden as she walked through the doors. It was always this way when she was unconscious, and she steeled herself as she relived the horror once again...

*She felt herself falling, the feel of a hand on the center of her back still lingering as she dropped. The ground thrust towards her, and she hit, torso first. Her body snapped like branches in a storm, rent from the tree to pierce the air and soil, cascading to the stone floor in a cacophony of crunching ivory and bursting blood vessels. She felt the pain of impact at first, then her neck hit, and she felt nothing else. Dust from the stone filled her nostrils, cut with blood and the taste of metal, and one of her teeth fell down her throat, stabbing into the side of her windpipe. Her body came to rest and she saw the light above wreathed in heads and shoulders of her attackers. Then the heads disappeared, one by one, to leave a rectangle of light. Stone on stone scraped the air and the rectangle became smaller and smaller until it was gone...*

Catriona stepped the rest of the way through the church doorway, and collapsed. She had no idea what the vision was, but it was persistent. Treachery sang through her body, as strong as the taste of iron and blood in her throat. She felt betrayal that the people above her had put her there, the feel of the hand that pushed her into the pit writhed on her flesh like maggots. She felt the life ebb out of her as she lay in the dust and she had to fight to regain it once she was in the safety of the church. It exhausted her and she spent several minutes on her hands and knees inside the doorway of the church, forcing her lungs to draw breath.

She didn't know why her subconscious gave her this vision, this horrible dream, but being here in the church was both pleasant and unsettling. The safety she felt here let her think about things unhindered and that gave her a sharpened perspective upon waking up, but it also meant her body was totally helpless, as she only encountered this place when unconscious. At first, she had thought this whole place a dream, a vision made up by her own mind coupled with the thing that knocked her out. The priest here was familiar to her though, a man she had met when her son was born, during the time she was a captive of a sadistic Mandian named Marco Giovanni. He had been kind to her during her captivity and responsible for her escape. She felt protected here and secure from those things in the dark that beckoned her and showed her death.

Father Benjamin knelt before the altar and Catriona stood slowly, then moved to a pew near the middle of the church. She knew he was aware of her presence and her dilemma; he always was, so she waited patiently for the priest to nod his final benediction to the Saints, rise, and then walk over to sit beside her. She believed this realm was one beyond the plane of the Living World, yet not quite the Realm of the Dead. Rather, she thought it was a doorway between the two, where time worked a little differently, but the inhabitants were real nonetheless. She had asked the priest before if he was actually dead and he had assured her he most certainly was, but that his sacrifice has bought him the time in the afterlife to redeem his actions from life. Thus, he was here for her, but only accessible when she was unconscious and unable to awaken for a time, for then she was most like the spirits who walked between worlds.

"Hello, Father Benjamin."

"Hello, Catriona."

"What should I do?"

"You should start by looking at what you know."

"The king's Chancellor, Myrgen, has told me to kill the king. He has implied Alan and Tanglwyst's destruction should I refuse. I don't know if he knows about my soul sight but the drug that was used on me to get me in that cell blocked my visions and made me groggy, but not unconscious. He has access to these powerful drugs, but he doesn't make them himself. If he was the one who made them, then the drug on the darts used by the black guard would have done what the guard believed it would, not killed me, like I determined they would have. The drug on the original dart tip was strong enough to have put me to sleep instantly. However, I also think they're being betrayed because they fully expected the drug on this other set of darts to put me to sleep and it would actually have killed me. I also know my jaw will hurt quite a bit after having it hit so hard, which means Myrgen knew enough about me to surround himself with people that knew an opportunity when they saw one, and to not underestimate me.

"That's all I *know*," Catriona added.

"And what did you perceive?" Father Benjamin leaned in closer to her. "What did you *see* about Myrgen?"

"Not much. My Sight was affected, but I can tell from foreknowledge he has many secrets."

"Which one is his most important?"

"His vulnerability. You never want your enemy to know your weakness."

"Myrgen's must have something to do with the king. I would imagine that's why he wants him dead," Father Benjamin said, leaning an elbow on the back of the pew in front of them.

"No. That doesn't feel right. He was hostile about the assassination, like he didn't want to do it this way. There's something else going on."

"Any ideas?" The priest stroked his cheeks and chin, his cowl almost hiding the shadow of a scar which slid around his entire neck.

"One thing for certain, he seems to have Alan. He also has taken Tanglwyst." She looked at the pew, at the rosary in his hands. The beads were carved into the shape of roses and he was constantly turning them as he thought.

"Why would he take Tanglwyst if he has your son?"

Catriona blinked, trying to assess this information. *This* was the primary reason she appreciated her presence in this place at a time like this. There were loyalties involved here regarding the Mervol merchant woman, and Catriona felt their pull, but there was something wrong with this situation. Father Benjamin was right. There would *be* no reason to take Tanglwyst if Alan was the leverage, unless Alan wasn't Myrgen's original target. "Be… because he… Benjamin, I don't think he took…"

She was about to explore this with the friar when she heard a heavy tapping. She looked at the stained glass scene of the Ascension of Saint Giles on the west wall and saw a young, blonde woman rapping on the window.

"I guess it's time for me to go. It looks like Gwen has found me this time." Catriona had discovered years ago the signs of her returning consciousness. If someone interacted with her unconscious body, they appeared to be rapping on the windows. Catriona suspected it was because they probably could not enter this place. "Father…," Catriona looked again at her friend and took his hands in hers. "You have a bond with Alan. He's described this church to me from one of his dreams. Please, can you see my son? Can you tell me if he's safe?"

Father Benjamin closed his eyes and seemed to listen to his feelings. When he opened them again, he said, "He's safe, but scared. You need to find him, Catriona."

"Can you guard him, Father? Protect him like you did at the end?"

"No, my dear, I cannot," he shook his head sadly. "I cannot leave this church. But you know ways to ensure his safety, do you not?"

"You mean my connection with the Land? It is strange here in Mervolingia. It's as if she is blocked from me, stifled. Like the way I felt when I was captured. The drug dulled my senses but didn't let me come here, where I could connect to you."

"There are forces in play to limit your connection with the Land. You need a location where the patterns that block you cannot see you. Seek that place, Catriona, and protect your son."

Catriona took a breath and nodded. "Thank you, Father."

Father Benjamin nodded quietly as Catriona walked outside the church and dissolved into the night, and into reality.

Gwen's usually pale face was flushed red with effort as she tried desperately to pull the water-logged body from the well. She heard a horse ride up outside her small house and the familiar voice call out to her. "Gwen?"

"Dominic! Back here! Quick!"

Lord Dominic D'Medici spurred his horse immediately to the back of the small house and dismounted, fearful of the panic in his lady's voice at such a late hour, being just past two in the morning. He often crept to her home at this hour when the Lady Tanglwyst was in the throws of her current lover and he could escape to a similar endeavor. So far, he had made progress towards that end with Gwen but had yet to bring it to fruition. He honestly wasn't sure he'd go through with the marriage if she gave herself to him without it.

When he saw her frantic grasp upon the rope in their well, he ran over and helped pull the feminine form from the hole. Gwen bent down and listened at the woman's chest, brightening as she heard faint breathing. She looked up at Dominic. "Help me get her inside."

"By the Saints. What happened to her? Who is she?" He looked at the woman but her face was successfully obscured by Gwen's long blonde hair and the woman's own ebony tresses.

"She's my Mistress. Someone threw her into the well, and then rode off." The fear and emotion in her voice told Dominic the only thing he felt he needed to know: whoever this woman was, she was as important to Gwen as his own Mistress, Lady Tanglwyst, was to him.

They carried the woman into the house and lay her before the fire to dry her out. Gwen ran to get some bandages, water and healing herbs. Dominic cleared the hair from the woman's face and felt his heart skip a beat as he recognized her. "Catriona," he whispered, and her eyes fluttered open at the sound of her name, her gaze sharp and penetrating. Gwen returned and Dominic did nothing to hide the vehemence in his voice as he hissed at his betrothed, "This woman is your *Mistress*?"

\* \* \*

Gweneviere Douglas, known to her friends as Gwen, closed her door behind her and walked over to Dominic, standing by the well. She had insisted they take their discussion outside to avoid disturbing her recuperating charge, although she knew Catriona would know the specifics of the discussion without Gwen's offering. Dominic didn't speak, but merely reinforced his question with a glance. Gwen sat down on a log by the back door and looked up at her Mandian fiancé.

"You have an explanation for your association with this criminal?" Dominic folded his wiry arms across his slight chest, his intense dark eyes scoring an accusing glare into his betrothed. A perfect example of power in attitude rather than muscle, the D'Medici would be identified by a trained eye as a man accustomed to delegation. Full black hair and tan skin only offered to emphasize his good looks, causing women, and some men, to ignore the lack of bulk beneath his elegant robes.

His betrothed, in his measured symmetrical opinion, made up for his lacks in muscle and imposing build. She was a very attractive woman, with blonde hair of an impairing length and robin's egg blue eyes which watched all with an assessing mindset. Her figure and form belied the hard farm life she was born into in Glarren, where her family owned a sheep farm and she had spent her life climbing hills, traversing woods and lifting bales of lanolin-soaked fleeces onto the backs of mules, as well as spinning and weaving the wool for her own clothes. Her understanding of the full process of the wool industry, from sheep to shawl, gave her a competency and self-confidence which carried over into everything she did. It was this competency which attracted Dominic to her, recognizing the strength of his opposite.

"I know this woman better than you do," she said, successfully managing to keep her emotions in check.

"How?" Dominic glared, his stance unforgiving.

"When Tanglwyst came to Kilmory three years ago, I said I'd never been to sea before. That wasn't exactly true. About two years before, my father had decided to marry me off to one of the Lord Kilmory's sons. I was not interested and ran away, planning to leave Glarren and make my own fortune. I found a hidden cove a day's ride from the keep and in it was a black ship. I decided it was sign and stowed away in the hold before it set sail.

"That ship was the *Enigma.*"

"Catriona's ship," Dominic confirmed.

"Yes. She set sail and Catriona was inspecting the hold when she discovered me. I wasn't doing very well, having never been to sea before, and the smell of my vomit gave me away, I think. She took me up to the deck and had me watch the shoreline until I was stable. This helped me quite a bit and afterward, she allowed me to stay on board. I traveled with her as her maid-servant for two seasons, learning everything she would teach me, until the summer you came to Kilmory with Tanglwyst. She told me to return to my father, that he would be grateful to see me again and wouldn't press the marriage. I didn't know my intended had been married that spring to my younger sister, but she seemed to, and my father gladly let me be about it."

"I suppose I should have known you had lied to us when you weren't seasick on the Nostromo."

"You were a little too occupied with tallies and counting, I think. I figured you were Tanglwyst's lover the way you never left her side the entire trip."

"Loyalty to one's employer should be seen as an asset, not a liability," Dominic proclaimed, his posture tossing his nose in the air in a way which, usually, Gwen found charming because he was like a little boy trying to prove to his older brothers he could eat the insect they were daring him to. Tonight, though, he seemed simply pompous and insecure.

"Interesting point of view. Then we obviously have nothing more to discuss seeing as Catriona is *my* employer." Gwen gestured toward the cottage. "Simply consider her my asset. Putting it in that light should resolve everything." Gwen folded her arms across her chest in a gesture of triumph.

"And as such, I now have to determine whether *you* are a liability." Dominic's gaze judged Gwen harshly as she tried to convince him. "I can definitely see her influence in your actions and words now. Your feelings in this matter are clear, and apparently quite strong."

"I have many reasons for what I feel for her. This woman has saved my life many times before. She…."

"I am unconcerned about what she'd done for you in the past," he interrupted sternly. "I *am* concerned with your honesty with the Lady Tanglwyst. You lied to her and more importantly, you kept this from *me*. You must have suspected I would never approve of this association, and therefore hid it from me. She's a thief and a killer, Gwen, and trucking with this pirate does not instill trust," he said, turning his back to her. With a backward glance, he added, "Perhaps we should 're-evaluate' our engagement."

Crushed, Gwen swallowed and turned away. "Perhaps." She tried to call forth her voice of reason to handle this situation. Instead, this voice brought up an entirely different point, instantly dissolving her sorrow with suspicion. She turned toward Dominic to enable her to observe him, and asked, "What is *your* connection to Catriona, my Lord?"

* * *

"*My* connection?" He blinked in quickly-hidden guilt and Gwen fought to hide her victory smile. *How did she figure that out so quickly?*

"Yes, *your* connection. No one knows of my relationship to her, but someone must be aware of yours or else she would never have been brought here. They were expecting you to save her life."

"You know, they could have been just trying to kill her."

"Then why drop her in when there was someone so obviously in the house?" Gwen gestured to the house blazing with light.

"Convenience?" Dominic offered.

"What's wrong with those houses?" She pointed at the rows of houses up the road a bit farther, and the three farm houses in sight, one of which was dark. "Why ride all the way over here when that one there could have done her in without anyone knowing?"

Dominic glanced at the house, then around the yard, trying to decide how to deal with getting caught with this. He decided to turn the tables of suspicion back on her. "What makes you think no one knew of *your* connection?"

"Because I never left the ship except in the guise of a man, and she assured me she never noticed anyone thinking I was otherwise. None of her crewmen would ever say anything to anyone off the ship. She'd know and kill them for betraying me and her, and every one of them knew that and respected it. That leaves the abductor of Catriona to drop her off here for *you* to find."

"Why would they toss her here and not at my own home then?"

"Because you always meet me here for dinner these days. I don't think you've had a single dinner this year at the Holloway Manor house since Twelfth Night."

Dominic tried to determine how much of himself to reveal. He loved this woman, he knew, but to draw her into the ugliness of his own intrigues was not only inappropriate, but he was uncertain her handling of intrigues wouldn't be with all the grace of the way she handled baled fleeces. Her very upbringing indicated she wouldn't have the finesse to deal with these things, and involving her would only endanger her life. Still, he now saw he had a direct connection to Catriona, which he decided would definitely serve his purposes in the future quite nicely. Finally, he decided to leave her hanging a bit. "Let me just say we look after our own. Unfortunately, it's late and I need to go now." He walked to his horse and mounted up. He turned his head slightly to watch her reaction as he rode off and felt wicked delight in seeing her turn to storm into her house, flipping her long ponytail with enough force to decapitate the abundant horseflies milling around her door.

*Chapter Four:*
*"Better is a dinner of herbs where love is, than a stalled ox and hatred therewith."*
*~ Proverbs 15:17*

Charles IX Maximillian, King of Mervolingia, skulked through the city like an oil-drenched rat, keeping to smelly alleyways and hiding under bridges as he made his way to the cottage on the edge of Patras. It was just after dark and he had always loved to sneak away from his dominating mother and the vile bantering of court, but these days, it seemed more necessary than ever for him to be away from the palace. The horrors of the massacre still haunted him and he had frightening visions of his death and those of the people he loved.

A figure came down the street and Charles ducked into a shadow and waited for it to pass. The thrill of escape commanded the best of his senses but this was the barest of reasons for his liberation. The true reason for his flight lay behind the beautiful blue door at the end of this road. He crept up to the door and used his key to enter. He pushed the hood back from his face as he closed the door behind him and drank deeply the smell of dinner cooking. The hearth was warm and cozy, simple and modest because the lady of the house refused to have it otherwise. Marie Touchet had the world at the asking, yet she demanded simple surroundings to keep unwanted eyes from her window, and Charles respected that. He looked around for her as he shed his disguise and hung the trappings of a poor man on a hook by the door.

A large iron kettle hung from a hook over the fire, bubbling with a thick stew as bread cooled on the table. Charles took a wooden bowl from the cupboard and spilled several pieces of fruit from a sack he had brought with him. He took out a bottle of wine from the cellars and a couple of packages wrapped in silk. He looked into the bedroom, at the comfortable bed with the hand sewn coverlet Marie made from the silk wrappings of his presents, but didn't see her in the room. He checked the small bed against the wall and found his year-old son lying on the linens, his woolen clothes clean and warm against the early spring chill outside.

Charles knelt next to little Francois' sleeping form and watched him sleep, tears forming in his eyes as his heart swelled with love for the boy. He looked so much like his mother with his golden hair and stolen grey eyes. He reached down and touched his son's hair and the baby began to stir, and then fell back asleep. Charles picked up the boy and held him close, cuddling his only son. He went into the common room and sat in the rocking chair, waiting for the boy's mother.

Charles smiled warmly at the very thought of her, his heart brimming with immense love for the simple peasant woman, their home, their son. Charles had always dreamed of having a family which was nothing like his own, far away from his mother, and so he had set this home up to live that very fantasy. Marie told their neighbors and her parents he worked as a sailor and they all seemed to know when he visited because their lovemaking would be vigorous enough to alert the nearby households. They were very pleased, and a couple had even met him and didn't seem to put together the fact that Marie's husband and the face on their coinage was the same.

*They had met at a festival in her home village five years ago, when he and his brother had sneaked away from their duties. Charles had won a kiss from any girl at the festival and the prettiest girl sauntered up to him, expecting to be the one. Charles had looked around for the girl who was the least full of herself at the event and his eyes had lit upon Marie, who was helping with the children's activities. Charles stepped up to her and told her he had won the "Kiss from the Prettiest Girl" contest and he was there to collect his prize. Marie had smiled faintly at what was obviously a cruel joke from the pretty girl, who was sneering at her, and she had denied him his prize until she was finished with her work, figuring that would put him off for the rest of the festival. Charles simply pitched in and helped, and in so doing, had the finest time ever.*

*A year later, he planned to go to her and propose, but his mother had found out about the girl and threatened to have Marie exiled. Charles had wanted to marry Marie instead of Elizabeth of Krakte, but his mother wouldn't hear of it and even threatened to have Marie killed if he persisted with this affair. Charles went to Marie in great heartbreak, but Marie had reassured him she would always be there for him.*

*Charles had married Elizabeth reluctantly and had lain with her three times the first month of their marriage. After that, he slept with her dutifully once a month until Elizabeth became pregnant in May of 1571, and then wouldn't touch her again. Elizabeth was annoyed by this, but then seemed to get past it. Charles figured she had gotten herself a lover and he would have a plethora of heirs which would solve the lineage problem, and still be a secret deceit, a subtle rebellion against his mother.*

*When his daughter was born, he named her Marie, after his true love. Alexander, ever the more sensitive one, told the Bishop the child's name was Marie-Elizabeth, in a vain attempt to appease the queen and the Queen-Mother. Catherine was intent on seeking out and destroying Marie Touchet but she was distracted by the assassination on Plantyn and never quite got back to it in the wake of the massacre's repercussions. Charles knew it was only a matter of time before Catherine's distractions were no longer a priority and his family would again be in danger. During the meantime, Charles could enjoy a simple life with the people he cared most about in the world.*

Charles heard a key enter the lock and a small, plain-seeming woman entered carrying a bucket of water. She started at first when she saw someone was in the room but her surprise turned immediately to joy and she set the water on the floor and ran to her love. Marie was an immense dichotomy. She was born of simple folk, but had incredible intellect and clarity of vision. She claimed it was just common sense, but Charles believed she was the smartest woman he'd ever met. She seemed to understand the difference between love and duty and had forgiven him the ultimate sin of marrying another.

As such, he was always there for her. She had never come to the palace, even though she had been given the means to do so. He had once tried to blindfold her and take her there, but she had recognized the sound of the fountains in the courtyards as they came on for some reason, and she had balked. When he asked her about it, she told him she wanted nothing to do with the people and activities of that horrible place.

She had eventually met his brother however, an act he wanted to regret but found he quite couldn't. *Marie had been having some trouble with the last stages of her pregnancy and when he came to visit her, he found her in an impossible pain. He feared he'd lose both her and the baby and got a neighbor to sit with her while he ran back to the palace. He grabbed Alexander and threw an old cloak over him, and the two grabbed common horses from the stables. In the middle of a frigid January night, the two brothers galloped through the streets of Patras to save two precious lives.*

*Alexander had leapt to the task immediately upon entering the small home. He opened the woman's stomach and removed the baby carefully, removing the umbilical cord which had wrapped itself around the child's neck four times. Had Marie tried to birth her son normally, they both would have died. As he cleaned his hands after sewing Marie up, Alexander had stated, "You owe me."*

"What are you thinking, over there so quiet?" Marie had a smile on her face of sweet playfulness.

"The night Francois was born." Charles reached across the table and held her hand. "You?"

"How wonderful it is to have you home. I wish I could have you all to myself all the time."

"So do I, my love. So do I…"

Marie looked at him carefully. "How are the headaches?"

Charles rubbed his eyes and temples. "It's getting worse every day, Marie. I find the pain so blinding at times, it's maddening. The only time I get any relief at all is when I come to you, and every hour in that place makes the pain that much more unbearable."

"Did you take the powder I mixed for you?"

"Yes, and it has definitely eased the pain, but you said you didn't have any more of it, so I'm using it sparingly." He looked up at his love, shame and fear clotting on his face. "Marie, I hit Elizabeth last week."

Marie sat up in her seat, pulling her hand out of his grasp. Her voice was stern and tinted slightly with fear. "You what?"

"She came into my chamber after dinner to talk last Monday. I'd been away from you only a night and wanted to return, but she caught me trying to leave through the secret passage. She threatened to tell my mother. Mother's been in the Papal City for months on our behalf, trying to clear up that St. Michael's Day mess but I know she would return if she thought she could find you. She'd return immediately for any threat to the Crown and you and Francois would qualify in her eyes."

Marie squeezed his hand in comfort and he accepted it with a kiss on her fingers. "Regardless, I had the headaches back again, and stomach cramps as well, but the headaches were worse than they've ever been. She began yelling at me, calling me a weakling, a simpering whelp who only listens to his mother. She quite tore into me, and suddenly, something within me snapped, and I struck her."

Charles let his tears crawl down his cheeks, his shame was so dominant at that moment, and Marie took his hand again. "Darling, don't worry about the powder being all I have. Please take it. I don't want something like that happening here."

Charles looked slowly up at her, nodding. "That's why I haven't returned sooner. I was afraid I was truly going mad from it all and didn't want to hurt you and Francois." He squeezed her hand and she answered it reassuringly, her smile returning and filling his life again with light.

Charles and Marie sat and ate together, enjoying the gifts Charles brought and talked until they heard the church bells toll the hour. "Will you be going?" Marie asked as they stood up from the table.

"No, not tonight, Marie." He kissed her forehead and held her to him. "Not tonight."

*Chapter Five:*

*"I discerned among the youths a young man void of understanding, passing through the street near her corner; and he went the way of her house in the twilight, in the evening, in the black and dark night..."*

*~ Proverbs 7:7-9*

Lord Dominic rode off into the dismal darkness, disturbed by his conversation with Gwen. Granted, his connection to Catriona was dubious, and she *was* family in a rather inconvenient way, but his lady had never even indicated a relationship between herself and the dark she-pirate before. Now it appeared her connection was deep, deeper than the one he counted on between the two of them and suddenly, he was no longer certain Gwen would never betray him. The feeling of deception chilled him and he reflexively drew his light cloak about him to ward off the angst.

"But you're not terribly interested in admitting your own relationship to her either now, are you," he muttered to himself. The horse's dun-colored ears swiveled back in response to his voice and he felt slightly foolish in spite of himself. As he approached the city, he came upon Lady Tanglwyst's estate and decided to pay her a visit as he saw a light on in her study. Here, he thought, was another person who kept her relationship to Catriona very private.

The house in which Tanglwyst lived was extravagant, with twenty-five rooms all told and numerous secrets. As he approached, Dominic saw the light in the study go out. Damn, he thought, she's going to bed. Well, maybe if I hurry, I'll be able to catch her. If she's sleepy, she may slip up and divulge something about the dark woman.

As he approached the door, he heard a thumping, as if a large man were coming down the stairs. *Ah,* he thought, *she has a man with her again. He must just be leaving. I'll wait over here to see who it is this time. Probably Nicolai.*

He waited a few minutes but when no one came to the door, he entered the house using his Chancellor's key which Tanglwyst had given him when he took the job of governing her finances. He looked around for the person and finding no one, went to the wide bank of stairs which would deposit him at the doorway to Tanglwyst's study. His foot struck something near the bottom.

He knelt to examine it and found the body of Simon, one of Tanglwyst's young valets. His soft brown hair splayed on the steps, a small amount of blood trickling from his ears. Quickly checking the boy, Dominic discovered the body was still warm and he checked to see if the child was indeed dead. Unfortunately, he was and the cause of death seemed to be that his neck was broken, presumably from a fall down the stairs according to the story told by his body's position. Then Dominic noticed blood spreading on the stairs and he carefully lifted the boy's head to reveal a round dent in the back.

Dominic stood carefully, looking up the stairs and listening. This was obviously the sound he mistook for a lover of Tanglwyst's, but he now believed there was an intruder in the house. He'd seen enough murdered bodies at his cousins' houses to recognize a victim when he saw one. A familiar scent lingered on the steps, but he hardly noticed it because it belonged here. He ascended, cautiously avoiding the Nightingale Stair, a squeaking stair employed in Yndia and installed by Tanglwyst's carpenters as an early warning system at her brother's suggestion. Dominic looked through the open door into the study.

The full moon lit the room in dull pastels through the stained glass window imported from Tanglwyst's Mandian glasswork factory, striking the darkness unabashedly, offended by its advances. The room was cold, a telling sign that Tanglwyst had not been the one in here. One of his Mistress's idiosyncrasies was that Tanglwyst seemed always on the verge of freezing to death and thus, even in summer, had a fire going wherever she was. Dominic called her a reptile, but he meant it as a compliment, comparing her to his own glacial demeanor.

He walked over to the desk and saw it had been hardly gone through. The intruder had obviously known exactly what they were after. Suddenly, Dominic thought of Tanglwyst herself. Where was *she*? He looked to the door which bridged her bedroom to the study and started to move toward it when he was grabbed from behind. He saw as well as felt the dagger pressed to his throat, the filtered moonlight glittering off the ornately carved bit of handle he could just barely see.

"If you ever want to see the Lady Tanglwyst again," a steely voice hissed from by his ear, muffled by cloth covering the mouth, "you'll not interfere with the black witch's mission." The gloved hand holding his chest had some sort of paper in it and Dominic could barely make out the words "...to get Catriona to assassinate..."

*I've got to get a look at that letter!* Dominic contemplated elbowing his captor in the kidneys, knowing he might suffer a nick on the neck but not enough to kill him. The man was slight, like a thief would be, and was shorter than him by a head, but was probably nimble and quick. He tensed slightly and his captor pressed the dagger closer, whispering, "Monk's Hood." Dominic froze at the mention of the deadly poison, recognizing the faint smell at once. He seized, haunted by the childhood memories of people dropping dead from the poisons administered to them by his D'Medici cousins. As he shook in uncontrollable fear, his captor released him and pushed him down behind the desk. "Remember, D'Medici, stay out of this."

He heard no sound when his assailant left, and found his limbs unresponsive until long after the mysterious visitor's retreating horse's hooves were but a memory.

*"Assassinate" the note had said, but assassinate whom? And what did Tanglwyst have to do with all this? What was Catriona's role in all this? And what was Gwen's?* "I've got to talk to them," he spoke to the darkness. He held out his hand and tried vainly to quell the near-violent dance of nerves it displayed. "Just not tonight."

* * *

Gwen closed her door behind her and looked around. A fire was singing in the hearth and Catriona spoke from the shadows dancing to its melody. "How bad is it?"

Gwen went to the chair opposite the one her Mistress had taken near the fire, leaning her forearms on a homemade blanket draped across its back. Catriona's hands encompassed a mug of mulled wine as she recovered from her unpleasant dumping in the small well. A wool blanket eased the bulk of the chill from her form and the cold water had calmed the swelling in her jaw so there might not even be much of a bruise in a week. The damp was finishing its last wisps of steaming away in the heat of the fire.

"Pretty bad. He wants to 're-evaluate' our relationship. He thinks I've lied to him about our association."

"No, I didn't get that from the conversation," Catriona volunteered. "He never asked you before about an association with me because he had no reason to suspect one. You were on the other side of the world. How could you possibly know me?" She leaned forward so the light of the fire showed her concern. "His own dealings with me are dubious and full of intrigues. He therefore suspects everyone of the same."

"What *is* his connection to you?" Gwen pulled a long, blonde hair off the blanket, wiggling it to the ground.

"I did some work for him about a year ago and the consequences were not quite what he expected. Let's just say he now owes his family a lot of money, and that makes for a very shaky foundation amongst the D'Medicis."

"So, what happened to you today?"

"Well, I was at an Inn in town with…"

Gwen perked up. "Grymalkin?"

Catriona leveled a gaze at her protégé and arched an eyebrow. "No, my little romantic, Anika and Drake. They had just arrived from Rouen and I was setting them up in the Inn so they could rest before returning to Caratia with Alan. Nevertheless, as I left the Inn, I was poked with something tiny and my head got muddled. It even impaired my Sight. I was taken to a cell in some dungeon where Myrgen the Grey told me he wanted me to assassinate the king."

"Charles? Why?"

"That's actually what I want to figure out."

"Well, I would assume it's for power, knowing Myrgen. Dominic says he's rather power mad." Gwen took the bowls from the table where she had planned to eat with Dominic and took them to the stove, dishing stew.

"Dominic is wrong. Myrgen is calculating, not spontaneous. Although killing the king would grant him power because of the amount of responsibility he would suddenly have to assume, it would also make him vulnerable because he would have to hire new people to keep up with all the work, and that opens the door for spies. Myrgen's a little too secretive for that. Too many naughty skeletons under his bed for him to rest easy."

"You feel this request was unplanned?"

"And angry. Trust me, there's a plan involved here, but not his. He let too much of himself show here for me to think this is his idea. Odd as it may sound, I think he's being manipulated, and he's chafing a bit at the collar."

"Myrgen? I find that hard to believe."

"So do I, but nonetheless, that's how it feels." Catriona sipped the mulled wine, inviting its warmth to quell her chills. She set it aside as Gwen handed her the bowl of steaming meat and vegetables. Catriona took a bite.

"Perhaps you're wrong this time. I mean, who could possibly manipulate Myrgen the Grey? The Queen-Mother?"

Catriona swallowed and reached for the slightly cooler wine. "Perhaps. By the Stones, she's managed to manipulate enough other people." Catriona's voice had a sadness to it that puzzled Gwen and she looked inquiringly at her Mistress. "The Saint Michael's Day Massacre. She told Alexander and Charles Plantyn had something to do with my capture a decade ago, when Alan was born." She blinked out of her mournful reverie and drank.

"I thought that was someone named Giovanni?"

"It was. But she used her knowledge of Giovanni and his depravity to implicate Plantyn as well. She had no idea exactly how volatile the suggestion was." She set down the wine on the floor away from her feet. "Alexander told me after the massacre, trying to explain his actions. Apparently, Catherine handed them a letter from Giovanni to Plantyn, implying a connection that was over a decade old. Alexander and Charles assumed more to that connection because of their own experiences. It was only after the order was given to kill Plantyn and the Emilianites in the city that Charles figured out Catherine had played them both. Charles was devastated, and Alexander has hated her for that ever since. I don't know if she realizes how much she lost with them both, and Alexander wouldn't trust her judgment now if she told him the sun rose today." Catriona retrieved her goblet from the floor.

"What's that going to mean when Alexander is king?" Gwen  scooped up a bite of stew.

Catriona felt a shiver run through her soul at that statement, and she looked up at Gwen, studying her. "When? Don't you mean *if?*"

Gwen looked up from blowing on her spoon to look at her

intuitive mistress. Catriona knew Gwen had always wanted the strange gift her lady possessed of amazing intuition, but never had she felt what Catriona dealt with every day. She blinked and set down her spoon. She shook her head, looking her mistress full in the face with shocking certainty. "No, apparently, I mean *when*." Gwen sat back in her chair, surprised.

Catriona sat up again, her wine forgotten, trying to figure out how to explain the most important part. "Myrgen took Alan."

Gwen dropped her spoon, splashing a tiny bit of stew on her dress. "Has he hurt him?"

"No. Neither of them will hurt him. The Nubian will be sure of that. It is not his nature to harm women or children or to allow them to be harmed. I read that much in his nature and I think he'll protect him if something slips out of Myrgen's control. Alan is safe enough."

Gwen glanced down at her dress and wiped the stew from it with a kitchen towel. "Uh, if he's against hurting women and children, why is there a spreading bruise on your jaw?"

Catriona reached up and touched the tender flesh. "Well, that was my own stupidity. I swallowed."

Gwen wrinkled her brow, confused.

"Unconscious people don't swallow, Gwen. They just drool. Apparently, he knew that."

"Oh. Yeah, I guess you're right. I never thought about that, though I have a very hard time picturing you drooling."

"We all do it, Gwen. Just because I'm the Stâpâna of Caratia or the captain of a ship doesn't mean my body doesn't function just like yours. I have all the indignities the rest of the humans suffer."

"Could you leave me my illusions, please?" Gwen picked up her spoon and took a sip of her stew. "Still, that was incredibly stupid of Myrgen."

"Yes, I know."

"He can't possibly expect to survive this now. You never threaten a woman's child. Especially one you assume can assassinate somebody as powerful as a king."

"He also took Tanglwyst, possibly to keep me loyal or to keep Alan calm. I'm not sure why, but you can see why I have to go…" Catriona stood up, but the speed with which she moved made her dizzy, and her body rebelled against her commands.

Gwen barely caught her before she hit the floor.

"You're not going anywhere, except to bed." Gwen lifted her in her arms and laid her in Gwen's small bed. "You have been knocked out and dumped in a well today. Your body needs to heal. Now you stay there and rest. You can run off tomorrow when you're up to it, but tonight, your body had better be in that bed."

"Poseidon's beard, Gwen. I just stood up too fast..." She closed her eyes and focused her energies, trying to heal herself but the drug in her system fought that option. Catriona's head began to throb then as her blood pressure evened out, and the dull pain in her jaw reprimanded her for her thoughtless physical activity. She lay back on the bed with a sigh. "Then again, maybe you're right. What about you?"

"I'll be fine. If I need to sleep, there's enough room there for two if we don't mind being close. It might be the only way I have of making sure you don't leave in the middle of the night."

Gwen got up and pulled the heavy woolen blanket over Catriona's form. Catriona looked up at Gwen, a plan rising in her stead. "Is there a place where I might be able to observe someone without being in the palace itself?"

"There's a hedge on the east side of the gardens next to one of the palace walls, near a window. There's room enough for two people to hide behind it for hours." Catriona looked at her pointedly and Gwen blushed in admittance, swallowing visibly. She walked over to the wine pitcher and poured some more wine. "Why?"

"I might need to watch someone without being seen, obviously."

"Alexander, perhaps?"

"I don't know who yet, but the garden is a good spot, especially with everything blooming right now. People have been shut up indoors all winter and they'll want to get out. It's only logical the garden is the spot for interludes. Also, I need you to deliver a very important message for me."

"Ah. *This* one's for Alexander."

"Gwen, stop it. I can't let him know I'm here. No, I want you to bring word to Anika and Drake that there are some problems with taking Alan away right now, and ask if they can wait a few days. I'll gladly pay their expenses."

Gwen nodded. "What should I say if they ask what's

wrong?" She had met the Duce of Caratia and his Ducesâ a couple of times while traveling to Catriona's regular home port, back before Nicolai came into their lives, and she had written them often over the years. Catriona had wintered in Patras instead of Caratia for the first time since Alan was born, keeping to the house so as not to attract Alexander's attention. The Duce had a power about him that was unsettling, but Alan preferred it there than in Mervolingia and had been asking about returning.

"Tell them it has something to do with Nicolai. That should explain everything."

Gwen nodded, then thumped her fingers on the door frame. She knew Catriona avoided even the possibility of seeing Alexander all winter, so he would not be tempted to seek her out. Their time at the cabin had changed everything, and the meeting later had changed it all back. It irritated Gwen to no end. "Why not?"

Catriona looked at Gwen, her sight flashing in the darkness to see what was on her friend's mind. She exhaled audibly, not having the energy at the moment to fight this fight. "Because I am still married, Gwen. It is inappropriate and counter-productive for me to see Alexander, no matter what we might have meant to each other. Now, please, I'll do as you've asked if you'll not mention it again." She rolled onto her side and glanced at the floor, then closed her eyes. "At least not tonight."

Gwen bowed deeply. "I am and always shall be at your service, my Captain." Gwen began to close the door. "Now, go to sleep." The door bit off the flow of firelight, spitting the darkness all over the room.

Catriona rested on the fleece which covered the straw-stuffed mattress. Gwen's romantic ideals were pretty, but she didn't understand what she was doing to Catriona's heart. She had a hard enough time dealing with the night she and Alexander had spent together without Gwen's hopeful machinations. She had been so incredibly lonely for so long, and Alexander had been there for her yet again. It wasn't hard to see why she would fall prey to her own sorrows and seek solace at last in the arms of the one man who had been there for her for so many years.

Catriona rolled onto her back and actually let herself think about him, something she had avoided for nearly the entire winter. Alexander was handsome by any standards, and his devotion to her was unquestionable. She didn't need mystic sight to see that, but she could never use her Sight on him anyway. She wouldn't have if she could. He had never done anything to make her think he would betray her trust, and she couldn't envision a circumstance that would make her believe differently.

He had sought her out often during the past few years, ever since they had reconnected in Cheryb. She had been so shocked to see the Prince of Mervolingia skulking around in the seedy port like he belonged there, she had almost blown his cover. A clandestine meeting later revealed he had actually heard of a woman ship captain fitting her description and had used it as an excuse to escape court and all those inane people who sought his favor. She had told him not to endanger his life by looking for her again, but she had been happy to see how he'd changed.

Their next meeting, and nearly every meeting after that, had ended with him healing her from some scrape she had gotten into. Her own healing abilities were limited when it came to healing herself, and Alexander's hearth wisdom, gained at the side of the midwife who had attended her convalescence after the attack at the church, had served her time and time again. She had never revealed it, but she had been more reckless after they had started keeping company, in the hopes she would need mending at his hands. She never dared to call her emotions for him love, too caught up in the picturesque memory of her relationship with her husband. She had been told Nicolai had died years before, and it was only after a serious injury that required Alexander's help for several weeks did she decide to actually let her husband's memory go and move on.

But Fate or Karma had other plans, and a month later, Catriona had walked into a meeting with Tanglwyst and saw her husband sitting, alive and well, at the same table. Nicolai had gone after her when she tried to leave, insisting on knowing what had happened to her all those years ago. He had apologized when she told him and had left. It was almost a month before they would be able to speak again, and after they did, Catriona had come away with the knowledge of his illness, blindness and deafness. He had needed her and she had not been there, yet he had been the source of her inner strength during her imprisonment. Her guilt crushed her beneath its weight.

She was embarrassed and ashamed and she had tried to

forgive herself for seven years. She had thought he died alone and crippled only to find he had survived and held her memory faithfully while she had sought solace in Alexander's arms. At the end of last season, after saying goodbye to Alexander, she had gone to Nicolai's ship and asked his forgiveness. He had been gracious enough to give it, and they had decided to try again.

She had felt unworthy ever since, though she barely admitted it to herself, much less to anyone else. Sometimes she felt so lonely she could barely breathe, and bedding Alexander had not stopped that feeling. She didn't know what to do, and this new development in the drama just added to the pressure.

At least it was a distraction. She blinked out of her self-examination and tried to think. *Who would want to kill both her and Charles?* She hadn't told Gwen about the poison because she didn't want her to worry, but one of her ship captains, who couldn't have cats on board, had a housemate who was a poison maker to deal with his rat problem. The more effective poisons were ones which let the rat return to the nest where it would die and the other rats would devour it. That was how she recognized the cyanide on the dart tips, because she had seen the same reaction on the spoons the poison maker used to stir the mixture.

Whoever had put the poison on the darts had planned on killing her, but it definitely didn't seem to be Myrgen, or his guard Michael, which meant she was expendable to whoever supplied the poison for the darts. Myrgen had gone to a lot of trouble to secure *her* services specifically. Had she been killed, kidnapping Alan or Tanglwyst would have done absolutely no good to whoever was the next choice. Unless, of course, that choice was Nicolai.

Catriona wanted to pace, to encourage her limbs to fight their fatigue, but when she sat up, slowly of course, she just didn't feel up to it. Unfortunately, it was Gwen's turn to be right, and the girl had foolishly wasted it on *this*. Ah well.

Catriona breathed in as deeply as her bruised ribs would allow and let the breath out slowly, centering her focus. She had tried for years to learn to heal herself by focusing her inner energies but had yet to succeed at clearing away more than a few minor cuts and bruises. Alexander had always been able to do better with his herbal poultices and she had discovered she could heal others easier than herself, relieving the need for a chiurgeon on board, much to Alexander's dismay. She managed now to breathe away the cut on her cheek and the bruise on her chin and eased the pain in her ribs. They would still be sore, but not evident. She looked and even the marks from the ropes on her wrists were gone. It was the best she could hope for without Alexander's help. Catriona lay back down on the bed and drifted off into sleep.

## Chapter Six:
## *"The wicked shall be a ransom for the righteous, and the transgressor for the upright."*
## *~ Proverbs 21:18*

Michael lit the torch in the hallways as he moved slowly down the labyrinth corridor leading the Queen of Mervolingia in safety through. He had hoped his treatment of the Catriona woman had not been too harsh the previous night. He had gotten to bed shortly after two in the morning and was grateful Myrgen had made certain he did not have other guard duty the following morning. He had no idea how to check on the lady's health without giving away his involvement in her condition. It had been most of a day, being just after evening mass, and he hoped she had recovered.

Michael touched the wall and it moved, admitting the queen to enter the small, dark room in the labyrinth where Tanglwyst was being kept. The room was part of the old chapel which had burned twenty years before and this room was the simple, tiny scriptorium. A large bed covered with heavy blankets and furs dominated the room, accessorized by a well-lit desk and about fifty candles on the ledge at eye level around the entire room. Originally a bookshelf for the chapel's library, the candles were meant to try and compensate for the lack of windows or fireplace and seemed to be working.

The Mervol woman looked up immediately, her lush green eyes sparkling in the flickering candlelight. The sun had set an hour ago by the feel of things and Tanglwyst felt her adrenaline rise as the door opened. Her chestnut hair was loose and brushed, splaying merrily across the quilted silken robes of luscious purple she had chosen to wear. Knitted woolen hose warmed her legs and feet in the chilly room, and Elizabeth glanced around, impressed with the accommodations. As Her Majesty entered the room and closed the door to maintain the heat, the Lady stood, the small lantern behind her casting fluttering shadows across the two women, and bowed respectfully.

"Stop that," Elizabeth said in a mock chiding, and the two friends embraced, re-establishing the bond between them since their childhood days.

Elizabeth's Kraken accent was all but gone after years of

living in Mervolingia, but her Teutonic beauty had lingered poetically, lush and well cared-for. The candles shimmered on her green velvet gown shot with gold. Oak leaves embroidered in gold and copper accented her figure while fur flowed around her head and neck in a tall collar and echoed in the cuffs of her forest green kidskin gloves. Neat velvet shoes of the same motif peeked out from under her hem, covering knitted silk stockings and velvet garters with gold tassels. Her mahogany hair was fetched up in a golden snood decorated with emerald glass beads, softening the look with a frame of delicate curls about her face.

They sat together on the bed. "How are you holding up?' Elizabeth asked, holding her best friend's hand.

"Well, the view isn't much," Tanglwyst joked with a glance around the windowless dungeon room, "but I insist on staying here out of sight. We can't afford for me to be seen. Thank you, by the way, for the use of these incredible clothes. It's good to be the queen, eh? This wine you brought me is interesting, too. The flavor is odd, but it helps me survive this far more than I thought possible." She smoothed a stray hair of Her Majesty's back in place. "How are *you* holding up?"

The queen stood up and walked over to the desk where her friend had been sitting when she'd arrived "The waiting is killing me. I don't know if Myrgen managed to accomplish what we planned. If he did manage to do it, I'm not sure what we will do next. Catherine is due home in a week. If Charles isn't dead by then, she'll catch us and kill us for treason." Elizabeth started to have trouble breathing, and Tanglwyst took her friend's hand and squeezed it.

"Calm down, Beth. Don't make this worse than it is. If he is still alive by the end of the week, I'll kill him myself."

"Tanglwyst, I would never allow you to endanger yourself like that."

"I wouldn't do it unless I had to, but it is not the first time I have had need to remove a man from my life by violent means."

"I just don't know. Killing him? Is that the only way?"

"Beth, don't falter now. We have a plan and it's a good plan. Charles dies and we tell Alexander when I am rescued that Emilianites with foreign accents took us. Alexander will rush off to war to destroy his brother's killer. He's a healer, not a fighter. He'll die in the first battle. But before that, we have to secure your own claim to the throne. Once Alexander marries you out of convenience, he'll leave you in charge in his stead. Upon his death, a new era will dawn in Mervolingia, and the lineage of rulership will fall to the female of the family. It is the only way to be certain a child is legitimate anyway. This foolishness of having a male inherit the throne has never been practical."

"How are we going to get Alexander to marry me before he goes to war?"

"I'll see to it a little bug is put in his ear. I have connections here at the palace. He'll never even think to associate it with you. And he won't be able to go to war immediately. It'll take time to amass the armies and supplies and then winter will arrive. He can't attack in snow so he'll wait for spring. That's more than enough time for us to convince him to marry you and make you queen again. Your experience will be necessary while he's away."

"And what of Charles?" Elizabeth's eyes were wet and concerned.

Tanglwyst stood up, angry, and walked away from her friend. "Why do you *care* so much about him? He obviously doesn't care about *you*. Need I remind you of the cruelty he's already demonstrated on you? His dispassionate consummation of your marriage? His ignoring you during your pregnancy with his daughter? Then, to name that daughter, *which you bore him,* after his *mistress*? He blatantly pursues her, spitting on your marriage, your family, even the Church and the sanctity of the Holy Vows which we all witnessed. Then, to top it all off, he's probably contracted some disease from the whores he's undoubtedly keeping which is causing these fits of madness, fits which are violent in nature." Tanglwyst turned to face Elizabeth. "Do you want to further endanger your self? Or, if you truly have lost all respect for yourself, do you still want to endanger your daughter*?*"

The words slapped Elizabeth hard, cowing her. They had always admired strong women when they schooled together, and Tanglwyst had always been the strongest of them all. Tanglwyst, after being raped during her first marriage, had been given a device which she wore inside her privates. The device was a multi-bladed knife in a flexible sheath which, when pushed back, would flay anything trying to enter her by force. This sort of ingenuity and strength was demonstrative of the sort of backbone and self-esteem Elizabeth needed to emulate. Elizabeth was the one of the three companions at the abbey where they were educated who had a chance to become that which they all dreamed: Sovereign in her Own Right, and Tanglwyst wanted to make sure she got that chance. She was very interested in forwarding the rights of women in Mervolingia, and Tanglwyst felt this idea was one which would ultimately strengthen the kingdom as a whole. Powerful women abounded in this country. It was wrong for them to be seen as less because of their gender.

Tanglwyst took a deep breath and dropped to her knees, then took and held Elizabeth's hand, trying to comfort her after the scathing reprimand. "You have to be strong here, Beth. You're the hope of all of us, of the entire kingdom. If Charles is dead, at least he'll be free of this horrible condition of his that is slowly making him insane. Between the incessant pain, and the lack of sleep, he's becoming more and more unreasonable each day." Tanglwyst implored as she saw Elizabeth's resolve convalesce. "He can't even stand the light of a cloudless day because of the pain. You said so yourself. He rages constantly, he's cruel to the servants and officers. He's a danger to this kingdom, and to his family."

Elizabeth straightened, Tanglwyst's strength and support invigorating her to do the right thing, with no regrets. When she spoke, Tanglwyst heard as well as felt her determination. "You're right, Tanglwyst. I don't want our land to be destroyed by a selfish king's illness, like so many others have been. I won't have it, not when I can prevent it. And Alexander *will* marry me. We'll see to it. We'll make sure the kingdom has a fit sovereign. Anyone would be better than Charles."

Tanglwyst nodded and smiled.

The door opened and in walked Myrgen just then, carrying a tray of food and wine "Hello, my dear sis…," he began, then lost his voice as his eyes met the queen's. For the past two years, he had been in love with this woman, but as yet, had only confided his affection to his sister.

Tanglwyst walked over to him, took the tray and whispered, "Breathe, Myrgen," then excused herself to see if Michael was hungry.

* * *

Tanglwyst closed the door and let her eyes adjust to the

dim. Michael was standing at the end if the hall and nodded to her when she came out. He moved up the hall and stood by a torch, waiting for her. Tanglwyst sat the tray on the floor. "How did it go tonight?" She took a bite of cheese and offered some bread to the handsome guard.

"Not quite like I'd planned, but well enough." Michael reached for the bread but Tanglwyst dodged his hand and brought the morsel up to his lips. His lips smiled but his eyes did not, yet he allowed himself to be fed.

"What do you mean, well enough? Didn't the sleeping agent I gave you work?"

"Not exactly. She had a scrape along her cheek but I couldn't tell if she got it from the dart or not. I actually ended up punching her to knock her out."

Tanglwyst looked stunned. "You hit her? Did you stick her with the sleeping agent afterward?"

"To tell you the truth, I trust my abilities with my fists much more than any drug, my Lady. I have been trained to fight. I can hit someone effectively without even bruising them. She was a tough fight though." Michael took the bread from Tanglwyst's hand and ate another bite.

"I'm not sure that's encouraging. I don't like changes to the plans we have gone to all this trouble to lay. You did coat the tips right? So it's possible she got nicked by them?"

"I suppose it's possible, yes."

She looked down the hallway toward her door. "Did you leave her in Dom's room?"

"No, I left her at Lady Gwen's home. Lord Dominic's patterns indicated he would be there about that time instead of at his own room at your house."

"Ah. Of course. Smart thinking." Tanglwyst poured some wine for both of them and handed Michael a glass. "It's nice to know you planned this out."

"I had a good teacher," he glanced at the door where Myrgen and Elizabeth were talking.

Tanglwyst glanced over at the door to her room. "The vials I bought for the darts. Did you return them to my house? We can't have Dominic discover they're missing from my stores."

"Yes, I put them right where you said I should, in the dining room across the main hall from the stairs. There's a problem though. There was a body on the stairs."

"What? Whose?"

"A young boy. Light brown hair."

Tanglwyst looked stricken. "Simon?"

"There's more. It turns out Dominic was there."

She snapped out of her shock. "Did he recognize you?"

"No, he never saw me, and I rarely speak in the palace. I believe he thinks I'm dumb. He left before I did. He came from upstairs a few minutes after I entered the manor."

"He was probably there to do some late work or get something from his room. Thank the Saints he didn't see you. Dominic's snooping could ruin the whole thing."

Michael's eyes narrowed. "Well, if necessary, we just cite the dead body at the foot of the stairs. He probably killed him on his way up. He didn't check the boy on his way out."

Tangl shook her head. "I can't think of a single reason why Dom would kill Simon, unless the boy saw something he shouldn't have. If that is the case, he may have inadvertently saved us."

*Chapter Seven:*
*"Stolen waters are sweet, and bread eaten in secret is pleasant."*
*~ Proverbs 9:17*

"How are you doing, my Queen?" Myrgen asked, not daring to look at her directly for fear of having her face etch itself permanently onto his retina where everyone could see it. As it was, he could still see her behind his eyes when he blinked.

Elizabeth stood by the desk wreathed in a nimbus of candle glow from the walls, looking upon the man who, unbeknownst to her, loved her. "I'm doing well, Myrgen. How are you?"

"Well, as best as can be expected, I imagine. This Catriona woman has been captured, threatened and sent on her way with a new mission. I don't know her personally so I'm not sure if she'll carry out the m… mission, or even if she can, but I've done what has been asked of me."

"Did Michael use the sleep agent? It was supposed to be very effective, according to the alchemist who made it."

"I believe he did, Your Majesty. I know he rode off into the woods with her limp body on his lap. According to the plan, he was going to leave her where she would be found easily by someone who would have a vested interest in her. I don't know where he took her, but he came back alone and unharmed so she obviously didn't wake up while they were en route." He glanced over at his secret love and sipped from her beauty, the familiar taste of his desire like fresh water on his tongue.

"Good," she said, nodding. "Now comes the hard part: the waiting." She came over to him, her voice wavering, then steadying as she spoke. "We are doing the right thing, Myrgen. He's in such pain, and our enemies are watching us, looking for a weakness. His displays have been public twice now. As it stands, when Alexander is crowned, they may go to war with us."

Myrgen dared a look at her face and she caught him in her eyes like a sunbeam catches a cat. She seemed to be trying so hard to be strong, but it almost appeared to be unfamiliar territory for her. Myrgen reached out instinctively and touched her hand. "Your Majesty, you shouldn't dwell on this. It will be fine."

They blinked at each other, then both looked at their joined hands. Myrgen realized he had just touched an angel without asking and his stomach flopped as he feared she would toss his hand aside in disgust. She closed her eyes and Myrgen started to retrieve his hand, fumbling with the words of an apology. He tripped over his own breathing as Elizabeth brought his hand up to her cheek. She looked at him with welling eyes full of pain and desire and he took a small step forward. His hand opened, taking in the entirety of her cheek and he slipped his fingers up behind her head and under her snood, enveloping them in her silken finery.

Myrgen felt her responding to his touch as if it were the most natural thing in the world. She tilted her head up to meet his and flowed into him as their lips met. Myrgen's artistic fingers reveled in the feel of her hair as his other hand cuddled her waist, pressing against her rigid corsetry and drawing her to him. Her arms encompassed his neck, blending into him like a watercolor in the rain. The moment lasted an eternity, ending with the full realization of the emotions present.

A knock on the door startled them like a thunderbolt in darkness, and Michael called through the door. "Your Majesty, you should be getting back."

"Yes, of course," Elizabeth said to the door, then looked back at Myrgen. He slowly released her, his fingers lingering in her hair, then he turned away, freeing them from the moment so they could compose themselves before facing the world. He went to the door and waited for her to nod before opening it for her. Michael stepped aside to the wall, making room for the queen and his Lord to pass. She looked at Myrgen. "Thank you again for your clemency in this situation. I knew I could count on you."

"I am forever at your service, Your Majesty." He took her hand and kissed it, his eyes never leaving hers. The contact was brief but powerful and unfortunately Tanglwyst caught the change in countenance in both their faces. She pursed her lips tightly over a smile. Myrgen realized he and Elizabeth were covering for each other, like guilty lovers who just barely escaped getting caught by the woman's husband.

When they turned the corner, out of sight of Michael and Tanglwyst, Elizabeth allowed herself to tighten her grip on Myrgen's hand, privately acknowledging the intimate moment they had just experienced. They moved silently through the dark, uncertain of anything but the route through the passageways. At the secret entrance to her chambers, she turned to face him again.

He touched her hand as it rested on his arm and she drew a breath, visibly melting. She looked at him like she had never seen him before, and he was suddenly very grateful for the time he had spent in Yantap, Yndia, studying romance from those novels and instruction manuals. They had shown him how to kiss a woman and who knew if he would get the chance to demonstrate his other studies? He smoothed a lock of her hair back into its fetters and she responded to his efforts with a smile that caused her eyes to dance.

His own dark hair was long and had a wavy curl to it, and he usually kept it bound like now, out of his way. His slate grey eyes had just a hint of blue to them like fine marble, a sweet complement to her own pale green ones. His hands were strong from handling horses and bows as a hobby, as were his thighs and back, betraying his activity as more than just a book reader and gold counter. He generally preferred to wear grey, keeping his more resplendent colors for fancy occasions, but suddenly, he felt underdressed for being in the presence of such a resplendent creature.

The faint candle glow mesmerized him, her features looking hauntingly like those of his portrait of her. He searched her eyes for a reason for this encounter, to see if, perhaps, she had somehow planned it. *Had she wanted this as much as he had, as long as he had?* He touched her face and found his heart singing when she didn't stop him. Perhaps this wasn't a dream after all. She tilted her head toward him and he cupped her chin, drawing her in for another endless kiss. They blurred together, becoming a single entity in the darkness, and he saw her need for him swell as did his for her.

"Join me tonight, for some wine," he asked as the kiss ended.

"When? Right now?"

"Well, I have some questions to ask Michael about how things went with Catriona. May we meet in an hour?"

"An hour would be perfect for me. Where?"

"Here. We'll go to my quarters. I have something I'd like to show you."

His uncommon smile caused her to blush, and she lit up the dank hallway with it. He opened the way to her door and she slipped inside, her fingers lingering the longest in his company.

Tanglwyst gave Michael a kiss and walked with him into her room as Myrgen escorted the queen through the corridor. "Will you join me tonight? Help me stay warm?"

"Forgive me, my Lady. I cannot tonight," Michael replied, expertly dodging her sexual entanglements yet again. "I must meet with your brother regarding the mission and then check on the boy. Nicolai has also requested the guard do some extra duties around the palace tonight." Tanglwyst's eyes dropped to the floor at the mention of Nicolai, then strayed over to the bed for a moment. "How is he?"

"Nicolai? He was edgy today, and looked like he hadn't slept well." Michael stepped into the hallway. "Do you need anything else, my Lady?"

"No. Thank you, Michael." She slowly closed the door as he went down the hall.

So, Nicolai was out of sorts today. Well, splendid! He would be worried about her, and when she emerged from her captivity safe and unharmed and possibly even close to his son, she was certain to be the only love in his life. Alan was a beautiful child and deserved a mother and father who wouldn't abandon him. That was easily going to be Tanglwyst and if she had Alan as well, Nicolai would cast aside his worthless marriage to Catriona and be hers entirely. Catriona didn't love Nicolai regardless. If she survived but lost Nicolai, the pirate would probably be grateful. If, on the more fashionable hand, she died or was put to death for murdering the king, the woman's entire family would embrace Tanglwyst as their savior. She lay back on the bed and fantasized about her soon-to-be-perfect life.

* * *

Outside the room, Michael breathed easier now that the door separated them. He didn't want to offend the lady but he also felt it inappropriate to bed Myrgen's sister, regardless of *her* desires. There was also something else which felt wrong, though he had never quite been able to put his finger on what that was. It was almost as if she had a loyalty to his enemy or some other insidious motive. Myrgen had warned him to avoid being touched by her, but he had never once wanted that. It had not yet stopped her though, and that put him off even more. Michael picked up the tray he and Tanglwyst had left and walked on down the hallway where he met Myrgen.

"How is the queen?"

Myrgen took the tray from Michael, a smile daring to try to play across his face. "She's holding up under the strain, but just barely. It will be well when this is all over." Myrgen looked at Michael. "Do you think it will work, Michael?"

"Your plan is a sound one. Alexander is a good man. He will not allow the kingdom to go to war. When you recommend he marry the Mandian Princess Isabelle, he will see how this would unite Mervolingia and Mande and end the threat between your kingdoms. They will be strong allies and the people will be safe and prosperous. The queen will be able to retire to Anjou, the Queen-Mother to Angloume and your position will be secure in the aftermath."

"I'm not concerned about maintaining my position here. I care mostly about the destructive nature of Charles and his mother." He thought briefly of Elizabeth and felt it necessary to get his business finished here. He had always thought he might retire with the queen to the ducal estate to administer her finances, but now he had hopes of something more between them. "Do you know anything about the woman? Catriona?"

"No, sir, but there was something in her eyes which reminded me of home. I don't know what that means, if anything. When she was out, I, um, checked to be sure I hadn't done any permanent damage and noticed subtle things, like the fullness of her lips and the shape of her eyes. They belie a Nubian bloodline. You can see it in the boy as well, though not as prominently."

"Nubian? Is that so? You mean, like perhaps your home tribe?"

"Yes. Her coloring, her features, they speak out that one of her recent ancestors was from the islands where my people settled."

"So she's not merely Nubian, but from the older bloodline."

"I believe so, sir. There are enough traits which are

Saintlandian so she would not be treated like a slave anywhere but the Papal City, perhaps. I have seen this sort of thing before, in places where the races have blended. If one parent were of the continent and the other Nubian, this sort of person would be the result."

"Yes, I have seen some of these people before. They are the most beautiful people I've ever laid eyes upon. It would explain a lot of things. How is the boy?"

"I was just about to check on him, sir."

"Good. Make sure he's not frightened, if you can. Make sure he's warm enough and has what he needs to survive. See if he needs any toys or anything else."

"I shall. I brought some things from the princess's nursery but I don't quite have anywhere else to go for such things."

"Understood. How about bringing him a pet, then? A dog, perhaps?"

"A dog might bark and alert the servants," Michael cautioned.

"I doubt that, where we have him. The old chapel isn't near enough to the new one and the walls around here are thirty feet thick to support their own weight. Even a barking dog wouldn't be heard. Besides, any servants who came down here would be lost before they found their way to the boy *or* out again. They would undoubtedly simply assume it was one of the Prince's animals and ignore it. Regardless, a dog might make his captivity easier to endure. We're both unwilling participants in this drama. I don't want to make things worse on him, if I can help it." Myrgen looked back at the tunnels. "Perhaps I should go speak to him."

"That would be unwise, Sir. The fewer people he sees, the better. There are kennels where the Prince's dogs have been kept for their training. I believe there are some young ones there who would be about right."

"That's right. Now that you mention it, Alexander said something about offering up a wolfhound from Heracles' line as a gift to someone, some foreign woman. They would be about the appropriate age for a young boy. Get one of those, if you wouldn't mind. Take some money from my room to pay for the animal."

"I'll get him one first thing in the morning."

"Perfect. Thank you, Michael. Get some rest and I'll see you in the palace tomorrow. Good night."

"Good night, sir," Michael said with a nod and went off to check on the sleeping Alan.

*Chapter Eight:*
*"Keep thy heart with all diligence, for out of it are the issues of life."*
*~ Proverbs 4:23*

*In the dream, Alan watched the darkness from an alleyway. He could see something lurking in the shadows, something terrible, something frightening. He wanted to run, but he knew that would be useless. If he revealed himself, he would be caught by the Terrible Thing and it would hurt, or even kill him. Instead, he shuddered in the cold, listening to the sound of pounding and roaring.*

*He heard a horse coming and it frightened him even more, though he didn't understand why. He knew the Terrible Thing wasn't on the horse, but somehow, the horse's arrival would bring the Terrible Thing out. He saw a rider on the horse come up before the alleyway and then he saw his mother come up to the rider. She was surrounded by a glowing nimbus, and she was happy and beautiful. She went to the rider and greeted him, excited to see this person.*

*Alan looked into the place where the Terrible Thing was and saw its muscles tense as it prepared to leap on his mother. Alan cried out but she didn't hear him and she turned her back on the place where the Terrible Thing was waiting. She and the rider began to walk away and the Terrible Thing leapt out of the shadows onto to them, and Alan knew the Terrible Thing was going to kill them. He ran out to them as the Terrible Thing used a Terrible Claw on the rider, slashing at him..*

*Alan's mother turned on the Terrible Thing, her face a mask of horror and fear as the Terrible Thing struck out at her too. The rider kept the Terrible Thing away from his mother but he got hurt in the process when the Terrible Thing clawed his leg. Another rider and horse came out of another alleyway, knocking the Terrible Thing to the ground. The Terrible Thing disappeared and his mother ran to her ship. She got her sword and stood, watching. As the riders helped each other, Alan saw the Terrible Thing rise from the shadows behind his mother, drawing his claws to tear her apart...*

Alan woke up with a start, sitting up in the small, dark room he was being held in. He was frightened by the lack of sounds of the dungeon room, though he could hear a few strange sounds occasionally, like water dripping or sometimes people talking. He sat back on the bed and thought about things which would help the bad stuff go away. When he had been on the ship with his mother, she had taught him to listen to the sea and think of wondrous things to relax him until he got used to the *Enigma* and the noises she made.

He tried to listen to the walls around him, determining what could make the sounds he could hear, but he didn't have a guide and he didn't know where he was, so his imagination simply made the things he didn't know into Terrible Things. He closed his eyes and tried to go back to sleep but he couldn't, so he got up.

The people supplied a lantern for him, and even a few things to keep him occupied, like charcoal sticks for drawing and a woolen ball. He thought about possibly drawing on the walls, but he wasn't sure what to draw. He lit the lantern carefully, like he had been taught to do by Drake. He missed Drake and Anika. It had been a while since he had seen them, and the men who had grabbed him were not nice people. Two men, one scrawny with red hair and a pimply face, the other a hulking great man who didn't speak very well, had grabbed him as he entered the Lady Tanglwyst's home with her. They had poked him with something sharp, a pin or thin knife or something, and he had fallen asleep and woke up here.

Alan was worried because Anika and Drake were supposed to take him home. He didn't like living in a land where the people worshipped the Saints like they had power over things. Alan knew the only true power was that of the Land, like Drake had taught him. He wished Drake was there now. Alan picked up the charcoal stick and drew Drake on the wall facing the side of the bed. He drew him big and strong, holding a black sword and wearing armor. All around him, the Land was on fire, jagged rocks piercing the ground and standing tall behind Drake.

He looked at his project and smiled. He felt much better now. The Land would protect him. If he was here, there must be a reason for it, for the Land to have let him be taken. Maybe this was the Land's way of getting him back to Caratia. Even if his father wanted them to, his mother would never allow them to stay in

Mervolingia after he had been stolen. He set the charcoal stick down and wiped his hands on his pants, putting long, black marks all over his thighs. He turned around and saw something on the stone floor: a small doll.

He didn't know where the doll came from. He hadn't seen it earlier with the other toys, and it was unusual for Mervolingia. He recognized the other toys as belonging to Marie Elizabeth, the king's daughter. They had played together a few times when his father had brought him to the palace, but her dolls were wearing fancy clothes and had real hair. This doll had dark skin and hair done up in beads, like his mother described his grandmother. Maybe this doll had belonged to his mother. This one was wearing strange clothes too and looked a lot like the black guard he had seen around the palace, the one who brought him the toys. He looked at it carefully and a great calm came over him. He held the doll close and the stone walls seemed to whisper to him to be patient, his mother was coming for him.

Alan curled up with the doll on the bed again and fell asleep, certain he would be free again soon. The doll rested next to his cheek, and as he drifted off, he thought he heard Anika's singing far, far away.

*Chapter Nine:*
*"Men do not despise a thief, if he steal to satisfy his soul when he is hungry."*
*~ Proverbs 6:30*

Elizabeth was thinking about the kiss in the chamber downstairs as she refreshed her appearance. She found herself preparing for their meeting with special waters and perfumes she usually reserved only for meetings with Alexander or the king. Not that anything like this had ever really happened with Charles, or with Alexander either. Not yet, in any event. She had plans for her and Alexander to join when Charles was gone, and not exactly for the sake of the kingdom, as Tanglwyst had said. She had never told anyone about her secret infatuation with the Prince, but she had seen often the qualities she admired in a man displayed in him.

She remembered hearing about his involvement in the Saint Michael's Massacre. When Charles had given the order to kill Plantyn and the Emilianites, it had been Alexander who had carried out the orders himself. Elizabeth had been in Patras to attend the princess's wedding, along with her family. A commotion had drawn her attention and she had gone to her window, only to overhear Alexander telling Lieutenant Marcel to kill them all, regardless of age or gender. Marcel had sworn it would be done, a horrible glee to his voice. Elizabeth had known at that time she wanted Alexander for her own, and had even mistaken him for his brother for they looked quite similar in the miniature portrait she had been given.

Elizabeth saw herself as a strong, compassionate woman, having studied the Yorkish queen's tactics as well as Catherine's examples for acquiring power. Make them think you are weak, then strike with strength. It is said men could wage war upon the land but women waged wars upon the soul, and were therefore the deadlier enemy. She agreed with this. The Saints knew she had managed to fool everyone here.

When Charles had struck her last week, it had been completely unexpected. She had been lonely and mindful of the need for a male heir. She took advantage of the fact Catherine wasn't around and the peace that brought and planned to seduce Alexander. She had crept down the hallway in nothing but a robe, hoping to ply Alexander with drink enough to make him open to her will. She assumed Charles was either asleep or with his mistress, but Charles had come out of the privy, looking haggard. She had told him she was about to visit *him*, to offer herself for her wifely duties in the hopes of securing a male heir.

Charles had told her to go, that he had no interest in what she had to offer. She had followed him into his room and berated him, calling him less than a man. He had slapped her, knocking her to the ground, and she had wept and ran off. Once outside his room, she decided to run to Alexander and get his support. She hoped he would heal her with his poultices and in so doing, she would feign vulnerability and request his protection. With a bruise like this marring her cheek, she anticipated his outrage with glee.

But he had not been there. She had run into Myrgen in the halls on her way back to her room and he had insisted she speak to Tanglwyst. He had escorted her to her room and after she had gotten dressed, she wrote Tanglwyst a note describing what Charles had done. She had wrapped it in another piece of paper to hide the content from prying eyes, sealing it with her royal sigil. Not comfortable with the possibility of giving the note to Myrgen to deliver, she had gone with him to Tanglwyst's home. As she suspected, Tanglwyst wasn't home, probably off with Nicolai. Elizabeth had produced the note and left it in the drawer of Tanglwyst's desk in her study, explaining to Myrgen that she had come prepared for this.

Elizabeth had never before thought of Myrgen as a possibility for her desires. To her, he had always been Tanglwyst's brother. His concerns for her safety and sanity had always struck her as being fraternal. The kiss downstairs in the catacombs had suddenly changed all that. She felt certain Myrgen would support her overthrow of the Angloume males, if necessary. After all, she had won his heart. He would do anything for her. With Marie-Elizabeth on the throne after her, the kingdom would be in the hands of a level, sensitive ruler for the first time in history.

Now *she* was going to see what it was like to be Sovereign. She was going to take a lover, like her husband had, and drink the pleasures of power. Elizabeth couldn't wait for Charles to be out of the picture. Catherine had ruled here long enough through Charles. It was time for a change, and even though she wanted Alexander by her side, Elizabeth had no intention of ruling through any man. Even he would be expendable, like his brother.

She thought back to Myrgen's eyes in the darkness, the bit of blue summoned forth by the black around them and their treasonous circumstances. It had opened her eyes about something she hadn't quite noticed, or understood, before, something which seemed painfully obvious now. He loved her. She felt a strange exhilaration at that knowledge, alongside the buoyancy of infatuation. It was more a security in knowing he would never betray her because he loved her, even if their plan was discovered. It meant she would have to make sure she did absolutely nothing to endanger that emotion. It was too valuable, too important. Too exhilarating.

She touched up her light make-up, then decided to let her hair down and brush it to silken softness because he seemed to like the way it felt. She toyed with the idea of getting undressed, going to him in her shift and robe. She tossed the thought aside with a flip of her brush. No sense turning this tawdry. He may have a vision of her which precluded such physical messiness. She would play this by ear, distancing her emotions so she would not be dissuaded from her plans for the future.

She brushed her hair calmly, begging for the time to pass quickly, surprised to find herself anxious for the chance to see him, in spite of herself. She had not realized before just how attractive Myrgen was, but indeed it was so. This was going to be easier than she thought.

* * *

Myrgen entered his chambers from his reverie before the prayer room portrait and glanced around quickly. The servants had been there that day to clean the room, and he was finally grateful for such intrusions. His documents were always locked within his desk and he had long ago installed a poison needle trap to keep the drawer secure from prying eyes. The trap had broken last year but the first few servants who died mysteriously and almost instantly from cuts in their fingertips after placing their hands in the drawer insured no one had touched his papers since.

Thus he had little tidying to do to prepare his room for the visit from the queen. He stoked the fire so the embers caught the log again and before the hour was upon him, the glow of firelight was the only light he wanted to allow in the room. He found he was so caught in the rapids of her appearance in firelight, he feared he would drown in her flickering beauty. He went to the cellars and got a bottle of the best wine, returning just in time for his meeting in the passageway. This room had belonged to Charles originally and Myrgen's presence here was designed by the king as an affront on several levels. Not only did it place a commoner on the same level as the royalty, which offended his mother greatly, but Charles had also left it in part because of this passage. Charles wanted nothing to do with Elizabeth, and definitely didn't want her creeping into his bed in the night. Myrgen didn't mind at all.

He stepped into the passageway and heard her footsteps padding down the hall from her room. Elizabeth had let her hair down and the beauty of the simple act seized his heart in an almost painful grip. He took her hands and drew her to his doorway in the dark. They entered his portrait room and Elizabeth looked around the room, her eyes widening as they played upon the portrait. She looked to Myrgen. "Did *you* do this portrait?"

He watched her surprise and delight with a smile and nodded. "And the one of you in your Coronation gown."

She looked back at the portrait and shook her head, astonished. "We never knew whom to thank for it." She turned to him in the fluttering light and her hand brushed his cheek. "Let this be a start, to show my gratitude." She pulled him to her and kissed him lushly, the beginning of a night wherein none existed except the two of them.

Elizabeth put his hand on her bodice and pulled. Some thread popped where she was sewn into her bodice and she arched an eyebrow at Myrgen, daring him to do the rest. He took her up on her offer and pulled her bodice apart. Her bare skin melted under his touch, moaning escaping her lips under his. She dragged him to the wall, kissing him, and he obliged. The floor was cold under Myrgen's fingers and he looked down at her. "Do you want to move this somewhere more comfortable?"

"No. I want to feel you inside me in front of that portrait."

"As you wish, my love." He pulled her skirt up, noting the undergarments still in place. It was going to take a bit of work to do as she wanted, and she was not forthcoming in giving him direction. He felt foolish, fumbling in the dark with her, but the fact he had not been with a lover for over two years did not leave him unprepared. He ran his hands over her legs, listening for that intake of breath that indicated her preferences. He kissed her, mirroring her passion and was surprised when she reached down and started fondling him. He was solid to begin with and a few strokes brought him to full strength, rigid and screaming for release.

She moved down their clothes without bothering to remove them and pulled him into her. Myrgen once again obliged, entering her deeper with each thrust. The pleasure of her pussy, smooth and wet, was blessed further by the surroundings and he got very close very quickly. He stopped, not interested in finishing so soon, but she apparently had other plans, kicking her leg around his back and pressing her heel into his rear as she moved her hips to cause him to orgasm. He pulsed into her, his gratification almost forcing a scream of pleasure from his throat. He twitched and rested a moment, then looked at her. "That was unfair."

She smiled, a satisfaction on her face that had nothing to do with her own pleasure or lack thereof. "Well, I guess you'll just have to owe me then."

"Oh trust me, I will pay." He sat back, pulling himself into a bit more semblance of decorum as she adjusted things. He stood and helped her to her feet. She kissed him and started to go for the door to the catacombs. He grabbed her wrist and stopped her progress. "Hey, I'm not done with you."

"Aren't you done though?"

"Oh no. That was just the beginning." He drew her into the room and closed the door to the prayer nave.

* * *

Hours later, Elizabeth opened her eyes and blinked at her surroundings. One of the things that surprised her about this room was the lack of a window for a room that used to be the king's. She heard a heartbeat beneath her head and glanced at the man sleeping beneath her. Myrgen was more beautiful unwrapped than she ever suspected, muscles toned by riding and archery. His hair, unbound, draped across the pillow like silk sheets and she felt the birth of passion engulf her senses. He was an attentive lover, unexpectedly versed in multiple forms of pleasure. When she had asked him about it after a shuddering orgasm, her first in years that wasn't self-administered, he merely explained an interest in reading certain rare and scandalous books. Their explorations of each other would have put cartographers to shame and it was the morning movements of the changing of the king's guard which finally broke them apart.

Elizabeth tapped him on the chest and when he opened his eyes, she put her finger on his lips to keep their proximity a secret a while longer. They got up and Myrgen placed a robe around Elizabeth in her chemise and helped her carry her clothing through the passages, clad only in some riding breeches, their bare feet padding on the cold stone. They exchanged a final kiss with emptied arms at her doorway to the labyrinth, and she smiled. "You surprised me last night."

"I'm glad I was able to return the favor."

"What are you going to do today?"

Myrgen scratched his shoulder. "Well, first, I'm going to try *not* to whistle or hum my way back to my room." She giggled at that, pleasing him even more. His grin drifted to a bit more serious expression as he realized something he needed to focus upon. "Then, I'm going to start making a few preparations toward the inevitable end of your imprisonment. I don't want certain documents to fall into the wrong hands. We're dealing with a very dangerous woman here. If we mishandle anything, she'll exploit it."

Elizabeth found his respect for Catriona to be a little inappropriate for a man who had just spent the night making love to her. "How well do you know her?"

"Personally? Not at all. But once we got her to do this, I started do a bit of investigating. The things I have heard about her make her a very dangerous woman."

"Like what?"

"Like there's no proof, but rumor says she killed a Mandian noble named Marco Giovanni and his son. Or rather, she got the man to kill his own son, then himself. There's also a tale I heard about how she brought down the Black Sparrow, the pirate that was plaguing Tanglwyst's ships a couple years back. She's also taken out several members of the Black Hand, a group that serves the D'Medici family. Those people don't go down easily, yet she's taken out five of them, according to my sources. I understand she's the Stâpâna of Caratia but I don't know what that means since that country is as secretive as she is, but she's been seen often in Patras all season. That's how I was able to capture her. This was the only time I've had any kind of idea where to find her."

"How often have you looked for her?"

Myrgen arched his eyebrows. "Are you kidding? Someone who can take out Black Hand assassins? I would give half my year's pay to have someone like that available to me. But she's not for hire. It was pure luck that Michael happened to see her entering that inn where he managed to get the dart on her. Otherwise, I was about to go with my contact in Leone."

"Would you have preferred that?" Elizabeth secretly wanted this because his talk of this woman so soon after their all night session was irritating her.

"On the one hand, I'm thrilled to death to have the chance to work with her. I want to see what she can do. But the *way* this has been done?" He shook his head, a flicker of anger tainting his eyes. "This is just wrong, and stupid. You don't threaten a woman's child to get her to do something like this."

Elizabeth was about to loose her temper upon her lover when a knock on the door saved his life. Her head lady-in-waiting called through the door. "Your Majesty? Are you awake?"

She pushed him toward the tunnel and gave him a quick peck on the lips as a goodbye before closing the door on him.

*Chapter Ten:*
*"The righteous is delivered out of trouble and the wicked cometh in his stead."*
*~ Proverbs 11:8*

*Smoke.*

*She looked at the stain it made in the sky in the late afternoon light. The men had stopped the villagers from putting the fire out in the small house, killing two people in the process to emphasize their point. They watched the flames take the roof, scarring the wood that both supported and decorated the outside of the building. She had escaped the fire as they were killing the rescuers, a chunk of the stone back wall falling down to put out a small patch of the flames temporarily. The child had been coughing and the sound had carried through the building. Then the stone started screaming, the heat causing the water within to shatter it in a horrible retort. The men's faces had shown their satisfaction at the ending of the screams while the villagers had cried out in horror at the silence.*

*She muffled the child's coughs in the wool blanket she had grabbed to cover her face from the smoke, then slipped away to the river. Her assailants would sift through the ashes, looking for proof of their deaths, but not before nightfall, and probably not before morning. She needed to be gone before then. She saw in the twilight a ship at the end of the river, waiting in the deeper waters off the delta. The small village had been a learning experience for understanding the seafaring folk and she hoped her lessons would save her and her infant now.*

*Winged lions of gold maintaining a sword between them, the point to base, upon a black field.*

*There was something helpful, something peaceful in the standard the center mast flew, almost familiar, though she had never seen this country's flag before. The sword was not pointing up, to the sky, ready to destroy. It pointed down, to the land, the soil between them. Creatures of the Land, borne upwards, exalted. Unity, protection.*

*Home.*

*She knew they would help her and her child. She knew they would take her to this place, that she would find help and solace there. She knew, beyond knowing, that her son would be safe from those who hunted her. Confident, she moved through the reeds to the ship and the ladder which hung over the side…*

Catriona awoke in the morning feeling depressed and mournful and aware of a full day passing while unconscious. The dream reminded her of the kindness she had found on the ship, the protection of the sailors. They had taken her home, to Caratia. She and her son had been taken in by a kindly couple who had turned out to be the Governors of the Kingdom, the Ducé and Ducêsa of Caratia. The ship captain had been the Ducêsa's brother. She missed Drake and Anika, and wished she could return home to them. Alan had taken to life in Caratia like he was born there. Although Catriona had long ago accepted their offer to call Caratia her home, her obligation to Nicolai had interfered with it. Still, she was glad to be able to send Alan to be with them for the season. The boy was ten years old this year. This was the year, by Caratian reckoning, where he found his place in the world and became a man.

She felt better this morning, and was glad for the rest, but knew the time had come for her to get on her task. She wanted to get a message to Charles, warning him about the murder assignment, but wasn't certain how to do it. It wasn't like she could just walk in and request an audience, not with Nicolai in the palace as a guardsman.

More important, not with Alexander around.

The thought made her heart ache even more and she felt her eyes stinging as she bit back tears. She was in far too emotional a state to risk seeing Alexander and decided to go to Nicolai instead. Although they had had their intimate moments, lingering tenderness which fought against the tides of anger between them, he was usually bitter toward her. This was preferable to the angst which would encompass a visit to Alexander. Her relationship with him had been strictly utilitarian for years, but a moment of loneliness had changed all that last summer. She was so tired of being without that human touch in her life that she had allowed herself to get entangled in more than one inappropriate relationship. Now, she needed to figure out what was real and what was just because of a desire not to be alone.

She got herself dressed properly and crept past Gwen, still sleeping in a chair by the drowsy hearth, and slipped into the early dawn. She also needed to tell Nicolai about Alan's kidnapping. Although he would blame her and probably be cruel, he deserved to know. Maybe he would surprise her and be supportive, like he used to be. There was always hope.

Catriona shifted into the shadows of the burgeoning dawn and moved along the streets toward Nicolai's home. He had bought this home with his severance pay from Tanglwyst, and it was not lost on Catriona that she could see the rooftop of Tanglwyst's manor house from their bedroom window. She could not blame him for wanting that reminder of happier times after so much pain. She herself could see the palace from Alan's window and hear the docks from the front door. It was a fine house, with a separate room for Alan and close access to a public privy. But it was not home to any of them.

Catriona was about three blocks from Nicolai's house when she saw a blue door open in a modest house and a man kiss his wife goodbye. She waited a moment, not in a hurry to talk to her own husband, and watched the couple so obviously in love. The two disengaged and he put his hood up over his head. At that moment, she recognized the profile of the king, and her breath caught in her throat. He slipped easily into the role of a man going off to modest work and he kept to the less traveled streets.

She followed him, closing the distance between them slowly, until they were very near the palace. The man she needed to murder to save her son went into the gardens and slipped behind a hedge on the western side of the palace. She looked around, then waited a few minutes before pursuing him into the hedge which hid the secret entrance to the catacombs.

Catriona followed the passage Charles entered, stopping frequently to listen and make sure she wasn't discovered. She checked the walls as she went along, looking for other passages and doorways but found none. She touched the timbers supporting the passage, counting them as she went in the dark so she would have some idea how far she had traveled and noticed her hands sticking to them every once in a while.

The passage ended in a dead end, but there had been no turns at all, not even the hint of a turn, and she felt around the walls for some sort of a switch or catch. A small click from pushing on a stone popped the clasp holding the stone door closed and she caught to door to keep from making a noise. Catriona eased the door open and looked around inside carefully.

She seemed to have opened the door on a prayer room, moderately sized befitting the king. A very few votives were burning, in fact only two provided any light at all. Catriona slipped fully into the shadows of the room and watched Charles. He put his clothes of the street into a trunk at the foot of his bed and locked it, then went over to the window and opened the curtains, letting the springtime morning into the room. He pulled a silk ribbon from a pocket in his breeches, rich purple in the sunlight, and smelled it. She figured it belonged to the woman at the blue door, and by the looks of it, Charles was desperately in love with her.

Catriona studied Charles, looking for signs of the sickness Nicolai had mentioned in passing about two weeks ago, but seeing none. According to her husband, the king had been experiencing foul headaches which were overwhelming in their pain. They made him light sensitive, grouchy and violent of late. He had trouble moving when they hit him, sometimes incapacitating him completely. He had a physician who had tried several different remedies and had no luck, as had Alexander, and Catriona trusted Alex's diagnoses far more than those of some pharmacist.

A tray of food was on the table in the room, supposedly from the night before, and Charles poured himself some wine. There was some bread on the tray as well and Charles tore himself a piece, wiping it across the slab of butter on the tray before sitting in a large chair facing the window. He watched the birds and the fountains out his window as he ate the bread and Catriona moved to where she could see more of the room.

The pitcher of wine was an ornate brass ewer, and the dishes which he ate and drank from were gold and silver. The bed was a magnificent carved thing and he needed a step stool to climb onto the mattress to sleep. Huge blue velvet curtains with gold fleurs-de-lis adorned the bed and the windows, and a large robe of similar material hung on a special frame near the wardrobe. There was a beautifully carved desk with papers, sealing wax sticks and a candle lantern where Charles drew up decrees, and a large table in the center of the room for meals and meetings. Catriona looked at the tray of food and noticed the butter had strange blue streaks across it.

She heard Charles moan and lay his head back against the back of the chair. He picked up his goblet and put it back down again, practically upsetting it as he did so. He leaned forward and placed his head in his hands, rubbing his face and hair. He shouted for his guards who then came immediately into the room from their posts outside. He kept his hands on his eyes and asked the guards to close the curtains for him. They exchanged a glance, and Catriona saw silent suffering and apprehension in their faces, as if encountering an ongoing torment.

The men left him alone after they closed the curtains, apparently accustomed to this routine, and Charles rubbed his head and moaned. A few minutes later, there was a knock on the door and three servants entered with a breakfast tray for His Majesty. They cleaned off the table of last night's dishes and set the new tray in its place before announcing to the king that his breakfast was ready. Charles looked at the tray of food and rose, his face becoming a mask of evil and horror.

*Chapter Eleven:*
*"The fear of a king is as the roaring of a lion. Whoso provoketh him to anger sinneth against his own soul."*
*~ Proverbs 20:2*

Myrgen awoke, and dressed in blue because Elizabeth had asked him to before they parted company early that morning. He didn't have many blue things which weren't extremely fancy and settled for a shirt which had turned blue when a new washerwoman had added too much bluing and several whites had changed color, this shirt among them. He had a dark blue shaub and a grey doublet and breeches which went well together and he hoped this would satisfy Her Majesty. He worried overdressing would alert others to the fact something was going on, and snooping and gossip could be crippling right now.

Myrgen put on some tall boots and went to the privy down the hall. He had just left the room when he heard the king ranting and then the crash of metal. Two servants ran from the room and Myrgen heard another crying out in pain. The guards usually stationed outside the room were inside when Myrgen got there and the chancellor was impeded at the door by them. "Forgive me, Your Lordship, he's in a rage and we've been told to keep everyone out."

"Told by whom?" Myrgen was anxious, looking in to be certain it wasn't Elizabeth in the room being attacked.

"By me, Myrgen," came the Prince's voice from behind them. "Excuse me." Alexander pushed past Myrgen and the guards and surveyed the situation. Charles had beaten an old servant man into a corner with a belt. The man was bleeding from the ears and had several defensive wounds across his arms. Charles reared his arm back to deliver another blow when Alexander grabbed it, staying his hand. "Charles. What are you doing?"

Charles turned quickly, eyes wild and angry at who would dare interrupt him, who would be so bold as to touch the Royal Person. He saw it was Alexander and seemed to calm a bit. He pointed at the man cowering on the floor. "He's trying to kill me."

"Arnold? Trying to kill you?" Alexander looked straight into Charles' eyes and tried to get through to him. "Arnold has been with us since were children, Charles. He would never try to hurt you."

Charles broke free of Alexander's grip and strode over to his breakfast tray which was, unremarkably, the only thing still on the table. Silverware and a couple of goblets lay strewn across the floor and Charles bent over and picked up a butter knife from the mess. "What do you call this?" Alexander helped Arnold to his feet and looked him over quickly before turning to see what Charles was holding.

"I would call that a butter knife, Charles." Alexander patted Arnold on the shoulder.

"A *knife.* Exactly." Charles strode back over to stand before Arnold, who brought his arms up again to ward off another series of attacks. "He picked it up and pointed it at me, Alexander. He threatened to stab me with it."

Alexander looked at Charles sternly and suddenly slapped him. "Get hold of yourself Charles."

Charles put his left hand to his cheek, stunned for a second as his brother chastised him. "You *dare* strike the king?"

"You won't be king for long if you keep this up."

"He drew a *knife* on me."

"It's a *butter knife,* Charles. It's not a dangerous weapon. It's just an eating utensil."

"Not dangerous? *Not dangerous?*" With that, Charles plunged the blunted knife into Arnold's belly. With no bones to stop the assault, the old man's thin skin was penetrated immediately.

"No!" Alexander cried out and grabbed Charles' hands too late to save the servant man. Arnold slipped to the floor, the pain incapacitating as blood and bile flowed between his fingers as he grasped his stomach. The blow was a deadly one that would kill him slowly and painfully over the next twenty minutes. Charles looked in horror at what he had done and dropped the knife, its impact with the floor spewing small blood drops onto the king's feet. Alexander looked immediately at the two guards. "You!" He pointed to the one on the right, "Get me some bandages. Now!" The guard took off quickly.

Myrgen stepped into the room when the doorway cleared and ran over to Alexander. "Is there anything I can do?"

Alexander was a little surprised to see Myrgen by his side but took advantage of the situation. "Can you find his wife? I think she works in the kitchens. Her name is Evelyn."

"Sure. Do you want me to do that right now?"

"Please. I can't stop him from dying, but I can at least have his wife with him when he goes."

"I'll be back with her immediately, if I have to carry her up the stairs myself." Myrgen rose and took off toward the door.

"I'll have him in my room. Bring her there."

Myrgen turned back at the door and nodded his understanding. He threw a glance at Charles who was watching the whole thing from the other side of the room. Alexander called the other guard to him and told him, "Help me take this man to my room." The guard carefully lifted the old man in his arms while Alexander kept pressure on the wound to keep the blood flow to a minimum.

Charles looked at the scene around him. "Alexander, I... I didn't mean to..."

Alexander looked at his brother and let the disgust show in his voice. "Yes you did, Charles. I'll be back to speak with you."

Charles leaned heavily against the bed and began to cry and Myrgen ran down the hall toward the stairs.

* * *

In the shadows of his prayer apse, a figure blended into the darkness like a whisper in the wind. Catriona waited there, trying to piece together what she had just seen and what to do. She wanted to go to Charles, to soothe and help him, but in his current state, she doubted he'd be able to understand. She tried to think of what could be going on here and was drawing a blank. Charles was acting so very unlike himself, so unlike the man she had first met ten years ago.

Alexander, on the other hand, was as he had been then, kind and helpful, mindful of what would comfort and giving no thought to his own station and how it differed from that of his patient. To Alexander, the old man was a person, not just a trusted servant, and if he could, Alexander would give his own life to save another's. She wasn't sure she could heal the man, but she could prolong his life, provided she could get there in time. She wanted to go to her friend, to watch him work and give him her support in this time of chaos and she would have in a second, if she'd had a way.

However, she had looked in the escape route which she followed to reach the king's chambers and it had no forks and no hidden doors to connect it to even the queen's escape passage. She knew palaces usually had escape routes from the kings and queen's chambers to get them to safety in the event of a siege, thinking it odd there was no passage connecting the king's room to the queen's, and decided to figure out why that was. Perhaps it was pertinent to the situation and if she could find it in time, she might be able to save Arnold.

She stepped back out into the secret passage, the balanced door belying better craftsmanship than the castle at the Giovanni estate. She also noted this passage was done more recently. The timbers supporting the walls and ceiling were still sticky in places, the sap and pitch not quite dried out. This passage had been built in the past few years. It couldn't have been more than four years old at the most because the sap, though very sparse, was still present in some of the timbers and they would be bled dry completely by this time next year.

That would mean Charles hadn't always been in this room, and that the room he was originally in would be the one with more than one passage. She thought about the rooms and where each was positioned, but she didn't quite know the palace layout and came up short on where to look next. She was about to go back to the garden and look for other ways into the castle when she heard Alexander's voice in Charles' chambers.

"Charles, how are you feeling?" Alexander asked as he closed the king's bedroom door behind him.

"I'm feeling very strange, Alex. I don't know what I'm doing." Charles looked up at his brother with red-rimmed eyes puffy from crying. "I was *so sure* he was trying to kill me, *so sure…*"

"Why did you think that?" Alexander approached him, slow steps ready for trouble.

"I can't, for the life of me, think of a reason, now, but then, it was so clear. I'm frightened, Alexander. I'm scared out of my wits."

"Me too, Charles, as is nearly everyone who comes in contact with you. What's going to happen when Mother comes back?"

"Saint's Blood, I don't know. I can't deal with the pain,

Alex. Make the pain go away, please…" Charles gripped his own hair, threatening to pull it out and Alexander helped him into bed.

"Maybe you should rest now. I'll send in your physician."

Charles nodded and lay down on his bed. Alexander closed the door behind him and Catriona left lest she be tempted to see Alexander in his time of need. The only place to meet him would be in the halls of the palace and she was just as likely to run into Nicolai there as Alexander.

* * *

Alexander met Myrgen in the hall. Myrgen nodded toward the door and asked, "How's he doing?"

"Terrible. He seems to know what he's done, but he can't understand why. How's Arnold?"

"Dying. Evelyn is with him, but he'll be gone soon." Myrgen folded his arms across his chest and leaned up against the wall letting out a tortured sigh. Alexander agreed, having witnessed the elderly couple's love for one another before, and knew it was the right thing to do, letting the two of them spend the man's last moments together. He longed for a chance for a love like that, and knew instinctively it would be like that with Catriona. He glanced at Myrgen and saw he was near tears himself. Clearly, the incident had effected the man and Alexander had no idea the Chancellor was soft-hearted when it came to servants.

Alexander gestured toward the gardens and Myrgen accepted, getting his tears under control. They walked to the garden, feeling the springtime air lift the weight of the scene upstairs from their shoulders a little bit.

"Did you know Arnold well?" Alexander asked as they walked by the roses.

"Me?" Myrgen pointed to himself. "No, not particularly. Why?"

"Well, you seem to actually be upset by this. Forgive me for being rude, but you don't strike me as being all that concerned for the common man normally."

"Why not? When it comes right down to it, *I'm* 'the common man.'" His slight chuckle held no mirth. "No, I was thinking about Marie-Elizabeth. What if that had been her in there to see her father, and not some servant? Would you have been able to stop him?"

Alexander shook his head. "I don't know. A child in danger is an entirely different thing. You can be sure I won't allow her in there from now on."

"What about Elizabeth, or your mother? What if he had gone after them?"

"He would have killed Elizabeth, to be sure, but Mother's a rather scrappy fighter. On the other hand, if Mother *did* survive an attack from Charles, she'd have him out from under that Crown before the sun set."

Myrgen looked surprised. "Is that so? She always struck me as the 'royalty can do as they please' sort of person."

"She is, to a point, but if Charles keeps this up, he won't be king much longer. Once Mother gets word of this, there will be an investigation. With the Augustinian Church angry at them both right now, she'll take decisive steps to protect him from any Papal decision that he's being possessed by Lucifer, or other such nonsense."

Alexander caught a hint of movement in a shadow behind a hedge and stopped Myrgen with a gesture. He watched the shadows there for a minute. He adjusted his eyes to the surroundings and thought, for an instant, he saw a viridian gaze return his eye. His heart leapt in his chest and he began to move toward the hedge when a valet came up to the two men.

"Your Highness," the boy said, bowing, "I'm to tell you Arnold is dead."

Alexander looked at the boy and at Myrgen, then quickly back at the hedge, which was less shadowy now, as if whatever was capturing the sunlight on the other side was now gone and letting it flow freely. Alexander turned back to the boy and the three went inside.

## Chapter Twelve:
## *"Evil pursueth sinners, but to the righteous, good shall be repayed."*
## *~ Proverbs 13:21*

Michael opened the door to the boy's chambers and looked around. He was asleep again, a common thing for captives to do which helps pass the time without them having to occupy it. By sleeping, their captivity seems less long, less difficult to endure, but it also weakened the person, letting their muscles grow soft because they no longer used them. When he had been a slave, he saw this often. Michael looked at the boy, and saw Catriona prominently in his features. Since the boy had been brought here, he had wanted to talk with him, but the surroundings didn't seem to foster such intimacies.

Michael set the tray on the small table and stepped outside the door again to fetch the sack. The puppy inside whined a little and the boy stirred, opening his eyes. He saw Michael and sat up, undoubtedly afraid the sack was for him. Then the man reached inside the sack and brought forth a puppy, setting him on the bed next to Alan. The puppy looked around for a second or two, its sleek form and soft curly fur shining in the lantern light.

The puppy found the boy and leapt up onto his face, causing him to smile. Michael stood up and moved toward the door, and Alan said, "Wait." Michael turned back to the boy and dog. "Do you know why I'm here?"

Michael nodded.

"Can you tell me?"

Michael weighed his response. He wanted very much to talk with this boy, to ask him about his mother and her background, to learn about them, but he also worried it would be very inappropriate. He looked around the room and thought it was so horrible the boy had to be imprisoned in such an inhospitable environment. The boy had drawn something in the night, a frightening man with a black sword and jagged surroundings. Michael wondered who the man was.

"Come on and sit down. It's fine." Alan patted the bed and Michael closed the door and sat down next to the boy. The boy had a foreign accent, one Michael had heard before. It was Caratian, from the Land near Nubia. Nubia, Caratia, Yokotama and Yndia shared a common sea, according to maps he had seen on trips with Myrgen. The dog bounced over to Michael and licked his face as a matter of course, then bounded back to Alan. The boy smiled at the act. "He likes you, even though you had him in a sack. That's means you're really a good person."

Michael smiled. It seemed the boy was trying to reassure Michael.

"Does he have a name?"

"The hounds keeper called him Wolf, but that seems rather unimaginative. After all, he's a wolfhound. That may confuse the dog when it comes time to hunt."

"You're not retarded," Alan said in the blunt, innocent manner of children.

Michael laughed and shook his head. "No, I'm not. Does that surprise you?"

"Sort of. One of the men on my mother's ship is like that and she trusts him completely because he isn't the sort to betray anyone."

Michael appreciated the opening. "Your mother has a ship?"

Alan nodded. "Oh yes, a great black carrack that's magic. It has ghosts on it and it was sealed with fae pitch and it never needs repairs. Her entire crew is loyal and she's the bravest ship captain in the world!"

Michael nodded at the lively imagination of the boy. He nodded to the drawing on the wall. "Who is that?"

Alan petted the dog. "That's Drake, the Duce of Caratia. He's invincible. He sits in the great castle at Zara and the Land rises to protect him."

"I see. Does he protect you too?"

Alan nodded, a little worried. "Yes, but he's not here right now. Does that mean you're going to hurt me?"

"No. I have no desire to hurt you at all."

"Then why am I here?"

Michael took a deep breath. "You're here because your mother wants to keep you safe."

"Does she know about the Terrible Things?"

Michael cocked his head. "What Terrible Things?"

"The Terrible Things which want to hurt her."

"Who wants to hurt her?"

Alan opened his mouth to say something, but then he closed his mouth and looked over at the puppy. "I can't say, or it will come true."

"Did someone tell you they would hurt your mother if you told?" Michael was immediately defensive, prepared to confront whoever would say something like that.

"No, not exactly. I just have dreams about things that happen later, but sometimes, if I don't tell, they don't happen."

"And you had a dream about your mother? Was she in danger?"

Alan nodded his head.

Michael furrowed his brow. "Was the Terrible Thing me?"

Alan looked up at the large, dark-skinned man. "No, it was my father…" Alan clasped his hands over his mouth, very worried now that he had told about the dream. No matter how much Michael implored, Alan refused to tell him more and Michael left the issue alone for a while. The guardsman got up and moved toward the door.

"I have to go now, but I'll be back in a little while. Do you need anything?"

"Where is the puppy supposed to, um…" The boy glanced at the chamber pot in the corner.

"Ah, well…I'll tell you what. When I come back later, I'll bring some straw for him. Will that be enough?"

Alan nodded and went back to petting the young dog. He looked up at Michael as he left. "Thank you for talking to me. And for the dog."

Michael nodded, smiling. "By the way, it was my Lord who decided to give you the dog. He didn't want to involve you. It's his way of apologizing." Alan blinked, then returned to playing with the puppy as Michael left the room.

***Chapter Thirteen:***
***"Much food is in the tillage of the poor, but there is that
that is destroyed for want of judgment."***
***~ Proverbs 13:23***

Catriona sat in Gwen's house and thought about the situation. She was waiting for Gwen to return from the marketplace with groceries and Catriona had needed desperately to get away from the palace. She had barely gotten out of the passage and across the large walkway in the garden when Alexander and Myrgen had emerged from the palace, and she barely had time to hide. Every time she laid eyes upon the Prince, her heart cried out to see him, to touch him. She had been so focused upon Alexander, she had almost forgotten to read Myrgen. It was a distraction which she could ill afford at this time. Her son was missing, and she needed to find him. She went to the door and opened it, looking around to see if Gwen was in sight yet, but saw no one coming her way. She picked up a handful of dirt before Gwen's threshold and said a whispered prayer to the Land to keep him safe, then cast the dirt into the air so the wind would carry the message. She dusted off her hands and closed the door.

She thought about what she had seen in the garden. Myrgen *had* cared about what happened to the servant, and he was telling the truth when he said it was Elizabeth and her daughter which were his greatest concern. She recognized the appearance of new love, the fury with which it consumes a person's soul. She needed to determine if the queen also was in love, for if this was the case, she now understood Myrgen's desire for the king to be removed from the picture. If the two were truly in love, Myrgen would do anything to free her from her marriage, and since the Augustinians did not condone divorce and Catherine would destroy Elizabeth in a prison before she allowed the marriage to be annulled, the only choice left was that of murder. It had to be soon, before Catherine returned.

Catriona went to Gwen's cupboards and got a piece of paper, a quill and some ink. The manufacture of quills had not been completely removed with the invention of the printing press, but it *had* made such former extravagances like paper and writing utensils more accessible to the common man. Still, not everybody could write, so the demand went to those of the middle class and higher. Even though Gwen was illiterate, Dominic used these items frequently around her and thus she kept a supply of these items on hand.

She looked around the desk area until she found what she needed: an inventory list in Myrgen's handwriting, complete with his signature. Catriona wrote a note to determine the queen's part in this play and blew on the ink until it was dry, then folded it carefully. The message inside was enigmatic enough to instill extreme caution. It also would probably not require discussion between Elizabeth and Myrgen so Catriona's ploy wouldn't be discovered.

Catriona thought back to Charles' fit in the palace. She dwelt most on the event right before the occurrence and his behavior. He had been fine when he was in the streets of Patras, and he hadn't eaten much, probably just enough to convince the servants he had been there all night. The symptoms hit him suddenly, and without warning, making his behavior erratic and uncontrollable. He seemed to have delusions and paranoia, mixed with rage and adrenaline-enhanced furies. This, she observed, was immediately after he ate the bread which left blue streaks on the butter. The rage had been so sudden and so fierce, she had been completely stunned by his actions, but had almost stepped into the room to stop him just before Alexander had walked in. Even so, neither of them had been able to save Arnold and that made her feel ill.

Catriona paced over to a wardrobe and rummaged around in Gwen's clothing for a few minutes before coming up with a simple set of skirts and an apron. She topped it with a simple unboned bodice and a kerchief in her hair and pocketed the note for the queen so no one would stumble upon it while she was gone. She left her dagger strapped to her thigh, but left her sword behind, there being no place for such an extravagance on a working woman's hip. Lastly, she stripped off her ever-present gloves and left them stuffed in a pocket.

She walked through the streets of Patras, passing knots of people doing their daily chores and businesses, and up to grounds of the palace. The hedges around the grounds marked the line the populace saw, but Catriona had escaped here an hour ago and went back in the same way she had left. A few turns and sniffs of the air later, and she was at the building that housed the kitchens to the palace. She gathered a bundle of wood for the fire from the stacks outside. She entered the kitchen from the doorway facing the palace and asked the large woman there where she would like this load of wood.

"Bring that right over here, dearie," the woman said pointing. "Who are you?"

"I was told to help out today for a little while," Catriona answered humbly, "to fill in for Evelyn."

"That poor dear…Has anyone heard what happened," the woman washing dishes asked the group.

"Only that her husband was wounded and the High Chancellor himself came and got her," replied the woman kneading bread.

"Is that so? That Myrgen fella?" The dishwasher looked astonished. "What would happen that would bring him out of his hole?"

"I can't say as I know," replied the woman in charge, "but I *will* say he was lookin' right dressy this mornin'."

"Antoinette! You're too old to be lookin' at a young man with those sorts of sinful thoughts."

"Well, it's enough for me to pay that Claudette to spill more bluing into his laundry." The entire gaggle of women broke into laughter and continued to gossip as they worked. Catriona slipped away from them and looked around the baking area for anything suspicious. She figured if what she thought was happening was happening, then there were three places she needed to look: the bread, the butter, and the wine. Both the bread and the butter were in the kitchen and the wine would be either in the cellars or in kegs, although the problem could be from the goblet rather than the bottle.

She glanced at the spice rack and noticed something interesting. An apothecary's bottle was among the spices in the locked cabinet. Catriona glanced around to make sure she was being ignored and looked carefully at the label. It said, "Herbspyce. For King Only." The case was locked and required a key, and Catriona had nothing with which to pick the lock. Besides, the kitchen was a high traffic zone right now and she needed more privacy than this to work on a lock. Her lock-picking tools were actually on the ship at any rate, to assist in the "preemptive salvaging" business she occasionally engaged in for

Tanglwyst's company.

She ducked back out of the kitchen and went to the lower area of the palace where the servants entered and left. The kitchen was a separate building from the main house, with the food brought in through tunnels barely four feet wide. The tunnels went generally to two places: the dining hall and the stairs. If a feast was being served, the food was dispatched as quickly as possible to the tables, but still usually was cold by the time people began eating. The passage which went to the stairs was to facilitate the feeding of the Royal Family in chambers.

Catriona looked around, trying to determine where in the palace the physician would be, or if he would be arriving from town. She spied a young man in neat robes leaning against a wall, a small box with catches and a handle next to him. The box was similar to the one Alexander kept, but the young man was probably an assistant and not allowed near the king. Catriona glanced around to be sure they were alone for the moment, then stepped out into the hallway, tripping herself on the edge of the door and sprawling across the floor a little way away from the young man.

As expected, the gentleman ran immediately over to Catriona. "Goodness, are you all right?"

Catriona turned over, her face flushed with embarrassment. "Yea, Oi think so. Nothing 'urt but me pride, Oi think."

The young man smiled at her in a forgiving manner. "Here, allow me to help you to your feet." His voice was cultured but as fake as her own affected accent. He probably believed it made him sound more upper class. He lifted her with both hands and she stood, then suddenly collapsed as she put her weight on her right foot.

"Apparently you're not all right," the man observed, his cultured accent slipping a bit into normal tones. He helped her over to where he had left the box.

"Oi'm so sorry," she explained. "Oi don't mean to be any trouble. Oi'm sure it will be fine."

"Don't worry," he replied, setting her down and crouching to take a look at her foot. "I was just waiting."

"Wha' for?"

"My Master, the King's Physician, is upstairs with the king right now. I'm his apprentice."

"Indeed? Wha's wrong with His Majesty?"

"Oi, I mean *I* don't know," the apprentice replied as he examined her foot, touching it carefully. "He's recently gotten massive headaches, rages and other things. Apparently, he killed a man today."

"Saint's Blood. Ow."

"Sorry. Indeed. I'm rather surprised my Master even came."

"Why wouldn' he?"

"Does that hurt?"

"A lit'le."

"Let me bandage this."

"Thank you."

"Well," the apprentice began as he got out a bandage from the box, "my Master isn't at his best these days. He's effectively useless because he's succumbed to the drink. Passes out every night until dawn, when he mixes up something for the hangover, usually in a glass of wine. If he's sober three hours out of the day, it must be the Sabbath."

"Oh dear. Wha's he…ouch…Wha's he doing with the king then?"

"He gives him powders and teas. They just make everyone think he's good at this, but his only skill is staying out of the king's way when he's in a rage."

"Oi saw a bot'le in the kitchen which was different from the other bot'les. Antoinette said i' was only for the king."

"Yes. It's called Herbspyce. He got it from an old herbalist in a monastery. It's sea salt and iodine."

"That sounds ut'erly useless."

"It is. Well, you should be fine now." The young man helped Catriona to her feet and she stepped gingerly on the limb. She limped a bit and he helped her stand against a wall. "Try to stay off it as much as you can. I know that sounds kind of ridiculous here, but maybe you can peel onions today?" His easy smile indicated a great bedside manner and she had the feeling he would be an excellent physician.

"Oi'll work on that. So le' me ask you this: wha' would *you* prescribe to the king if you had the chance?"

The apprentice looked at the ceiling as he contemplated his answer. "Probably fresh air and clean water, two things Patras isn't known for." He smiled again and she returned the gesture. There were noises of someone coming down the stairs and Catriona recognized Alexander's voice speaking to someone who slurred his words.

She looked at the apprentice . "Oi guess Oi'd bet'er go before Oi get in trouble. Thank you again."

"Don't mention it." Catriona limped off through the door just in time to be missed by the Prince.

* * *

"Good Lord. What have you done to your foot?" Gwen leapt out of her chair as Catriona came into the house.

"Nothing. I spoke to the assistant of the king's physician and he did this."

"Why didn't he bandage your head while he was at it? There's obviously something wrong with that too, the way you keep running off without letting anyone know where you're going."

Catriona sat down and unwrapped the bandage. "What did you want me to do? Leave you a note? Here. Don't say I never give you anything." She tossed the rolled bandage to her maid who put it in a small box with a few other such items. "Did you get the message to Anika and Drake?"

"Yes. They said they would stay as long as you needed them to, and Drake said his blade was yours, should you require it."

"That's what I thought they'd say." Catriona stripped down to the bare shift under the clothes she borrowed. "Have something to eat. I've got an errand for you to run for me today."

"Another one?"

"You will be delivering a message to Her Majesty from Myrgen. It will say, 'Be on guard- M.' You will watch her and observe what she does and how she reacts. Be sure she doesn't look at it where anyone else can read it but try to get her to read it in front of you, if you can."

"And where will you be?"

"I'm not sure yet, that's the problem. I want to observe her personally, but I don't know where I can do such a thing without being detected. I also need to get some sleep tonight. I have to be up at baker's hours tomorrow."

"Where will you be at baker's hours tomorrow?"

"Calling on a baker, obviously." Catriona smiled and went into the bedroom to lie down for a nap, her body still not quite recovered from the ordeal yesterday. Gwen set about puttering around, preparing for an early dinner.

## Chapter Fourteen:
*"There is a way which seemeth right unto a man, but the end thereof are the ways of death."*
*~ Proverbs 14:12*

Queen Elizabeth sat at her embroidery hoop that evening, uninvolved in the distraction before her. Her auburn hair shone in the firelight, giving her a faint halo. Try as she might, her heart did not seem to want her to rest, even though visible support of the king during his insanity-inducing illness was exhausting, as was the night's activities with Myrgen. He had been present at the meeting this morning when the physician had told the queen and the Prince the news of the king's increased sickness. It had been very difficult for her to keep from smiling during the sad news of Charles' attack on the servant. She didn't even remember the man, but Myrgen had seemed very shaken by the whole incident. That had sobered her enough not to act inappropriately in front of Alexander.

A knock on her chamber door nearly put her in the rafters and it took her a moment to recover before she had her attending page admit the visitor. One of the king's guardsmen, Nicolai Moriarity, entered the room and bowed respectfully. "Your Majesty, there is a messenger in the antechamber for you. She says she must deliver the message personally."

"She?"

"Yes, Your Majesty. It is Lord Dominic's lady, Gwen."

"Gwen? How odd." Elizabeth rose and went with Nicolai. A ship captain for Lady Tanglwyst's fleet during the sailing season until last winter, the Latian sailor took the position at the castle at Tanglwyst's urgings and recommendations. Always eager to employ skilled fighters capable of making life-saving decisions, the captain of the guard, Gomez de Santander, hired Nicolai. From what Tanglwyst had said, he was in charge of a group of guards now.

As he bowed before Elizabeth and turned to lead her to Gwen, she noticed the masculine appeal of his midnight-colored hair laced with sexy streaks of premature grey and the concealed strength of his frame and visage. He was strong and lithe, his skin looked supple and his muscles well-toned. His coloring was the olive of the Latian Isles, enhancing his dark brown eyes which seemed to glitter in the sunlight. This *is why Tanglwyst loves him,* she thought, *this and so much more.*

Tanglwyst had told Elizabeth of their relationship, how he had been so terribly sad when she found him in that fishing village. His wife had gone off somewhere years before and had never returned. Someone told him they thought she had been killed by highwaymen because there was a church that had been burnt to the ground by bandits in the vicinity where his wife had been seen. When he had asked about it, he was told there were several bodies found in and outside the church, and at least one of them was a woman. He told Tanglwyst he realized at that moment his wife was dead. He had lived in sorrow and pain for the next two years, barely surviving, but wanting to die.

He had left his home eight years ago, intent on ending his life, when he met Tanglwyst. She was looking for sailors to refit a ship and she had been beautiful. Nicolai had taken a position on the ship, leaving behind his father's failed company and the house which had reminded him daily of his dead wife. He sailed on the refitted ship for two years before Tanglwyst had seen him again and when they did, sparks had flown. She arranged for him to sail on her flagship, the *Sulocco,* and she had fallen in love with Nicolai during the course of the next year. Tanglwyst told Elizabeth he had fought his attraction for almost a year, not wanting to violate his wife's memory. When Tanglwyst told him she was a widow herself, he had fallen prey to the sharing of grief, and the two had rescued one another's hearts in a kiss on a perfect night at sea.

Just before they went into the chamber where Gwen was waiting, Elizabeth got an uneasy feeling, like she was being watched. She turned to Nicolai and whispered, "Would you stay, please?"

Nicolai blinked, confused, and reassured her he would. Visibly hiding her relief, the queen entered the chamber. She found herself unsure as to why she was worried about Gwen and decided it was probably just paranoia. Gwen was in a deep curtsy as Her Majesty entered, and did not rise when the queen came over to her.

"You have a message for me, Gwen?"

"Yes," the strong, blonde Glarren woman replied. "I suggest you read it to yourself, as the walls have eyes, and ears," she added, glancing at Nicolai.

Elizabeth took the small message Gwen offered her and turned away from Nicolai slightly before opening it. Her breath caught as she read the message:

"Be on guard. -M."

She touched the writing briefly, then quickly concealed the note in her bodice. "Is there anything else, Gwen?"

"No, my Queen."

"Then be on your way, but be careful. Someone said he saw foreigners in town today, and I'm told there's an ill moon out tonight."

"Thank you, my Queen."

Elizabeth turned and left, moving quickly past Nicolai as he held the door open for her. She and Myrgen had resolved not to see each other in their chambers tonight because she was afraid they would be discovered by a servant who might enter to tell her Charles was dead. This note indicated perhaps he had seen evidence of the murderess in the castle and Elizabeth needed to destroy the note lest someone link the killing with her and Myrgen through the missive. He was wise to use Gwen for this, she thought. Dominic would have read the note first, being the type who collected people's secrets.

Gwen smoothed her woolen skirt as she stood and walked purposefully out of the chamber, almost knocking Lord Dominic down as they met in the corridor.

* * *

Dominic had just finished the day's work for Myrgen and was on his way to see Gwen and apologize for his behavior last night. He hadn't felt right all day with them being at odds and he desperately didn't want to spend the night lonely in his apartment in Tanglwyst's home. Especially not after the experience with the intruder with the Monk's Hood.

The two looked at each other, then he saw the retreating back of the queen over Gwen's shoulder. A horrible feeling enveloped him as he remembered the note he'd seen just a scant twenty-four hours ago, and he had the feeling the queen was the one who was to be killed. He looked at his betrothed with a sickening feeling that she had somehow decided to assist her "mistress."

"What are you doing here, Gwen?" The slight shake in his voice was quickly hidden.

"Just delivering a message."

"For *her*?"

She looked at floor and wall, not meeting his own piercing, but non-magical gaze. "Where were you two this morning? I thought she was so injured, yet when I went to your house, both of you were gone."

"She left to go see Nicolai and I followed her, to make sure she was safe. Unfortunately, she must have detected me and lost me. I arrived at Nicolai's house but she never showed up."

"Gwen, you need to avoid her. She's dangerous. She's…" He began to say she was a killer, to tell her about the note, when Michael came around the corner, heading for the kitchens. He swallowed, looking away from his love to regain his control. He began feeling that sense of betrayal he was worried about and knew he needed to show her where his own loyalties lay. When he looked back into her sky-colored eyes, the concern in his own brown ones was hardly noticeable. He led her outside to the garden to talk in private.

"Gwen, I understand you have some kind of connection to this woman, but I assure you, she has no such loyalties to you or anyone else."

"What makes you think you know what's going on with her, or with me?" Gwen seemed irate, but was exhibiting an uncharacteristic amount of control. "You ran off, refusing to even listen. Now you come to me the next day saying she's *dangerous,* assuming I'll take your side over hers just because we were betrothed? Especially after *you* indicated you wanted to break with me over some perceived insult or betrayal. What makes you think you know something *I* do not?"

He looked into his lady's determined eyes and decided his suspicions were right about Gwen. "I know a lot about her. More than you think, in fact. I know what she does, and how."

"Oh?" She crossed her arms. "And exactly how long did *you* sail with her?"

"She did some work for me a year ago. Since then, she's killed six of my relatives."

"Your relatives, huh?" Gwen stroked her chin and looked into the sky, her brow furrowing. "Since you don't actually care about any of the other ones, you must be talking about your *D'Medici* relatives. And exactly how were *they* trying to kill *her?*"

"That's beside the point, Gwen. The fact is she's very accomplished at murdering people. I don't want you to get hurt. I don't want anyone else to get hurt by her either, but especially not you."

She looked carefully at him, and he tried nonverbally to convey that there was more here than he felt he could talk to her about at the moment. He saw her wavering and felt this was the time to strike, while she seemed to be in doubt. "Gwen, I do care for you and believe in you," he said, taking both her hands in is, "but I know what Catriona's doing here, and you need to realize I... can't allow her to do what she wants."

Gwen looked into Dominic's eyes and he saw her resolve solidify, like she believed he knew nothing at all about the situation. Her opinion of him seemed to change, going from love to anger and disgust with the blink of her eyes. With a stony coldness he felt Catriona would have been proud of, Gwen disengaged her hands from his. "And you need to realize I can't allow you to stop her."

Gwen pushed passed Dominic, leaving him in shock.

*Chapter Fifteen:*
*"The hearing ear and the seeing eye, the Lord hath made both of them."*
*~ Proverbs 20:12*

In the small vortex formed as Her Majesty passed him, Nicolai's heightened sense of smell caught a whiff of body scent the queen had not entered with, a scent as familiar as his own. *Catriona?* He looked quickly about the room Gwen was in but saw no sign of his wife, so he hurried to catch up to the queen.

Nicolai studied the queen's manner as she entered her chambers, then he sniffed the air to see if the traces of his estranged wife were upon the queen herself or if he should look elsewhere. Several years before, immediately after his wife had disappeared, he had been struck ill by some disease which passed through the town. The effects it had blinded and deafened him. As a result, his other senses became sharper, allowing him to distinguish things and surroundings, even people, by touch and smell. During the entire time, Nicolai had kept a favorite shift of his missing wife's with him, smelling her every day lest he forget her and not know her if she had survived somehow and were to return to him.

A year after he'd contracted the disease, he had dropped and broken an old pitcher which was used to draw water from the well. He replaced the pitcher with an earthenware bowl that Catriona had made years before for grinding herbs, planning on getting a new pitcher at some other time.

Apparently, either the herbs had left residual healing properties or the pitcher had been renewing the disease in him because a few nights later, he was awakened by something completely unexpected: a sound. A pair of cats were fighting outside his window, something he would neither be able to smell, taste nor touch, yet knew was happening. It took several months for his full hearing to return and the rest of the year for his sight, but since he still had to rely on his other senses so heavily, they remained sharp. Now, after years of sailing on Tanglwyst's various ships, calluses had stolen his fine touch and strong drink had dulled his taste buds, thankfully in some cases, so the only thing remaining was his olfactory perceptions.

"Hey, Pierre," Nicolai said to the other guard on duty,

"Increase the guard on Her Majesty. I need to go check something out." Without wasting any time answering questions, Nicolai took off to the antechamber where the queen had just had her meeting with Gwen.

By the time he got there, the room was empty and he sniffed the air to try to determine where his wife had been during the meeting. Oddly enough, it was in the middle of a wall in plain sight, an interior wall. He inspected the area and felt a slight draft coming from the wall itself. He felt around it until he found the place where the mortar was missing. The wall was an interior one so there should have been no way for air to reach this point, but he could smell the garden as plain as day.

He went outside to the garden where the antechamber bordered and figured out there must be a passage inside the wall. He knew where the king's and queen's escape routes were, but this passage wasn't near either entrance. He looked closer and discovered a space behind a large hedge in the Royal Gardens, with room enough for two large men to hide behind indefinitely. Deciding internally to make certain this was sealed up later, the seasoned fighter knelt down to inspect the dirt by the passage opening.

At first he saw nothing, the shadows from the hedge effectively blocking the fading twilight from aiding him. He cut away some branches and there, barely visible in the last vestiges of sunlight, was the vague outline of a small boot print. The wearer must have been expecting to be followed because the print was barely visible and would have been missed by probably anyone else, but his experience with this particular individual had made him observant to her subtleties.

He stood and looked at the wall there. It seemed solid enough, but he was certain something must be hidden and felt the wall for a catch. One of the stones depressed and a balanced door swung open into the total darkness of the passage which traveled behind the wall of the antechamber. He was about to enter when he heard a horse's snort, then the sound of a gallop as it took off toward the woods. He left the hedge quickly and ran toward the other end of the Garden.

* * *

"Tell me what you saw."

The voice was like liquid night that seemed to flow from everywhere at once, and Gwen knew she had found her Mistress.

"I saw a hitch in her breathing when she saw who had sent the note. I saw her touch the writing and hide the note guiltily."

"What do you think she is doing right now?"

"Burning it. She can't afford to be caught with it. It would upset her plans."

"What are her plans, Gwen?'

Gwen sighed, defeated. "I don't know."

Catriona stepped from the shadows in an area not at all where Gwen had suspected she was, the darkness like a cloak billowing around her. Catriona stood near her former maid and looked up at the castle. "There's a secret passage into the antechamber where you were. The passage empties out behind that hedge where you left me. I leaned against the wall and hit a trigger. It enabled me to get closer to the conversation than I thought because, in the center of the north wall, the mortar isn't whole. I was able to *see* her as well as hear her. She knows something is going on.

"That's not all. While I was in the wall, I noticed something." She looked at Gwen. "I recognized the smell of the place." She nodded toward the palace. "That's where I was held when I was captured." *And that's where Alan is,* she added to herself. Obviously, she needed to spend more time there because that was where he was probably hidden.

Gwen looked up at the castle, then back at her lady. "You recognized the smell, you say?"

Catriona looked at Gwen and nodded. "Yes. Human beings don't have the capacity to remember colors accurately, but sounds and smells trigger true memory because our bodies never forget them."

Gwen was amazed at this insight, well beyond anything she herself had ever accomplished. *That is why Catriona was the Master and she was the student.* "Well, what do we do now?" Gwen folded her arms across her chest, anticipating another assignment in which to test this new knowledge.

"*You* go home," Catriona answered as she walked back to the shadows from which she had emerged.

"*Home?*" Gwen cried, disappointed. She walked over to

Catriona and noticed a passage in the hedgerow which she'd never noticed before. The passage went directly toward the woods where the kitchen staff had woodcutters harvest the wood for the royal fires, and the hedges hid a black horse which she had also not noticed before during the conversation. She vowed to be more observant in the future. Catriona patted the beast and looked over at Gwen.

"Yes. Home." She turned the horse around carefully in the passageway, "You've been seen at the castle. I can't afford to let you be implicated."

"Well, since I've already been seen here, won't I already be implicated?"

"Dominic will defend you if you're accused, saying you gave the queen the note to see if she meant to betray the kingdom."

"What makes you think he'd defend *me*?" Gwen asked, the memory of their confrontations of late fresh in her mind.

Catriona looked back at her friend. "He desperately loves you." She looked at the palace. "A man will do anything for a woman he desperately loves. Good night, Gwen." She turned and began to walk away.

As Gwen watched Catriona lead the horse away through the low branches, she mulled over the words just spoken. Her mind caught on the memories of Dom's damp eyes in the palace, his anger, no, *pain* at what he thought was some sort of betrayal. These things suddenly told her volumes, and she resolved to mend the relationship between her and her love, Dominic. She was just about to the edge of the shrubbery when she heard the horse gallop off and a moment later, ran straight into Nicolai.

Nicolai looked past Gwen but when he couldn't see anything beyond a thick part of the hedge, he asked sternly, "Where is she going, Gwen?"

"Why, Nicolai," she replied coquettishly, "what makes you think she'd tell me that?" She brushed past the guardsman who muttered something unflattering about enigmatic, willful women and went back inside to make sure the queen was safe.

*Chapter Sixteen:*
*"Good understanding giveth favor, but the way of transgressors is hard."*
*~ Proverbs 13:15*

It was still dark when the horse snorted, awakening Catriona. She had slept next to the animal to keep herself warm as well as to enable her to flee the area quickly should the need arise, and he acted as a perfect lookout on this particular morning. She looked in the direction of the kitchen and saw the baker, a middle-aged man named Lawrence, just opening the door and preparing the stoves and ovens for the day's baking. Catriona had carefully removed the wood normally piled outside by the door for the morning's activities and knew the baking would be at least in the ingredient stages before the Lawrence noticed there wasn't any wood.

She stood and dusted herself off, removing anything which might catch the light and reveal her at first glance. She waited for the baker to walk into the spice room before moving up to hide in the shadows of the eaves. The door was on the north side of the building, so Catriona knew she could conceal herself successfully between the shadows of the kitchen and the palace. The wood piles were at the back of the kitchen building and the process of fetching the wood should take a few minutes, allowing Catriona time to enter undetected. As expected, Lawrence came out about a half hour after arriving, looking around for the wood which was supposed to be piled by the door. He must have been a sailor earlier in life judging by the string of curses he used when he found the wood not where it was expected and, as he moved off toward the pile to fetch his own, Catriona slipped into the kitchen.

There was a large table dominating the room which served as both a working and eating surface. On one side was the makings of the day's bread, with one bowl set aside from the others. Near this bowl was the bottle marked "Herbspyce. For the king only." Catriona took the bottle and replaced it with a bottle she had gotten from the physician's assistant's chest while he had it open and was bandaging her foot. She had recognized the green herb in the bottle as an innocuous one and had taken Gwen's sea salt to fill the bottle, knowing *her* sea salt was not dangerous. The label had been replaced with one like the Herbspyce so Lawrence would be none the wiser.

Unfortunately, Catriona couldn't tell if the item was already mixed in with the dry ingredients so she moved the bowl so it teetered near the edge of the table. She was just about to duck back outside when she heard Lawrence return from the woodpile. Apparently the man was used to hauling his own wood, and was quicker than Catriona had planned. The dark woman faded into the still early shadows as Lawrence brought in the armload of wood and dumped it onto the floor.

The crash of the wood was promptly echoed by the crash of the ceramic bowl with the king's mixture in it and the baker began swearing oaths, in his anger putting curse words which didn't even belong together in a volcano of descriptive anger. Catriona waited until the man stooped to scoop up the flour mixture in a dustpan before slipping out past him. As she walked to where the horse waited to take her to the docks, she noticed the flour dust had coated her as she walked out of the room. It cast a luminescent glow around her and left a slight white cloud billowing in her wake, her cloak dispersing it into soft spirals near the ground. Her usual attire was a long coatdress, common and fashionable in Caratia and the cloak had protected the rest of her clothes from the white dust.

As she mounted her horse, she glanced back at the palace and saw a figure at the one of the windows, looking down at her. She saw the perfect outline of Alexander and watched to see if he had noticed her. His eyes were trained in the direction she had gone but she was sure he couldn't see her in the shadows of the trees. As it was, she could barely see him through the branches around her but she steadied the horse so she could watch him. Lawrence came out of the kitchen to gather more wood and Catriona's horse snorted and shuffled around. Catriona moved him back into the shadows but it was too late. Although the baker didn't seem to notice the movement, Alexander, who had been specifically looking for it, *had* noticed, and he moved away from the window with a purpose.

Catriona waited until the baker loaded his armful of wood, knowing a horse and rider would definitely be noticed if she took off at that moment, but also terribly aware of Alexander's potential appearance at the servant's entrance to the palace any moment. She contemplated letting herself be caught by him, then decided she couldn't afford to, not with the Herbspyce in her pouch.

Lawrence returned to the kitchen and Catriona spurred her steed to take flight. As she rode past the palace, she stole a glance and saw a tall shadow coming down the tunnel to the kitchens at a run. She hunkered down over the horse's neck and moved quickly out of sight. She worried Alexander might follow her, anticipating her arrival at the docks, but at least there, she felt more at ease. She could think clearer near the river that led to the seaport city of Rouen, the flowing water sharpening her senses, as if the city dulled her like strong wine.

*And what then?* She guided her horse through the familiar streets as she contemplated an encounter with Alexander. Would she tell him her suspicions? Would she tell him about Myrgen's betrayal, or Alan's abduction? No. She still didn't know enough to make any accusations. Myrgen might be as much a puppet in this as she was, and she didn't have anything to determine who might be doing that. She knew Myrgen was in love with Elizabeth, and she suspected the queen might return the feelings, but she saw something else, as did Gwen. The queen had plans, and the extent of those plans and whom they affected were still up in the air.

Catriona looked behind her as she approached the docks but she was not being pursued. As she reached the docks, she eased her horse to a walk and went to a nice house on the waterfront. The Seine River was a shallow river and thus the docks accommodated only barges and small vessels. These vessels transported goods and passengers to Rouen where the docks were sizable. Catriona knew Tristram Wulfschlager, the captain of the *Righteous*, was in town with the members of his crew which also wintered in Patras, and that they were setting out today.

She eased up outside the Captain's house, still checking to see if she was followed. She scanned the entire wharf for anything suspicious before stepping up to knock on the door. Captain Tristram Wulfschlager answered her knock personally and the two friends embraced. Tristram was beginning to show his age. His rich, dark hair was peppered with an appealing grey and his skin's color no longer paled over the winter months, now a perfect russet tone. Tristram had a baritone voice, though you would barely be able to tell from looking at him. He was tall and of a moderate build, getting on the side of heavy in the middle after a winter of Patrasian dining. His hands and legs still had a young man's fighting strength to them, a fact she could tell even with his gentle hand on her now.

"Is Armand awake?" she asked.

Tristram shook his silvering head. "Would you like some tea while I send for him? I was just about to have some."

"Thank you. I was hoping I wasn't going to wake you."

"Had you arrived ten minutes earlier, you would have had to get me out of bed yourself. Not, of course, that I would have minded." Tristram winked at Catriona, who tossed a smile his way as he opened the door to his home and admitted his employer and good friend.

Catriona walked with him as he motioned for the listening valet to get the poison maker. Several people from the *Righteous* wintered near each other and still others without families simply signed on with ships going elsewhere for the winter. The *Righteous'* regular crew worked other professions in Patras and Rouen, biding time before the sailing season began again. The poison maker was one of those, but since his profession was actually extremely profitable, he could afford to split the housing costs for this grand home with the Captain.

The smell of rich herbs filled the room. Tristram was a true tea fanatic and her best shipper for such items. He knew good tea from great tea and had an impressive stash which insured he would bring business to the better tea merchants. You couldn't bribe him with silver, but wave a good tea under his nose and he might be tempted.

With full knowledge of this, Catriona pulled a pouch from her belt. "I brought this from home, grown by an herbalist in the woods."

"Caratian tea? I understand the land there has special properties. Do they perhaps transfer once they leave her shores?" Tristram opened the waterproof pouch which had sealed the tea well against the moisture of the sea and the dust of land travel, and took a sniff. The aroma was heady and fragrant, pleasing Tristram heartily. "This smells wonderful. I must meet the source."

"Ah, but then I would have nothing to offer you as payment for your services."

The Captain arched an eyebrow at her, "I am always at your service, my Lady."

"But I would not take that for granted, my friend."

Tristram brewed the tea as they spoke of the shipping business and trade routes until the poison maker arrived, halfway through the first cup. Tristram was a bit annoyed it took him so long to arrive until he looked up. Apparently, Armand had wanted to make himself presentable before stepping into Catriona's presence because his hair was wet from being freshly washed, and he looked to have picked out his best clothes for this meeting, a red robe over a blue doublet and breeches. Even his red stockings were laundered, and his shoes had the look of a wet cloth being pulled across them minutes before. Foolish clothes to start the day, especially if he was going to be doing apothecary work which often involved acids and flame. Tristram smiled understandingly and shook his head at the man.

Armand des Mortes, poison maker, barber and sometime mortician, bowed respectfully to Catriona, his fresh smell brightening the dawn. Armand was an accomplished apothecary and made the ship's soaps, herbal salves and medicines, serving to make the *Righteous* one of the most pleasant for passengers to travel upon. This added a large amount of revenue to Catriona's shipping investments and she was very appreciative of Armand's versatility. However, she would never actually have him on her crew for the Enigma because he reveled in enticing lovers into his bed with his fancy perfumes and gifts, and knew she would be a very distracting target during a sea voyage, especially a long one. Plus, she had never saved Armand's life, which was a requisite for being on the *Enigma's* crew.

"My Lady," Armand said, taking her hand and kissing it while heavily flirting with his eyes. "It is always a pleasure to see you."

"Thank you, Armand. I'm sorry to trouble you so early in the day."

"'Tis no trouble at all, My Lady. I am always available for your use." He kissed her hand again.

Catriona extracted her hand and motioned for him to sit with them. Tristram offered him some tea which seemed to quite impress Armand. He graciously accepted and Catriona brought out the bottle. "Armand, do you think you could analyze this and tell me what it is?"

Armand took the bottle and read the torn label, which was now missing the instructions regarding the king. "Herbspyce?

What's that supposed to be?"

"Well, it's *supposed* to be sea salt and iodine, but I'm not sure if it is. I have a friend who has been given this as a cure for his headaches."

"Him?" Armand raised his eyebrows in mock sadness.

"Fear not, Armand, you're still my only love." She winked at him and Tristram let the comment go by unmolested. For the moment.

"Good. Well, what makes you think it's not sea salt and iodine?"

Catriona took a small bit of butter from the tray of breakfast breads Tristram had with his tea and spread it in a cracker. She uncorked the Herbspyce and sprinkled a small amount on the butter. A moment later, the butter turned blue. Catriona resealed the bottle as Armand and Tristram sat back and contemplated the new color.

"I saw streaks of blue in some butter which was served to my friend. They appeared after he wiped his bread across the butter on his breakfast tray. A few minutes later, he seemed to come down with an incapacitating headache, then flew into a rage, and declared his butler was trying to murder him with a butter knife."

Armand looked at the Herbspyce. "That doesn't sound like behavior brought on by sea salt and iodine."

"Exactly my sentiments."

Tristram asked, "Is this Grymalkin?"

Catriona looked at him but left the question unanswered as Armand, now totally distracted by the Herbspyce, contemplated what he was looking at. "The reaction took a moment to manifest, which tells me it's a quite fast poison treated with a buffering agent. Fast ones which need to be ingested would put off the victim if noticed. Was this agent in the butter or the bread?"

"The bread. The household baker was told to add it to my friend's bread, but only his bread."

"So heat doesn't kill the active agent. That's important."

"How long will it take for you to tell me what it is?" Catriona wanted to still look for Alan today but she also knew Tristram had plans to set sail soon. "Can you figure it out before you set sail or will you have to send the analysis to me?"

Armand used a knife to pick at the butter, noting the way it interacted with the metal as well as the butter. He looked at

Catriona, then at Tristram. "It will take at least a day to figure this out. The color is confusing. The manufacturer had specific things in mind for this or it wouldn't be this color, which means the same stuff which turns this blue would react poorly with whatever would stop it from turning blue while still being necessary for it to be effective. However, without proper equipment, I can only speculate, and I don't have the proper equipment onboard the ship."

"Where do you have this equipment?" Catriona leaned forward in interest, marrying her chin to her hand.

Armand looked over at Tristram. "Well, here. My lab is in that room," he pointed to a closed door on the downstairs level. Armand said to Tristram, "How long before you're back in Rouen?"

Tristram thought about this a moment and replied, "Not for two months."

"I can meet you in Bordeaux in a month."

"Or," volunteered Catriona, "I can sail you to St. Andrew in a week, if you don't mind making the trip to Rouen in a few days."

"St. Andrew would be more likely," Tristram conceded. "Do you have everything we need until then?"

"Your entire shipment of soaps and poisons against the rats are labeled and should already be at the ship. I sent it on yesterday."

"Then you should stay behind and assist our patron, here."

Armand smiled and Catriona sighed in relief. She asked, "When can we begin this?"

Armand said, "I'll start working on it right away. You relax and finish your tea." He got up and unlocked the room he'd indicated earlier, taking the Herbspyce. Catriona saw a lot of lab equipment, much of it covered with cloths in preparation for Armand's absence. He was so focused upon his task, he almost missed Tristram's suggestion that he change out of his nice clothes. Armand looked down and then smiled. "Good idea." He took the bottle with him as he returned to his room.

Catriona finished the tea with Tristram and he stood, preparing to be on his way. He took Catriona's hand in both of his. "Now you be careful of that fellow. He eats luscious young women like you for dessert."

"I'll do my best to resist his wiles." She refreshed him with a smile and Tristram kissed her hand before gathering up his Captain's bag and heading out the door. Catriona saw him off and then went to Armand's lab and knocked on the door. He called out for her to enter and she came in. The huge array of alembics, fluids, powders and papers amazed her. It was like a giant glass maze. Several tables still had covers on them, and the poison maker had several small chests out on the table, pulled from a trunk beneath a table. Armand was working on an empty section of the table, dividing the Herbspyce into several smaller amounts.

"I'm going to perform some tests to see if I can figure out what this substance is and isn't. It will take all morning. This afternoon, when I have a list of the ingredients, I'll perform some other tests to see what it will do under certain common conditions. This will tip you off to other areas where this poison may be found."

"When should I come back?"

Armand smiled at her. "About dinnertime?"

Catriona smiled at him and agreed. "Perhaps I'll even bring a friend."

"Oooh. I'll count the moments…."

Catriona closed the door behind her on her way out.

***Chapter Seventeen:***
*"A brother offended is harder to be won than a strong city, and their contentions like the bars of a castle."*
*~ Proverbs 18:19*

Alexander couldn't sleep. The incident with Charles the day before disturbed him greatly. *What could be affecting him so negatively, so suddenly?* Perhaps it was as Elizabeth had said during their fight last week and he had caught syphilis from a tryst, but Alexander doubted it. The venereal disease did cause signs of madness in certain people, but Charles wasn't exhibiting those sorts of symptoms. Besides, Alexander could cure syphilis and he hadn't yet made a dent in Charles' troubles. The signs he had almost suggested an internal issue, but Alexander couldn't put his finger on what was the real problem here.

The Prince got out of bed and poured himself some light wine. The water in Patras wasn't the best tasting and thus, Mervolingia's wine makers were among the best out of necessity. There were light breakfast wines, earthy lunchtime wines, heady dinner wines and sweet dessert wines. If one didn't care for wine, there were other drinks, but mostly, it was wine. Alexander took a swallow of the breakfast wine and went to his window.

He had opened his window that night before bed because the cook had made a drink which was incredibly unpleasant: hot chocolate with peppers. It was supposed to be Yorkish, a recipe sent with the chocolate, and Alexander considered it an act of war. He had thrown the mixture into the fire which had been a bad idea and it had taken all night to air the smell out. Still, the weather was warming up and he had enjoyed the fresh air coming in from the king's woods attached to the gardens. He went to the window and looked out, enjoying the easy chill of springtime.

A figure walked from the kitchens toward the woods, a dark yet ghostly creature in a cresting cloak. Alexander watched to see if he recognized the servant but when they walked past the wood pile, he determined this wasn't a servant. The person went into the trees and Alexander watched carefully to see if there was any sign of who it was. He was about to pull his head back in when the noise of a piece of wood dropping spooked whatever was under the leaves of the trees. He saw a horse with a rider then, well hidden by the darkness and shadows.

The rider had come from the kitchen and Alexander suddenly got the feeling maybe what was wrong with Charles was more intentionally induced instead of incidental. He ducked his head back in and grabbed a robe, pulling it on as he took off for the kitchens. There was a torch burning to light the way to the privy and Alexander grabbed it in case he had to search the trees. He ran quickly, but the palace was large and he was afraid he might have been spotted by the rider. He opened the door which led to a staircase outside by the kitchen and heard a horse galloping toward the palace.

He got there after the horse had past, but he caught a glimpse of the dark rider, a fine white dust flying in the air behind her, illuminating her trail. Horse and rider turned the corner and he could have sworn he saw long black hair. *Catriona!* He ran to the edge of the palace but it was too late, and he chided himself for chasing a horse in the pre-dawn hours in his robe. He also felt as though he was going mad. First, yesterday in the garden, he thought he saw her watching him from the dappled shadows of the foliage. Then, yesterday afternoon, he thought he heard her voice downstairs. He thought he smelled her there, too, as if she had just been with the physician's assistant. She had a distinctive spicy fragrance about her which defied him to determine whether it was perfume or just her natural scent. Now, in the middle of the night, he was seeing her riding a horse away from the kitchen.

He shook his head at his foolishness. *Wishful thinking actually, not foolishness.* It had been early November since he had last seen her, despite being here in town. She had told him she and Nicolai were going to try to make their marriage work, but Alexander had no confidence in that. He had avoided Nicolai because he found he hated the man on principal, yet he had read the reports daily, paying close attention to anything having to do with him. Alexander decided that, without more direct contact with the man, he needed to see more of him. He had recommended Nicolai for promotion, serving Alexander's own ends. Nicolai would be writing the reports then and Alexander could monitor his attitude and mood changes through his actions. He could also vicariously make sure the woman he loved was properly supported financially due to the monetary raise the position and extra duties brought.

The gamble had paid off. Alexander had noted a surliness

in Nicolai that was his usual demeanor, and he noticed he often smelled of excessive drink in the morning, though that wore off as the day progressed. It meant he drank at night, at home. Alexander knew the effects excess alcohol had on the libido, and every day Nicolai came in smelling of wine, Alexander found himself in a better mood. He also knew Catriona didn't employ drunks, gamblers, abusers or anyone with any other kind of addiction. She didn't trust them. He felt certain Nicolai was getting nowhere with his wife, and this relationship was unlikely to last.

Alexander caught the sound of wood being dropped in a pile in the kitchen and he remembered why he was there. He walked into the kitchen and Lawrence turned to see the unexpected arrival of the Prince of Mervolingia in his kitchen. He bowed his respect. "Your Highness? It's been quite a while since you've been down to the kitchens during my shift. Is something wrong?" Lawrence wiped the dirt from the wood on his apron and made to get some water heating. "Hot chocolate, Sire?"

Alexander scowled in disgust and Lawrence smiled. "Thank you, Sire. That Yorkish rot is the most dreadful concoction known to man. Their tea is worth the trouble though." He bent to hang the huge kettle on the hearth hook.

"Lawrence, did you see a black rider go by just now?"

"A black...*rider*, Sire?" Lawrence glanced out the back door into the paling darkness. "No, no Sire, I did not, but I was not paying much attention to my surroundings, Sire." The baker returned to his mixing.

Alexander looked around and saw the area where the flour had been swept. "What happened here, Lawrence?"

The man looked over his shoulder without taking his hands out of the mixing bowl. "That, Sire? That's just some spill't flour. Darn fae, as my mother would have said."

"Fey?"

"Yes. *'That's the trouble with being so near a wood,'* she would have said. *'Fey come in and fuss with things.'* Of course, I think it was just me being distracted by the lack of wood here in the kitchen. I'll be coming in tonight to give those boys a whipping for not bringing in wood for the fires. At least they got it cut."

Alexander folded his arms across his chest, arching his eyebrows. "Fey, huh... well, I beg your pardon for interrupting your work, Lawrence. I'll let you get back to it." He turned to go and asked at the door, "You're sure you didn't see someone on a horse?"

"I'm sure, Sire." He looked at him concerned, his mixing slowing. "Did you?"

Alexander looked out the door toward the woods. "No, I guess I didn't. Thank you," and turned to leave.

"Your Highness?"

Alexander turned back. "Yes, Lawrence?"

The baker put his bowl down squarely on the table. "I heard something yesterday... something about... Arnold."

Alexander took a silent breath to steady himself for the answer. "Yes, Lawrence. He died yesterday. Evelyn was with him."

"They say, well, they say the king did it."

"I'm afraid he did, Lawrence." Alexander's gaze dropped to his hands, unable to meet Lawrence's eyes for the moment. "I'm looking into it myself. Consequently, I'm going to be the one giving him his food from now on." He looked again at Lawrence.

The baker shook his head and returned to mixing his bread. "He's been different ever since your sister's wedding. Understandably so, too." Lawrence looked back at Alexander. "You be careful around him from now on. You hear me? I don't want to hear someone had to sit by your side as your life leaked away."

The vision of Catriona sitting by his side, holding his hand as he passed away into death, swelled into Alexander's mind, and he smiled at Lawrence. "I'll be careful, Lawrence. Good morning to you."

The torch from upstairs was in the torch holder next to the outer door and Alexander realized he didn't remember putting it there. *What now,* he wondered to himself. *Did Catriona now ride her silent horse into the hallway and take the torch from your hand?* fae were as good an explanation as he had, and he left it alone.

He walked back up the stairs to his room and noticed the door to his niece's room was open. He looked and saw a lantern lit in the privy and determined it was the nurse who was awake. He looked in on Marie-Elizabeth and she opened her little eyes of the clearest blue and looked over at him.

He stepped into the room and went over to her, expecting

her to have closed her eyes and gone back to sleep by the time he reached her. He was wrong. She looked up at him with fully awake eyes. "Alex."

"Hello, Marie. What are you doing awake?"

"I goin' get Alex," she answered in her sweet, perfect voice.

"You're coming to get *me?* What did *I* do to deserve a perfect little girl coming to get me?"

"I sa hungee."

"You're hungry?"

"Hungee."

"Well, I've got something to eat in my room."

"Hungee." Marie-Elizabeth tossed off her covers and got out of bed as Alexander stood up. She reached up for him. "Up?"

Alexander picked her up and turned around to meet the short, dark-haired nurse in the door, wearing a night dress. She arched an eyebrow in question, pursing her lips together in dissatisfaction. He shrugged his shoulders. "She's hungry."

"Hungee."

"Apparently so," said the nurse. "Your Highness, let me take her and feed her so you can get back to bed."

"Oh no, Chantal, I'll do it. You have to get up with her every night and I'm up. I've already done my exercises so I'm wide awake, and I have some fruit and bread in my room. We'll be fine."

Chantal stifled a yawn. "Are you sure, Your Highness?"

Alexander looked at Marie-Elizabeth. "Positive. Right, Kitten?"

"Hungee." The two adults laughed as Alexander walked off with the little girl to his room down the hall. Once there, he handed her an apple and a cracker and she took a bite of each in turn. Alexander stoked the fire so it would be warm in the room and retrieved his wine from the window sill. He pulled a blanket off the bed and sat in one of his wing chairs, then turned to call Marie-Elizabeth over to sit with him. The blanket would keep her warm in the early morning cold until the fire managed to heat up the room.

Heracles, Alexander's wolfhound, tried to get the cracker from the toddler and she gave it to him merrily. The dog towered over her by at least a foot, but he was terribly gentle with the Royal

Family. He wasn't fond of strangers but he recognized the royals and admitted them into his master's presence. Many of the servants had learned to clean the Prince's quarters when he had the animal outside on a romp in order to avoid the dog, and would refresh his food and wine at that time.

Marie-Elizabeth crawled up into Alexander's lap and snuggled under the blanket with him, then returned to her apple. The fire was cozy and worked its magic on them both and Elizabeth found them both asleep when she came to get her daughter a couple of hours later.


The queen had gotten into the habit now of leaving Myrgen's bed at dawn so her servants wouldn't find them together and this morning, she had awoken out of habit, forgetting their decision not to be together made the early rising unnecessary that day. Their sexual escapades were incredible, their bonding, especially on Myrgen's part, was more and more committing and Elizabeth caught herself fantasizing about Myrgen, Marie-Elizabeth and her living together as a family.

She had gotten up to get Marie-Elizabeth, looking forward to cuddling her, only to find her in the arms of her brother-in-law. She sat down in the other wing chair and watched them until Alexander stirred a few minutes later. He looked over at Elizabeth. "How long have you been sitting there?"

"Only a few minutes. I came looking for her this morning and Chantal said she came in here with you around dawn."

"Yes. I thought we were both pretty awake but apparently, I was wrong." Alexander looked down at his little niece, her soft lashes draped peacefully across her upper cheeks.

"Do you want me to take her?" Elizabeth stretched out her arms toward the child. "She's probably wet. So are you, by now."

"No, I don't want to disturb her. If I'm wet, then taking her away now won't change that but it might wake her before she's ready and start her day off badly." He looked over at Elizabeth who was smiling at him. "What?"

"You're so considerate."

"Well, just doing unto others, you know."

"Was that what happened yesterday? You brought that

man's wife in to be with him because you hoped they would do that for you someday?"

Alexander glanced down at Marie-Elizabeth. "Of a sort." He looked back at Elizabeth. "When I'm dying, I hope they'll bring the woman I love to be the last thing I see of this earth." His eyes seemed to mist up for a moment as he looked at Elizabeth and then he looked down at Marie-Elizabeth asleep in his arms as he got himself under control.

Elizabeth felt him tug at her heart then. She was so incredibly fond of Alexander and his kindness, and it seemed, just then, that he was trying to tell her something. She looked down at her daughter in his arms and noted how appropriate that picture was, like she belonged there. Marie-Elizabeth had some of the same features as Charles and Alexander, and Elizabeth caught herself imagining her daughter being of Alexander's loins instead of his brother's. Her eyes had been opened sexually through Myrgen and she suddenly believed Alexander would be the same sort of lover.

He looked back up at her. "You're doing it again."

"What?"

"Thinking things."

"Oh. Yes, well, I noticed you kind of dodged the reference to Charles' fit yesterday and I was just being patient."

"Ah. Sorry. I didn't realize you were asking. You should learn to be more blunt, Elizabeth."

"I'll work on that." She cocked her head at him as he looked off into the fire. "So what happened?"

Alexander took a deep breath. "He had one of his headaches, only this time, he thought Arnold was trying to kill him. He was defending himself against this imagined foe."

"I understand you had the man brought in here to die."

"I wanted him to be as comfortable as possible. I felt responsible, in a way."

"Why?" Elizabeth's tone was incredulous.

"Because I was right there." He looked over at Elizabeth. "I was standing right next to him, and I couldn't stop him from killing a man. Saint's Blood, what if that had been you? Or Marie-Elizabeth?" His eyes began misting again and he turned them back to the fire. "I just don't think I could live with myself if that happened."

Elizabeth's eyes misted up as well, believing he was telling her how much he loved her, and she felt her heart break. She felt as if she had been bombarded with a thousand choices in the past two years and had made the wrong ones at every turn. First, she had married Charles instead of Alexander, which wasn't a choice of hers but she had gone along with that. Then, after Alexander had proven his love to her over and over again, she had gone to Myrgen's bed instead of staying true to her original course. Once Charles was dead, Elizabeth was certain Alexander would be hers, but she had entangled herself with Myrgen now, and she wasn't certain how to extract herself from that emotional briar patch.

"Alexander, I… I'm sorry for all of this…."

Alexander looked back at her and saw how she was on the verge of tears over the issue. He reached out to her with his free hand and she took it. "Elizabeth, don't. There's nothing any of us could have done about this whole mess. It was out of our hands before we got the chance to grab it." His voice got an earnest tone to it. "Listen to me, now. I don't want you or Marie-Elizabeth anywhere near him right now, do you understand? I can't always be here and I wouldn't want anything to happen to you, do you hear me?"

Elizabeth nodded, her tears running down her cheeks now.

"Well and good." He let go of her hand and looked back into the fire. "If there's anyone to be put at risk here, it will be me."

Marie-Elizabeth stirred at that time and opened her flawless blue eyes and smiled at her mother, completing the picture in Elizabeth's mind of sweet, perfect love.

***Chapter Eighteen:***
***"For by means of a whorish woman a man is brought a
piece of bread: and the adulteress will hunt for the precious life."***
*~ Proverbs 6:26*

Nicolai opened his eyes to a perfectly silent house, and he didn't like it. He had gotten used to sleeping alone when Catriona had been off gallivanting around the world but then he had gotten used to having someone there again when he and Tanglwyst fell in love. After Catriona showed up, she had stayed in his bed until Alan came to live with them for the winter, then she had began spending more and more time watching over the boy instead of sleeping with her husband.

He lay in his bed and looked up at the tile ceiling, thinking about the past year. He had finally let go of his grief a year ago and given in to the emotions he had denied for the Lady Tanglwyst. They had been at sea for two months, but they were never hard months on Tanglwyst's flagship, the Sulocco. They had gotten an early start on the season that year, the first one without the pirate Black Sparrow on the seas, and the good weather offered a chance to set sail in April instead of May as usual.

They had sat and had dinner together in her cabin. She had asked about his wife and how she had died, and Nicolai had told her he didn't know. It was the hardest part of it all, the lack of knowing. He had no body to bury so there was no closure for him, no ending to the pain. Tanglwyst had said she knew something of what he spoke because she had lost a husband, had watched him die in front of her, his throat cut by street thugs. Nicolai was astonished to find she had been present for such a brutal death and he had reached out his hand to her. He had intended the touch to be reassuring, commiserating, tender.

Instead, he discovered himself hungry for her touch, and his hand trembled. She noticed and had looked at him then. *Her eyes, Saint's Blood, her eyes. They glittered in the candlelight, their gentle hazel color transforming almost to blue in the beautiful soft glow. Her eyes had hypnotized him then and he had leaned over to her and kissed her, beckoned to do so by those enrapturing eyes.*

*He had broken the contact first, suddenly feeling self-conscious at kissing his employer. The action felt at once so right and so wrong, and he pushed away from the table and left to get his confusion under control. He had waited on deck, smoothing through his thoughts like combing a long haired dog, and noticed the deckhand take away their dishes. He waited until he noticed the light in her cabin go out and then waited a little longer, although it seemed to him to be an eternity.*

*He returned to his Captain's cabin, which, incidentally, was next to hers, and disrobed. He had lain in bed, listening to the sea lap against the side of the ship when he heard a slight creak of a door opening. He saw a hidden door, which connected the two cabins, open and saw her step through, a small candle in her hand. Nicolai had sat up on his elbows and was about to protest when her chemise slipped off her shoulder as she turned and closed the door, and his comment caught in his throat.*

*She had been beautiful. The candlelight scintillated off her auburn hair which was brushed to silky elegance and flowed like the wind across a wheat field over her shoulders. Her eyes were vulnerable and full of desire and he couldn't say anything except, "You're beautiful."*

*She had smiled at that and came over to him, setting her candle on the table next to his bed. He managed to open his mouth to protest and she quieted him with a finger to his lips. She skin had been so soft, resting on his lips and he had closed his eyes and felt it there, smelling her, tasting her touch so close to his tongue. She had drawn her finger down his lips and replaced it with her own, even softer than her fingertip. He had wanted to protest, to send her away but his voice failed him and he could not.*

*The taste of her kisses still captured him in a bed of honey, her affection filling the void of his life. Never had he known how empty he was inside until she filled him. She had moved the blankets aside and lay atop him, her weight spectacular and as easy to feel as the sea. She had kissed his chest and worked her way down to his crotch, lingering there in sweet temptation without actually giving him the taste of her lips. He had never experienced anything like this and it completely overwhelmed him.*

*She hovered her lips over his erection, dusting it with her breath while never touching him. Then she lowered her mouth over him entirely, still maintaining the distance. He could feel the moisture of her mouth, the heat, the breath, then she raised herself off him again, allowing tingling brushes with no actual contact.*

She did this over and over, hovering, breathing, sometimes closing her tongue into a partial tube but never letting him feel complete contact until, just as he thought he would burst, she plunged her entire mouth onto him, full contact on every surface.

He had arched and almost screamed with pleasure, his orgasm threatening to come too soon. She bobbed her head up and down on his engorged cock until he thought he'd burst, then she suddenly backed off him. He heaved forward in his bed, his body convulsing from the denied orgasm. She then moved up and straddled him, poising herself over his straining erection. She licked her hand and lubricated herself to insure ease of penetration, then slowly slipped onto him.

He had thought her mouth was scrumptious, but her womanhood swallowed him whole. He thrust deep within her, penetrating her cervix, a sweet second orifice waiting deep within the first and she didn't seem to mind. She did, however, take control of the session. She pinned him to the bed by the shoulders and let her vaginal muscles take over where her mouth left off, lifting slowly up the entire length of his manhood, then slowly pushing back down. The rocking of the ocean seemed to assist her, as if the elements were entirely at her command.

Once, he tried to pick up the pace on the lovemaking, so hungry for her he wanted to throw her to the floor and take her, but she stopped moving completely when he did, pushing his legs down with the tops of her ankles and he folded like a house of cards, completely at her mercy. She popped him out of her completely but teased around it, never letting it get very far from home before plunging down onto him and bouncing quickly for a few strokes.

The pace was maddening and finally, he felt himself about to crest that final wave of pleasure. She held him off for a good ten minutes with this torture until eventually, he was so close, her sitting still and pulsating her vaginal muscles drove him over the edge. He erupted, more than he ever had before but when he was finished, she didn't stop and he did the impossible: he reached orgasm a second time, instantly.

She smiled down at him in triumph and removed her chemise to expose her breasts and waited until she could start all over again. They kept up like this for four of his orgasms and, by daylight, he couldn't be more hers if they occupied the same skin.

*Her lovemaking was amazing and over the next few weeks, he found even more reason to love her beyond the physical. She was so completely generous with her body, more than willing to try any and everything with which he wanted to experiment. She had been versatile, aggressive, passive and everything he'd ever wanted.*

*She still was. They were supposed to meet yesterday morning. He had visited her the evening before, after Catriona had fallen asleep in Alan's room. He had drunk too much and had had too much sex, but Tanglwyst had slipped him into bed just before dawn. Nicolai had awoken later and found both Catriona and Alan gone. He had been expecting that, what with the sailing season almost upon them all. He had gone to Tanglwyst's house, but she was also gone. He had been in a foul mood ever since.*

Nicolai heard a sound in the kitchen, a pan being pulled from the cupboard, and he hoped it was Tanglwyst. He got up. He needed to use the privy regardless, so he slipped on his boots, the need in his bladder too great to put on anything more than a robe. He went into the common room and Catriona was there. She looked over at him. "I'm sorry. Did I wake you?"

"No, I was awake. I'll be right back." He ducked outside and used the privy, then came back in, shaking off the early spring chill. He moved over to the fire and warmed himself by poking it around and helping it catch. He stood up and swung his arms to help improve his circulation. "I thought you had left for the season."

Catriona looked out the window at the sunrise, the palace still sleeping in the early morning glow. "Not yet. I still have some things to do here."

So, have you been up long?"

"Yes."

Nicolai waited for more than this but received none so he said, "I didn't hear you come in last night."

"I just got in. I was with Gwen. She and Dom are quarrelling."

"Oh? What about?" Nicolai moved over to the food prep area and took a piece of fruit from the plate of apples and pears she was cutting. He leaned against the wall and looked at her.

Catriona looked at him and smiled. "He doesn't approve of me."

"I didn't know he knew you and Gwen knew each other."

"He recently found out."

"Oh, I'll bet he took that well." He took another piece of apple. "Are these for both of us?"

"Of course."

"Oh. Good. I was hoping I wasn't being a pig." He watched her cut the fruit. She appeared to have something on her mind, and he wondered if she was going to volunteer it, or if he would have to coax it out of her. *Probably the latter.* "So. Sit down and talk to me. Tell me what you've been up to lately."

"Just saw Tristram Wulfschlager off this morning. He sent me home with some tea, of course."

"I guess you'll be off here soon too, huh?"

"Yes, pretty soon."

"Know where you're goin' yet?"

"I'll be heading off to St. Andrew first thing. I have a passenger to deliver before the end of June." She turned a chair next to the table around to sit down and leaned her back against it, facing the fire. The early morning light had always looked somewhat wrong on Catriona but Nicolai reflected that she sure shined at night. It wasn't that she wasn't beautiful, she was, but full daylight seemed to the wrong shade of color for her complexion or something. He was still feeling amorous from his remembrances that morning, and he wondered if he would be any more successful this time than he had been all winter. In all their months together, they had been intimate only once and he had made the mistake of calling her Tanglwyst during their coupling.

Nicolai saw that the water was boiling. He got up to get some mugs for the tea and grabbed the two little bags of tied cloth to which Catriona had referred, popping them in the mugs. He was thinking of mentioning that Tanglwyst had apparently left town already, but thought better of it. They seemed to be actually talking right now and he wasn't interested in having Catriona turn suddenly cold and unresponsive. He dipped the water out with a ladle without thinking to put the mugs down first and successfully scalded his hands with the water.

Catriona immediately grabbed the bucket of well water from the sink area and put Nicolai's hands into it, holding them under the water to stop the burning. "Damn. That was stupid." Nicolai shook his head. "What was I thinking?"

She looked at him. "I don't know. What *were* you

thinking?"

He looked back at her and recalled his waking thoughts, remembering he had been a total ass when it came to her and making love, and how he was paying the price for it now.

"Honestly? I was thinking about how beautiful you were, especially in the moonlight." He looked into her eyes and thought about kissing her, about seeing if he could wipe away the unpleasant experience of their only other recent intimate moment. She seemed to sense it and withdrew her hands from the water, going over to the prep area and drying her hands on a towel. He took his hands from the water as well, taking the towel from her very gently.

She looked down at his hands. "They're going to blister. Here." She held both his hands and closed her eyes. Nicolai watched as a slight breeze seemed to dance around them, fluttering her hair. He heard everything more crisply, like he had while he was still blind, the air bringing the sound of children laughing in the early morning sunlight, dogs barking, and young girls singing love songs. He felt an energy flow from her hands, moving into Nicolai's burnt ones. It was hard to let her do this because he objected to this use of "heathen magic," but he also knew he couldn't wield a sword for guard duty if he had burnt hands. The redness from the scalding water disappeared and she breathed out, releasing the extra energy back into the air from whence it had come.

He watched her, knowing this was something very intimate, that she had done for others on her ships but never for him. He regretted everything about them, but he especially regretted the loss of their closeness. They had loved each other so completely when they were young. He hated losing that in this late day of their relationship. Sometimes, he felt that love again, hiding behind the regret and interference from the outside world. Sometimes, he wished he could kiss it all away.

She looked at him and he kissed her unexpectedly, a gentle, grateful kiss. She reacted, confused and hesitant, but she didn't push away. Nicolai took that as a good sign. He reached out to her, embracing her with his strong arms and disciplined hands. He touched her face, her neck, her hair with his lips, and he felt a stirring in his heart, as if a sleeping bird were trying to awaken.

He kept kissing her as he began touching her side, inching

up to caress her breast, pulling her closer. She began to resist, but he just pulled harder, determined not to allow her to escape this time. She tried to speak, to tell him no, but he kept kissing her to quiet her tongue. He reached into her coatdress and pulled the front open in a jerk. She tried to push away from him then, but Nicolai had played this game before with Tanglwyst, and she loved it. Nicolai moved his hand into her coat, under her shirt to the bare flesh of her breast.

"Nicolai…please…."

"Certainly," was his reply, and he bore her down onto the table, spreading her legs with his hips.

* * *

Catriona trembled at the ravenous way Nicolai was acting. She felt his partial erection and took a breath. She wanted something in her life, some intimacy that was *right*. Nicolai was her husband, and they had loved each other once. She desperately wanted to believe they could again. She responded to him, hoping to be drawn closer by this act to him. She needed to be able to confide in someone, to have someone spark that emotion in her. She opened up her heart and her eyes to see that now. She looked at Nicolai, to see what he needed to bring that about.

Her Sight exposed him to her, exposed his desires, his dreams, his goals. She saw that he didn't know Alan was missing because he thought the boy was already with Drake and Anika. She saw he had been lonely and he, too, wanted that relationship with love and a deep devotion involved. She also saw the most important part, the one whom he needed most of all in the world, the one for whom all others paled or were a substitute.

She saw he needed Tanglwyst.

* * *

Catriona tried to push Nicolai off her but he simply took this as an opportunity to unfasten her hose with the same quick yank as he did her coatdress. He lay down on her again as he wriggled his hand inside his robe and she finally had to slap him to get his attention.

"Nicolai! Don't."

He leaned back, holding his cheek as she rolled off the table and began refastening her clothing. Nicolai cursed inwardly, then decided to voice it. "Damn it, Catriona. Why do you keep pulling away from me?" He looked over at her, eyes frustrated.

"Because the truth of the matter is you love Tanglwyst and I'm merely a substitute until you can be with her again. That's a role I just can't play."

"Look, I know I made a mistake that one time but…"

"Like what was going on just now? Try to tell me you weren't wishing it was… Never mind. I have some things I need to do."

"Things like what? Him? That Grymalkin guy?"

Catriona looked at him, reading exactly who he meant. "No, Nicolai. Unlike you, I haven't seen my lover all winter." She tightened the ties on her hose and tied them, her anger threatening to snap them.

Nicolai saw where this was going and stormed into the bedroom to get dressed and go to the palace. Catriona finished dressing, and was out the door before he found his shirt. He heard the door close and cursed himself again. She had been the most important thing in his life once and now, he couldn't be in the same room with her without fighting her. She had proven her willingness to work on this relationship, but a few ill placed, bad comments and it had destroyed her faith in their future. She had turned cold and he couldn't battle her heart's ice with his fists.

*So why don't you melt the ice instead of beating against it? Run after her right now. Stop her in the streets and kiss her. You could always melt her with a kiss, back when you meant it.* Nicolai almost listened to himself but then he backed down because that actually was the thing, wasn't it? Back when he meant it, he could melt her with a kiss. Back when he meant it, he could bring a smile to her face by talking of their future. Back when he meant it, he could tell her he loved her.

Back when he meant it, which wasn't now.

* * *

Catriona left her home and got onto her horse as quickly as she could, afraid Nicolai would come after her. She was nauseous from his touch, it had so resembled the Giovanni. She had never told Nicolai the true identity of the man she had met with last summer, too protective of Alexander's vulnerability if it was known where he went when he escaped the palace. Nicolai had no idea he guarded the very man who loved her, but she had been true to them both in a way, sleeping with neither and never seeing Alexander the entire winter. She had gone without sex for so long, she rarely thought of it these days, and when she did, she remembered Alexander up at the cabin on the cliffs and not Nicolai any longer. Occasionally, she thought of Yantap and her time there, but things had gotten so tainted since then, she preferred to try and put those times out of her mind. She found her heart aching to forget too much of her life.

Catriona looked back at her husband's door. She could still feel his hand on her skin and tears trying to crest in her eyes. Her heart no longer felt pleasure from being touched and it had been years now since she had wanted someone to make love to her, even Alexander. Her time with him had been an attempt at intimacy, but in the end, it felt false and forced.

That didn't mean she should hold others back who truly did feel desire for another's touch. She wheeled her horse and kicked his sides. It was time to release Tanglwyst from wherever Myrgen had her hidden and return her to Nicolai so they could have each other. She was no longer going to hold him back and he would no longer have to wish he had his true love in his arms instead of his wife. She had been declared dead once, and so had he. Best to go back to those days.

Catriona rode back up to the woods and slipped in through the hedgerow until she was able to slip up to the palace. She got behind the hedge on the more eastern edge of the gardens which opened into the secret passage behind the antechamber. She knew this one didn't go to Charles' chambers and figured it must go somewhere else, possibly to the queen's chambers and from there, possibly branch off into the places where Alan and Tanglwyst were being kept.

Catriona opened the passage, then pulled a candlestick, candle and sulfur stick she had borrowed from Gwen from her pouch. She set up the candle and lit it, then closed the passageway behind her. It occurred to her she should track down Michael and follow him, but he had managed to capture her which meant he was a little too well informed concerning her. Involving Gwen was putting a strain on her relationship with Dominic and Catriona didn't want to be responsible for yet another love being destroyed by her. She was on her own in trying to solve this problem

She stopped moving in the passage and leaned against a wall, suddenly out of breath. She was starting to panic about finding her son, about him being dead or worse. She feared she would look for him and never find him, getting hopelessly lost herself and die, screaming his name. She wept silently for a moment, letting the release refuel her determination.

She felt the cool stone beneath her fingers as she leaned against the wall, and remembered what Father Benjamin had said. *There are forces in play to limit your connection with the Land. You need a location where the patterns that block you cannot see you. Seek that place, Catriona, and protect your son.* She checked her light and the flame wasn't flickering in the slightest. The small candlelight illuminated very little and she almost felt she would be better off without it. She decided to give that a try, feeling she could always re-light the candle. She blew out the candle and waited for the wax to solidify before putting the assembly away in the pouch. The wait gave her eyes time to adjust and she sped the process by closing them and thinking. *What did she remember from her imprisonment?* The smell of this place was different from Charles' passage because it was older than his. His still smelled of timber in places.

This one smelled primarily of dust and… something else, under that…ash…yes, but, something else too. Something old…

Death.

Yes. Of course. *Death.*

The Royal Crypts. There were always passages under the castles and palaces, tunnels where the Royal Families were buried. The Chapels were sometimes even underground for the burial ceremonies. She thought back. There had been a fire in the old chapel about five years ago. Yes, Alexander had said once that Catherine even blamed it on Plantyn in an attempt to incite the people's ire that the Royal Remains weren't even safe. That would put engineers and workers in the catacombs to rebuild the chapel and Charles could have easily slipped in a crew which built the escape tunnel to his own chambers.

Catriona opened her eyes and there was a very dim change. She could identify the walls versus the passage but now she felt she knew more about what she was looking for. She stood up and began walking further into the tunnel, keeping her hands on the walls to keep her aware of any openings. The passage was about five feet wide, barely enough to accommodate the dresses in fashion these days, and she was once again grateful for choosing to be classified a pirate so she could wear breeches. That was simply one reason *not* to marry Alexander. The size of those gowns was completely impairing.

*One* of the reasons. There were so many. The Royal Line of Mervolingia was perpetuated through the males, unlike York, which was a matriarchy. Alexander held the distinction of being heir to the throne of Mervolingia, unless Charles declared a different male heir. He endangered his life enough seeking her out. Had any of those unsavory relatives of Dominic's in Cheryb found out who he really was when he traveled as Grymalkin, he would be captured and held for ransom. Likewise, if anyone knew he cared for her, his own enemies could threaten her for their own ends. Myrgen had taught her one thing: She was not as invulnerable as she thought.

Notch.

She also wasn't certain she wanted to be a Prince's wife. He could possibly mend the injuries from the Saint Michael's Massacre with the right political marriage, as Charles' own marriage had solidified trade relations with Krakte, the finest engineers in all of the Saintlands. They were probably the ones who designed these tunnels centuries ago. It would explain why they were still standing and hadn't fallen into ruin like other Mervol landmarks had over the centuries. Political marriages were the way of things here, and those in power could not afford the luxury of love.

Notch.

The resurfacing of her own marriage to Nicolai had come at an incredibly inconvenient time, but a part of her felt a little bit rescued at the same time. Her decision to be with Alexander was a product of loneliness, pure and simple. Karma and the Land probably understood that far better than she had and had brought Nicolai back into her life then. She had studied the principles of Karma during her time in Yantap, a time she still remembered fondly as the only time in the past ten years where she had been truly happy. She had learned to refine her Sight there, and the spiritual nature of the culture there had healed the wounds of her captivity. And there had been Alistair...

Notch.

Catriona stopped and felt the wall again. A notch in the wall marred the right hand side at shoulder level, marking the wall. A rise in the stone that seemed to be a natural occurrence, yet it was identical to the two before it. She realized she had felt three of them now and she moved forward slower, keeping her hands out at about that level. Sure enough, there was another in the wall about ten paces down and Catriona knew the chances of finding those notches with the small candle were very slim because the light would have focused her attention to only what she could see. She thanked the Land for her guidance and followed the notches as far as she could.

They eventually stopped when she reached a larger opening. She decided to actually light her candle at this time to be sure she wouldn't miss a detail on the floor. She figured she had found a crossroads in the catacombs and that this was probably the path by which someone traveled often enough to use the passages but not often enough to know the way by heart, hence the notches. On the other hand, the notches could be obsolete to the royal who used them originally and helpful for those who were just being initiated into the Royal Family and the series of labyrinths.

The small light cast enough glow to display a large set of stairs going up. These stairs were about ten feet wide and carved into the rock. Catriona inspected them and guessed they were to allow the king and queen the ability to escape and bring some of their retinue with them. She wandered around the open chamber. There were several ways to go, like the points of a compass. She could feel she was facing north at this point, the turns in the tunnel behind her shifting around obstacles beyond her awareness.

To the east were the stairs going up. She had gotten a look at the grounds and basic layout of the externals of the palace at this point and figured most likely, these stairs went to the eastern wing of the palace, where some of the royal chambers were housed. Alexander's window had been on the north face of the palace, the same as Charles'. Since Charles' passage was independent, she assumed the east wing had Alexander, Elizabeth and the princess housed there. Catherine would want to keep an eye on Charles so her chambers would be on the west wing with his.

However, since Charles had a separate passage built, that effectively meant the chambers he *used to* occupy were the ones connected to the other passages. That meant Myrgen's chambers used to be either the Queen-Mother's or Francois', Charles older brother whom he succeeded. That would supply a passage between Myrgen and Elizabeth without having to risk discovery by the servants. She wanted to explore these places. But first, she wanted to find Alan.

To the west, the wider passage continued, and she figured it hooked up with the chapel itself. They wouldn't build the new chapel on top of the old one and the multitude of crypts would pose a bit of a problem but she would be better off going in that direction.

The only question in her mind was exactly where that passage to the north went. She didn't have any idea what use it would have and it made her definitely want to look there first. She set off across the chamber toward the west, certain that someone had had a penchant for architecture which incorporated secret passages. They were everywhere. Underground, in the garden, in the ramparts over the Great Hall. The guards walked through a series of passages which went behind the walls encompassing the Great Hall. They were thirty to forty feet above the floor with no way to get to them except inside the walls, and had openings for firing arrows or crossbows into the crowd should someone try to harm the king or queen. There were a couple passages like that in the castle at Zara, but far fewer than this place.

The north passage got smaller quickly and soon she was almost brushing the walls with both shoulders, although she could still stand upright. Before long, she reached a dead end and she began checking the walls for some sort of trigger stone. A stone on the floor depressed, one generally inaccessible unless you were looking for something, and the stone in front of her gave way to reveal the western side of the palace grounds. This was the side where she rode her horse past the servants' entrance by the kitchen, but the hedgerow passage also came that way. She looked around to try to figure out what use this had and her hand brushed a small trigger in the wall. A section if the south wall gave way and Catriona beheld the inside of a cell. It wasn't the one she had been in but she could smell all the same things so she knew it was close.

She felt around the walls some more and located a passage

in the north wall which led down. This one seemed to be more of a natural cavern and the stairs cut into the ground led down to the room she had been in. The room had apparently been some sort of torture chamber, although the light and circumstances hadn't revealed itself to her when she had been imprisoned here. The cell was still in the center of the room and hanging from the walls were various other implements like a rusted spiked cage and an ancient iron maiden. Catriona looked around for any passages out of the room but saw none in the limited light, and returned to the main tunnel.

She noticed she was hungry and thought, for an instant she smelled food. She didn't see or hear any prisoners in the holding cells in the jail, so she assumed she smelled the food from the kitchens around the corner. It then occurred to her how she might find Alan. They were undoubtedly feeding the boy. She may not be able to trail Michael in plain sight but she could definitely shadow him down here. She'd already determined the presence of a light source actually limited one's perceptions here, and anyone carrying food wouldn't be carrying a large torch, especially in some of the smaller passages.

She settled into one of the hollows of the prison passage and waited.

*Chapter Nineteen:*
*"Do this now, my son, and deliver thyself, when thou art come into the hand of thy friend; go, humble thyself, and make sure thy friend."*
*~ Proverbs 6:3*

Michael went to the kitchens and prepared the trays for Tanglwyst and Alan. The kitchen staff was accustomed to him preparing trays for the royalty and officers of the guard and the tray he piled a bit higher with food was undoubtedly his because he was so large. There were some who refused to allow him to touch their food and still others who believed it was the role of the "lesser races" to serve their betters so he was never quite paid much mind either way. He was always well spoken and courteous so the kitchen staff had a tendency to be generous with their special treats.

Today, Antoinette had put together a special sausage and egg loaf, meat and eggs inside a loaf of bread. She told him it was supposed to keep the sausage and eggs warm and had some gravy inside to make things moist. He smiled and thanked her heartily, giving her a coin from his pouch for her kindness. She tried to wave it away but he insisted and dropped it into her apron pocket. Then he took the two trays of food into the servants' entrance to the palace.

Michael knocked on the door in the code they had established, and Myrgen called out, "Enter."

Michael came in with the two trays of food. "Breakfast, sir."

"Michael, you are a friend of mine. You don't have to call me 'sir.'"

"I am still a possession according to this society."

"Would you like to buy your freedom?"

Michael blinked, thinking about it, then said, "Not right now, sir. I'd have nothing to do and no where to go if I did so. If I may, though, what would be the cost?"

"One silver piece."

Michael nodded and went into the portrait room and the catacombs behind them, on his way by snagging with a little finger the small lantern Myrgen lit for him. He went down the lengthy corridor which ran behind the south wall, then turned left down the brief hallway to the wide stairs. He descended them in short order, not wanting the food to get excessively cold. He always covered the trays with heavy towels to maintain their heat but the long, arduous way through the passages taxed even the items right out of the ovens.

At the bottom of the stairs, Michael turned right and pushed the trigger stone in the middle of the wall with his foot. The passage swung open before him and he entered the ancient hallways of the old family crypts.

* * *

Catriona moved quickly to be certain she caught sight of the door. Most of the doors had a catch on both sides and so no one would be trapped if they knew where the triggers were. She noted Michael had to pick his foot up to about waist level to open the door, but when she got to the door, it was still partially open. She looked around and saw a small stone had gotten caught under the door, holding it open. The door was on such a balanced hinge, the stone had stopped the door but Catriona was careful not to dislodge it until she had slipped past in case the door was heavier than she thought. She could see the light of his lantern way ahead of her and she was grateful her own lesson with the darkness had been so timely. There were hundreds of shadows to become a part of in order to hide.

Michael came to a T in the passage and went left. She followed carefully, staying to the shadows and back far enough to avoid his light if he passed by again. She also hoped to have enough time to flee up the passage if he returned directly. She heard the squeak of metal door hinges, indicating an actual door instead of the rock closures. She also thought, for a second, that she heard a puppy bark. She waited up the passage, listening for the creak of the hinges again. The passage which brought them down to this place wasn't wide enough to hide her and let Michael pass by without noticing so she tried to give herself enough time to escape without getting caught.

She heard the hinges squeak and prepared to remove herself quickly and silently but Michael simply walked past her corridor and went down the right passage. A bit further down the hall, she heard a knock and Tanglwyst's voice mumbling something. The squeak of door hinges and silence. Catriona poked her head around the corner of the passage, then down the T and turned to the left.

As she approached the T, she noticed the wall of the corridor was scorched wood and realized she was probably in the old chapel. Unlike the current one, with street access, this one had been part of the original monastery which was founded on this site. She looked around for a place to hide in the hallway and found the access to the main hall of the old chapel. The chapel wall had collapsed here and there was barely a place to be out of sight across from the other door in the hallway but it would work. She got to test the theory immediately because the door at the end of the hall opened just then.

"I'll be back for your dishes this afternoon, my Lady." Michael closed the door and walked back toward the passage to leave, then passed it by and went to the other door. He unlocked the door with a skeleton key, the lock in the door obviously well oiled because it hardly made any noise. Michael opened the door and a medium-sized puppy bounded across the floor to him and she heard her son's voice say, "Hi, Michael."

"Hello, Alan. What are you drawing?" He stepped inside and she heard muffled voices from then on. The two seemed to be talking but she couldn't make out what they were saying. Regardless, Michael seemed not to be mistreating Alan at all and he obviously had things to keep him occupied so he was well. Catriona waited in the hallway for Michael to leave, thinking of her next move.

* * *

Michael closed the door behind him.

"I'm drawing a picture of my mother and Anika next to Drake. That's who I named the puppy after, Drake. It means 'dragon.' I figured it wouldn't confuse him as much as Wolf when it comes time to hunt."

Michael smiled at the boy's memory of the dog's primary function. He looked at the drawing. "What's your mother doing?"

"She's leaving."

Michael frowned. "Does your mother leave a lot?"

"Yes, every summer. See this? That's me as a baby. She left me with Anika and Drake when some Terrible Things were chasing her, trying to kill us. She left me there so I could be safe."

"Did the Terrible Things ever get her?" Michael was fascinated by the detail of the drawing on the wall. There was a castle and fields and a pretty good rendering of a ship, like he's seen them up close.

"They did when I was first born, but she fought them off then and every time they found her after that."

"How do you know all this?"

"Anika and Drake told me. They used to get letters from her and they read them to me all the time, even the old ones from when I was very little, not big like I am now." He emphasized this by nodding his head at Michael, who smiled at his adult manner. "They also told me every day that she would come back for me because her letters said so. Drake told me that if the Terrible Things ever got her, it was *my* job when I became a man to hunt them down and *kill* them for hurting her. That's the way things are done."

Michael was taken back a bit by this comment coming from a small boy. "How did you feel about that?"

"I didn't quite understand it when I was little but that's fine because Drake said he would teach me how to fight when I was big."

"Is Drake a good fighter?"

"He's fantastic." Alan jumped up excitedly. "He was a general in the Caratian army. He was a member of the Order of the Dragon. He was quite good at fighting." The boy began acting out the various battles Drake fought in, apparently raised quite a bit on Drake's exploits. Michael listened to the stories for about an hour before he realized how much time had passed and he stood up to leave.

"I'm sorry, Alan, but I have to go now. I'll come back later and you can tell me more stories, all right?"

"That'll be *great*."

Michael opened the door.

"Oh Michael?" Michael turned back to face the child and Alan asked, "Why do you have to lock the door?"

"Well, your mother wants to make sure you're safe. If I didn't lock the door, Terrible Things might get in here."

"But what if something happens, like Drake accidentally knocks over the lantern and the straw catches fire?"

"Did you have a dream about the straw catching fire?"

"No, but this place had a fire once, didn't it?"

"Yes, that's true."

"Well, what if that happens again?"

"I would come and save you. But here, let's alleviate that right now." He took the lantern and put it on a hook up out of the way but where it still cast the light well. "See? That hook was put there just for holding the lantern so it wouldn't get knocked over. Now Drake can't set the straw on fire."

"What if the candle burns out?"

"I'll bring a fresh one tonight. How would that be?"

Alan seemed to run out of things to protest about so he nodded, his mouth pouting a little. "Hey Michael?"

Michael turned back to him. "Yes?"

"When can I go home? When is my mother coming to get me?"

Michael came back over to him and knelt before him so he was at eye level. "Soon. Very soon."

"Promise?"

Michael pursed his lips and tried to think of the best thing to say. A small breeze flowed into the room and he noticed a familiar scent on the wind, a spice blended with vanilla and musk. He had smelled it when he carried Catriona from the torture chamber and it made him smile. He nodded. "I feel confident that your mother will be along very, very soon."

* * *

Catriona left the burnt chapel after Michael said goodbye to Alan and returned up towards the prison passages. Catriona knew she could get Alan out of there, but wasn't sure what kind of shape Tanglwyst was in.

They had also given Alan a dog to keep him company, which was a different problem all by itself. She couldn't ride away with a dog as successfully as she could without one, especially one of those wolfhounds the likes of which she caught a glimpse. It was too big and squirmy for Alan to hold but she was certain she wouldn't be able to make him leave the animal behind. She didn't really want to either. The dog was an act of kindness to help her son get through a terrible ordeal. To take the dog would be beyond cruel.

Regardless, she was going to need help with this one. She needed Drake. She had determined while waiting that she wanted to give Anika and Drake enough time to get far away with Alan, and that meant going in after dark, after Michael had brought Alan his dinner. They would have to have time to prepare for the trip, and that may take as long as a day. Securing horses for them to simply ride to her ship in its secret port might be possible but it was risky. That was a well known road to the town and night was a foolish time to travel it. On the other hand, they would be traveling with Drake, and Drake wouldn't let anything happen to Alan.

She decided to get her friends prepared to leave and let Drake choose the manner in which he would get her son away safe. She trusted him to make the best choice. After that, she would deal with rescuing Tanglwyst. She checked her corners and left the prison passage. She looked around, trying to decide where to go now. She knew she should go directly to Drake and make arrangements to get Alan out of there, but she also felt she had so many things to do.

She needed to find out if the Herbspyce was indeed poison as she suspected, then determine who was poisoning Charles and why. She needed to figure out why Myrgen was involved in this little charade, and who was manipulating him. As odd as that sounded, Myrgen wasn't behaving like his reputation dictated. He was known in the Underground as a ruthless spendthrift, someone who gladly paid for unsavory services, but they had better be done precisely as he directed. His plots were always well thought out and never got personal. Usually, the insalubrious types never even got close to him, and many merely suspected he was the one who put the contract out. In some areas, Myrgen the Grey was almost mythic.

Catriona decided to gnaw on this bone for a few moments. This job didn't involve money, partially because she had refused the job when it was presented to her through the Underground grapevine. It wasn't public knowledge that Catriona knew Charles and Alexander, and no one knew *how* close they were, that she owed them both at least one life debt. She had never seemed terribly attached to Mervolingia, or Patras in particular so there would be no Oaths of Fealty anyone would have witnessed. Thus, she felt safe in refusing the job to kill a member of the Royal Family, knowing there would be no connection for the client to determine why.

No, Myrgen had gotten Catriona specifically. When money didn't work, he got personal, then showed himself as the person hiring her and telling her directly what he wanted in no uncertain terms. This behavior was completely foreign when associated with Myrgen's legends and her studies of him, and Michael's involvement meant they didn't have any reason to have her and no one else. Michael was more than capable of killing Charles and he had access, yet Myrgen secured her. Myrgen could have kept his hands clean but he didn't. Why?

*Well,* she thought to herself, *Self, let's analyze the circumstances. Who would care about Charles dying? Marie, his mistress. Catherine, his mother. Elizabeth, maybe. Alexander. And me. What would cause such a thing? Who was behind this?*

Catriona felt like she was just going around in circles, missing something important, and she needed to be able to think clearly. She knew what she had to do, but she didn't quite know how to pull it off. The last time, she'd had a facilitator: Michael. Now, she couldn't just get where she needed to go as easy. Well, Alan was safe and Drake needed to make arrangements. However, she wasn't about to leave Alan down here with letting him know she had found him. He would never forgive her. She stepped up to door and took a knee to be closer to his listening level. "Alan."

The puppy barked, letting Alan know someone was there and Catriona cast around, hoping it was far enough away for Michael not to return to investigate. Alan came over to the door. "Momma?"

"Yes Alan, it's me."

"Have you come to rescue me?"

"Yes, but I can't do it right now. I need to get Drake. Are you okay?"

"Yes. I have a dog." The puppy continued to bark as they talked.

"So I hear. Are they hurting you?"

"No. The guard said they were very sorry for taking me. His master didn't want to. Drake! Be quiet."

"Drake?"

Alan shuffled his feet and the puppy clawed at the door. "Yes."

Catriona smiled and was about to say something about that when the door down the hallway opened and Tanglwyst stepped out of the well-lit room. Catriona noted the light did not reach all the way to Alan's door, but the sound of her silk robe carried well enough. She was certainly not detained in squalor. Tanglwyst called out, "Michael? Is that you?"

And she didn't sound frightened either.

Catriona glared into the light as her husband's lover crept back into her room and shut the unlocked door. She returned to her son's situation. "Speaking of Drake, Alan, they are in town. I have to leave you for a little while to go get Drake's help on this. Can I do that? Will you let me?"

"When will you be back?"

"As soon as I can. I have to wait a couple days for something to happen, for my friend to get better. Then I can come and get you. But don't worry. The Land led me to you. It won't let anything happen to you, especially down here. You are surrounded by it right now. You are completely protected. Do you understand?"

"Are you sure?" Alan's voice sounded weak and unsure.

"Yes, I'm sure." Catriona tried to think of a way to reassure him. She needn't have bothered.

"Then so am I." His voice was strong now, like he had regained his confidence. She smiled at his resilience. "You are the Stâpâna, momma. You have to protect me. It's your job. Drake said so."

"Yes. And the Land helps me. I love you, Alan."

"I love you too, momma."

Catriona kissed her fingers and put them to the ground, sending her love through the earth they shared, then stood and left the tunnels.

* * *

"Gwen?" Catriona looked around the small but neat house.

"Back here." The call came from the back of the house.

Catriona went to the back of the house where Gwen was seated at a large tub and stirring clothes in murky water with a heavy pole. Gwen looked up at her Mistress. "How did your visit to the palace go?" Catriona could tell Gwen wanted to ask about Alexander, but the girl showed great restraint in response to Catriona's request from the night before.

"Good. I found Alan."

Gwen blinked. "What? Where is he?"

"He's under the palace. He's fine."

"Did you see him?"

"No, but I spoke to him. He knows I have found him and I'll be back." She held up her hand at Gwen's immediate protest, seeing it coming. "I couldn't get him out without his captors knowing it, and there were a few complications. I stopped by the Inn where Drake and Anika are staying and gave them an update on the situation. We'll get him out. The trouble is the rest of the saga."

Catriona had left the catacombs by the same way she had come, more than a little furious at what she had seen. Tanglwyst could leave at any time, and although Catriona could think of several reasons why she might not risk leaving, the decadent surroundings of Tanglwyst's "cell" belied she was hardly a prisoner. Her head had been too muddled with the drug when Myrgen had spoken to her to read him and find out what was really going on, but she now thought it might be necessary for a private viewing. Those catacombs went to the royal chambers. She would see if she could connect to his. It was past time to pay him a visit. But she had to figure a few things out first. Catriona asked, "How busy are you?"

Gwen continued to stir. "Why?"

"I need you to administer a dosage to me. A knock-out drug."

"Where did you get a knock-out drug?"

"From Armand, the poison maker for the *Righteous*. I didn't exactly want to be unconscious with just him watching over me."

"I don't blame you." Gwen stood up. "It'll be good for those to soak a little while. What do you need me to do?"

"We need to prepare this first. After that, just be here for me for a little while. I have to figure out some important things and I can't do it on my own."

Gwen looked confused but she did as directed and mixed

the appropriate medium for the drug. "Do you need me to stay right here?"

Catriona drank the mixture and lay down on the bed. "No. As soon as I'm out though, place this pill under my tongue. Armand said it will slowly bring me out without the tiniest hangover. Then you can go back to what you were doing."

"Are you quite sure it's safe? The man is a poison maker."

Catriona smiled. "Yes. I read him when he gave it to me. It's legitimate."

"Did he know?"

"No. I only read him. That's usually innocuous and doesn't hurt them. The pain comes if I have to go deeper and force it from them. Besides, he's a man whose secrets I don't think I want to discover."

Gwen closed her eyes and shuddered. "Me neither."

Catriona gave the small pill to Gwen and closed her eyes. She took some deep breaths to quiet her nerves, and she felt the blackness closing in. She tried to tell Gwen she was going under but she didn't think she got the words out clearly, which meant Gwen would understand. She vaguely felt her mouth being opened and something being put there, and then the blackness consumed her.

Catriona opened her eyes and sat up. She looked behind her and, sure enough, there was the old stone church. She got up quickly and bolted for the door. The memories of her insight pummeled her, gratefully this time, and she pushed into the church not nearly as exhausted as she usually was when she fought the memories. She still paused inside the doorway, but managed to keep her feet. Perhaps fighting the memories made it worse, but she didn't have time to think about that now. Father Benjamin was already sitting in the pew, as if waiting for her, and it made her wonder for an instant why he usually was praying if he could be sitting right here, prepared to talk. She determined from looking at him that the other times, the prayer for her was for her survival during her presence here.

"I need help figuring out who is manipulating Myrgen."

"Who do you have as suspects?"

"That's the trouble. I'm not sure who's a suspect and who's a victim."

"What are the current circumstances, my child?"

"Myrgen hired me specifically, being sure to secure *my* services. That's why he took Tanglwyst and Alan. But he's shown his hand and that's not like him at all. He's connected it to him and he never does that."

Father Benjamin clasped his hands in his lap. "Well, what would make him want you in particular?"

"I don't know."

"Think. How are you special?"

Catriona thought out loud as she speculated. "I'm a woman…"

"How would that be an advantage here?"

"Well, if the manipulator believes Charles would bed me and I could kill him that way, my being a woman would be important."

"There are a lot more women out there who would be better than you at that, women who do that for a living. Besides, he's in love with Marie. It's not like he goes out whoring."

"That's my thinking too," Catriona reconsidered. "Well, I'm a mother, and he could take my child to blackmail me."

"Why would he do that? Has he ever failed to pay his minions?"

"No. He wouldn't want an unwilling killer in this situation because that could stab him in the back. If the money was an issue, he would have just gone with a cheaper assassin."

"So, what have you to offer the situation?"

"My perceptions?"

"Would Myrgen know about those? The details of them?"

Catriona nodded. "Yes. The drug that poked me muddled my Sight, although that could just be a side effect and not the purpose of that drug. Very few people know how I do what I do."

"Perhaps we should come back to this one in a minute. What else do you need to figure out?"

"Why he's doing this. Why would he show his cards like he has?"

"Well, he secured *your* services specifically, then threw the job at you."

"Yes."

"Sounds like he needs this done in a hurry and didn't have time to go through the proper channels to keep his hands clean."

Catriona looked at Father Benjamin, her eyes opening wide

in awareness. "Of course. Catherine. What ever happened to spark this action happened after Catherine left and Myrgen needs the deed done before she returns. She would see through this faster than I could and have Myrgen hung for treason. The woman is extremely sharp witted and if the catalyst had occurred before she had left, my services would have been procured long before now."

"She comes back in three days, doesn't she?"

"Yes. This means they'll be getting pretty desperate unless they see something happening, and it would need to be a concise effort with lots of impact or it won't be what they need."

"What do they need?"

"They need Alexander to be king before Catherine returns."

"Not necessarily. They may just need Charles dead before she returns. Now, what would happen if Charles were dead?"

"Alexander would be crowned king. Elizabeth would probably be retired to either Charles' lands or would return home to Krakte. Marie and the baby would probably starve without Charles to support them. Alexander would undoubtedly banish Catherine to her family estates," Catriona looked at her hands. "and Alexander would try to court me to become queen."

"So who would benefit from Charles' death?"

"Alexander, I suppose."

"But he doesn't want the throne," the priest reminded her.

"No, and I don't see him plotting to murder his brother."

"Well, let's let that dog lie for now, too. You said last time you were here that someone tried to murder you, too."

"Yes. There was poison on the dart tips. Neither Myrgen nor Michael seemed to know it was there."

"But they knew something was supposed to be there?"

"Yes. Michael specifically dipped the darts in front of me."

"They must have figured you would have understood it was a sleeping drug and not an actual poison. Why else would they show the instrument to you after going to all this trouble to secure *your* services specifically?"

"I think they truly believed it was something like what I used to get here today."

"Could the poison been produced by the same person who sent you here today?"

"Armand is very proud of his art. If there were some similarity between this drug and one he had done for a job this spur of the moment, he would have mentioned it. I didn't see in him the desire to kill anything but rats."

"Then who would have a reason to kill you?"

"And Charles too."

"No. The two assassinations could be completely coincidental. Go one at a time first."

"Me. Well, the only person who would stand to gain a lot from my death would be Dominic."

"Is he truly the only one? What are the motivations for murder again?"

"Power, money, love…"

"Love?" Father Benjamin seemed to be trying to tell her something.

"Love? Why would Dom want to kill me for love?"

"Maybe it isn't Dominic…."

Catriona had one of those moments where everything seemed to click into place. Tanglwyst was in love with Catriona's husband, who would stand to inherit a fortune from the Giovanni estate if Catriona died. Alan would be her will beneficiary, but Tanglwyst would press for Nicolai to assume his paternal duties in regards to the boy. Tanglwyst's company had been in trouble since the Black Sparrow had destroyed many of her ships two years ago. If she were to do in Urien and Catriona, then marry Nicolai, she'd be flush again.

Tanglwyst must have known about Myrgen's infatuation for the queen. She could have discovered it any number of ways but she must have used that to manipulate Myrgen to do this, and in such a sloppy manner. She would have been the one to suggest involving Alan to get Catriona to do this. That would explain her lush apartments in the catacombs and her unlocked door.

Catriona shook her head, disgusted that she had trusted this woman so completely. Well, prior to that moment, she didn't have any reason to not trust her. Then again, Catriona had seen Nicolai's infidelity revealed just this morning. She didn't think they were in on it together, but it might explain why he had not been concerned about Alan's whereabouts. Now, as Catriona figured out what might be the case, she felt the stab of betrayal threatening to enter her heart. However, she refused to assume on this one. It was too important a thing to base on suspicion. Catriona needed confirmation before she would slit the throat of *this* relationship.

This was Nicolai's love, and her freedom as well. If she wanted a chance at happiness, she had to hope Tanglwyst *wasn't* a willing part of this.

But Heaven help her if she was.

*Chapter Twenty:*
*"A virtuous woman is a crown to her husband, but she that maketh ashamed is as rottenness in his bones."*
*~ Proverbs 12:4*

Elizabeth left her chambers to walk in the garden in an attempt to clear her head. She found her heart pulling her in two different directions and she desperately needed to think. She had gotten to the stairs when the servant called out to her.

"Your Majesty?" She stopped on the stairs and looked back.

"His Majesty would like to see you…"

"What for?"

"He didn't say, Your Majesty."

Elizabeth looked around for Alexander or Myrgen, anyone who could interfere with this request. From here, she could go either path to Charles' room, taking her either by Myrgen's room or Alexander's, but she didn't know where either of them were. The servant noticed her looking around nervously and seemed to completely understand. They both heard footsteps coming down one of the halls and watched the hallway anxiously until Myrgen came around the corner with several papers in his hands. He stopped when he saw the pair looking at him.

"What?"

Elizabeth and the servant both exhaled when they saw it was Myrgen and looked at each other. Elizabeth held out her hand to Myrgen, who took it and drew her to him, almost too close in front of a servant. Elizabeth was reluctant to voice her concerns but the servant came to her rescue by answering the Chancellor. "The king wishes to see Her Majesty."

Myrgen looked at the servant, then back at Elizabeth, assessing the danger inherent in this statement and he took a deep breath as well and let it out, nodding to her. He looked back at the servant. "Would you mind getting His Highness ready to join us? Just in case."

"Instantly, Sir." The servant ran off toward the Prince's chambers, leaving Myrgen and Elizabeth alone.

"Are you all right?" Myrgen's concern was evident.

"I…don't know. After yesterday, I…"

"I know what you mean. I'll be there with you, if you want

to go. I'll also give you an excuse if you don't."

Elizabeth smiled at his gallantry. "With Charles in these moods, you waylaying me could be a death sentence."

"I'd rather me than you, My Love." He raised her gloved hand to his lips and kissed it, their eyes locked.

Elizabeth's face furrowed out of the smile Myrgen had just given her. "Let's see what he wants. If he seems lucid, we'll stay. If he seems twitchy, we'll make excuses to depart rapidly."

"As you wish, My Queen." Myrgen placed her hand on his arm and escorted her to the king's Chambers. He knocked on the door for her and admitted her when the king gave his leave.

"Hello, Elizabeth," Charles said formally. He was dressed well today and the curtains were open, but only partially. Myrgen couldn't tell if this was a good day or a bad day yet, so he stayed in the room, slightly behind and to the right of Elizabeth. "Thank you for coming. Would you like to sit down?"

"No, thank you, Your Majesty. I'm fine where I am."

Charles looked at her, at Myrgen's continued presence and her reluctance to enter further, staying within flight range of the door. He looked down at his feet, looking guilty and a little ashamed to Elizabeth. He tried again. "Myrgen, you may go."

"Her Majesty has asked me to stay, Sire." Myrgen's tone was laced with defiance, the subtle threat which said he was here to stop Charles from hurting the queen. Charles exhaled, defeated here as well.

He turned to face Elizabeth. "Very well. I had wanted to keep this private but I can see my actions of late do not inspire trust."

"That they do not, Your Majesty." The words were out of Myrgen's mouth before Elizabeth could reply in kind, but he clearly meant every word. The difference was that he could be put to death for speaking like that to the king.

Charles looked around her shoulder at Myrgen, eyebrows raising at the tone in Myrgen's voice. "I was talking to Elizabeth." He looked back at her. "Regardless, I wanted to apologize for striking you last week. It was inappropriate and rude. I have no good excuse, and I ask for your forgiveness." He stood straight up, hands together in front of him, and waited.

Elizabeth looked at him, trying to decide if this was genuine or if it was madness. She surveyed the room but saw no signs of a rage, just normal order as expected of a king's chamber. She looked back at him and bowed her head carefully, prepared for anything. "Apology accepted, Your Majesty."

"Thank you, Elizabeth. I understand things are proceeding for a party to celebrate mother's return in three days."

"Yes, Your Majesty."

"Do you know if there will be a ball?"

"I believe so, Your Majesty."

"Then perhaps you will save me a dance?"

Elizabeth curtsied properly. "It would be my pleasure, Your Majesty."

"Thank you. You may go, unless you have anything for me."

"No, Your Majesty." Elizabeth curtsied again and took Myrgen's arm, confusion not daring to show itself until she was away from the king's door. She looked over at Myrgen as he guided her into his room. "What was *that*?"

"I have no idea," Myrgen answered, shaking his head. "He seemed almost *remorseful*."

"He *did*, didn't he?" She looked around, eyes wide and disbelieving. "Myrgen, I'm more scared now that I was before." She looked at him.

"Don't worry. I'm sure he's practically dead now. Catriona is undoubtedly on the task and he'll be dead before long."

Elizabeth looked at Myrgen more intently. "Have you seen her or something?"

"No, but I'm certain she's on the job. Her reputation is impeccable."

"Well," she said, relaxing, "thank you for being there for me."

"I'm always here for you, Elizabeth." He leaned in and brushed away the meeting in the other room with a touch of his lips on hers.

* * *

Charles watched Elizabeth go, then closed the door behind her before relaxing a bit. He looked over at his prayer room and said to the darkness, "Feel better now?"

Alexander emerged from the shadows there where he had

watched the entire event and leaned against the doorjamb. "Yes. I do." He walked into the room and sat down at the table.

Charles joined him, leaning his elbows on the mahogany. He looked over at his brother matter-of-factly,. "She and Myrgen were pretty cozy there, weren't they?"

"Myrgen was probably available. What you did yesterday has everyone scared of you, Charles. Including me. I told her specifically not to be alone with you. I'm grateful for Myrgen being there for her." He sat back in the chair, draping an arm across the back. "Besides, what do you care if she were to find someone? You're not feeling jealous, are you?"

"Over Elizabeth? No." Charles shook his head, then buried his face in his hands. "No, it's not that." He looked back up at his brother. "What you said a little while ago struck the heart of the matter. What if that *had* been Elizabeth, or my daughter, and not Arnold? Worse, what if it had been Marie or baby Francois. I'm afraid to see anyone I care about because I never know when one of these blasted headaches will hit me and I'll lose control."

Alexander looked out the window at the rooftops of the city. "How are Marie and the baby?"

"They were fine yesterday morning. That was the last time I saw them."

Alexander's attention returned to his brother. "You saw them yesterday?"

"Just. Why?"

"Did you have anything unusual while you were there? Any potions or tobacco? Any new wines or different foods?"

"No. Half the things I ate were brought from the palace here. Fruit, a good bottle of wine. Nothing out of the ordinary."

"Did you drink the water in town?"

Charles thought about it, then shook his head. He leaned forward. "What are you thinking, Alex?"

"I'm wondering if you might be having an allergic reaction to something. Remember when we were children and you ate that entire pail of berries in the kitchens and broke out in hives? Something like that."

"Well, is there something you can give me to stop the reaction? I mean, it's a pretty serious reaction if that's the culprit."

"I can't treat it unless I diagnose it first. Maybe I should stop all food and treatments until I know for sure what's causing it.

I should have you drink just wine that you open personally for the next three days. You'll need to make sure the seal is unbroken, and clean off the bottle before you touch it to your lips, but it may be the only way."

"You want to know what *I* think?" Charles pointed at his brother. "I think I'm being poisoned."

"Poisoned?"

"Yes, poisoned. Poisoned by this place, by this crown. I can't breathe here. I can't love here. I can't even be king here. Between the Church and Mother, I'm a useless puppet, and the impotence of it all is killing me." Charles ran his fingers through his hair. "I've been king since I was ten, Alex. I'm twenty-seven now. That's too long. I should have at least had the chance to see the world before becoming responsible for an entire country." He looked at his brother with exhausted eyes. "I envy you, Alex. I envy you every day."

Alexander looked at his brother. "I know exactly what you mean, Charles. You see, I envy you. In spite of Mother's threats and objections, you still fight to stay with the woman you love, and you get to see her almost any day you want. You can go to her arms in the night and wake up with her in the morning. You can talk to her, touch her, knowing she's there for you and *accessible*. You can look out a window from here and see her home. I ache to be able to do that with Catriona. I'd give anything to be with her, Charles."

"Have you heard from her since November?"

"No, but I have the feeling I'm going to. I'm seeing her everywhere. I smelled her perfume downstairs when the physician left. I saw a rider which looked like her on a black horse tear out of the forest, although the baker in the kitchens said it was probably a fae. I thought I saw her watching me from behind the bushes in the garden earlier yesterday. I'm taking all of these things as signs that she's nearby."

"What will you do if you see her again?"

"I don't know. I know what I *want* to do. I *want* to take her in my arms and never let her go. I want to beg her to stay with me, to marry me. And if she won't, then I'll pack up everything here and leave with her."

"Well," Charles said, slapping the table in front of Alexander, "that's what it takes, my brother. That's what it takes.

You have to be willing to commit to the woman. You have to be able to stand in the face of your opposition and say, '*I'll not be turned aside from this course.*' When Mother gets in your way, you have to be prepared to push her out of it."

"I highly doubt Mother would be an issue with me. After that fiasco two years ago, I don't think she dares get in my way these days."

"Well, help me out on this one, Alex. What would *you* do if you were me?"

"If it were me? I'd banish Mother to Anjou, declare myself an Emilianite and divorce Elizabeth, and set Marie-Elizabeth up as Duchess of Angloume, with Elizabeth in tow. Then I'd marry Marie and declare my son legitimate, granting an heir to the throne and simultaneously freeing my favorite and only surviving brother to pursue the woman he loves. That would be my plan.

"Either that, or I'd stage my own death and run away to live with my true love and son somewhere far from here. I understand Caratia is a great place to hide." He smiled broadly at Charles. "What about you? What would you do if you were me?"

"Wow. Well, I'd convince my brother to declare an heir to the throne so I could pursue the woman I loved. I'd secure her love by any means necessary, traveling the seas by her side. Then, when my brother passed on, I'd see him off in ancient style, applaud my nephew's ascension and retire with my true love to a life of luxury as an advisor to the new king. Or I'd have him killed, banish Mother and, having not made the same mistakes my foolish older brother had, would spare no expense to set the woman I loved by my side on the throne. After all, you're a handsome Prince. Aren't women supposed to dream of being rescued by men like you?"

"Good point. What's wrong with her?"

"Exactly." The two brothers laughed and the sound of their mirth echoed down the secret passage's open door and out into the subtle, fragrant air of the gardens.

"So, when do you plan to see Marie again?"

"I don't know. I want to see her every day, but with these headaches and things, I don't dare. I couldn't stand to hurt her, and if I were to kill her or the baby?" Charles' eyes started to glitter with tears at the thought and Alexander stood up and patted his brother on the shoulder.

"Look, you seem to be doing pretty well today, but let's not push our luck. Why don't you get some rest and we'll meet for dinner, if you're feeling up to it. Sound good?"

Charles nodded and Alexander bowed and left as Charles lay down to rest.

## Book Two

*"Enter not into the path of the wicked, and go not in the way of evil men. Avoid it, pass not by it, turn from it, and pass away, for they sleep not except they have done mischief; and their sleep is taken away, unless they cause some to fall. For they eat the bread of wickedness and drink the wine of violence.*

*But the path of the just is as the shining light, that shineth more and more unto the perfect day."*
*~ Proverbs 4:14-18*

*Chapter Twenty-one:*
*"The righteousness of the perfect shall direct his way, but the wicked shall fall by his own wickedness."*
*~ Proverbs 11:5*

Myrgen woke to a beautiful day and a knock at his door. It had been several days since the kiss in Tanglwyst's chambers that began him enjoying his life and Myrgen had been in an irrepressible mood. Charles' illness and other stresses conspired to interfere with their meetings, but he and Elizabeth had still managed to find occasion to capture a kiss in the catacombs during the days. At night, they met in his chambers, to drink some wine and explore each other's mind and heart. Each morning when they spent the night together, they would part at her door in the catacombs to face a day of hidden smiles and excuses regarding discussion of the kingdom's finances. Never had he been so happy.

Neither of them spoke of their concern regarding Catriona's lack of appearance in the kingdom or castle, though it plagued Myrgen every evening as reports of the king's health came in. Last night, they decided to refrain from staying together again in case the king was finally done in. Myrgen found his years of longing for her were a mere pittance compared to the absence he felt this morning.

His attempts to appear, to the staff, to be unchanged had barely worked and his valet had mentioned his uncommon smile at breakfast yesterday. Myrgen had decided to be sour today in an attempt to throw them off. He bid the door be opened but was surprised to see Lord Dominic instead of his valet entering.

Dominic had accepted the post with Myrgen at Lady Tanglwyst's request, having agreed that Dominic was ready to move on to greater things than the chancellor's position of her familial company. As Myrgen's assistant and messenger between the Royal Chancellor and anyone else in the castle, Dominic's clean-shaven face and doe-like eyes had become quite a familiar sight in the area in the past year and the young D'Medici was becoming quite conversant with the way the finances worked here.

"Myrgen, you have a royal summons."

"A *royal summons,* eh? Well, I'd better answer that then, hadn't I?" Myrgen leapt from his bed and got dressed quickly. He primped a moment before the mirror, something he had never done in front of Dominic before. Usually, he would have gotten dressed quickly but without vigor and been polite enough to comb his hair before heading out the door. This time, he washed his face, combed his hair, splashed a little fragrance on his face and then popped a clove into his mouth to freshen his breath. His clothes were lying out, apparently picked the night before. A long blue silk robe with pale grey trim was worn over a pale grey doublet and breeches, also of silk. The shimmer looked good on him, but was extremely out of place in the palace during such sober times. His boots had even been shined. The Chancellor grabbed some hot water and sipped it, helping the clove oil do its work, then clapped his hands and smiled broadly, saying, "Let's go."

Dominic pointed to a small, black piece of clove stuck between his teeth and Myrgen confirmed it in the mirror and removed it. They stepped out the door and turned toward Her Majesty's chambers.

"Excuse me, Your Lordship," Dominic said, figuring it out and, no doubt, noting it for future blackmailing attempts. "*His* Majesty wants to see you."

"Ah." Myrgen turned slowly, recognizing the predator's tone in Dominic's voice and walked to the king's chambers, filling his thoughts with ways to help Lord Dominic forget the unfortunate slip Myrgen had just made.

Myrgen and Dominic approached the king's bedroom which was flanked by two guards, and requested to be announced. The guard on the left, Martin, said, "You are expected, Myrgen. His Majesty would like to see you alone," he added, looking directly at Dominic. Myrgen shot a slight smirk over his shoulder at Dominic who backed away from the door and sat, disappointed, on a bench across the hall. The two guards escorted Myrgen in, then stayed inside the room and closed the door.

The first thing Myrgen noticed was how uncommonly bright the room was, and Myrgen squinted to see His Majesty framed in the window, his back to the door, while the guards took up post on either side. The heavy curtains were not just opened, they were removed, lying in a puddle of heavy blue velvet at the base of the window as if pulled down from their rod. A slight breeze of fresh air filled the room with the scent of roses from the garden.

It was the Feast of Saint Hubert of Liege and His Majesty

Charles IX Maximillian was clothed in a rich, blue robe embroidered with fleurs-de-lis in flashing gold, so common in these last three weeks as his condition worsened to the point where the meeting room was moved to his bedchamber so he could rest while still feeling involved in the governing of his people.

"Ah, Myrgen. Good." Charles turned to face his chancellor, his dark blonde hair cascading neatly over his shoulders and looking almost holy in the morning light. Charles had apparently also taken the time to get groomed as he wasn't his usual disheveled mess at this hour of the day. "Please, sit down. Have something to eat," he added gesturing toward a plate of food. "I figure you probably haven't had the opportunity to breakfast yet."

"Thank you, Your Majesty." Myrgen gratefully took some bread and ate it. Charles watched him a moment, then continued.

"I'm sorry to call for you so early in the day but I have some very important business to deal with before the court celebrating Mother's return the day after tomorrow."

"I am at your service, my king. What do you need from me?"

Charles turned to look at him, mildly surprised at his offer and Myrgen saw the king was dressed in the beginnings of court attire. He was obviously planning on attending court in person instead of by proxy for his mother's return, possibly even to hearing court today, something he hadn't done in a month. "Well, thank you for being so accommodating. Perhaps you'd like to tell me who's planning the assassination against me." Charles smiled as Myrgen practically choked on the food in his mouth, then swallowed to banish the likelihood from happening again. He looked at the king, head tilted and eyebrows furrowed upwards.

"Sire?"

"Well?" Charles smiled charmingly at his Chancellor, laying an unshaking hand upon the back of his chair and the other one on his hip. "You did 'hire' the assassin, right? Blackmailed her by kidnapping her son, and the Lady Tanglwyst?" Charles stepped toward Myrgen, allowing his royal ire to spread like storm clouds across his visage. "What? Did you think I do not know what happens in my own castle?" Charles slammed a fist down on the table in front of Myrgen, and Myrgen jumped back, conscious of the king's violent behavior which had killed Arnold three days ago.

"You're… not well, Your Majesty." Myrgen said carefully, eyes trained on the king. Charles had narrowly missed him and he was reminded of the king's violence toward Elizabeth, which he had tried to dismiss with an apology the day after murdering Arnold. Myrgen felt his hatred brimming. "This sickness has caused you to imagine things."

"Has it now?" Charles growled. "Am I imagining her?" He gestured to the shadows of the prayer nave. Catriona emerged from the darkness like a whispered warning that wakes the sleeper in the middle of the night, and Myrgen felt fear seize him in a stranglehold when he saw her. "I would expect *you* to do a bit more research, Myrgen. Hiring my own assassin to kill me? How ill-advised."

Myrgen looked back at the king, weighing his options. His flight instinct howled fiercely in his head, nipped at the heels by his fear. But then he thought of Elizabeth, and knew she and his sister would be destroyed if he ran, left at the mercy of this black witch. Catriona leaned in the doorway of the prayer nave, her arms folded across her chest, burrowing into his soul with those vicious green eyes of hers. She looked at him, then blinked, understanding dawning in her eyes. *She knew. Somehow, she knew.* He closed his eyes, attempting to repel her and turned his own gaze upon the king. His only hope was to turn the king's ire fully on him. The two guards in the room moved closer to Myrgen and he noted this with a glance over his shoulder.

"Sorry Charles, had I known I could just walk up to you and stab you in the heart myself, I'd have done so. Would've made things much less complicated."

Charles blinked, his shock at Myrgen blatant treason unbalancing him. He shook his head, trying to regain his authority. "You… you *dare* to speak to me that way?"

"Why shouldn't I? Nothing left to hide now, is there? Yes, it was me. *I* decided the world would be better off without you in it. You attack women and old men, yet for some reason, you can't seem to throw off the yoke your mother has on you. You're a waste, Charles, a rabid animal and it's time you were put down before you and your mother really do cause this country to go to war."

Charles crossed the remaining space between them and backhanded Myrgen across the face in a sudden assault, his eyes wide and rage filled.

Myrgen slowly turned his face back to the king's raging presence and said carefully, "My, that does seem to be the way you deal with people who disagree with you, doesn't it? Watch yourself, *Cat*," he said, injecting a familiarity he hoped would incited *her* ire as well. "He has a predilection for hitting women too." He noted the king backing off a bit at the exposure of his own lack of control. "Not just any woman, either," Myrgen continued, cocking his head a bit, "but the queen. So you can see rank and station are meaningless to *His Majesty*."

Charles' face reddened with embarrassment from this exposure, and Myrgen realized then the man was afraid because of Catriona, of losing her respect in spite of his facade of familiarity. Myrgen decided to poke this bear. "Yes, beating up on people who are weaker than you, like that old man, Arnold, seems to be your new favorite hobby. Or maybe you just got a taste for it on Saint Michael's Day."

"Shut up. You know *nothing* about what was going on there!"

"I know enough to know you were too weak to stop your mother from convincing you to kill your best friend, Charles. I was right in the next room. I *heard* you give the order to kill them."

"But you don't know *why.*"

*"Enlighten me!"* Myrgen watched him closely, letting the challenge sit in the air. For the moment, there was just the two of them. He had forgotten everything else.

Charles leaned on the table and the room was dead still. He snarled, "It's not appropriate for you know why."

"You're wrong, Charles." Catriona's voice was silken, floating like a web in a sunbeam. Myrgen and Charles looked at her. "Of all the people in this room, he has the *most* right to know why." She looked at Charles. "Yes, he is guilty of treason, of plotting your death. He is guilty of many more things than these, but they are not a factor here at this time, and thus are not to be revealed. You know what you need to know." She walked over to Myrgen and leaned by his ear. "I do not hold you accountable for my son's involvement. I know now that you would never stand by as another child fell before your eyes. I'm sorry for your loss, Myrgen."

Myrgen blinked, her words bringing the vision of another

boy, barely a man, cut in half before him during that massacre while his mother screamed in protest. It cut through every emotion, bringing into focus the only thing that mattered, the only true feeling of value in this entire endeavor, and he felt shame for not remembering it before now. The Queen, the sickness, even his sister's insistence on bringing the boy into this were secondary at best and a distraction at their worst. The only person who he should be championing was represented, at least in part, in a cell below this very room and he had failed utterly to protect him.

Myrgen looked at her, saw a small glimmer of dampness on the edge of her eyes, then she turned and disappeared into the darkness. Charles nodded to the guards and they took Myrgen out of the room.

* * *

Outside the room, Dominic fell back onto the floor in shock at Myrgen's rage. He had been able to hear the conversation though the keyhole (provided he put his ear right over the thing), and was stunned at the king's accusation. He scrambled to his feet and got sat down on the bench just as the door flew open and Myrgen was escorted out. Charles was still leaning on the table and he watched them take Myrgen away.

As they left the room, Charles spotted Dominic in the hallway, looking aghast at the arresting of his superior. "Dominic!" The king's bellow shattered him out of the spell fascination had woven upon him and he turned sharply toward the king. "Get in here." The words spoken were softer, but still unquestionably a command. Dominic complied immediately.

"Lord Dominic, Myrgen has been relieved of his duties as Chancellor. He needs to be replaced. I am appointing you Acting Chancellor until such time as I designate a new one. Be at court this evening and I will make it official. Make whatever preparations you deem necessary." He turned and walked toward the desk and pulled the chair out as if to sit and work on decrees. "I have some business I want done tonight. Some of it is long overdue. Send me the Vox. I have some things for him." The king turned his back on Dominic, dismissing him.

The young lord looked around the room and saw a vague shadow in the prayer apse. Assuming this was the king's informant, he noted the rest of the room, the letters spread across the desk, each of them already signed and possessing the royal seal. Whatever information this person, was it a woman? Yes, he had heard the king refer to "her" in his rant and the name "Cat." However, nearly every assassin, prostitute and second story thief went by the name "Cat." That was no help. Be that as it may, whatever information this person had brought him, it had set the king in a frenzy of activity. Dominic wasn't even aware there was this much life still left in the man, from the meetings he had attended with Myrgen.

"Y-yes, Your Majesty… and what about Myrgen, Sire?" Dominic stammered, and, bowing.

Charles glanced at the new Acting Chancellor. "He'll be tried tomorrow, or the next day. Let him rot in the prison awhile." He turned his attention back to the view from the window. "I want my mother to be here for this."

Dominic suppressed a shiver at the thought of what Catherine D'Medici was capable of doing to someone who tried to hurt her family. Catherine was a royalist, and a D'Medici. He couldn't imagine the things she would do to Myrgen in the name of patriotism. He bowed to the king's back and left quickly.

*Chapter Twenty-two:*
*"Mercy and truth preserve the king, and his throne is upholden by mercy."*
*~ Proverbs 20:28*

After Dominic was gone, the king leaned forward, placing his elbows on his desk and his head in his hands. His fingers splayed into his hair, causing it to go wild. He sighed, still not up to perfect health yet in spite of the efforts Catriona had made. He looked briefly around the room again, noting she had disappeared by the time the D'Medici lord had come in. He believed Dominic still might have seen her, but didn't figure that quite mattered. She had saved the king. Charles would make sure everyone knew that, should there ever be a question. If she were ever going to be Alexander's wife, she would need to be seen as trustworthy, and being the savior of the king would be a good start. Perhaps this would work after all.

Catriona flowed into the room from the doorway of the king's small prayer room and deliberately stepped upon a dried bread crumb from Myrgen's breakfast, allowing the crunching sound in the quiet room to announce her presence to His Majesty. She had always been courteous regarding their station, calling the visions upon him and Alexander only once and inexplicably failing to get a thing. She had always felt it would be rude anyway, and she owed these men her life.

He moved slightly at the sound, then turned to face her. "What did you see, old friend?"

Catriona stood before the king's chair and looked at him unabashedly. "He is not the killer."

"Because he ate the bread?"

"Yes. He was completely unaware of the poison which has been administered to you for the past three weeks. In about an hour, he will feel what you were feeling two days ago, but he won't know why. Maybe less time than that considering his excitement level."

"Your alchemist friend confirmed the Herbspyce was the poison."

"Yes, but with the recipe in front of them, he said anyone could have made it. The components are common enough. The Royal Physician is a drunk who passes out every night and doesn't wake until morning, according to his assistant. Anyone could have switched the bottles in his kit. I don't know who is doing this or why specifically, but it's someone who knows poisons *very well*, and not Myrgen or Michael. Neither of them knew the dart was tipped in poison, not sleeping potion as they believed. They both would have been surprised to find me dead had it but grazed my skin."

Charles raised his head, arching an eyebrow in disdain. "I still think I should execute Michael for striking you." Charles folded his arms across his chest, disgusted.

Catriona smiled. "It was better than the alternative."

Charles smiled briefly, then dropped his hands and glanced down at the fading red places where he had struck Myrgen. He sighed heavily. "Catriona, what Myrgen said there was true. I am a waste. My violent reaction to Arnold…"

"It's a side effect of the poison, Charles. You had control of it today, didn't you?"

"Yes, thanks to you. Still, I'd hate to know you thought ill of me." He turned back to his desk, staring at the joyless papers and meaningless ink. "I did strike Elizabeth when I wasn't in my right mind. I would never do that to the mother of my child." He looked at her, sorrow aging him before her eyes.

"Either of them, right?"

Charles closed his eyes painfully, aware of her intimidating integrity, and embarrassed by his weakness concerning Elizabeth and Marie in failing to truly commit to his heart nor his Crown. "Either of them." He took a deep breath in order to change the subject. "So, the person trying to murder me is still out there. What can I do, Catriona? Help me." He opened his eyes to her, his strength returning a bit.

Catriona crouched at his knee, taking his hand in hers. "You have to be careful, Charles. Whoever is planning your death is waiting for you to be vulnerable. Don't give them the chance they seek. I'll do what I can. That means not going to see Marie, or your son right now. Just spend time with your princess, Marie-Elizabeth. She doesn't see you often enough as it is."

"I'm not sure I dare to." He looked at the upset table, the wine spilt on the floor turning the poisoned bread it soaked a nasty blue color. "Maybe tomorrow…"

"Tomorrow then."

"Thank you, my friend." He kissed her hand, reliving an old fantasy for a moment, then patted it, releasing her. Catriona stood and moved toward the secret passage in the prayer chamber, when the king said, "Catriona, promise me something. Promise me you'll consider Alexander's proposal."

Catriona did not turn to face Charles, but she did stop in the doorway, turning her head slightly to address him. "Charles?"

"He loves you. He's always loved you, from the day we found you on that road, surrounded by blood and carnage."

"And if I could, I would relieve him of that burden."

"I could command you to, you know. I *am* the king," he said halfheartedly.

She turned to look at him, their friendship renewed over this incident. She had missed that friendship, and she smiled. "You're not my king, Charles. I'm not of your kingdom. You cannot expect obedience from someone who is not your subject."

"I don't want loyalty to this kingdom to stop him from being with the one woman he actually loves. Don't damn him to the same fate I suffer, Catriona."

"It's not that, Charles. It's… There's a past to deal with here that precludes such intimacy."

"You don't mean his part in the massacre, do you? He was lied to. We both were. You can't condemn him for that night. He didn't know."

Catriona blinked. Her eyes got brighter in color, something he had not seen since he and Alexander had found her in the road. She had looked at them in a moment of wakefulness, but it had not felt like this. This was different. He could feel her eyes invading him, taking his secret and he suddenly realized the thought uppermost in his mind was not Alexander's love for this woman, but his part in the massacre two years ago. In an instant, the scene flashed through his mind…

*The assassin's second bullet had failed to kill Plantyn, just hitting him in the shoulder after the first bullet had taken out his First Lieutenant.Charles had been horrified and Catherine had declared the King the target, accusing Plantyn of treason on the spot. Guards seized him at the Queen Mother's command and he was bourn to the ground from his horse in a single, efficient gesture by Alexander. All Charles seemed capable of was gaping in horror at the betrayal. Even so, in Patras, Charles had taken*

Plantyn to a tower near the palaces, safe from further assault from external sources. He wanted to visit him, to ask why he would do such a thing but his mother refused to entertain the idea and Alexander advised similar caution.

Alexander put his hand on his brother's shoulder. "It's not as if he will tell you his plans, Charles."

Catherine's voice was soft. "No. It's not as if you are Marco Giovanni."

Both men turned to her, their faces bookends of shock. Alexander recovered his vocabulary first.

"What did you just say, Mother?"

Catherine looked up, as if surprised she had spoken aloud "Pardon me?"

Alexander's whole attention turned upon Catherine. "What did you just say about Marco Giovanni?" He took a step towards her. "You mentioned him just now. What do you know, Mother?"

She stepped back, her hand going to her chest, but not in a gesture of fear. It went to the left breast, not her clavicle. The difference was not lost to Alexander. He grabbed her and reached inside her bodice, his grasp neither that of son or friend. She protested but he extracted a letter, just the same. He pushed her back onto a chair and read the now slightly torn missive. He looked at her, his eyes accusing and merciless. "When were you planning on telling us about this?"

"Once we got to the Palace, I swear it!" She was nervous and Charles found himself almost afraid to read what was written.

"What does it say, Alex?"

Alexander's eyes never left Catherine, though her own gaze fell to the floor. He thrust the letter at Charles. "It says Plantyn was working with Giovanni to put a Mandian on the throne, or more blatantly, back on the throne." Alexander spat at his mother's feet. "How long have you been plotting this, Mother?"

She raised her eyes. "I have not wanted the Power of Sovereignty for myself in my entire life. If I had, I would have taken it when it was offered me by your father, after your oldest brother was born. I told him to pass it on through the children, that the burden was too great for a woman to hold on her own. I told your brother Francois the same thing on his death bed. I have had more opportunities to rule Mervolingia than you have, Alexander, and I have always turned them down. And you know it."

Charles looked up from the treasonous letter. Its contents were worse than he had originally thought. "Alexander, do you think Plantyn could have been around when... that he knew about the dungeon?"

Alexander's body went stiff. He turned to Charles who pointed to the letter "It mentions either one of Giovanni's kin, or one of his get. They mean someone he breeds. Could Plantyn have been in on the capture of those women? The breeding pens?"

Charles had never mentioned Catriona directly but Alexander had understood. They looked at the letter, Catherine forgotten for the moment. Charles shook his head. "I can't accept that. I can't believe he'd do something like this."

"He's a soldier," Catherine had said, drawing their attention back to her presence. "Soldiers are capable of atrocities the rest of us can't even imagine, if it fits their plan."

Charles recalled that Plantyn had said that very phrase in front of Catherine before, and that she was right. It took a while for them to convince him that the murder of his friend was the way to go, but in the end, Alexander had become more and more convinced that Plantyn had something to do with Catriona's capture and Charles had been unable to offer an argument to counter Catherine's accusations. Eventually, even Charles had been convinced and when he gave the order to destroy them all, Alexander had taken the task directly to Marcel without hesitation.

It was while he was gone that Charles had taken the letter out to the balcony. After that night, his friend would be dead and he would be alone again. He didn't want this letter around anymore. He had actually wanted to destroy the evidence of Plantyn's treason, out of deference to the friendship they had shared. It was as he was setting the letter alight, burning this stain from his mind that he saw, for just an instant, a watermark. The same watermark used to write Writs of Destruction. Someone had forged this letter with his own stationary. The letter fell from his fingers and he turned to his mother.

Words had failed him while he looked at her, but when he heard the mobs forming below him, Alexander's cries leading Marcel's troupe, he shouted out to stop the assassination. Then the shot that killed Plantyn broke the room in twain and the letter burned away, taking with it the proof it was a lie.

Catriona blinked again and the memory faded. Charles staggered a bit and Catriona gave him her hand to steady him. "Was… was that…?"

"That was my ability, yes."

"By the Saints…" He realized what she had seen and looked into her eyes. "Catriona, he was duped. Please, don't hold that against him."

"He was willing to kill all those people for revenge against one man. How can I not hold that against him?" She let go of him. "Charles, you're going to be fine now. I'm going to go."

"Please don't leave like this. See him. Talk to him."

"I'm suddenly not sure I want to hear what he has to say." Her eyes had gone cold, like two pieces of jade, and Charles was suddenly afraid he had ruined his brother's life by revealing his secret.

"You owe me a life debt, then," Charles said, getting to his feet. "We saved you that day. Had we not come along when we did, you'd have surely bled to death."

She nodded towards the poisoned bread. "My debt to you is repaid."

"Then do it for a friend. Please." Charles was almost begging now, and this attitude seemed to soften his dark companion. He took heart at the fact she still stood in the room. He felt he was making some sort of progress, and persisted "I had always thought that Alexander would have gone to the healing arts had he not been the king's brother and heir. Seeing him save your life like he did amazed me." Charles went to her, putting his hand on her shoulder. "You probably don't remember that day, what happened after you were left to die. The smoke from the church was what brought us there. We never saw who did that to you, but Alexander and I ran up and saw you lying there. I've never seen Alexander so bent on doing something. A couple was there, trying to move a friar and I helped them get the baby, but Alexander focused on only you. I swear he mended your cuts and bruises by virtue of his will alone.

"He fell in love with you then, fighting desperately to close your wounds and take away the brutalities of your captivity. After you were healed enough to move, the couple took us to their home.

He stayed right by your side, even though I couldn't. He would have stayed there throughout your convalescence but Mother sent for us. As it stood, he returned often. Then, one day, you were gone, and the house was burnt. He was never the same after that. He became dark and bitter. It wasn't until found you again that he has been happy. He's practiced his healing and gotten good at it again. He cares about others and he won't even speak to mother now. He's a better man now, because of you."

"It's a pity he couldn't have been one before that." Catriona turned away. "By the way, I've looked at Catherine before. You shouldn't be so hard on your mother. As much as she has her faults, the thing she is trying to do now is for the benefit of all your people. She has been fighting against civil war since your brother died. It is through her strength that you have a throne at all. She saved both your lives by making you return to Patras instead of staying on the Giovanni lands."

"It never felt like that, to either of us. I think that's why he started leaving in the night, staying away for weeks at a time. It irritated both Mother and I, but I handled it a little better. I think he was looking for the man who hurt you, to try and finally settle those demons that seized his heart." He studied the intricate weave of the lines on his hands, noting the royal signet ring's fleur design. "That's actually why he left. To kill him personally. When I heard the man was dead, I never asked Alexander how he did it. I just respected why he did it. It was enough."

"It wasn't him. Alexander didn't kill Giovanni. I did."

Charles turned to face her. "You?"

"If I had any way to stop it, I would never allow Alexander to bloody his own hands. His hands are for healing. If he ever used his gift for evil, it would destroy his soul. He left Patras because he needed to find his own way." Catriona's voice softened as she spoke, which gave Charles hope. "His course needed to be charted by his own nature, not the restraints of the accident of his birth. Once your wedding was imminent, he felt no longer necessary. Just as I am no longer necessary here."

He swallowed, a touch of desperation dotting his brow. "I see. You've saved my life now, haven't you? Your life-debt is repaid, and unless I can stop you, you're going to walk away from this place and never set foot in here again. You deserve more than just being released back to the sea."

"No, Charles. That is exactly what I deserve. It is what I want."

"Then promise me you'll see Alexander, to tell him goodbye. You'll betray no one by doing that."

Catriona shook her head, her eyes threatening tears. "Why do you wish so earnestly for our union, Charles?"

He looked away from her questioning gaze and looked at his wedding ring from his political, arranged marriage, the weight of which was a convenient excuse for the mistress he kept. "Because I love my brother. Because I don't want him to make the same sacrifices I've had to. Because somebody in a position like ours should be able to marry for love. Because I wish him to be happy." He looked back at her. "You can make him happy. You have before. Last summer…" Catriona looked away, embarrassed that Alexander had told Charles about the cabin on the cliffs of St. Giles. He looked at her a moment, weighing what he was about to say. "I love you too. I've admired your strength from that very first day. If that man who hurt you is dead and gone now, then there's nothing to stop you from marrying Alexander. Please, talk to him. If you won't marry him, at least tell him in person. Tell him why."

"Alexander already knows why."

"Then tell *me* why."

Catriona sighed, realizing he didn't know. "That day we three met, when I was escaping captivity, I was fleeing enslavement from my own arrogance and its consequences. I had foolishly tried to entice Giovanni's money out of him to save my village, and paid dearly for my hubris. I know you have always appreciated the fact I kept the baby which you have assumed was the product of the captivity, but you are wrong. That baby was the child of my husband."

Charles blinked. "You were married?"

"Still am, although we are… estranged at this point in our lives. I'm trying now to decide what to do. I'm surprised Alexander didn't tell you, when he didn't mind revealing our intimacy." She found herself angry that Alexander had bragged to his brother about his conquest.

"I actually guessed that. He came home grinning like I'd never seen him. I recognized the look." Charles sat on the desk chair again and she looked at him, realizing that was the truth. Her anger was stolen away from her, which irritated her too. "You said you are estranged. What do you mean? Do you want an annulment? Will the church not free you of this bond?"

Catriona shook her head. "Well, the legal bond ended long ago. He believed I was dead, I believed he was dead. In fact, he was recorded as dead in the ledgers of our home village, as was I. We are both ghosts."

"I see. And if you were to publicly marry the Prince of Mervolingia, you would be obviously alive and anyone with a grudge against you could have you burned for adultery. Do you need him dead?"

That comment returned her anger to her possession, and she felt herself bristle at her friend. *Was this the solution the royalty had for everything?* "That would only remove one barrier to our union, and I think your family has enough blood on its hands right now."

Charles looked away, guilty. Now that she could read him, she seemed unable to stop, and delved again into his soul. She recognized the impotence he was feeling in his life, being so familiar with it in her own. She took pity on him and sighed. "I will see him, Charles. For you."

Charles brightened. "Thank you. I'll take you there. There's a secret passage in Myrgen's room. I'm pretty sure he won't be there right now," he let a wry smile punctuate his comment, "so we can get you there undetected." He opened his door carefully while Catriona ducked back into the shadows of his prayer room. The guards who had taken Myrgen had not yet sent up replacements, but it was only a matter of time before they did. He waved her over and they slipped quickly down the hall to Myrgen's room. Charles pulled out a key and opened the door, closing it as he heard heavy boots arriving around the corner.

He stepped over to the wall and opened the secret door. The glow of twenty candles illuminated the room and both Charles and Catriona stopped, caught by the painting of Elizabeth. The likeness was so good, it appeared almost alive. Charles said, "That's the same as the painting in my room, the one of Marie-Elizabeth. Did Myrgen do this?"

Catriona stepped over to the painting. There was a very small signature in the bottom right corner: "Yes." She stepped back to admire the work. "I believe he did." She looked at Charles, a cutting remark present on his tongue and she decided to interrupt before he let it out. "Come, where is the other door?"

Charles remembered his purpose here and closed the first door. "You have to close this outer door once you enter this room before you can open the one to the secret passages. It's a fail-safe." Catriona nodded and Charles activated the other door and grabbed a votive from the shelf to light their way. He stepped through the passage and Catriona recognized the smell of the place. This tunnel connected with the other one, where Alan was. Off to her right was the wide set of stairs she had seen earlier. She knew where she was, and now knew a secret way to Alexander's room. She swallowed, realizing the danger in that knowledge.

"You said before that your husband was only one barrier to being with Alexander. What are the others?"

"Private."

Charles stopped. "I'm probably never going to see you again after this moment, Catriona. Please, what harm will come from me knowing more?"

"Knowledge is power, Charles. I don't want that knowledge causing trouble for you."

"Is it the sort of knowledge that could get me killed?"

"Yes."

Charles pursed his lips. "This way." He resumed walking down the long corridor that hid in the walls of the Palace. He stopped at a dead end and turned to the left wall. He used the candle to find the catch stone, and turned to look at her again. "Thank you for doing this."

"When is court?" she asked in the doorway.

"After I pray, eat, get ready..." he replied, smiling. "When I say. After all, I'm the king. It's not as if they'll have it without me. Not tonight."

She smiled. "How well do you know this passage?"

"Well enough."

"Good," and with her hand on the catch stone, she blew out the candle.

## Chapter Twenty-four:
### *"The desire accomplished is sweet to the soul…"*
### *~ Proverbs 13:19*

Catriona carefully moved the stone door and slipped into the darkness of the prayer nave. Alexander sat in a chair by the hearth, staring into the fire. The scene sparked a memory of a similar fire and a similar chair only a few months ago, when the air was warm from the sun and the nights were shorter. Her anger at his part in the massacre faded as the memory emerged.

*Alexander awoke in his chair to find Catriona alert and trying to get out of bed. Her bandages were clean and still tight, so he helped her rise. Even so, she cringed at every step on the wounded leg, but was still able to stand. Gwen came in at her request and Alexander had left as Catriona got dressed, going on deck to await her summons. The* Enigma's *decks were bustling, as usual, and she had wanted to feel the wood beneath her feet since she had been brought back on board in Cheryb. The leg wound was healing nicely though, the rapier fight with the D'Medici assassin having given mostly superficial cuts and bruises which Catriona could heal herself. The only exception had been her opponent's dying lunge which had stabbed her leg from behind.*

*She walked onto the foc's'le, her leg fighting against her desires but her will winning the battle, and stood facing the sea, arms folded across her chest, the wind and spray enveloping her features. Once there, drinking in the view, she surprised him by asking how he was doing. He laughed and replied, "I'm fine. Your bleeding has stopped, you have good color and the herbs are doing their magic in assisting it all. There may not even be any scarring, although I think that must be my own wishful thinking rather than reality."*

*"You have saved me again, my Prince," she said in response. "This sort of life debt is difficult to repay." The wind blew her hair behind her and the waves crashed in an attempt to cover his heartbeat as he watched her.*

*"Oh, I don't know. You've seen the places I frequent. My life is threatened all the time. Obviously, you just need to be there to stop my assailants." He smiled easily, welcoming the opportunity to release some of this tension from the previous days.*

*She smiled lightly,. "Perhaps I should simply find a safer place for you to stay." And with that, she turned and left, speaking to her First Mate on the way. There was a cabin she had outside one of the port towns not too far away, with a private beach to access it. First Mate Octavius gave some orders and the ship changed course.*

*Alexander turned his gaze back to his beloved sea, feeling it caress him with a lover's fingers. He had grown more and more fond of the sea because of the connection it had with seeing her, and he always felt closer to her when the sea was nearby.*

*They sailed away that night and arrived a few days later at another cove, this one with steps carved in the cliff face. The crew prepared for some shore leave in the nearby town and Catriona waited until dusk before she took Alexander to a stone house which overlooked the sea and the cove. The house was alone and protected from view from the road by a small forest. It had a comfortable feel to it, like a purr. Gwen was leaving it as they arrived, looking a bit dusty, and the evidence of her work there was prominent in the tidied appearance of a place rarely used. Fresh linens were everywhere, food was cooking in the hearth, and wine was poured in a decanter on the rough hewn table.*

*Catriona offered him some wine and they lazed away the evening talking of business and royal goings-on. He told her the gossip, she regaled him with stories, and they enjoyed each other's company until late in the night. Around midnight, he stretched and stood, preparing to take his leave and return to the ship for the night.*

*She had not stood, not said good night, just stared into the fire, her hands warming a cup of mulled wine, and he had the oddest feeling of not being dismissed. Having not allowed someone his leave to go before, he thought it odd he would think that when she had not said a word. He stood by the unopened door and watched her as she seemed to wrestle with something which was vexing her.*

*"Catriona?"*

*Her eyes fluttered a moment at the sound of her name, and she closed them, a sigh of deep longing escaping her soul. "I have been alone a long time now, Alex," she said, opening her eyes. She looked up at him from her chair. "Too long now." She stood then, placing her cup in the table in the center of the room, and gliding over to him in the doorway. She had stood before him, looking up at him, and had touched his hair. He was entirely unprepared for this and found himself devoid of words or even thought as she bent his head to hers and kissed him.*

*He had experienced fear before, during the bloody massacre when the mob mentality could have turned against the Royal Family in a moment. He had watched the Church burn heretics, had seen battle wounds, and even been chased by a pack of wolves in the woods during a hunt where he was separated from his party, yet never had he let his fear rule him. Nevertheless, at that moment, as he found himself in the very place he had always wished to be, his fear overwhelmed him and he almost panicked. Then she touched his hand, and the world evanesced and there was deep silence as he felt himself dissolve in her kisses.*

*They had made love, the likes of which he thought didn't exist in this world, and he held her in his arms until dawn, afraid of sunrise lest he wake from this perfect dream. As the daylight touched their faces, she had awakened and he remembered thinking, "If I never see another sunrise, I will ever have this moment in my mind."*

*"Thank you for staying with me, Alexander," she had said, sitting up enough to lean on her arms over him. Her eyes glistened in the aurora of dawn, and he had to catch his breath before he could respond.*

*"I could have done nothing else had it been asked by the Saints themselves."*

*"I have thought about you often these past years, since our first meeting. I always thought to visit you but never quite dared believe you would remember me."*

*"Not remember you? You have dominated my thoughts every day since we left you in that cottage. That first month in your presence, learning how to help a person heal, and bonding with your son, are the most vivid memories I have." He shook his head and touched her hair as it leapt from her shoulders to caress her breast. "You have been the Morning Star which guides me through the reefs and rocks of my daily life. I can't think of a day in which I haven't written you or spoken to you in my heart, hoping somehow you would find those letters or hear those words across the world. My life has begun and ended when I've seen you, and disintegrated when we've parted company. Not remember you? I've never been*

*able to forget you."*

*She smiled, a full, encompassing smile like she had never given in his presence before. "My, and you were so quiet last night. Apparently daylight is your best time."*

*He had sat up and kissed her then, gathering her into his arms. "My best time is when I am within sight of you." He kissed her again. "I love you, Catriona. I can't bear the thought of going away from you again."*

*"I have been alone so long, Alex," she said softly, worry flashing across her brow. "It's not that easy to abandon those habits."*

*"Aren't you interested in trying?"*

*Catriona had looked into his eyes, full and penetrating, yet open and revealing as well. "Desperately so...." They fell together in a kiss, and when he stretched above her, watching her hair cover the pillows, she had told him she loved him too.*

***Chapter Twenty-five:***
*"A man's heart deviseth his way, but the Lord directeth his steps."*
*~ Proverbs 16:9*


Alexander sat staring into the fire flickering on the hearth. The firelight seemed to hypnotize him, calling out to him to join in the dance, but Alexander rarely danced these days. Catriona watched from the doorway of the catacombs, wondering if she should truly interrupt his reverie. When she would sit at the window sill and watch him in his own window, she imagined he was remembering the night he had spent in Catriona's cabin on the cliffs, but often, the memory was accompanied by the unpleasant flavor of the aftermath a month later. He had wanted to fight for their relationship, but she would not hear of it. She could barely look at him. Had he but seen Nicolai in that moment, he would have torn the man apart personally, but in the end, his desire to remove the obstacle to their love was no match for her determination to try again with her husband.

Heracles, a large wolfhound Alexander had acquired on his travels, raised his head and looked toward the prayer nave. A small growl crept from his throat, drawing his master's attention. Alexander looked into the shadows apathetically, probably figuring the intruder was a rat or something of that nature. Catriona tried to slip back into the catacombs, but she had unintentionally moved towards Alexander as she observed him, and the door slid shut as she bumped it closed with her rear. She slipped into the room, out of sight and hoping he did not decide to investigate Heracles' growl.

She heard him get up and leaned her head back, holding her breath. Ever since the Massacre, Nicolai had said the entire royal family had dealt with threats from Emilianite affiliates and Emilianite believers, though she doubted anyone had ever made it this close before.

Alexander stepped up to the room preceded by a dagger, Heracles on his feet beside him. All but one of the votive candles was extinguished, making the small chapel darker than the main bedroom. This advantage hid her, and he let Heracles enter first. The dog sniffed around, and she crouched, holding out her hand to him. He had traveled back to Rouen with her on the ship after

Alexander had bought him and he remembered her. He lay down just inside the doorway, tail wagging.

Alexander entered behind him, dagger drawn, ready for anything. Catriona stood carefully and the small rush of air she brought caught his attention. He sniffed, short at first, then a second breath through the nose, closing his eyes to savor it. She smiled, knowing she was undone, and reached out for his dagger hand.

A soft voice to his left whispered, "You won't need that." A gentle hand touched his own, putting the blade down and drawing his eyes open again. Shimmering azure eyes glittered like stained glass in the glow of firelight that leaked in from the bedroom and he blinked at the vision before him that he dared not believe was real. "Catriona?"

"Alexander."

"My lady," he said, his eyes steady as if she would disappear in a blink, "if you are a dream, I beg you, do not wake me."

"I'll not wake you, my Prince, for it is only in dreams that I may do this." She removed her glove and touched his cheek, her rarely bare fingers lingering on his velvet skin. Alexander closed his eyes, then opened them with a snap, still reassuring himself he was not dreaming, but she was still there, glittering in the shadows. She smiled at his boyish antics.

He touched her hand on his cheek and kissed her palm.

"What are you doing here?" His voice was elated, as if all his dreams had unexpectedly come true. He took her hand from his cheek, squeezing it a little before releasing it.

Catriona retrieved her hand and removed her other glove. "I was in the area."

Alexander laughed. "Come." He gestured to the doorway. "Sit by the fire with me. Prove to me you aren't some ghost or faerie glamour." He moved into the open room.


Catriona looked into the beckoning comfort of his bedroom, his large, cozy bed, the warm fire, the wine, the tray of food, the curtains covering the windows to keep the cheerful sun away during his more morose periods like today. She took a step towards the room, but stopped at the doorway.

Her hesitation caused him to turn to her and the half-light heightened the splendor of his elegant features. It was hypnotic, falling peacefully into sapphire eyes, graceful hands, auburn silk hair. His flesh was sculpted by training and travel, his mind by study and exploration. His healing ability was a gift from heaven, one not widely known, but she was well-versed in it. He had removed three musket balls and stitched two sword cuts on her since they had met up again and she couldn't even see the scars which should have marked their encounters. She had a skill of her own in healing, and he always claimed she used it to heal the scars were gone before they met again, though they both knew she could heal others but not herself. Next to him, here, in this place, she felt out of her element, as ugly as the scars he had never seen.

"Not…yet, please," she whispered. Alexander looked at her shadow-clad form and eased back into the room, questions drawn on his face. She looked down at her hands, noting that, even with gloves, they were working hands. Far too rough for such surroundings.

He touched her down-turned face, raising it to look into his eyes. "Is something wrong?"

"I'm not certain I'm up to stepping into full light," she explained, taking a step back into the darkness. "Not here. Not with you." Catriona drank in his gaze a moment, lost in the intensity of her emotions for him. She should not have come here, not to him. Her will was only so strong. She had withstood imprisonment, beatings and a thousand other tortures, physical and mental, but having him so close he could touch her was destroying her ability to see what was right and wrong. She was still married, his faith was not her faith, and she was still not the person for him. She needed to leave before she lost control and everything ceased to matter. She turned away from the temptation, breaking out of the spell.

Alexander leaned back against the wall by the doorway. "I know exactly how you feel. We'll wait until you're ready."

"And if I never am?" Catriona stepped away, pretending to examine the votives, trying to locate her sense of appropriateness which she seemed to have misplaced somewhere in this very small room.

"Then they will find my bones leaning against this wall in a hundred years."

Catriona smiled, realizing she was still in the presence of a master craftsman of language. He did have a command of beautiful speech, and he could melt her heart with a well-phrased sentence.

"What made you come here?"

"I was with Charles. He asked me to see you."

"You were with Charles? Why?"

Catriona heard the odd tone of jealousy and concern for her safety in his voice and turned to see him. "He wanted me to tell you why I couldn't accept your proposal."

"Is there a new reason?"

She let her lips don a tiny smile from their wardrobe. "No, but I thought it interesting you had never told him why. You obviously had told him about the proposal. I wanted to see what had happened to keep the rest of the story from him."

Alexander looked at the floor and shuffled his feet. "Pride mostly, I think. He had been so happy for me. Remember, this was on the heels of his wedding to Elizabeth and he was hoping I wouldn't have a cold bed to go to on my wedding night. He had been forced to give up everything he loved for the sake of the kingdom and he didn't want that to happen to me." He sighed, shaking his head. "Mother has so thoroughly ruined him, Catriona. She has utterly destroyed everything that matters to him, save the things which matter to her, which she allows him. If he could, he'd run so far away from here, no one would ever find him." He looked back at her. "So, when he learned it was *you* I'd found, he was ecstatic. I have loved you for so very long, ever since I first met you, and the thought of being able to live vicariously through me was very appealing, I think.

"Plus, I think he was in love with you too, long ago. He told me to hang on to you, no matter what, to protect you from Mother and be certain, above all, to follow my heart, no matter where it takes me. I believe he meant for me to run away from this place and this life, taking nothing with me save what I needed to provide for you because, when it came right down to it, it was what he wanted to do for Marie.

"Besides," he said, a smile seeping into his voice, "aren't women supposed to dream of handsome princes rescuing and marrying them?"

"I have heard that," she replied, unable to keep her own smile from her lips. "Of course, I've never felt the need to *be* rescued. That's just something you keep doing on your own."

Alexander let her smile cheer his features. "I'll try to be more considerate in the future." He reached out his hand to her. "Come, sit with me. Please."

She took his hand again and this time, the two of them walked into the room. The bed curtains were lush black velvet, his covers were golden griffins, a fantastical monster he had always loved in stories as a child. He'd often said he would have griffins as his personal arms if he'd been allowed them. There were other griffins scattered about the room; a pillow on the bed, tiles set into the hearth, a set of stone ones flanking the fireplace, and a ceramic decanter for his wine.

Alexander went to the hearth and stoked the fire to a strong blaze. An ember spit itself onto the hearth and bounced to the rug behind him. Catriona stepped in absently and delivered it back onto the hearth, mindful of crushing it into the fibers of the rug where it could smolder and ignite. Suddenly, Alexander stood up and turned and the two found themselves within a breath of each other.

She started to step back but he grabbed her hips and kissed her. The force of his sudden passion caught her off guard and she gave in, folding into him like a flag when the wind stops. Her hands had gone to his chest, and they slid gently, then eagerly up to his neck, her hand slipping into his hair as she let her need for a human connection take flight.

The kiss finally ended, the passion surging around the room like a rampaging ghost, leaving them both breathing heavily. She swallowed. "This isn't exactly sitting."

"No, it isn't." He looked into her eyes. "Stay with me. Please."

"Tonight?"

"Forever."

"I can't."

"Then tonight will do." He kissed her again, and she joined in the kiss, grateful for the fact she would never question whether Alexander was thinking of her at that moment, and more grateful that she never could.

The desire to be the only one in his life turned bittersweet in her mouth and she felt sorrow instead of passion. If she gave in to his ideas, she would put him and his family in danger. Catherine would never tolerate a half-Nubian to sit the throne of Patras, much less a pirate and adulteress. If she left Nicolai as she intended, the most she could hope for would be that Alexander leave his home and lands to sail with her. If she maintained her duties and responsibilities at the expense of his, what kind of a person would she be?

Catriona broke the kiss's spell, her conscience pushing them apart. She turned and walked from him a few steps, the pain of her convictions warring between them.

"Don't, Catriona. By all the Saints in heaven, I beg you, don't turn away from me again. It almost killed me when you left before."

"I never meant to hurt you, Alexander. Not then and especially not now. But I have obligations we've never discussed."

He stepped over to her, touching her back. "Then tell me what they are. Enlighten me so we can dispel their hold over you. I'm the heir to the Crown of Mervolingia, for Heaven's sake. Just tell me what they are and I'll remove them from our lives. I'm begging you. Don't walk away from me again."

She was almost swayed. She was leaving Nicolai already. What would be the harm in telling Alexander? But then she realized the harm would be in what it caused him to do, to throw away. "Alexander, I would stay if I felt I could but I can't. You would make me your princess and that is a role I would never be able to play, even if your family allowed it."

"You mean if my *mother* allowed it. Charles would celebrate the chance to have you and I together."

"Yes, I mean your mother."

"Catriona, not to disparage my mother's scrappy fighting, but I'm pretty sure you could take her."

"Alexander."

He stepped over to her and took her hands in his. "Mother has taken everything he loves from my brother, save those he values more than all others: his true love and son. Even Mother is not omnipotent."

"She doesn't have to be, Alexander. She just has to be sneaky. I can't stop a threat I can't see coming, and neither can you. Do you really want the majority of our days to be spent making sure my food isn't poisoned? I don't. And that's only if I made it to the altar. She could turn the entire kingdom against me with a single, well-spoken sentence, and you have her gift for saying the right thing at the right time." *The Land knows I've fallen before his well-spun song before.* "No. I cannot stay here with you. Even if you managed to get rid of her, there's still Nicolai to contend with, although, well, that may be dealt with soon enough."

"What do you mean, 'dealt with'?" Alexander searched Catriona's eyes and when she looked away, unable to keep eye contact, his own eyes narrowed in understanding. "You're leaving him, aren't you?" Catriona tried to move away from him but he held her tight. "You are. By the Saints, you're leaving him." He took her in his arms and kissed her hair. "Thank you, Heaven."

"Don't move me in just yet, Alex. Drake and Anika are here to take Alan with them and I have plans to take the *Enigma* home to Caratia." She looked up at him, trying to get through to him the seriousness of their situation. "But I'm not free yet. I may never be. If he wants to, Nicolai can decide to call me an adulteress, and he would be right. If I'm caught, it would be the obligation of your brother to put me to death, by your own laws. I'm just thankful he doesn't know it was with you."

"I could have him killed."

She put her head against his chest, letting him encompass her with his arms. "That isn't funny."

"Maybe I wasn't trying to be."

Catriona looked at him, searching. Alexander blinked, a bit of a hard edge coming into his eyes. *He couldn't mean that, could he? This is Alexander, not Charles or Dominic.* She moved back a little as Alexander eased his hold on her.

Alexander took her chin in his hand. "I could, you know. I would too. Anything for you." He kissed her again and she tried hard not to cringe, and harder not to find the idea appealing.

She put her hand on his chest and pushed him away. "Alex. Please. This isn't right. Even talking about such things is a violation of your laws."

"I'm the Prince of Mervolingia. I have the right, for matters of State, to do what I must to end any threats I perceive."

"Nicolai is a guard here, not a threat." She stepped away from him, not liking where he was going with this. "Alex, listen to yourself. Don't let this drive you to do or say something you will regret. Nicolai is not a bad person. He stayed true to me for six years going exclusively on his memory of me."

"And what have *I* done? Have I not also lived and breathed for the very chance of seeing you again?"

"Yes, you have. I wish I could explain it better. It's as if the Land has not yet released me from his side. I feel this pressure to stay and I can't wait to leave."

"But you said you have arranged things with Anika and Drake?"

Catriona looked down at her hands again, then sighed deeply and looked back at the man fighting so hard for their love. "Yes."

"Why?"

Catriona looked away, ashamed to tell him what Nicolai had done to her. Alexander turned her back to face him. "Why, Catriona? We have avoided each other all winter, and that has been no small feat on my part. You wanted an opportunity to try again with him and were determined enough that you broke all contact with me. You have never backed down from a challenge as long as I've known you. So, why now?" He blinked and suddenly a thought seemed to dawn on his features and a look much harder than steel and sharper than broken glass invaded his eyes. "Did he… What did he do to you?" He looked her over quickly for signs of violence but she waved his scrutiny away.

Catriona closed her eyes, tears wetting the edges of her lashes. "He… has gone back to Tanglwyst's bed." She opened them and looked at him. "I just can't stay here anymore. Between not being able to see you and not being able to stop him from seeing her, I get so angst-ridden I can barely breathe."

Alexander calmed down, reining in his anger and frustration in light of what Catriona had revealed. "Then I'll go with you," he said with sincerity. "I can be ready to go in a matter of minutes."

"And abandon your obligations? That's not you, Alex." Catriona shook her head. "No. You're the brother of the king, a king with no male heirs."

"He has one. He just can't acknowledge him." Alexander sat down in the hearth chair, his elbows on his knees, and put his hands in his hair. Catriona smiled as she recognized the gesture Charles had made in the next room. It seemed to be a family trait. She walked over to crouch before Alexander and put her hands on his legs. He sat back and closed his eyes, holding her hands.

"That's all there is to say, isn't there? You can't stay and I can't leave." Catriona reached up and stroked his hair, soothing his sorrows and his tousled mane as best she could.

The fire crackled loudly in the room as they tried to reconcile their feelings with their duties and it was Alexander who spoke up first this time.

"I was just thinking about you, before you arrived."

"You were?" Her voice was soft, like her touch.

"About the cottage on the cliffs. Do you still go there?"

There was a pause while she stopped stroking his hair, putting her hand back on his knee and standing. "No. It feels… inappropriate… to be there without you. I felt you in everything I touched when I was there last and it almost destroyed me." She turned and stood watching the fire as the memories pulled her into the flames. "I found myself clutching the cup you used, trying to feel the warmth of your hands. Finally, I left and I couldn't bring myself to return."

He leaned forward, resting his elbows on his knees and letting his hands and head dangle. "At least you had that. I was left with nothing to touch, nothing to prove it had happened at all." He looked up at her. "Just the sense my heart would never recover if you left me again."

She folded her arms across her chest, running her hand up her arm as she had often done when she thought about being held by him. "I suppose it was wrong to make love to you before I had told you about Nicolai, but I decided I wanted that memory just in case you didn't want me."

Alexander stood and put a hand on her shoulder, watching the firelight dance on her black hair. "What made you feel I might not want you just because you had been married before?"

"It wasn't just the marriage, but the fact I had let my own vanity and pride destroy the marriage when I left Nicolai without telling him where I was going. Then, after I was freed, I still refused to go to him, abandoning him in what turned out to be his most desperate hour. It was possible you would believe I would do the same to you."

"But you could just look at me and tell that wasn't true. You have the ability to look into people's souls."

"I've never been able to look into yours. I'm blocked from seeing through you. It's because of the life debt. Since I owe my life to you, you have the right to take it at will, and my sight will not allow me divination so I can't interfere with your collection of the debt."

"How do you know all this?"

"It is a tenet of faith in Yndia. Karma demands payment of the life debt, one way or another. When Tanglwyst summoned me to Patras for an emergency meeting, I was going to see about retiring from her service so I might be able to be with you. Then I walked into that room and saw Nicolai sitting there, alive and well. It was the most horrible experience of my life. Karma. I had just decided to stop grieving and he turns up not dead."

"Imagine how I felt when he turned up *here*," said Alexander, shaking his head, "as a Royal Guardsman, no less. At Tanglwyst's request. I'm pulled in a thousand directions every time I lay eyes on the man. I know he doesn't know it's me you were with, but I avoid him as much as possible as if he can smell you on me still." Alexander snorted a laugh. "Hell, sometimes I think *I* can smell you on me too, and it's maddening."

She touched his hand once more and then exhaled. "Alex, I have to go. I have things I need to attend to."

"Anything I can help with?"

"I hope your skills will not be necessary, but if they are, I will send for you. Charles has plans for tonight and there are several things I have to do before then." She turned to leave.

Alexander caught her wrist. He looked at her, a plea in his eyes, though he never let it get to lips. She turned back and Alexander kissed her again, drinking from his life's blood one last time before she slipped through the cracks of the catacombs in a whisper of stone.

*Chapter Twenty-six:*
*"A friend loveth at all times, and a brother is born for adversity."*
*~ Proverbs 17:17*

Charles opened his bedroom door with barely a look at the flanking guards and closed his door behind him. The exchange with Catriona had been exhilarating and he was quite pleased with how it had gone. She had consented to see Alexander and he hoped that was enough. Alexander was a skilled diplomat. Charles felt certain he would be able to convince her to stay a while, maybe longer. All he needed was time and Charles intended to give him that time. Charles had always had a fondness for the lady and when he had seen the happiness his brother had found with her, it had made his own situation that much more bearable for that month. Charles had been almost as crushed as Alexander when she had broken things off although he had never known why she had done so. Now he knew.

There was a large comfortable chair facing the window and he stood between the two and looked out at the deafening blue sky. The Vox should be by soon and Charles looked over at the desk to make sure he had everything he needed. Catriona had restored so much by showing up when she did. She had stopped the disease of spinelessness that had been draining his life for years. He had lost his integrity at the Massacre and it was time he regained it. Marie and his son deserved someone who was not a puppet, and he was breaking those strings which bound him today.

He realized how much Marie had been there for him, risking her own life and their child's against the judgment of the omnipotent Church and the Royal Family. If the queen chose to, she would be completely justified in the eyes of the law and the church to have his family put to death, and the Queen-Mother would be just the person to manipulate Elizabeth into such an act. He was so terribly disgusted with how little control he seemed to have over his own life, but seeing Catriona in so similar a situation actually made him angry. Some creatures were born in cages, and some were born free and put in cages. Charles wasn't about to let her stay in that cage, not when he could do something about it.

He sat down at his desk and began to write one more document. This was the last of three which needed to be done by his hand and he needed to make sure they were done today. Mother would be home soon and she had blocked decrees like these before. Her tendrils claimed things they never should have and Charles was not about to let her get her claws on these documents. Thank the Saints Catriona had stopped the poison. Having a clear head for this part made the writing easier.

He picked up the quill and dipped it in the ink, writing quickly while he had in mind what he wanted to say. Usually he wrote the decrees on blotter paper in order to get his wording right, but the first two of these particular decrees had been in his mind for four years and he knew precisely what he wanted to say, to the last syllable. This final one was something which had just come to him, and he needed to word this one properly. No reference to anything or anyone specifically except Catriona, and maybe not even then. What had been the name of her ship? The *Enigma* Alex had said. There can only be one captain of that ship, especially who had a husband.

As he finished the wording on the blotter paper, Charles suddenly realized something else, upon reflection. Catriona *did* love Alexander. Her desire to keep Charles alive was more than just friendship. It was also the only way Catriona believed she and Alexander could ever be together in any way. As long as Charles remained king, Alexander could travel as he had for the past several years, keeping to the seas and seaports, waiting for a glimpse of that ebony hair, those enchanting green eyes. Charles thanked the Saints Catriona had discovered the poison. Alexander would never forgive him for dying and taking that away from him.

He knew Alexander loved her, and, although Charles had also believed he loved her too, back when he was younger, he understood something about himself now. He had long ago discovered his "love" for Catriona was more akin to desire or lust, that every image his mind recalled was lingering on the physical instead of the substance within, unlike his feelings for Marie. It was this realization which explained to him why *he* had never been the object of Catriona's affection. She would see that for what it was in the first glance.

No, Alexander deserved her, and she him. They complemented each other very well in their personalities, each being the strength where the other was weak, thus making the ideal pillar. A perfect foundation for a lifetime romance, for building a marriage upon if the Church could be appeased, and money could often do that. She had such an integrity in her soul, as displayed that very first moment he and Alexander had laid eyes on her. Battered and broken, with the smoke of the church blackening the sky behind her, she had been crawling over to a beheaded priest, muffled cries of an infant coming from beneath him. There was no possibility of her moving the body in her condition, and the king and Prince of Mervolingia had grabbed a dead man and saved a living child. Charles still felt pride over that selfless act that introduced the three of them.

*Catriona had fallen unconscious as soon as she saw the baby was rescued and Alexander turned his attention on her. He had put his hands upon her and Charles remembered a glow spreading from his hands into her body. Her breathing had been choppy at best, but it had evened out under Alexander's hands. Charles had seen Alexander heal cuts and bruises that would have gotten them in trouble with their mother, but nothing like this. It was almost like Alexander was panicking and the intensity of the emotion was causing a surge in his healing ability.*

*Catriona had moaned and moved a bit then. Alexander had picked her up and looked around for a place to take her. A couple ran up at that moment, a midwife and her husband, who had them take Catriona and the baby to their home. The midwife had worked on Catriona's injuries, but Charles already knew what she would find. His brother had healed her through force of his will alone, and the woman would be fine. Charles saw the brutality Catriona had endured, wounds that were not from the fight and Alexander had told him later that her wounds were very deep. Charles had suggested they leave but Alexander had not wanted to. He had asked the midwife if he could help and she had asked him to hold the baby and make sure he was not injured.*

*Charles had watched as Alexander walked cautiously over to the baby and the midwife's husband told him how to hold the child. Alexander had become captivated by the boy as the husband had him hold the child next to his skin and heart, giving the child the human connection his wife had discovered helped babies right after birth. The child had snuggled into Alexander's chest and Charles had watched his brother cry for the very first time since he'd become a man. From that day forward, Alexander had lived his life for this woman, and Charles felt his devotion was not misplaced.*

Charles looked down at the letter he had written, Catriona's liberation. *This is the very least I can do for her*, he thought. Unbidden, another voice, perhaps Marie's, perhaps Alexander's, floated to the top of his head.

*What would be the most you could do?*

He looked up at his daughter's portrait hanging on his wall. It was a wonderful likeness, showing her chubby little cheeks and beautiful eyes like the sky, a true credit to the artist, who Charles now knew to be the newest inhabitant of the dungeon. One day, it had appeared at the palace and he never found out whom to thank for it. There was one of Her Majesty as well, dressed in a gown of gold and green from her Coronation, and Marie-Elizabeth was wearing the same dress, only her size, although he didn't believe his daughter had one like that. This little girl had captured his heart, as had his son, Francois. He wanted the best for both his children, and hoped his actions today, coupled with the decrees on the desk, would do that very thing.

There was a knock at the door and the herald's assistant came in. He looked nervous. "You sent for me, Sire?"

"I have some things which need to be announced at court tonight. Please take these decrees to the Vox so they can be put upon the roster for court business." Charles sealed the other one and put it in the drawer of his desk.

The assistant took the two sealed documents and, bowing, left. Charles looked back out the window, yawned, and decided to take a short nap, to give his beloved brother more time with the woman he loved. He went over and sat in the comfortable chair and looked out of the window, smiling over his new decrees. They were on their way now. Even Mother would be unable to stop them. The one in the drawer was special and would require a bit more clandestine delivery. Regardless, he felt certain the recipient of that particular letter would be up to the task. Duncan McVryce was a reliable man.

He reached over to a small table next to the chair and picked up a goblet of wine he had forgotten in all the chaos. He drank it and noticed a strange flavor that should not have been there. He felt his throat get thick and full of mucus, his hands and arms shaking. He rose from his chair, hoping to call out for his guards before he could no longer speak at all, but his voice was already gone.

He started to pitch forward, the goblet falling from his fingers. He prayed for the sound to bring the guards running, but he hit the ground, his fall broken by the puddle of velvet curtains pooled on the floor by the window before the goblet did. He turned, using the last of his energy to see a delicate gloved hand had caught the goblet before it hit the stones, and Charles fell into darkness and silence.

## Chapter Twenty-seven:
## *"All the days of the afflicted are evil..."*
## ~ *Proverbs 15:15*

Tanglwyst took a chance and left her cell. Myrgen's last report was that there had been neither hide nor hair spotted of the pirate woman and Catherine was due back tomorrow or the next day, so Tanglwyst decided they couldn't wait any longer. Apparently Catriona had figured out they were trying this now because Catherine was gone and had decided to merely wait it out. This meant Tanglwyst's back-up plan had to go into effect.

She had been improvising since the beginning and, luckily, was quick on her feet. When she had been listening to Dominic talking about his relatives in Mande and all the poisons and death and faked deaths they had, she had gotten the original idea to poison Charles. Charles dying would free Elizabeth from this hurtful marriage and maybe Tanglwyst would be able to convince Myrgen to leave his post at the palace to go with Beth, retiring to Angloume. Once together, Tanglwyst was *sure* Elizabeth and Myrgen would fall in love. Myrgen was already there.

But Tanglwyst didn't have any way to administer a poison to Charles, not with any surety. There was also the added problem of Catherine, who knew more about poisons and their effects than Dominic did, and would surely identify an amateur's attempt to poison Charles. Elizabeth occasionally still slept with Charles, too, and their daughter might accidentally be the victim if it was on his papers or something like that. Tanglwyst didn't want to run the risk of collateral damages on this one, especially not *those* damages. That meant either something he would use exclusively or something he wouldn't use at the palace.

She didn't know his habits in the palace well enough to come up with a way to place it there, but she *did* know where his mistress lived. She had discovered Charles leaving Marie's one morning a few weeks ago as Tanglwyst made her way home from Nicolai's house earlier this year, while both Catriona and Tanglwyst's new captain were in Rouen refitting their respective ships for the sailing season. Tanglwyst had gone to the house with the blue door right then and there, and watched carefully. She saw Marie and the baby, and decided that course was also dangerous because of the baby. Tanglwyst had two older children of her own and couldn't bring herself to endanger a little one any more than Myrgen could. So she had put the idea out of her head.

That is until Charles hit Elizabeth. He had come down with something which was causing rages and he was with Elizabeth when one of them took him. Catherine had gone to the Papal City as soon as the roads were clear in late March, or Tanglwyst might have suggested they take this matter to the Queen-Mother. As it was, they had to deal with the situation themselves, so Tanglwyst had suggested they bring Myrgen into this. Elizabeth had been confused until Tanglwyst explained the little known fact that Myrgen knew his way around the more unsavory circles of Patras. He could find the person to ease all their pain.

Then the idea to serve her own ends came to her. She knew she could get Myrgen to contract Catriona to do the assassination. The woman was a killer, as Dominic had proven, and had absolutely no morals other than doing what Tanglwyst said. She was a shallow, vicious monster who had a hold on Nicolai and Tanglwyst wanted him free to be with *her*. She figured Catriona could be set to the task of regicide and Tanglwyst would simply tip him off. The image of her lover catching his nefarious spouse in yet another heinous exploit would seal Catriona's fate. He would either kill her or imprison her, either one of which was more than acceptable to Tanglwyst.

She had suggested Catriona for the murder and she had been met with incredulous looks by both her companions.

"Murder the king?" Myrgen had asked. "Actually *murder* him? Are you insane?"

"Clearly," Tanglwyst had replied, only half-joking. She had long suspected her tender formations of right and wrong had been so terribly corrupted by her destructive treatment at the hands of her first husband. She had walked out of that alley where he was murdered before her very eyes and bought that block, building her first house so that her study window looked directly upon that perfect alleyway. She had felt her sanity slipping from her grasp then, and this was just another step on that ladder into the dark abyss.

Elizabeth had become very quiet at the suggestion of doing away with Charles, and Myrgen tried to be reasonable with his sister, but Tanglwyst was very persuasive in her arguments and before the day was out, he had set about trying to contract Catriona for their cause. They all agreed they needed to do this while Catherine was gone, knowing her experience with this was likely to reveal their conspiracy, but they had quite a while before they needed to worry about that. It was two week's travel from the Papal City to Patras in royal style and she would surely send word before she set out so the palace would be prepared for her arrival home. They waited patiently for word from their chosen savior as to her acceptance of their noble task.

Then, a week later, Myrgen had told her Catriona refused the job, and had said he had a back-up assassin he could use instead who lived in Caer Leon. The assassin was reliable and could be there in a week. Tanglwyst insisted they *had* to come up with some other way to get Catriona to commit this sin. She had suggested kidnapping Alan, knowing that would get her to do the deed, but Myrgen had protested, saying this was completely unnecessary. The Leon assassin would be quick, easy and to the point, fulfilling his contract for money. Myrgen stated he trusted a man whose loyalty could be purchased for large sums of gold more than that of a woman trying to recover her child.

Tanglwyst realized she was fighting with two conflicting goals, and she had to choose between the two. She had already figured on Catriona never surviving the ordeal because Tanglwyst planned to alert Nicolai to his wife's evil action and that served the one goal. The other goal was actually that of killing the king, freeing Myrgen and Elizabeth, as well as ridding the kingdom of Catherine's Machiavellian politics with Alexander's Coronation and her subsequent exile. Both were noble purposes, but each required different tactics.

The ideal in Tanglwyst's mind was to have Catriona kill Charles and to have Nicolai catch her. Her refusal to accept the contract now ruined everything, and Tanglwyst was scrambling for a way to have her original plan take root. Then Nicolai had visited her in the night, telling her of Catriona's intentions to have Alan go away for the summer which would enable him to stay exclusively in Tanglwyst's bed for a solid five months and she saw her chance. Just after midnight, when Nicolai got completely drunk, Tanglwyst had escorted him to his house.

She knew Catriona was in Rouen and would be back the next day, so Tanglwyst tucked Nicolai into bed and carried off his sleeping child as soon as the man was snoring soundly. She took the boy to the secret passages inside the palace and put him into one of the rooms in the abandoned chapel, locking the door behind her. She then stole up to Myrgen's room and told him what she'd done. He was angry at first, but she had said the deed was done now and to carry on with the plan.

She asked him to help her prepare a room down in the bowels of the catacombs for her so she, too could be considered kidnapped, to further persuade Catriona to do the homicide, but Myrgen said no, that this plot was too complex and too prone to pitfalls. She needed to return the child before he was discovered missing and let his professional do this. Tanglwyst lied, and told Myrgen she had already been spotted by one of Nicolai's neighbors and it was already too late for that. When he growled at her about it, she claimed she had told the neighbor who stopped her she was Nicolai's employer and that Nicolai was drunk again, and she was taking the boy to her house for the night, to take care of him until his father was recovered. The neighbor seemed to have bought it. The rumor, Tanglwyst insisted, could be spread that she and the boy were taken on their way to her home that very night.

To add to the viability of the ruse, though, she told him she would also have to come up missing, of course, and the two lives in the balance would be all that was necessary for Catriona to take on the contract. Myrgen was furious with her, but he decided the deed was in fact already done and insisted she follow *his* plan from here on out. She nodded and he left. She looked around for a room for herself and found the old scriptorium. The room was a good choice, by the scant firelight of the lantern she had, and she had lain back on the old straw mattress and slept, satisfied with her work.

The next morning, Myrgen and Michael had arrived at her little cell, and brought her some supplies, blankets and candles. All that day, Michael brought her things which were sent down by the queen, whom Myrgen had informed of the new developments, and Tanglwyst got set up pretty comfortably. She had entertained herself with thoughts of their success. Catriona's mephitic reputation had now put Nicolai's son at risk, an enterprise which would *certainly* sit ill with Nicolai. After her original sin of leaving, Nicolai would be completely against Catriona. Tanglwyst wouldn't be surprised if he even released the door to the gallows himself when they hung his wife as a traitor.

Tanglwyst was grateful she had seen the need to not be available for Catriona to consult or petition for resources on this one. Catriona could see through Tanglwyst like a stained glass window, and she would expose her involvement in the whole matter. Nicolai could conceivably turn against Tanglwyst completely upon discovery of her active participation with his son's imprisonment and the common foe might be all that was necessary to re-forge the solid love Nicolai had for his wife in the first place. He had gone for years on the *hope* she would return; Tanglwyst wanted to avoid *that* devotion, at least as it applied to Catriona.

When Myrgen had brought her dinner that night, he seemed to have accepted the situation, albeit reluctantly, and he told her he didn't like working this way. He didn't approve of being manipulated, especially by his sister, who should know better. She apologized and said if Catriona didn't work out, the boy would be returned to Nicolai unharmed and they would go with the assassin from Leon. The conversation had turned to how they would get Catriona to the place where they would "acquire" her services.

Myrgen's research had indicated she would be a very deadly opponent, especially if she were an unwilling one. It was then that Michael, who had joined them after taking dinner to the boy, suggested a sleeping agent to render Catriona helpless. He told them it could be administered through something like a blow gun like the ones his tribe used to hunt for the village, and would enable Myrgen to put this Catriona woman under without even getting close to her. They could hit her with the drug and send her on her way.

Then things began to go wrong with Tanglwyst's improvised plan. Myrgen had received word that Catherine was due back on the first of June instead at the end of the summer like they had believed. Tanglwyst was no longer sure they would be able to insure Charles' death by then, which meant Catriona would escape as well. Tanglwyst decided to take things into her own hands then too. She found the pouch with the sleeping drug Michael planned to use to knock Catriona out to bring her to the catacombs and she tampered with the fluids, using the poison she had originally gotten for killing Charles if she had to do it herself. When Michael told Tanglwyst that he had put her out with a punch instead of using the darts, Tanglwyst felt a tinge of fear. Who knew what had become of the poison?

No one had seen Catriona since she was set to the task of murdering the king. Tanglwyst began to suspect Catriona had probably figured out their timeline and decided to wait out their demands, knowing Catherine's arrival would do them all in, and the plan needed to be altered again. It was Tanglwyst's perspective that when one hit a wall, to turn it into a corridor until another opening presented itself. That way, she could leave behind an impenetrable maze which would throw off investigation, or at least slow it down, enabling her to destroy any evidence linking her to the situation. That was something she had learned from Myrgen.

Charles needed to be dispatched so Catriona could be charged. If she wasn't going to do it, Tanglwyst decided she would. She was already missing. Nicolai would undoubtedly have verified that by now. He was probably looking for her already. No one would ever suspect Tanglwyst had anything to do with Charles' death if she stole into his room and stabbed him as he slept. Only Catriona might know the truth and she'd damn herself by saying anything. Her new course of action determined, Tanglwyst had stripped out of all her clothes except her shoes and partlet, which went almost to her ankles, and crept outside to the secret passages.

It was daylight, unfortunately, but she knew there was no way to get to Charles' chamber within the palace so she went through the passages to Myrgen's room. The hallways were oddly empty, and she took a dagger from Myrgen's room and quietly crept toward Charles' chambers. They were unguarded and the door was open a little, so Tanglwyst simply slipped into Charles' room. It never occurred to her to wonder where the guards were, and for some reason, she never thought they would be a problem. She closed the door behind her in the dim room.

She thought she saw a form on the bed so she went there first, but the bed was empty. This was the first time she suspected she might not be able to pull this off and she began to panic. Then she turned to leave and saw the hand laying extended from the chair. She carefully walked over to the chair, dagger poised to cut Charles' throat, but when she got there, she was greeted with a horrific sight.

Charles' was *covered* in blood. It was everywhere. There was no sign of what could have done this and Tanglwyst reached down to touch his hand. That was when his eyes had fluttered open and he grabbed her wrist, his hand and arm bathed in blood. She was so scared she couldn't scream and jerked her hand back out of his grip.

The knife flew across the room, hitting the table behind her with a thunk before landing in the blood pool by the chair with a clatter on the floor. She turned and began to flee the room, but tripped on the large area rug by the chair and fell, face first onto the ornate rug that greeted her proximity with a splash. The rug was soaked in blood coming from the bottom of the chair Charles was in. She realized the guards could return at any time and ran for the door, checking quickly for the guards. Elizabeth came around the corner and put her fist to her mouth to stop her own scream.

* * *

"Tanglwyst, what have you done? What are you doing out of your cell?" Elizabeth glanced into the room and didn't really see anything at first, but the bloody footprints from the room to the door were enough to mobilize the queen before they were seen. She guided Tanglwyst to Myrgen's room and closed the door behind them, making sure she didn't add her own footprints to the bloody trail.

Tanglwyst seemed unable to speak and Elizabeth looked directly into her eyes and shook her. "Tanglwyst, what happened?"

Tanglwyst blinked. "Blood… he was covered in blood. He grabbed me. *He grabbed me, Beth!* Like he *knew!*"

"Tanglwyst!" Elizabeth's whisper cut through Tanglwyst's panic like an arrow. "You need to get out of here. You need to go now. Get back to your cell and get out of those clothes immediately. Get rid of them. We can't have you discovered like this. Go!" She opened the door to Myrgen's secret shrine and closed the door behind her friend.

Elizabeth watched Tanglwyst disappear into the darkness of the passageway and then slipped into the hallway which would lead to Charles' room. Tanglwyst had been bloody, and that excited Elizabeth, and frightened her. There were drops of blood on the hallway floor from Tanglwyst's partlet leading to the bedroom down the hall, and the queen proceeded carefully but quickly, rubbing the blood away with her shoes. At first, Elizabeth had thought her friend had been injured but now she suspected otherwise, and she advanced cautiously to see what she could see. She poked her head around the corner and realized something very important, and very unusual: the guards were missing. Elizabeth assumed Tanglwyst had arranged for them to be sent on some errand before she had entered the room.

She went to the room and entered it, her heart pounding in her throat, excitement dripping from every pore. She was greeted with the glorious sight of Charles dead, his vital fluid of life cascading all over the floor. Those stains would never come out of the carpet. She had looked around at the scene and reveled for only a moment, then got her wits about her. The guards were gone but they would be back, and Elizabeth definitely didn't want to be in the room when they returned. Too much precedence for it to be *her* who did this, and exposing Tanglwyst would damn them all.

Elizabeth was about to leave when an incredible idea came to her. She could frame Marie Touchet for Charles' death!

She went over to look at Charles' body, careful not to step in the mess surrounding him, then looked around for the knife obviously used by Tanglwyst to murder him. She found it over on the floor sitting in the vitae dripping from the chair. It was one of Myrgen's, ironically the one Charles had given him when he awarded Myrgen his Arms. She thought of going to Myrgen now and telling him her plan so he could help her implement it but she was in a bit of a rush, so she moved now with a purpose.

Tanglwyst had evidently dropped the knife on her way out, probably when she had realized fully what she had done. Tanglwyst was no killer and the deed would scar her beyond a doubt, but she had done what no one else had, and Elizabeth planned to reward her for her ingenuity. She had to step into the puddle of blood to get the blade, holding on to the chair back to steady herself.

She wanted to reach over and stab Charles again herself, but she knew she only had a small amount of time and resisted the urge with great difficulty. She moved over to the two portraits on the wall. She knew now the portraits were painted from complete fancy by Myrgen, and she was saddened by what she had to do here, but she pulled the desk chair over to the wall and climbed onto it.

She used the dagger to slice the throat of her portrait, the motion flicking blood droplets across her rendered face. Then, for good measure, she moved and sliced the throat of her daughter's portrait. That, she decided, would implicate that whore of Charles' completely. Elizabeth pushed the chair back over to the desk and saw the blotter paper with his writing on it. She picked it up and began to read it when she heard the guards returning. Elizabeth thought fast and quickly ran over and locked the door. She leaned in and listened carefully by the keyhole to make sure they would stay where they were. One of them tried the door, then said, "He must be sleeping again. The Prince said he would."

Elizabeth sighed, relieved, but then the guards went on, capturing her attention. "What do you think of that Myrgen character?"

"I don't know what to think about that. He certainly put up a fight when we threw him into that cell. He's pretty strong for a guy his size."

Cell? Elizabeth didn't know what had happened, but if Myrgen was in a cell, she knew she couldn't go to him for help. She had to take care of this one on her own. With the guards stationed outside, she looked around the room of death for a way out. The only way available to her now was the passageway, and Charles had made certain his never connected to anyone else's. It was terribly risky, but she had to move right away. Elizabeth activated the doorway and left, her skirts brushing the entrance as she escaped.

She moved quickly through the passage, knowing it had only one destination. She slipped into the garden undetected, but had a definite problem when she got there. A host of servants were tending the gardens, preparing for Catherine's arrival. Luckily, it looked like they might be finishing up and she waited for an intolerable ten minutes before the way was clear. She moved hastily to the hedge which hid the passage to her chambers. The doorway opened easily and she escaped into the secret byway.

She ran through the corridors, knowing her way from memory. When she arrived at the large crossroads, she took off up the stairs, her adrenaline rushing in her veins. She reached the top of the stairs and stopped to catch her breath and be sure she knew what she was doing. Myrgen had apparently been taken to the dungeons this morning so she knew he would not be in his chambers. She went to the doorway and opened it into his room, careful to be as quiet as possible in case servants were cleaning or something.

It looked as though they had not been in here yet today and she realized she had to move quickly. She went over to his bed and stuffed the bloody knife under the covers, glad to see bloody streaks staining the places where she touched the blankets and sheets. The servants should find this easily. If Myrgen's already in prison like the guards had said, then there's no way he could have done this deed. Charles had been seeing things and acting insane for days, had even killed an innocent servant just the other day, so Elizabeth was *certain* she could clear Myrgen of these charges.

The important thing is that *Marie* couldn't have known Myrgen had been taken, and therefore was completely without an alibi, especially in the face of a queen's accusation. Elizabeth would be rid of both Charles and his harlot in one easy action. She hadn't even had to get her own hands bloody. Then Elizabeth looked down at her hands and saw they were, indeed, still a little bloody from handling the knife. Easy enough to fix, she thought. She needed to be in her room when they came to tell her of Charles' death.

She left quickly and returned to her room via the cool stone of the catacombs.

* * *

Tanglwyst ran into her room in the catacombs, her skin pale and her eyes wild, blood clotting on her face. She closed the door quickly, as if being pursued and stood in the center of her room, trying to think. Her mind was racing, thumping in time with her heart.

Charles had grabbed her. The Saints only knew how, but he had grabbed her. She looked down at her right wrist and saw the grip of his fingers imbedded in blood on her partlet cuff. Her visage in the borrowed mirror showed her face and clothes covered in gore and the sight of it almost made her scream.

Tanglwyst looked at her clothing and remembered Elizabeth's instruction to get rid of it. She stripped and went to the washbasin to clean the blood away. With every bit of blood she removed, she felt the horror of the incident wash away as well. She thought about what she had seen and determined she was transposing the order in which things happened. Charles hadn't been bloody when she went into the room, but afterward, after Tanglwyst had obviously killed him. He had grabbed her wrist after his throat was cut because *she* had cut it, and of course, by then it was too late.

As she cleansed herself of the activity, she felt her pride in the achievement start to fill her. She had done it. She had freed her friend, her family and her kingdom from the tyranny of the D'Medici pawn. She celebrated her resourcefulness by taking out some of her perfumes which she had brought, and dousing her skin with the expensive scents. She glanced around the room, trying to decide what else to wear and spotted the bloody partlet in a heap on the floor.

She grabbed Elizabeth's velvet robe and was about to don it when it occurred to her the partlet was still wet from Charles' blood and the presence of blood on the royal clothing would be an unwise move. Tanglwyst picked up the partlet and went, nude, into the catacomb passage. She looked around in the light afforded her by her open door and saw the ruin of the chapel wall about fifty feet down the hall. She went to the place where the wall had collapsed and stuffed the partlet into a hole in the burnt rubble.

Suddenly, she realized the light illuminating her way was growing dim. She looked back and saw her door falling slowly closed. She pulled her hand back and the sudden movement pulled a small board down on her hand, trapping it there. The door closed, leaving her naked and alone in the dark. Tanglwyst began to panic. Her breathing became heavy and labored, as if she were toting a huge boulder on her shoulders. Her mind went blank and she began to hear things, shuffles in the dark nearby. She thought she felt things brush by her, raspy fingers on her back and neck. She thought she heard whispers in the blackness, accusations delivered on apparition's wings. Sounds, scents, and sensations bombarded her, confusing her until she passed out.

When she came to, she had no idea how long she had been out, but the black out had cleared her head. She noticed her caught hand was asleep and it occurred to her that might be a good thing. If she had to do something which might cut or bruise her, having the feeling gone might make it easier to do what she needed to do. She also noticed she could see, a tiny bit. There was a very dim light leaking from under a door nearby and Tanglwyst realized that must be where Alan were being held.

She focused on the board which trapped her hand and reached in with her other hand, managing to lift the fallen board enough to free her other hand. Her wrist hurt a bit but the feeling was coming back to her hand quickly now and she didn't seem to sense any other damage. Her backside was sore from where she had been sitting on the ground and her head hurt from the fainting, but that seemed to be the extent of her injuries.

Massaging her wrist, she crept back down the corridor toward her room. Her mind was clear of panic now and she was a bit worried about her sanity. Had she truly killed the king? It was more than she had ever done before, but it didn't feel right. No, it hadn't been her. She had found him like that. Catriona had actually done the deed! Tanglwyst almost shouted with joy. Now, her destruction was complete. Nicolai would discover Tanglwyst this evening and she would tell him that Catriona captured her. It would be *perfect.*

She opened her door and looked in the mirror. She still had blood on her from where she had fallen in the kings' chamber and she used the ewer and basin to clean herself up. She was exhilarated and felt very amorous. The sex with Nicolai when they got together would be amazing and she could barely contain herself. She wanted to run to him now and it was only the savoring of the revealing of his wife's sin that stayed her feet.

The door opened and Michael came in carrying a tray of food. *Was it that late already? How long had she been unconscious?* Michael looked at her and then stepped back behind the door. "My apologies, Lady Tanglwyst. I should have knocked first."

Tanglwyst looked down at herself and realized a very interesting opportunity had just walked in the door. "Please, Michael, don't worry." She lowered her gaze, shifting her body and licking her lips. "I won't tell." She stepped toward him and pulled the door open, one thing on her mind. She was not going to be denied this time.

***Chapter Twenty-eight:***
*"...but he knoweth not that the dead are there; and that her guests are in the depths of hell."*
*~ Proverbs 9:18*

Michael poured the queen some wine after he returned from delivering dinner to the hostages, specifically requesting he go through her chambers to take the captives their food because she had some things for Tanglwyst and it would be more convenient for him to go through her passage instead of Myrgen's. She had also asked Nicolai to assign him to her around noon today, and had been anxious and edgy all afternoon.

She knew Michael delivered food for Tanglwyst and the boy twice a day, then always occupied his time right after breakfast with menial tasks which took him into town, coming on duty after midday. She told Nicolai to have Michael guard her today if he didn't mind, as she was concerned about His Majesty's temper and wanted somebody large to protect her should Charles come after *her* in a murderous rage. The truth of the matter was she wanted to be sure a servant discovered Myrgen's room and not Michael. Michael might try to conceal the evidence planted there and Elizabeth needed it to be found like it was in order to clear Myrgen later.

She smiled graciously, accepting the ornate goblet from the Nubian guard, thanking him. She sipped some wine before asking, "How's Tanglwyst doing?"

"Fine, Your Majesty. The same as always, only more so today." Elizabeth saw a small look of annoyance cross his face and was tempted to ask after it, but thought better of it. "She is ready for all this to be over."

"So am I, Michael. So am I." Michael bowed and left to take up his position as guard outside Elizabeth's door, nodding to Nicolai on the other side as he did so. Lord Dominic walked by on his way to speak to the Prince. Elizabeth smiled to herself, grateful for what she had seen today. She'd gotten nothing as far as news about any of the occurrences of this morning and was actually quite disturbed to discover how slowly the rumor mill worked here despite her rank and station. Ah well, she thought. She had a sweet satisfaction at present which outweighed that of already being in on the gossip. She glanced over at her desk.

The Vox had been by earlier and picked up her own personal decree creating a new order, the Knights of the Golden Garter, and naming Myrgen its Premiere, which should dispel all doubts as to whether or not he quite slew the king. The Golden Garter recipients were set to be placed above all others in the Order of Precedence, this Order now being the highest in the kingdom. It displaced Charles' familial Knights of the Blue Garter, which served the king's family. It was a bold move, but after Tanglwyst's move this afternoon, Elizabeth knew she had to proceed while she still had her control of the throne. Catherine was due back tomorrow and, between her and Alexander, it would all be gone soon.

She knew this Order would seal her legacy in history, and show the populace a woman monarch was just as powerful as any man, just as the Yorkish queen had done in her realm. Elizabeth wanted to form an alliance with Elizabeth Tudor but Charles refused such a bond because of something having to do with Alexander's rejected courtship of the woman. She never found out what the issue was, but whatever had happened, it would send both brothers into fits of laughter at the mere mention of her name.

Elizabeth wanted an alliance with the York because she had conceived of an idea which would empower the women of Mervolingia. Her vision involved setting up a Matriarchal society which enabled women to rid themselves of their husbands, and would bring peace and prosperity to the lands, creating a unity which would be unrivaled by any Patriarchal lineage. When men were in charge, they thought of how to prove they were the strongest, but women in charge proved who was the kindest. Tanglwyst and Elizabeth had talked of this many years ago as they were educated, their tender minds growing together in a desire to no longer be at the whims of men.

Tanglwyst's first husband had beaten her, used her and in general been a nightmarish bastard, and Tanglwyst had vowed to never allow such treatment of her or her daughters again. When Charles hit Elizabeth, it began the entire discussion all over again, and this time, Elizabeth was convinced. Men were not equals, they were lesser beings, war-like creatures with no concern for beauty or grace except for how to destroy it. They were resources to be used, and she had vowed to free herself from their restraints and use them to bind her captors.

This decree was going to start it all. Tanglwyst had once told her the best way to get a man to do what you want is to get him in bed, then reward him for it. If anyone deserved a reward for his lovemaking prowess, it was *definitely* Myrgen.

*And Alexander?*

Well, he was her first love. In fact, she knew she loved him even now, and the torment between choosing someone who was totally devoted to her and someone to whom she was totally devoted was absolutely maddening. Something would inevitably happen which would cause her to choose, and she wasn't prepared for that yet.

\* \* \*

There was a knock on the Prince's door an hour after Catriona left. Alexander had spent the time resting in the chair she had occupied and reveling in the very scent of her for as long as it lingered. He had wanted to make love to her, to capture her here like a brilliant bird that would illuminate his nights with her smile and his days with her voice, but, like caging a perfect wild thing, he knew she would have died under the suffocation of life in the palace. Tragically, he had watched her go, fighting the urge to follow her. He figured she was with her son and her friends now and looked forward to when she would return.

He opened the door to see Lord Dominic. "Hello, Dominic. What can I do for you?"

"The guards and servants have requested your presence. It is His Majesty's supper time and his door is locked. The guards think he may be sleeping and want to know if it would be best to disturb him or let him rest. Regardless, they would ask Your Highness's opinion."

Alexander said, "Come in, I'll be right with you." Dominic entered and waited as the Prince of Mervolingia prepared for the meeting with his brother. First he took off his linen shirt and replaced it with a heavy silk one which would aid in the stopping of anything from an arrow to a musket ball. Then he put on a doublet which was lined in silk, buttoning it to his chest. He picked up his physician's kit. "Let's go."

Dominic nodded and the two men left, walking towards the king's chambers. They saw Nicolai and Michael standing guard outside Elizabeth's door, and Alexander frowned at how threatened everyone was with Charles' condition. The guards bowed as the Prince passed and Alexander acknowledged their respectful gesture. Dominic nodded greeting to Nicolai and Alexander caught an exchange between the two men. Dominic looked guilty and Nicolai looked vigilant. Alexander wondered if it was for the same reason. *Had Dominic done something to bring on Nicolai's ire?* Alexander knew about the Giovanni connection between Catriona and Dominic, and wondered if Nicolai did as well. Regardless, now was not the right time to investigate such things. Alexander still felt Catriona's body in his arms and talking to Nicolai would put him off severely.

Then they heard the scream.

Nicolai looked at Michael. "Stay here and guard Her Majesty."

Elizabeth opened the door suddenly, a scared look on her face. "What is it?"

At a run, Alexander, Dominic, and Nicolai covered the hall to the king's chamber where the door stood open. The Castellan who had opened the door, a frail man named Nigel stood by the table, the tray with His Majesty's supper an offensive heap on the floor at his feet. His hose were splashed with clotted gore and Alexander could see Charles hand draped over the arm of the chair, splattered with blood. Nigel had a young boy with him and the boy was screaming, but Nigel seemed not to hear him. Alexander moved through the room and walked around to the front of the chair. Full moonlight illuminated Charles' body which rested back in the chair, the front of his shirt and robe a violent vision of red and blue silk. His eyes were closed and blood had flowed across the floor soaking through the chair like creeping death. Nigel looked down and saw he had inadvertently stepped in it. He leapt back and the boy's scream reached a crescendo.

A sharp sound drew Alexander's attention and the boy stopped screaming. He stood up and saw Nicolai crouched before the boy, who had a red handprint on his cheek. "Boy, did you see anyone leave this room? Anyone at all?" The boy shook his head and wiped his mouth with his sleeve. Nicolai stood and turned to Nigel. "Did you open the door, Nigel?"

"Y, yes. We had his dinner."

Nicolai asked, "Why didn't you wait for His Highness? I

told you no one was to enter this room without him."

"I insisted. I told the guards I wasn't going to incur the king's wrath by bringing him a cold meal."

Dominic said, "Nigel, let's take the boy out of here." He put his hand on the child's shoulder and Nigel and Dominic moved them to the door. The guards stepped over to Nicolai and talked to him as he asked questions. Alexander looked back down at his brother's limp body and reached out to touch him, his healing instincts moving him to look more clinically. The amount of blood indicated a heart wound, and the position of the body indicated he had been sitting when it happened, but there was something not right about this. The blood pattern was wrong and there was so much of it. The body had been moved and placed in this position. Alexander glanced up at Nicolai and then reached down, picking up one of the velvet curtains on the floor. He draped the body with the velvet, covering it completely.

Nicolai came over. "Your Highness, the guards said there has been no one in this room since Myrgen was arrested this morning."

Alexander looked at him. "Why was Myrgen arrested?"

"Conspiracy to regicide." Alexander and Nicolai looked at Dominic who was returning to the room. He said, "I was there. No one told you?"

"No, I had a visitor from out of town come by today and I spent the day there. I never came out of my room." He looked at Dominic. "Regicide? When did he try to kill Charles?"

"That was the conspiracy aspect. Myrgen didn't try to do it himself. He hired someone to do it." He looked at Nicolai. "Apparently His Majesty knew her because she was Myrgen's accuser. I saw her. She was still there when he dismissed me." Nicolai looked sharply at Dominic at this, as did Alexander, and Dominic finished, looking at Nicolai. "It was Catriona."

The Prince's face shattered and Nicolai closed his eyes in pain and fury. "I'm sorry, Your Highness. The woman he's mentioning is…"

"I know who she is, Nicolai."

Both Dominic and Nicolai looked at Alexander, but the Prince was caught on what he had just heard. *She had things to do before tonight. Saint's blood. Did she kill Charles?* "Gentlemen, please give me a few minutes. I'd like to say goodbye."

Both men muttered, "Of course, Your Highness." They moved out the door to the hallway and closed the door behind them as Alexander closed his eyes in pain. He leaned against the door and put his head back, letting the tears forming in his eyes sink back in to his head. He couldn't do this right now. He needed to make sure the woman he loved did not do this.

He stepped away from the door and went back over to his brother's body, uncovering it. He moved his head and shirt, looking for the wounds that caused all this blood to be spilled. He picked his brother up and carried him to the bed, the blue robe Charles had been wearing dragging through the blood, leaving streaks across the flagstones. He laid his brother out, inspecting him for signs of injury. There was nothing. It was then he thought he saw a dark stain on his tongue. He started to reach in and a soft voice from the prayer nave said, "I wouldn't do that, Your Majesty." Alexander spun on the hidden speaker, recognizing the voice instantly. "You wouldn't want to suffer the same fate."

**Chapter Twenty-nine:**
*"Rejoice not when thine enemy falleth, and let not thine heart be glad when he stumbleth lest the Lord see it and it displease him, and he turn away his wrath from him."*
*~ Proverbs 24:17-18*

Elizabeth closed the door behind her and waited for the news of Charles' death with a grin on her face. She noticed the smile in the mirror and realized she needed to remove that immediately lest she be found out at this crucial moment. No one must know she had anything to do with this, no one except Tanglwyst and Elizabeth knew her loyalty was unquestionable. She also decided she needed to plan her responses carefully. A look of utter shock at Charles' demise wasn't quite appropriate since she knew he was ill. Everyone in the palace knew he was ill. She decided to seem saddened, but expecting the worst. Then, she could look surprised when they told her *how* he died. Yes. That was it.

Elizabeth sat down at her vanity and practiced her look of horror, preparing for the inevitable moment when someone told her the king was murdered. She also needed to be angry and scared when they told of the slashed portraits. She wanted to be in denial when they tried to blame Myrgen, and righteously indignant when some fool tried to claim he must have done it.

She wasn't completely satisfied with her appearance and looked around the room for something to help her. A knife to cut her hand or something would suffice. She could say the scream had scared her as she was cutting a piece of apple, causing her to slice her hand. She was reaching for the knife when she noticed the hem of one of her farthingales peeking out from under her skirts and was horrified to see blood staining the hem. A sudden knock at the door just then, and Lord Dominic's voice calling her startled her into action. She panicked and lifted her skirts, undoing her hoop quickly and throwing it and the petticoats into the secret passage in her prayer room. She quickly closed the stone door and moved, visibly disturbed, to admit her visitors.

She opened the door to find Michael as well as Dominic outside. She searched both faces for news. "What? What is it?"

Dominic gestured inside and Michael stepped in, guiding her to a chair by the fireplace. They sat her down and Dominic knelt next to her side, facing the hearth, looking into her eyes. She looked up at the guardsman, then back to Dominic. "Your Majesty," Dominic said. "The king is dead."

The queen, prepared for this, searched Dominic's eyes, looking confusedly for falsehood, then desperately for it. Dominic rewarded her acting as he looked away, unable to give her what she sought. She stood and walked away from him, her discovery of the blood on the farthingale causing her hands to shake visibly. "Alexander and I talked this morning about what would happen if Charles died from this condition," she asked quietly, careful not to let her fear, or her relief, show in her voice. "Please tell me, did he die while sleeping'?"

"I, I'm afraid not, Your Majesty. He was murdered." Dominic stood, ready to catch the queen should she faint at the news. Elizabeth saw this, and almost obliged. They took her quickly to the chair again and she looked more desperate and frantic the more her color faded. "How? What…what happened?"

"He was stabbed. We're not sure why, but there was a bloody dagger found in Myrgen's room."

"Myrgen?" Michael stood, looking at Dominic.

"Y, yes. You can speak?" Dominic looked nervous now and Elizabeth tried to bring his attention back to her.

"Don't worry, Michael. It must a lie. Someone must… be…trying to set your master up." Elizabeth let the comment explain her shock as well as her denial.

Dominic recovered from his surprise. "Yes. It looks like someone intended to frame Myrgen for the murder. Obviously they didn't know he had been arrested this morning."

"Arrested?" She was actually proud of how shrill her voice had become under tension. It quite added to the illusion, in her opinion but this news was still a genuine shock. "What for?"

"Treason, Your Majesty." Dominic swallowed. "Apparently he hired an assassin, a rather accomplished one, and His Majesty found out about it." Dominic took her hand. "I found a letter a few days ago. We believe Myrgen kidnapped Tanglwyst to get the assassin to kill the king."

*By the Saints*, Elizabeth thought, her fear now becoming slightly more real. *How much does he know?* She looked frantically back at Michael who was holding his own anger in place, and was therefore a well for her to draw from. "Where is

Alexander? Does he know?"

"He's with the Charles' body right now. In the king's chambers."

"Take me there. Now, please."

"Your Majesty, I don't think…"

"Take me there."

Elizabeth stood and Dominic rose and offered his arm as Michael opened the door. The young Mandian noticed the queen's skirts were dragging noticeably on the ground and asked, "Your Majesty, do you want to change? Your hoop is missing."

Elizabeth looked down at her dragging skirts. Dominic had helped the Lady Tanglwyst get dressed on several occasions, mainly because she was trying to bed him, but according to Tanglwyst, he never took the bait. Consequently, he was quite familiar with all the underpinnings necessary for a dress of this style and how unusual it was for her to be without it. Her hem was sagging a little more than the others in the back, a consequence such a hasty removal of the undergarment. He began to look around for the missing item. "Dominic, I removed my hoop because it got singed by a cinder a little while ago. Tell me, do you really think His Majesty will care at this point if I'm dressed in the latest fashion? Come." She waved him over and he stepped up immediately, apologizing for his insensitivity.

He moved them quickly into the hallway and walked beside her to the king's bedroom. The door was mostly closed when they got there and Dominic knocked before entering. Alexander saw who it was at the door and he held up his hand to Dominic. Dominic and Elizabeth waited in the hallway as Alexander covered the body again with the velvet curtain. When he had done so, he walked over to the door. "Elizabeth, I'm sorry."

Elizabeth stepped in to the room, pushing past the men and Alexander grabbed her arm, stopping her. He shook his head and she put on her look of horror at the giant pool of blood seeping out from the rug edges and soaking the back of the chair. She turned into Alexander's chest, closing her eyes tight against the view. Alexander held her and she clutched him desperately, her powerful emotions for him surging to the surface as she huddled in his muscular arms. She listened to the beating of his wounded heart, not certain how to react to suddenly finding herself in the very place she had wanted to be in since she became Charles' queen.

She melted visibly into the hollows of his body and begged the Saints not to think ill of her now for her gratitude at this moment.

* * *

Nicolai came upstairs from seeing to Nigel and the screaming page and saw Dominic and Michael outside the closed door. "Is the Prince…?"

Dominic nodded. "Yes, he's still in there. The queen is with him."

"The princess is looking for him. Her governess just asked me what that scream was because it frightened the little girl." He knocked on the door, opening it as Alexander released Elizabeth.

"Yes, Nicolai?" Alexander inquired about the guard's interruption while Elizabeth tried to compose herself.

"The princess is looking for His Highness."

Elizabeth looked up quickly. "Don't let her in here. Saint's Blood," she said, turning to Alexander. "What am I going to tell her?"

"Nothing. *I'll* tell her the truth. She deserves that." He escorted the queen out of the room and turned to Nicolai. "Please remove the chair and that rug and destroy them, then get some servants up here to clean up the room. Don't touch the body."

Nicolai got a gritty look in his eyes. "Should I send for the mortician?"

"No. The Rituals involving the transfer of rulership have to be done by the heir. If he is touched by anyone else after he dies, it makes the transfer much harder to accomplish. I'll take care of it when I return."

Nicolai nodded and Alexander took Elizabeth away.

* * *

Dominic watched as the Royal Family departed and Michael went off the other way to see to the arrangements before venturing toward the king's bedroom. Nicolai watched him for a second, then said, "Dom, what are you doing?"

"Something's nagging at me." He opened the door and entered quietly, Nicolai behind him. He looked around the room a moment, then walked over to the desk. He opened the drawers, looked underneath it, behind it and finally found what he was looking for. He held up some blotter paper.

"What's that?" Nicolai looked at the paper Dominic was inspecting.

"Blotter paper. His Majesty always used this to make notes regarding court. Rough drafts and such, so he could do the decrees clean. It was a quirk of his to write up his own decrees, even the long ones. When I was in here earlier, there were several decrees finished on the desk, here. They're not here now. It might explain who killed him and why." He flipped through the pages that were there but found nothing pertaining to that evening's court. He continued to rifle through the desk as Nicolai looked around the room.

A shadow on the portrait of Marie-Elizabeth caught his attention and he moved over to look at it. His eyes widened. A cut was across the throat of the little girl in the portrait and there was blood in the wound. As he stepped closer to examine it, he caught a whiff of a scent which chilled his blood. "Catriona's been here," he said darkly.

Dominic looked up from the pages. "Yes, that's right." He looked at him oddly. "I said so earlier, remember? What makes you mention her now?"

Nicolai looked back at Dominic, then up at the portrait. "Look up there."

Dominic walked over, seeing nothing at first. It wasn't until he was directly under the painting he saw the cut. "Saint's blood, did she do that?"

"I don't know why she would, but it's so subtle, it could be." He looked over at the portrait of Elizabeth where the slash across the throat was more obvious. "Look. She did that one too. And she has been in this room, though whether it was before or after the murder, I can't be sure. The scent of blood is overpowering."

Dominic said. "It was before. She was in here, I believe, when Myrgen was arrested."

Nicolai looked at Dominic. "That's right, you mentioned that earlier. What was the charge again?"

"Treason. Myrgen kidnapped Tanglwyst in order to blackmail Catriona into killing the king. Apparently, it worked."

"He what? He kidnapped *Tanglwyst?*" Nicolai thought

about the last time he had seen her. He had gone to her house to grouse about things at home, knowing in the back of his mind he would get plenty of comfort and sympathy from her, usually in the form of sex. He had gotten terribly drunk on her personal vineyard's wine and she had walked him home because Alan was at home alone. She had taken Alan home with her to keep him safe, but he hadn't seen the boy again. Foolishly, he had believed Catriona had picked the boy up and turned him over to her Caratian friends for the summer just as Tanglwyst left for the sailing season.

Being told now she had been kidnapped quite possibly meant something had happened to Alan as well, and the thought chilled his blood to the bone. "He hasn't been executed, has he?"

"I doubt it. The king wanted him to rot in jail for a few days first. Why?"

"Alan was with Tanglwyst the last time I saw him, and that was several days ago. If he took Tanglwyst, he may also have my son but only he would know for sure. If he's the only one who knows where Tanglwyst is, she may die before we find her." Nicolai took off toward the door.

"Wait. What if he won't tell you where she is?"

Nicolai looked back from the doorway with deadly certainty. "I'll make sure he talks," he growled. "Believe me."

Dominic glanced at the sheaf of blotter papers and stuffed them into his doublet before running off after Nicolai.

*Chapter Thirty:*
*"The way of life is above to the wise, that he may depart*
*from hell beneath."*
*~ Proverbs 15:24*

Catriona and Drake slipped up to the garden as dusk descended. They had acquired a couple of horses and other things to spirit their charges from their confinement and Drake was, as always, prepared for trouble. Catriona had told him of the cramped quarters they were dealing with so he had left his broadsword with Anika, but had still brought three daggers of various sizes. Catriona actually was grateful for this. Myrgen wouldn't be coming after them but Catriona knew Michael was still out there and would be alerted by now to her disloyalty, although she got the impression that Michael was involved in this solely because of his allegiance to Myrgen, and she'd gotten used to following her impressions. Besides, she found she liked the man, in spite of their introduction.

They had wanted to wait until darkness because the cover of night would aid them, as would Michael's obligations elsewhere, as a guard against whomever might be trying to assassinate the king. She believed he would not shirk his duty to feed his hostages, but would probably also not linger or he'd be missed. Catriona motioned for Drake to follow her, and they ran silently to the hedge which hid the passage entrance.

She had told him to feel the walls for they were marked and they moved without a light or a sound through the stone corridors to the crossroads. They listened carefully for sounds of anyone in the underground passages and were rewarded for their caution by the opening of the secret door across from them by Michael. The large guard stepped through with two trays stacked upon each other, holding a small lantern. He dropped a brass mug as the door began to close behind him and he set down the trays and held up the light to retrieve it.

He inspected the mug to be sure it was not ruined and seemed to notice something in the shiny bottom. He held up the lantern and Catriona and Drake saw what the issue was at the same time. Michael wiped his mouth of the red lip rouge smear, irritated by its very existence, then when it was gone, he retrieved the trays and moved on toward the passages above. Catriona and Drake waited until his light was gone, then moved quickly across to the door to where her son and Tanglwyst were being held.

There was a lingering scent near the door, but it was overpowered by the smell of wine which was spilt from the mug. Catriona activated the door and the two colleagues entered the corridor. The farther away from the door they got, the stronger the other scent was until Catriona stopped them and turned to Drake, sniffing. "Do you smell that?"

Drake sniffed the air as well, then asked, "Jasmine?"

"Yes."

"What's it doing *here*?"

"Tanglwyst wears that scent. She's down the hall."

"She's a prisoner with perfumes?"

"Trust me, Drake, it has crossed my mind as well. First things first though." Catriona moved on down the corridor and turned left at the bottom. She felt along the wall to the door to Alan's cell and stood before it, concentrating. "A citizen of Caratia stands behind this door," she intoned, speaking the command. "The Stâpâna demands passage." The door lock popped and the door swung open. The dog and Alan came bounding over to them both, the puppy running back and forth down the corridor. Catriona hugged Alan. "Are you ready to get out of here?"

"Yes!"

Drake reached out and snatched the puppy as it barreled past him and scooped the animal up. He said, "This is not an animal of Caratia. I'm not sure I can settle it down."

Alan stepped over to the dog and touched his head. "Drake, it's time to calm down. You don't want to have to be put in a sack again, do you?" The dog looked at him and stopped squirming. Alan looked up at the Duce. "He'll be fine now."

Drake the Man looked at Drake the Dog, then at Catriona, smiling. "The Land blesses us all. Let's go." They walked down the corridor and left the catacombs through the prison passage. They escaped to the woods in very short order, Catriona knowing the way almost instinctively by now. Outside, they moved in haste to where the horses were hidden. She put Alan on the black horse she had ridden and Drake handed her the puppy as he mounted his own choice. She handed the dog to Drake and then got on behind Alan.

Alan looked at his mother. "What about Lady Tanglwyst? Aren't you going to save her too?"

Catriona looked at Drake and Drake returned the look. Drake said, "No, Alan. We won't."

"Why? Is it because she isn't a Caratian?"

"No," Catriona replied, reining the horse around. "It's because she isn't a prisoner."

They made it quickly back to the Inn and Anika was ready to leave. She, too, had a horse picked out and they had made arrangements for passage with a barge captain a little way down river. Anika took the dog from Catriona and promptly put him in the sack with his head sticking out of the top then popped him into one of the saddlebags on her horse, again with is head sticking out the bag. The puppy started to whine and Alan said, "He doesn't especially like sacks."

"He needs to be contained for the ride, Alan. You don't want to lose him, do you?" Alan shook his head and started whispering to the dog, who calmed down readily.

Drake pulled his horse up alongside the women,. "Let's go." Catriona nodded and glanced back at the palace, trying to say goodbye. She started to mount up when Anika grabbed her arm.

"Wait. You have to go back." Catriona looked at her friend, and Drake turned his horse around to see what the hold up was. Anika stood there, clutching a large black stone with gold flecks that she wore on a chain around her neck. It glowed and pulsed. "The one for you needs you right now. You must go to him." She turned and pointed at the palace. "He is there. The Land will guide you."

"Now?"

"Yes."

Catriona looked at the palace and swallowed, then back at her Ducesâ. "Take care of Alan."

Drake said, "We won't let anything happen to him. Go."

Catriona got on her horse and rode away from her family.

* * *

Alexander sat in the chair in Marie-Elizabeth's room and told her about the death of the king. The governess was in tears and weeping quietly so as not to disturb the little girl. It wasn't working. Marie-Elizabeth was crying because the adults were and Alexander felt sorry for the child. They gave her some food and he put her down for the night. Elizabeth and Alexander had just stepped into the hall when they overheard the guards at the end of the hall talking.

"No, he just came in and said he wanted to question the prisoner alone. Looked angry as hell but that Myrgen deserves whatever he gets at the hands of Nicolai, after what he done."

Elizabeth said, "Saint's Blood," paling visibly and took off toward the stairs. "Alexander, what if he kills Myrgen?"

"What if? He conspired to kill my brother. He'll be hung for treason anyway. If he dies now or dies later, he's still dead."

Elizabeth turned on Alexander. "I'm not going to stand by and let him be killed. If he is, we may never find Tanglwyst. Now show me where the holding cells are."

Alexander took the lead and Elizabeth followed him into the dungeons of the palace. Their rush alerted the guards and a group of them followed the pair quickly. The sight which met their eyes, though Alexander had no love of Myrgen to lose, only served to emphasize Alexander's loathing of Nicolai.

The floor of the holding cell was splattered with blood and Myrgen's face was badly bruised. He was lying on his side, bound and curled in pain as Nicolai delivered another bloodying blow. Dominic entered the room then and drew back a bit as he surveyed the carnage before them. Nicolai grabbed Myrgen by the bloody robe. "Tell me where Tanglwyst is or I swear I'll kill you right here."

Myrgen summoned up reserves of strength from inside. "If you kill me, you idiot, you'll never find her. She'll die before she's discovered."

"Where's my son, you *cur*? Did you take him too? Or did you just kill him?"

"Maybe I sold him. You ever think of that?"

Nicolai moved to swing again when Alexander grabbed his fist, restraining him. "What are you doing?" The Prince looked into the guardsman's rancorous eyes for a moment, and saw the beast within the man up close, much closer than he ever wanted to be. Elizabeth ran over to Myrgen.

"He took Tanglwyst three nights ago. My *son* was with her that night and I haven't seen him since."

"You haven't seen your son in three days and it's just bothering you *now?*" Alexander suddenly had more than enough reason to hate this man.

"That's because he's such a loving father," Myrgen stabbed.

"*Shut up.*" Nicolai looked back at the scrutinizing gaze of the Prince and explained, "My wife and I are separating. I thought *she* had taken the boy with her."

Alexander had restrained his own beast until now only because he saw such an ugly creature in Nicolai right then. If Myrgen had taken Alan, Alexander would kill him personally. The problem Alexander had was why Catriona wouldn't have told him that. Regardless, he refused to turn into the monster Nicolai seemed so ready to be. He released Nicolai's arm, who shrugged off the Prince's cautions with a glare but didn't lash out again. He wished he could see Catriona now and have her explain herself, explain this whole thing, but he knew what he would get: Enigma. She couldn't read him, so she kept as many secrets as she did in an attempt to maintain a balance within. He had always found this exotic and alluring, but now it was irritating.

Elizabeth pushed over to Myrgen and inspected his wounds. He looked at her with restrained affection, and turned away from her. "Your Majesty, please…"

Nicolai echoed Myrgen's restraint. "Your Majesty, get away from that creature. He's dangerous."

"The only 'dangerous' one I see here right now is you, Nicolai. Are you drunk again? That's usually when you solve things with your fists." She returned her attention to Myrgen as Nicolai took a step back, her intimate knowledge of his temper unseating him.

Alexander looked at the man again. *Elizabeth would only know that if Tanglwyst told her, which would mean Nicolai has raised a hand against someone in a drunken rage. Saint's blood. If he's hurt Catriona or Alan, no amount of distance would be enough for him to survive my wrath.*

"He's responsible for murdering the king," Nicolai said, trying again.

"No. You're wrong." She looked at the three men in turn. Alexander cautious, Dominic judgmental, Nicolai just vicious. "You said yourself, Dominic, he was imprisoned this morning. He couldn't have done it."

"Regardless, he is guilty, Your Majesty," Dominic said. "This morning, the king revealed Myrgen had hired an assassin to kill him. I told you about it, remember? He's kidnapped Tanglwyst and may plan to kill her too, if he hasn't already."

"Don't be ridiculous, Dominic," Elizabeth said, looking into Myrgen's still handsome face and untying his hands. "He wouldn't kill his own sister." Elizabeth regarded Myrgen's eyes nonchalantly as they scolded her for letting that secret out, then looked over at Nicolai who stood stunned by this news, his anger knocked out of him as surely as if by a punch to the stomach.

"His sister?"

"Yes," Myrgen said, wiping the blood from his mouth with the back of his hand, "so I don't think you'll be getting my blessing on your wedding anytime soon." He coughed and spit out a mouthful of blood.

Dominic recovered quickly, having known this for months but only now remembering,. "Regardless, Your Majesty, he *did* order the king's death. He's a traitor. Whomever he had kill the king is planning on killing the princess as well as you, we believe."

Elizabeth looked up at Dominic, as both Myrgen and Alexander stared in disbelief at the young Mandian. "What?"

"The portraits of the princess and the queen in the king's bedroom have had their throats cut with the very blade which murdered the king. They were both marred with his blood."

Myrgen looked at Elizabeth, trying to ascertain what was going on. Elizabeth stood, looking down at him, her eyes and voice turning cold. "Regardless, you won't get the names of his conspirators from him, Nicolai, by any means. They would be killed immediately. All of them. That probably means the boy as well." Myrgen's eyes widened at her comment and dropped in shock to the floor. Elizabeth turned to Nicolai. "So you can stop this brutality immediately, Nicolai. As Alexander already said," she looked over her shoulder at Myrgen, "he's dead already. Nothing can change that now." She returned her attention to the other three men. "Does anyone know who the assassin is?"

"Well, yes, Your Majesty." Dominic looked quickly at Nicolai. "I believe I do. Her name is Catriona."

Myrgen sat up and looked at his accuser. "How do you know that?"

"I saw her in the prayer niche after you… left this morning."

"You actually *saw* her?" Elizabeth had a shaky edge to her voice that caught Alexander's attention. "Are you sure?"

"Well, not exactly, Your Majesty. I saw a shadow in the prayer room."

"A shadow…And you didn't tell anyone a shadow was in His Majesty's prayer room who might be an assassin?" Elizabeth's tone was deadly, implying she was in a hanging mood.

"He knew." Myrgen spoke up, concern on his face that Dominic might end up where he was. "He showed her to me, gloating that she was his personal assassin I had tried to hire. But only I hired her, Alexander. Dominic didn't know anything about this. No one did."

"But you knew her already?" Alexander looked at Dominic, trying to sort out what he was hearing. "In the chambers, you said you knew her."

Nicolai said, "So did you."

Alexander glanced at Nicolai like he was an annoying gnat beneath his notice and kept his focus on Dominic.

"She's killed half my family in her time," Dominic said.

"Killed them…? Which family members?"

"Marco and Jean Giovanni, among others."

Alexander spat. "Close family?"

Dominic's eyes flicked to the strong reaction to the names, and spoke very carefully. "No, Your Highness. Despicable vermin."

"Good answer." Alexander turned to leave.

Elizabeth said, "What about him?" She nodded to Myrgen.

Alexander looked at Myrgen, who flicked his eyes between the assembled individuals. He was filled with rage that Myrgen would lay a hand on Alan, and fully expected Catriona to exact her revenge upon him. However, she couldn't very well do that with a hundred guards and onlookers. Alexander smiled. "You threatened a woman's child, Myrgen, a woman you clearly know nothing about." He looked at Nicolai. "You want to know the fate I choose for him, Nicolai? Remove every guard from this area immediately." He returned his gaze to Myrgen. "I want him unguarded and alone. Fewer witnesses." Alexander turned and left, Elizabeth right behind him.

*Chapter Thirty-one:*
*"The fear of the wicked, it shall come upon him, but the desire of the righteous shall be granted."*
*~ Proverbs 10:24*

"Alexander, may I speak with you?" Elizabeth made sure they were out of earshot of the others with a glance.

"I'm afraid I'm not feeling very talkative right now, Elizabeth." She looked away, and he sighed, leaning his head back against the wall. "I'm sorry. Please, what did you need?"

"I had a question about this Catriona person everyone seems to know, including you, and Charles. Did, did you know he knew her?"

Alexander looked down the stairway towards the cells. "No. I didn't know they kept in touch at all."

"But you knew they knew each other."

Alexander nodded, almost to himself. "Yes."

Elizabeth leaned against the wall as well, letting out a long breath. "Could they have been... Was she his mistress?"

He looked at Elizabeth, feeling her pain at the king's blatant infidelity, then looked away, the thought of Catriona and Charles together blistering on his soul. *Where was she? Why did that image keep coming up?* "I don't think so. Catriona never would have allowed such a thing with Charles. He's married."

"What other kind of relationship could they have had, Alex? If she was in the prayer room, she obviously has been through the labyrinth, otherwise the guards would have prevented her from entering. That place is a knotwork of passages. I have my ways marked so I know where I'm at, and *I* live here. How can she know the way into his bedroom unless she's been there before?"

Alexander disliked the precision with which she managed to nail his fears to the wall. "The same way she knew her way into mine. She has infallible direction sense. It's necessary on the sea. Besides, the passage to Charles room is direct. No twists or openings that connect with the labyrinth. He designed it that way."

Elizabeth looked stunned at what she was hearing. "What do you mean *your* bedroom?" She stood, jealousy prickling her anger to waken in her voice. "When was she in *your* bedroom?"

"She came to me today, about midday. She said she had been in the area. We... talked... for a while before the servants brought up supper."

"In the area? Through the catacombs?" The queen's glare accused Alexander. "And the two of you '*talked*,' did you?" Elizabeth looked incensed. "So she killed my husband and, to reward herself, she bedded to you right afterward? What kind of monster is this woman?"

Alexander bristled. "Watch your step, Elizabeth. I said we *talked.* She wouldn't sleep with me, even though we wanted to. Besides, I'm sure she had nothing to do with Charles' death. For one thing, there was no blood on her anywhere."

"*Anywhere*, eh?" Elizabeth crossed her arms angrily. "I'm sure you inspected her thoroughly."

Alexander looked at her pointedly. "Yes. *Anywhere*. That mess in his room would have gotten on whomever did this, at least somewhat. There were bloody footprints and drops of blood in the hallway, the prayer nave, everywhere. If Catriona were going to murder someone, there would be no trace of her. Catriona's a good person though. She would never hurt Charles. You're going in the wrong direction, Elizabeth." He pushed off the wall and started up the stairs again.

"Then where *should* I be looking, Alexander?" Her voice maintained its edge and she stood with her hands on her hips, eyes flashing anger.

"At whomever might be wanting to clear Myrgen of these charges. Killing the king while he was in prison is a pretty good alibi. Get some sleep, Elizabeth."

\* \* \*

Myrgen listened intently to the conversation between Elizabeth and Alexander. Stairwells were perfect sound funnels, even the curved ones like the ones that entered the holding area. Myrgen listened to the two of them and caught the flash of jealousy she was striking out with. *What was going on here? Were Alexander and the queen sleeping together? And Alexander's biting remark to Elizabeth to watch her step. He had all but admitted to the desire to be with the pirate woman. What did the Catriona  mean to the Prince?*  Myrgen sighed, his strength waning in the night as he felt sick from the fight, and lack of food. He had no idea what the dynamic was here, but he clearly didn't know one tenth of what was going on. Catriona knowing the king was one thing. Knowing the Prince was not a far stretch, but to hear they were on intimate terms was quite another story. She knew her way around the labyrinth enough to get into not only Charles' room, but Alexander's as well. That worried him.

*Tanglwyst had been adamant about not being seen by Catriona. Something about her being able to see through people.* Myrgen leaned against the stone wall of the cell, his stomach churning and cramping. He had been sick earlier shortly after he had gotten thrown into the cell, but he figured that was just nerves. The sound beating at Nicolai's fists didn't help him at all. He focused his energies, trying to draw from an area that wasn't wounded, and eventually found his feet weren't all that sore. He closed his eyes and thought of healing poultices and stitches closing his wounds, cold water slowing the swelling in his cheek and the throbbing in his jaw. He was grateful no bones got broken. He exhaled, expelling the pain in his body and opened his eyes.

He looked around the cell and crawled over to the pile of ancient straw. He rolled onto his back and closed his eyes, trying not to listen for things traveling through the mattress. Alexander was right. Whomever killed Charles had absolved Myrgen of the crime, whether intentionally or not. But Myrgen shuddered at the thought that Alexander felt the best punishment he could throw at Myrgen was to leave him unguarded so Catriona could get to him. He felt absolutely certain he was right in his assessment.

*Ah, I deserve what I get. I never should have allowed that child to stay taken.* Myrgen sighed. Elizabeth had made herself immensely clear. If he told about her or Tanglwyst's part in this, they would both be put to death as traitors. She was right. He had to keep it as just his idea.

* * *

Dominic and Nicolai stood outside the prison area, Nicolai giving orders to the guard to leave the prisoner alone. The palace holding area was rarely used, especially with the State prison nearby, and Dominic wondered why Charles had chosen to house Myrgen here instead of in the Bathory like other enemies of the State. The more he thought about the whole thing, the more confused he became. The king knew Catriona and seemed to trust her, but Myrgen hired her to kill Charles. She betrayed Myrgen to the king because Myrgen kidnapped Tanglwyst and blackmailed Catriona into doing the deed. Then why turn Myrgen in? Wouldn't that endanger Tanglwyst's life? And Catriona's son? He never thought of Catriona as a maternal sort, but she wouldn't endanger her son. He felt quite certain of that.

"Something's not right, Nicolai," Dominic said as the guards went off to their other duties. "This smells like a set up."

Nicolai looked at the thin young man. "What does?"

"This whole thing." Dominic said, throwing his arms open. "The king is murdered and all the evidence points to Myrgen. He kidnapped Tanglwyst to blackmail Catriona into killing the king. Except Tanglwyst is Myrgen's sister and not likely to be in any real danger. So where is she? Some country manor house somewhere? Does she even know she's reported missing?"

"I don't know, but that's an interesting point. It's one *I'd* prefer. That way, if she's still got my son, he'd be safe."

"It's all wrong."

"Well, I agree with that."

Dominic looked around. "I'm going to go. Good night, Nicolai." The young D'Medici stepped out of the corridor and headed upstairs.  He needed to talk to Gwen. She may not be literate, but she was sharp and, more importantly, she knew Catriona. Dominic had some theories, but he wanted to talk them through, or at least think them through.

Ever since the other night when Gwen had showed up at the palace for the meeting with the queen, Dominic had been certain Catriona's target was Elizabeth and he felt pretty certain Nicolai must have suspected something because he put extra guards on her immediately. Dominic remembered the Prince signing a receipt for extra pay for guards working longer hours and he had seen the extra contingent at her door.

Now the queen was showing mercy to a man accused of conspiracy to commit regicide, a man who had just this morning responded like a man in love who was no longer unrequited.  He was accused of a murder so sloppy, Dominic couldn't do it that badly, and he had never killed anyone. He couldn't even claim responsibility for the destruction of that Giovanni cretin. For all he had been saying what the Prince wanted to hear, he was also speaking the truth. The world was a better place without that man.

Dominic's own experience with the man had been enough to convince him of that. It felt like he was being duped, and he absolutely hated being duped.

Gwen. Gwen would know what Catriona was doing with the queen. It was unlikely Catriona was working with Myrgen, but someone was. Maybe Gwen could help him figure it out.

The time had come to actually ask her.

## Chapter Thirty-two:
*"A false witness shall not be unpunished, and he that speaketh lies shall not escape."*
*~ Proverbs 19:5*

Michael watched the queen return to her chambers for the night and stood outside in the hall, thinking. His experience with Tanglwyst had disgusted him beyond his level for tolerance and he decided he didn't want to return to that place again. She had been naked when he had arrived and had grabbed onto his hand, almost dumping her supper onto the floor. Michael had set the tray of food on the desk and tried to extract his hand from her deceptively strong grip. When he succeeded, she had grabbed him by the penis, his simple breeches sporting a modest codpiece which she had reached right under to take hold of him. She then pulled him toward her, laying back and spreading her legs. He had moved forward but not fast enough, and she had actually gotten a good part of his member out of his breeches before he stopped her.

She had gotten rude then, demanding his submission to her because she was his superior. She then grabbed him by the doublet and kissed him, very much against his will. He was trying to tuck himself back into his breeches and her effort unbalanced him, causing him to partially fall upon her. She reeked of perfumes and was made up almost to excess and she offended him intensely. Mervol women put him off immensely. He had pushed off her and staggered back against the door, ready this time to slap her if she came at him again but she had just lay on the bed and he took the chance to leave her.

Despite this repeated aggression, he found he couldn't walk away at that point, however. The boy needed him to survive. Myrgen wouldn't betray the queen or his sister, regardless of whether or not they would betray him, but that meant Michael needed to keep bringing them food so they would be able to survive long enough to be rescued. He didn't know exactly how that would happen but he hoped it would happen soon. Part of him wanted to go down to the dungeons and sleep outside the boy's room to make sure he was safe but he knew the boy's door was locked and Tanglwyst's wasn't. Michael was especially grateful for that now because at least Alan was protected from Tanglwyst's presence, although he was sure her lustful flesh only cried out for fully developed men.

Michael decided to go to Myrgen's room. There were two guards outside it and Michael requested entry. "What is your purpose in the room, Michael?"

"I was told my Master is accused of treason because of things found in his room. Is this true?"

The guard on the left said, "Oh yes. The room is covered in damning evidence. Once the Queen-Mother sees this, Myrgen's head will roll *that* dawn."

"May I see it?"

The guard on the right said, "I don't know...no one's supposed to go in because they want the room intact when the Queen-Mother returns."

"I won't touch anything and you can watch me, if you like."

The guard on the left nodded to the guard on the right and they opened the door. Michael looked at the planted evidence and found something which he wasn't expecting. He perceived a scent of perfume, and thought at first it was a holdover from the incident in the dungeons with Tanglwyst. Then he realized that the scent was a different one than the one Tanglwyst had been wearing when he saw her an hour ago. This scent was also hers, he still recognized it, but it was the one she was wearing yesterday. He found it odd he would notice something so minute. That had never happened before.

What that told him was that Tanglwyst had been in here before she got washed and made up for Michael's visit. This meant she had put this blood here, betraying her brother. He shook his head and left the room, thanking the guards as he did so. He walked down to the unguarded holding cells and went to Myrgen's cell, but the man was thoroughly unconscious, clothes belying a severe beating. They weren't as bad as they should have been, judging by the damage to his clothes, but he also knew Myrgen could heal himself of most superficial wounds through some mental technique he learned in his travels before he met the man. If the damage were too great, and internal injuries could be fatal, Myrgen couldn't heal those and Michael watched his companion's breathing to make sure he would not die in his sleep.

Myrgen's chest fell and rose with no trouble and Michael left him to sleep. He couldn't risk moving him at this moment.

There were too many people around. The guards were gone from this area for some reason, but they were everywhere above, like circling vultures, waiting for the lion to finish. Michael found he could no longer tolerate being ordered by Nicolai. His ruthless bludgeoning of Michael's master had been spoken of with great reverence by the guards, and snapped that cord as well. They say the guilty will get some sleep once they are caught because they know they have an ordeal ahead of them, and there was no doubt Myrgen was indeed guilty of conspiracy against the king. But not of murder. The blood in his room indicated someone was a lot more bloody than him, and Michael now knew who it was.

He stood before his master's cell and tried to think of what to do. He needed help. With Myrgen being held, he wasn't sure how long it would be before he would likewise be thrown in a cell. Myrgen had always been a buffer between the guards and him. With his master accused of murder, it wouldn't be long before he, too, would be implicated. And he was no good to Myrgen if he was in the cell next to the man. He decided to go to the dungeons and check on Alan and his dog, and perhaps he would stay down there for the night. He didn't like having the boy so close to that woman unguarded, especially if she was capable all this. Michael left the holding cells with haste, the image of Tanglwyst trying to open the door to Alan's cell flashing across his mind's eye. He didn't know what this new perception was or why he felt so aware all of a sudden, but he considered it a gift of the Land and was going to use it. He closed the door to the holding cell area and proceeded to the garden.

* * *

Catriona sat on the floor of the catacombs and wiped the tears from her cheeks. Her entry into the labyrinth to see Alexander had been interrupted by the sound of voices from the area where she had first been taken. She worried that someone was being tortured, possibly Myrgen, and she was not yet comfortable with that idea. She could see he was but a pawn in this and all the signs indicated he was a very reluctant pawn at that. He had tried to protect her son, not use him. It mattered to her. She had heard Nicolai's fury through the stone walls separating them and tried to find a way in to the area to stop him. She knew Myrgen's situation better than Nicolai did and she wanted to stop him from destroying this man. It was made worse by Alexander's comment that, after three days, Nicolai was only now realizing Alan was missing. His lack of concern for their son was disgusting and she was glad to be rid of him. She would accept no more pain at his hands. Alan was safe.

The thing that hurt the most was the knowledge now that Charles was dead. She had sat in the corridor and let the tears roll down her face, apologizing to Charles for not being there for him when he actually needed her. He had been there for her at her critical time of need, but she had failed him. Yet another man she had abandoned when he needed her most. Well, that wasn't going to happen again. She stood up and started moving towards Tanglwyst. She wasn't going to let Myrgen take the fall for this, even if it meant throwing herself on the mercy of a Mervolingian court led by Catherine D'Medici. One look, and Catriona would know whether or not Tanglwyst was the one doing this to them.

She walked down the passageway, then went to the passage where Tanglwyst was. If Catriona was going to do anything with Tanglwyst, it needed to be tonight. Tomorrow, when Michael came down to feed his charges in the morning and found Alan missing, the smart money said they would move Tanglwyst and Catriona would have missed her chance.

It was surprise which registered on Tanglwyst's face when Catriona entered the room. She was definitely not expecting to see Catriona and almost screamed. The mysterious pirate billowed in as was her normal wont, and stood in the doorway, blocking Tanglwyst's exit. "Ah, so *here* you are."

"C-Catriona...."

"My Lady," Catriona said in a strong, quick voice, "I believe it's time we got you out of here."

"Get me out? What do you mean?" Tanglwyst asked, worried.

"Well, the king is dead and Myrgen's been arrested. I thought that might be important to you."

"Yes, of course it is...but why are *you* here?"

"Well, after we got Alan out of this place, I noticed the light on here in this room and decided to come back and check it out. I'm impressed your captors let you have so much luxury. Not very common among the torture set."

"Well, my captors understood the amount of trouble they would be in if either me or your son were injured in any way. Consequently, they treated *me* very well. How was your son?"

"They gave him a puppy to keep him company. I thought that was a very kind gesture."

Tanglwyst smiled. "Yes, that was." She looked around her and grabbed some riding breeches.

Catriona watched her, timing her moves and comments carefully. "May I ask you something, My Lady? Why did Myrgen choose me? Why didn't he go with someone else?"

Tanglwyst looked around for her riding doublet and began pulling it on, carefully weighing her answer. "Probably because you were local, and you had a distinct advantage to understand their cause. After all, you have been abused and destroyed by men, yet still managed to rise above all that. You are ruthless and can be counted on to do whatever job you've been set to do. Why *wouldn't* they choose you?"

"Because I told them no."

"Well, they must have been very determined." Tanglwyst pulled on her traveling shoes and stood up. "Shall we go?"

Catriona turned around to open the door. Tanglwyst grabbed a knife from the tray of dishes from supper and followed the dark woman out the door. Catriona caught the gesture and prepared herself for the attack, smiling. They had barely cleared the doorjamb when Tanglwyst lunged at her back. Catriona was in front of her enemy specifically so she could watch the rich woman's shadow and sidestepped the blow, grabbing Tanglwyst's arm and throwing her into the corridor. Catriona reached back and closed the door, plunging the hallway into utter darkness.

Catriona listened to Tanglwyst try to get her bearings plotting her escape through the catacombs. She probably thought she could trap Catriona in the ancient chapel by closing the stone door behind her but Catriona knew the Land would never allow that. Catriona could feel it in the pulse of the stone around her. Air held no quarter in this place and the earth empowered its champion. She felt the movement through the ground and gauged her opponent's location by the tremors. She brought her booted foot down on Tanglwyst's ankle, pinning her, and the Mervolwoman cried out in pain. Tanglwyst swiveled around and struck out with her knife toward the offending foot. Catriona anticipated the attack and moved her foot out of the way a mere moment before the knife plunged down, causing Tanglwyst to impale her own foot.

Tanglwyst screamed out in agony and Catriona stepped in and kicked the woman in the face. Her scream ended suddenly, and Tanglwyst growled in the dark.

"You set me up," Catriona spoke into the blackness, her voice silken poison once again. The tunnel hurled the sound everywhere and Catriona could hear the fear in her rival's voice. "What were you going to do if Myrgen or Michael had killed me with that poison?"

"Do? I'll tell you what I was going to do. I was going to *celebrate*.... I was going to bed your husband and remind him what a *real woman* was like. I was going to collect the money Dominic owed me from *your wretched Giovanni inheritance* and then sit back and raise *your son* while Nicolai showered gifts upon us bought with *your blood money.* That's what I was going to do."

"I see. And your brother? Where was he going to be in all this?"

Tanglwyst panted, her breath ragged from what sounded like a bloody nose. "Elizabeth. He was going to be with Elizabeth."

"Except that Elizabeth was not going to be there for him."

"You can't know that."

Catriona got right in Tanglwyst's ear. "Oh, can't I?" she dodged back as Tanglwyst sliced out with the knife in Catriona's direction, but she misjudged and Catriona heard her slam her hand into a rock. She screamed and Catriona crouched on the ground, turning her head to project her voice off the stony ground. The sound bounced everywhere, surrounding Tanglwyst and disguising Catriona's true location. "I am going to give you what you want, woman. I am going to give you a man who will be incensed to rage over your welfare. A man who will stop at nothing to be by your side, who will scream your love from the street corners. I will give you a man who will demand he is the only one, and who will ensure it. You want this man I left? He's yours."

She stood and sent a violent, well placed kick to Tanglwyst's chest, slamming her into the wall. Tanglwyst lost her breath and vomited. The small amount of light coming from the room Tanglwyst had inhabited was like daylight to Catriona and as she stepped up to her former employer in the velvet darkness,

Tanglwyst looked up behind her just in time to see the bottom of Catriona's boot heel crash down. Her grip on the knife melted away as the darkness became thick and muddy, enveloping her completely.

* * *

Michael stepped into the catacombs behind the hedge and walked purposefully to the crossroads. He had gotten very accustomed to the tunnels beneath the palace and had even gotten permission to put some torches in the crossroads in the past but found them unnecessary. Once a person got to the crossroads, there was a lot more ambient light from the chapel by the crypts. He stepped into the crossroads and decided to light a torch for the trip down the steps into the former chapel's foundations because the stairs could be treacherous in the dark.

The torch from the wall cast the light onto the hidden doorway to the area where Tanglwyst and Alan were being held and Michael was about to trigger the opening when the door fell open in a whoosh. Michael stood with the light expecting Tanglwyst and got a very different face looking at him than he ever anticipated. Catriona looked into his eyes and his gaze met and matched hers. She had no signs of their last meeting but she seemed to have been in a bit of a tussle more recently. He looked down at her feet and saw Tanglwyst, unconscious, on the stairs behind her.

Catriona called the visions on Michael. She saw his kindness to her son, as well as his dislike of Tanglwyst. She confirmed his loyalty to Myrgen while still maintaining his own convictions and she saw he was coming down to watch over her son right then. Michael leaned over and shed the torch light upon the still form on the ground behind Catriona, then straightened up and asked, "Is she dead?"

"No."

"Is the boy gone?"

"Yes."

Michael looked at the body on the floor again. "Would you like some help?"

**Chapter Thirty-three:**
*"An inheritance may be gotten hastily at the beginning, but the end thereof shall not be blessed."*
*~ Proverbs 20:21*

The pounding on the door made Gwen jump, her heart leaping into her throat in fear and surprise. She got up and pulled on a blue tartan Caratian coatdress Catriona had given her and answered the door. It was made of blue wool which was woven with a simple plaid and the mixing of cultures had always made Dominic cringe. Gwen opened the door, actually expecting Catriona, and was surprised to find Dominic outside. It was cold and he was dressed in a heavy cloak, giving him a rather ominous appearance. Gwen got worried that something had happened to Catriona and asked in a frightened voice, "What is it?"

Dominic, mindful of their last encounter and how it was not yet resolved, asked, "May I come in?"

Gwen blinked at his use of manners towards her, not sure if she should be grateful or insulted. "Of course. Let me grab some wood and I'll get the fire going again."

Dominic said, "I'll get it." He went to the side of the house and picked up several pieces, carrying them in past a very surprised Gweneviere. She stepped inside and closed the door.

"What's going on?"

Dominic looked up from setting the wood in a stack next to the fireplace. "Nothing. I just need to talk some things through and I thought... Why?"

"You never do menial tasks. Ever."

Dominic went back to stacking the wood by the hearth, then took the last piece and put it on the coals. "Maybe I realized how foolish I've been recently." He turned his doe eyes on her and stood. "I'm sorry, Gwen. I was an ass."

Gwen came over and hugged him and he smelled her hair and smiled. She looked up at him. "I'll get some wine mulling."

"Thank you." He turned back to the fire as the log caught. His cloak swished in the silence, and the sounds of a simple home warmed his heart. Wood popping, ceramic mugs clunking together, the splash of poured wine from a modest salary. *Simple pleasures making heaven available to the masses, if they would just take the time to see them.*

"What did you want to talk about?" Gwen brought the ceramic ewer over to the hearth and set it on one of the many ring stains on the stones, making a new one.

"When you came to the palace the other night, you were doing something for Catriona, right?"

Gwen sat down. "Yes. I was delivering a note."

"From Catriona?"

"Not exactly."

"I'm sorry, but this is rather serious, Gwen. The king is dead and there are a lot of unanswered questions."

Gwen swallowed, her eyes wide. "What? Charles is dead?" She looked at the fire, dazed, then she blinked, turning sharp, worried eyes on Dominic. "What about Alexander? Is he hurt?"

"No, no," Dominic said, raising his hands. "He's fine." He watched her as she settled down. "See, that's why I wanted to talk to you. Charles has been sick for a month now, and you know that, but you immediately thought it was something violent that did him in."

"Was it?"

"Oh yes. You were right to be worried. It was horrible." Dominic wet his lips and undid his cloak clasp as the room became warmer. "Thing is, I want to make sure others aren't in danger too. Gwen, tell me what you know. Tell me what's going on."

"Well, I don't know everything, but I'll tell you what I can. A few days ago, Alan was taken from Tanglwyst home along with her. Catriona got hit with a dart or needle coming out of the Inn where Drake and Anika were going to be staying and ended up in a cell or something in the catacombs under the palace. Myrgen was there, and so was Michael. Myrgen told her he needed her to murder the king. He left and then Michael was going to hit her with a dart or something but Catriona got a look at one of the things. She said it was coated with poison, the killing kind, not the sleeping kind."

"That doesn't make any sense. Why go to all the trouble to secure her services specifically, then try to actually kill her?"

"She didn't know, but she got Michael to knock her out with a punch instead."

"How did she do that?"

Gwen arched an eyebrow and cocked her mouth.

Dominic nodded. "How could she be sure he wouldn't poke

her with the poison?"

Gwen kept her facial expression.

Dominic waved at her and sat back in the chair. "All right, all right. So then she got dumped here, so I would find her. That must have been Myrgen's doing. That feels very much like him. So much of this feel like him and so much of it feels exactly the opposite."

Gwen leaned forward, soaking up some of the heat now seeping into the stones around the hearth with her feet. "Well, how can you be sure? How well do you know him?"

Dominic raised his eyebrows, taking a deep breath as he thought about his answer. "Well, I met the man through Tanglwyst, that one Twelfth Night after he returned from Yndia. Remember? He brought her all those bright colored silks? Before that, I didn't even know she had a brother, but apparently she has a few. Morgan, who lives in St. Marguerite, Caiaphas in Mande and Myrgen. I didn't know him at all then but in the past year I've worked with him, I've come to respect his abilities quite a bit. He's so insidious sometimes, I was beginning to think he was Mandian. I've seen investigations into activities I'm almost certain he's involved in suddenly hit a dead end, emphasis on the 'dead'

"That's how Myrgen is. He decides what he wants done, then hires someone to hire someone to hire someone to do it The third person down from him comes up dead and there's absolutely no way to trace it to him. He's very meticulous about such things. He'd never get caught up on something like hiring the king's personal assassin to do this. Someone would have told him, or he would have suspected."

"Wow, he's that good?"

"Let's put it this way: I want to be Myrgen when I grow up."

"'Personal assassin?'"

Dom shrugged. "That's what he called her."

Gwen reached out and turned the ewer to warm the other side of the pot. "So, you think he didn't have anything to do with the poison, or what?"

Dominic shook his head. "No. Personally, I think the two are isolated. I think we're looking at more than one entity working here. If Myrgen hired Catriona, he would have done it with money. He would never kidnap her son. That just makes a person who has a reason to seek vengeance upon you, and if he even knows who Catriona is, he knows she's not the kind of person who you want to give a reason to seek vengeance upon you. I can vouch for that."

"You can?"

"Oh yes. I hired her to deal with Giovanni." Gwen's questioning look was met with a nod. "Granted, she took the job immediately but the *way* she did it? Amazing. I had some spies on hand, keeping track of her progress and the report they sent back said the Giovanni was on the roof of his castle the night before his wedding. He was raving about a ghost or something. He turned and saw his son and heir coming out of the castle onto the courtyard and he pulled a crossbow from on of the battlements and shot him, right through the heart.

"The son fell and Giovanni screamed in rage and charged at someone else, hurling himself off the other side of the casement. He had lost an eye in a battle with invaders in a nearby village years before and they suspect he couldn't properly gauge how far from the battlement he actually was. However, Catriona came back to Patras a week later and I knew it was all her. Your mistress, Gwen, she's a very dangerous individual to get on the wrong side of."

"So you don't think Myrgen did this. You don't think Catriona did this. Who do you think did this then?"

"I don't know. Who would have a grudge against both Catriona and Charles, but still be crafty enough to pull this off?" A long, slow heartbeat later, the two looked at each other.

In unison, they said, "Tanglwyst."

* * *

Catriona and Michael carried Tanglwyst's limp form out of the tunnel and into the crossroads. They looked around and Catriona said, "This way." They moved down by the passages that went near the cells and the torture chamber where she had met Michael and Myrgen.

He seemed to realize where they were because he said, "I'm sorry about all this."

She looked at him. "All this?" She backed down the stone corridor, glancing over her shoulder.

"The boy was never supposed to be involved."

"I know."

"Neither were you."

"I know that too."

Michael took a deep breath. "He's not a bad man."

"What?"

"Myrgen, he's," Michael shifted his hold, going under her arms to get a better grip, "he's not a bad man. He's just been forced to do some bad things."

Catriona stopped and looked at Michael. She took a deep breath and called the visions forth. *Michael captured with the blood of a lion on his hands from his rite of passage, fighting his way out of a bar, Myrgen stopping him from being put to death for attacking his captors, Myrgen treating him like a person.*

*And something else... Alexander giving something to Myrgen, saying "He asked me to give you this." Myrgen opening his hand to see a silver piece, then closing his hand over it, his heart breaking.*

She looked at Tanglwyst's body and then back at Michael, overwhelmingly saddened by the final vision. "Then help me make it right. Who gave you the poison to put on those darts you were trying to stick me with when we met?"

He nodded to Tanglwyst. "She did."

"Where did she get it?"

"I don't know. The vials were at her house. I had to go there to get them after she was taken. I suppose she had it made."

Catriona nodded. *Apparently, I have a visit to make after we're done here.* She continued down the corridor that led outside.

## Chapter Thirty-four:
### *"The sprit of a man will sustain his infirmity, but of a wounded spirit, who can bear?"*
### *~ Proverbs 18:14*

Nicolai grumbled at the darkness as he left the holding cells. He didn't agree with Alexander's assessment of how to deal with this problem. He must figure Catriona might return and kill Myrgen if given the chance, to cover her tracks. Either Alexander really didn't know the woman, or Nicolai didn't. He had searched for word of his wife for five years after he left their village and never heard a thing. She knew how to disappear. Whether Myrgen breathed or not would mean nothing to her if she had killed His Majesty. She would leave, probably never to be seen again on Mervol foam or soil.

It bothered him that Alexander might know Catriona. She had told him that she had given her heart to another last summer, someone he found out later was named Grymalkin. That name was insufficient for him to find the man, but apparently, he was from St. Giles or Genoa. That didn't really narrow the area, since those towns were on entirely different ends of this continent. She never revealed his identity, especially after his blunder with telling her he almost called out Tanglwyst's name during their last and only coupling. He had foolishly thought if he told her that, she would tell him the name of her lover. But she had seen through his ruse, and not spoken to him for a week.

Nicolai needed to think this through. He wished he had someone to talk it through with, but the only person he would do something like that with was missing. He could not believe how much he missed his Tanglwyst. Every hour, he caught himself having to stop and exhale as a vision of the last time they made love would suddenly dominate his brain. He would smell her skin or feel her touch and it was maddening. He needed her more than he needed his next breath. But mostly, he needed a drink.

He walked down the busy halls, the clunk of his boots striking the stones blending so far into the ambient noise of the castle as to make them soundless. The palace never slept. There was always someone up, someone moving, someone doing things. The shifts in the kitchen rotated like large gears, the ovens baking or the stoves bubbling. The stables were one of the few places that was quiet in the night, with the only sounds often being sleeping horses and occasionally coupling young people.

He went off the palace grounds, looking for a drink. The tavern near the palace here, the Gilded Cage, was one where the guards usually frequented, but he had been thrown out of there and told never to return after getting into a fight with the owner over how many drinks he had one night. The stupid man had insisted Nicolai had imbibed far more than he could have, and had paid for his insolence. Catriona had said she would go and heal the man, but Nicolai had forbidden it. He would not have the world know his wife was a witch.

The next nearest tavern and the one after that had similar restrictions on them for similar reasons and he was annoyed to find, at this moment that the one tavern he could still drink at in all of Patras was on the other side of the river. He thought about returning home, thinking there might still be a bottle there, but that would bring him again back to his facing something beautiful he had destroyed. He thought about what he had just done to Myrgen in the cells. Again, destroying something beautiful. Tanglwyst would be livid when she found him. He leaned against a building and tried to sort out his situation.

Myrgen and the Prince's accusations regarding Alan had hurt like the truth. They had definitely hit the mark with their comments and they would never know just how badly they had hurt him. He doubted anyone could understand his pain and guilt, and the feeling left him terribly alone. He looked back at the comfortably warm windows of the palace and felt the inner voice of his urging him to make amends with the queen, to go back and apologize for being such a boor. He didn't have many friends right now, and to lose face with Tanglwyst's best friend for beating up her brother was a pretty deadly blow to his self-esteem. In the end, he ignored the voice like he had so many times with Catriona and walked on into the night.

He stopped under the eaves of the Gilded Cage, listening to the drunken laughter of the patrons but he did not feel cheered by the sound, and proceeded on toward his home. As he approached his door, his chest tightened and he began to feel the weight of his neglect surround him, like a pack of thieves on the highway. He stopped, afraid the guilt would suffocate him if he walked into the house, the sheer emptiness of his marriage bed and his son's bed would destroy him. He began to cry.

He felt he had failed at every important turning point in his life, mostly because he had never protected the people he should have when they needed him. His father had died and he had failed to keep up the contracts which brought in the money. Because of his mismanagement of the business, Catriona had left to secure funding from the richest house in the land. Because he failed to protect her and go with her, she had been captured, raped, and beaten over and over again, all the while carrying his son. Because he failed to go looking for her, she had been chased to the point of having to hide their son with a warlord in Caratia while she fought her pursuers alone.

Because of his illness, he had never noticed the chip out of the finish in the water pitcher which caused him to go blind and deaf for two years, and he had never quite thanked Catriona for using the wooden bowl to mix medicinal herbs in, which he truly believed restored his sight. Because he had been weak, he had fallen to the sexual wiles of a married woman and lost his soul to her. Had he but waited a few more months, he would have been reunited with his beloved Catriona, but because he had failed, the fates had opened the way for Catriona to fall as well, and now, because of their sins, they had re-entered the house of marriage without their hearts.

Because of a stupid admission, he had turned his wife's heart to stone on the verge of regaining their happiness. Because of his inappropriate love for Tanglwyst, he had alienated his wife and son, a son who had come to be with him. Because of his guilt, he had failed to foster that relationship with the only perfect thing left from his former life, back before everything went wrong.

Now, because he was drunk and lazy, his love and his son were prisoners in a trap which they had nothing to do with. Because of his misinterpretation of the signs he was given, he failed to protect the life of the king. Nicolai felt he might as well have murdered the king himself, just as he had murdered happiness at every turn. His life seemed to be overwhelmingly devoted to making bad choices.

Now, he couldn't face the empty house he owned and he turned away from it, walking through the streets again. He began toward the only tavern left to him but decided he didn't need to drink himself numb. He'd done that enough. He looked toward

Tanglwyst's home but knew that would be as bad as his own home for haunting him and he turned to the palace. He had a barracks bunk there for when he needed it and the guilt of the king's death could at least be shared there, plus he figured he could get something to eat, even at this late hour.

He thought about the death of the king and how it happened. Dominic might be right on that one. It didn't exactly fit. Myrgen may have ordered the murder, but if he contracted Catriona by blackmailing her, she never would have followed through, especially after revealing to Charles Myrgen had employed her to kill him. But why would she do that with Alan also being held? She must have found the boy because he didn't think she knew about the connection between Tanglwyst and Myrgen. *He* didn't know, and he figured he was a lot more intimate with Tanglwyst than Catriona was.

Nicolai decided he needed to locate Catriona, to find Tanglwyst as well as the boy, and his closest link to Catriona was Myrgen. He figured, at this point, Myrgen would be his best bet to locating his wife because he had known enough to track her down in the first place. He'd already been accused of treason and would therefore be put to death unless someone stopped it, like the queen. That actually looked rather likely, but it would be political suicide for both her and Myrgen.

The trick would be making the former Chancellor believe he wouldn't make it to the trial. There were a lot of guardsmen who took it as a personal offense that someone so trusted would order their Sovereign's murder right under their noses. Nicolai figured he could be convincing regarding a pre-sentencing brawl with the scrappy accountant. If Myrgen thought the guards might kill him in the holding cells while the queen slept, he might decide he had nothing to lose. Myrgen was smart enough to figure out the guards may get in trouble, but they wouldn't betray each other to the headsman. If Nicolai put it to him like that, Myrgen might feel enough of a vested interest to spill what he knew, especially if Nicolai offered to protect him from the guards.

He liked this idea and decided that night might be just as good as any other night to interrogate the prisoner, so Nicolai picked up his pace in anticipation. First, though, food. Nicolai got to the palace and entered the grounds, thinking about what to say to Myrgen, and was on his way to the kitchen when he thought he saw someone moving around in the stables. He saw a person, either a man or a woman in man's clothing, slip out of the stable and disappear into the shadows. He decided to check it out. Perhaps there was a young serving girl recovering in the straw from a sexual escapade. He noted how lustful his thoughts were, but continued to creep toward the stable.

As he neared the stables, he registered an odd scent, one decidedly out of place: blood. He sniffed the air, wondering if the scent were perhaps from a mare in season or something simple like that. He suddenly stood straight upright from his crouched position as he recognized Tanglwyst's perfume. He ran to the inside pens and let his nose be his guide until he determined her whereabouts. A pile of hay moaned and he dug her out of the fodder.

Tanglwyst was an absolute mess. Bruised and bloody, she had the look of someone who'd survived a barroom brawl, but only just. Nicolai called out for help, his cries echoing throughout the palace grounds.

* * *

Catriona heard the cry and recognized the voice. She smiled and preceded into the shadows of the woods, where Michael was waiting for her with the horse he borrowed from the stall where they put Tanglwyst. She got onto her own steed and Michael mounted the borrowed stallion. "That was fast," he said.

"A little quicker than I expected but fine, nonetheless. They deserve each other. C'mon. We need to not be here." She spurred her horse toward the darkness of the woods with Michael right behind her.

They traveled through the moonlit trees of the king's Forest until they reached a clearing near a small river. Catriona pulled up her horse and stopped near the edge. Michael pulled up beside her and Catriona moved the horse over so it could drink. Michael dismounted and checked his horse's hooves.

"Something wrong?"

Michael glanced up at Catriona. "I felt the horse step on something back there and falter just a little. I wanted to make sure he was not injured." He returned his attention to the horse and pulled out a knife. He focused on the task and removed a rather sizable rock from the stallion's hoof. The animal's tail swished and he walked over to drink beside Catriona's mount. The night was quiet, despite the proximity of this place to the palace. Catriona had half expected to hear Nicolai's cries from here but the only sound was the creek chuckling over something the rocks were saying.

Michael put his knife away and looked back at Catriona. "May I ask what the next step is?"

"We need to get you away from here. I have a ship that is readying sail as we speak for the coming season. I'll have you deliver a message to my First Mate, telling him what has happened. He'll make preparations for you. You can't stay here. It's only a matter of time before you are implicated in this mess."

"And you would not call that justice?"

She looked down at the large man, who was able to lean his arms easily on the back of the stallion. "No. You are also not a bad man. You are as reluctant a pawn in this as your companion. The thing is I was able to get you out. I don't know about getting him out."

"I will go with you then. Myrgen is my responsibility."

"How are you going to get him out?"

"The Land will provide a way."

Catriona blinked at this common Caratian belief. "Michael, may I ask where you are from?"

"Nubia. Why?"

"That phrase, it is the mainstay of faith in the land of Caratia."

Michael shrugged. "I have never been to Caratia. That was the belief of my people back in Nubia. My parents converted to Augustinian to avoid being burned by a Latian man named Giovanni, but at home we always worshipped the Land."

Catriona couldn't believe what she was hearing. *"Giovanni?"*

"Yes. He was a very bad man according to my mother. Destroyed a neighboring village to steal the holy woman. My mother's family fled and when they met up with another white man, they began to say praise to the Saints, to keep us safe. It did not work. I still ended up here."

"Do you want me to return you to Nubia?"

Michael thought a moment. "No. I want you to save my friend."

She knew from her visions he truly felt Myrgen was his friend, and she really hadn't seen any evidence to say otherwise. The image of the silver piece and Myrgen's heart breaking flashed across her heart and she drew in a breath to stop the rush of emotional pain. "Then I will, but you need to take care of the rest for me. Ride to Rouen and go to the *Enigma*. Tell Octavius I will be arriving in a hurry and probably with a few passengers. Ask him to prepare cabins for the guests and I'll be along in a day or so. Tell them to prepare for sailing to St. Andrew. I will endeavor to save Myrgen because you are a servant of the Land, and I am its Defender. I swear on the life the Land has given me that I will find a way, but only because I truly believe he is not responsible for the death of my friend. If I should find out otherwise…"

"You won't." Michael mounted up. "What are you going to do?"

She looked over at the palace. "I have no idea, but I'll come up with something."

"I believe you will. Thank you, my lady." He nodded respectfully to her and she returned the gesture, then they rode off in different directions.

**Chapter Thirty-five:**
*"It is the glory of God to conceal a thing, but the honor of kings to search out a matter."*
*~ Proverbs 25:2*

As Gwen stood up, mulling over their revelation, Dominic leaned forward on his knees and rubbed his cheeks. *Could Tanglwyst have really done this?* It was possible. Few people outside of Mande were as crafty as Tanglwyst. Dominic heard a crinkle and remembered the blotter paper in his doublet. He pulled them out and set them on his lap. Gwen saw the movement and came over to see what he was looking at. He leafed through the notes but found nothing of true consequence. A few notes regarding decrees he wanted to have Marco announce but that court wasn't going to happen now.

Then he noticed a piece of paper that he had thought were notes but was apparently the piece underneath a different one. It had spotty marks where the ink had bled through from the paper above it. It caught Dominic's attention because of this fact. Decree paper was vellum, and heavy. It did not bleed through. Dominic looked a bit more carefully and he could see a couple letters and words. He couldn't quite make them out. Gwen looked at him as she came back over. "What's that?"

Dominic shook his head, lowering the paper and frowning at it. "I don't know. I can almost make out some words but I can't... quite..." He held it up to the light.

Gwen said, "Wait, let me see that." Dominic handed it to her and she took it over to the table. She went to her cupboard and got out some tea and her mortar and pestle. She poured some of the tea into her mortar and started grinding it. A couple minutes later, she had made a fine powder and she carefully sprinkled it on the paper. She sifted it back and forth on the paper and Dominic saw the letters actually come more into view. He looked at her, astonished. "How did you know to do that?"

"I haven't always been a shepherdess, Dom. Catriona showed me this trick on the ship. It never thought I'd need it because I can't read."

Dominic kissed her and took the paper over to the firelight again. It took a bit of work, but what he saw made him twitch. "By the Saints, Gwen. It's a Writ of Destruction."

"That doesn't sound pleasant."

"It's not. It's something a king can commission to destroy someone or something they feel is a threat to the State."

Gwen looked at the marks on the paper. "So which is it? Someone or something?"

Dominic concentrated, moving it in the light. His eyes got wide and he looked up at Gwen. "Nicolai."

"What?" She took the paper from Dominic and looked at it. "Are you sure?"

Dominic leaned back in the chair. "Gwen, this is very damning evidence. If Tanglwyst knew this contract was out on Nicolai's life, then it would explain why she did all this. It would mean she was actually *behind* all this. Gwen," he looked at his fiancé, "she'll be put to death over this."

"But what if she didn't know about it?"

"I don't think it will matter. They're looking for the person responsible for this and I think Tanglwyst might be that person."

Gwen crouched down beside him as he ran his fingers through his hair, eyes worried. "Dom, don't think the worst. Tanglwyst isn't known for her faithfulness. Wasn't she with that Duncan McVryce person all autumn? She wouldn't do something this dangerous for her latest lover."

"Don't count on that, Gwen. I've heard men say that, if you can get Tanglwyst's attention focused upon you, it is well worth the trouble. And Nicolai has secured her full attention. There's nothing she wouldn't do for him."

"Well, then, why haven't we heard of several other marriages she has destroyed?"

"She isn't attracted to married men, or men in serious relationships."

"Is that why she's never tried to seduce you?"

Dominic blinked. "What makes you think she's never tried to seduce me?"

Gwen put her hands on her hips and stood up. "Is that so? So you know first hand what it is like to have her full attention, then?"

"No. Truth be told, Gwen, I couldn't handle her full attention. It takes all my faculties to keep up with her and she just showers me with moderate attention. If she were to put the full weight of her personality upon me I'm pretty sure I'd crumble beneath the onslaught. I can barely stand it now."

"Stand it?" Gwen's brow furrowed. "You mean it's unpleasant?"

Dominic chewed his lip. "Tanglwyst requires a lot of maintenance. It would be decidedly difficult for me to maintain her."

"But she's rich. You shouldn't have to maintain her at all."

"I don't mean monetarily, Gwen."

Gwen blinked and shook her head. Then she figured out Dominic meant sexually. She nodded. "I see. And you know this because…?"

"I've lived in the manor house for six years now. I must say, that Duncan fellow certainly gave her a run. I'm surprised she was able to walk."

Gwen looked over at the fire, fighting a yawn. She lost. Dominic noticed. "We should get you to bed."

"I don't think we can afford to do that, Dominic. If Tanglwyst has done this, she might escape now that Myrgen's been captured. Then she'll get away with murder."

"Only if she knows about the Writ. I don't think Charles has had a steady hand for weeks, yet he was writing decrees this morning. If this was from this morning, then Tanglwyst doesn't know."

"So how do we confirm this?"

"Well," Dom stood, "the only person I know of who could know would be Myrgen, but I'd need to talk to him tonight."

"Why tonight?"

"Well, to be brutally honest, I don't know if he'll survive past dawn." He kissed her on the cheek. "Thank you for the help."

"Wait." She started unbuttoning her coatdress while walking into the next room. She came out a few minutes later with a skirt and apron over her chemise. "I'm coming with you."

"Why?"

"Because."

"Oh well, when you put it that way…" Dominic opened the door and they both woke up a bit at the slap of crisp early spring air.

* * *

Alexander lay in bed, half-sleeping. He kept hearing noises in the night and fought the urge to check out every one of them. He finally had to put Heracles in the kennels with the other hounds because he kept startling the animal by jumping at every sound. He kept dreaming that Charles came into his room, covered in blood. He kept dreaming Catriona came into his room, covered in silk. He couldn't stop himself from falling asleep but he had no control over what his mind decided to dwell upon.

He heard the door to the catacombs open and he opened his eyes, tired of sitting up to find nothing. The sound repeated as the outer door closed, and he watched it carefully. He saw the shadows move and he waited. A dark figure entered the room, keeping to the shadows. He watched it closely until he saw it come over to his bed. The banked embers from the fire hid nearly everything, but then he saw the distinctive outline of a female form and he sat up, alert. "Catriona?"

She put her bare fingers on his lips and leaned down to kiss him. He drank in her lips and she opened her mouth, her tongue questing for his. Alexander started at this uncharacteristic behavior and stopped the kiss. He sniffed, but this was not Catriona. He pushed her away and got out of bed. She jumped onto him, her body grinding against his crotch and he backed into the hearth chairs, knocking over the bottle of brandy and sending the glass he had been nursing into the fire place. The brandy flared a flame and Alexander saw his assailant in the sudden light.

"Elizabeth! What are you doing here?" He grabbed her wrists and threw her off him.

"I came here for you, Alex. You need me."

"Need you? How? For what?"

"To protect you. This Catriona woman, she's dangerous."

"And you are going to protect me from Catriona? Don't make me laugh, Elizabeth."

"It's not just her assassination abilities, Alex. Her reputation is evil. She's killed people before."

"In self defense."

"How do you know? Were you there for any of them?"

"Yes."

Elizabeth fell silent in the darkness. "You were?"

Alexander crossed his arms. "Yes. And I have patched her up afterwards. She is quite familiar with my skills."

"Your *medical* skills, right?"

"All my skills, Elizabeth. Now, get out of my room. This is not the time or the place for such indiscretion. In fact, it will never be the proper time for such a thing."

Elizabeth stepped up close and her face was lit by the dying flames on the coals. "You need me, Alexander. This kingdom loves me."

"And they will love her too. I'm sovereign now, Elizabeth, or will be by this time tomorrow and I have already chosen my queen. You will be sent with Emmy to the Anjou Ducal Estates and my Mother will be assigned to the Papal City as our ambassador. Once you're both squirreled safely away where you can't interfere, I'll bring her back and marry the woman I have loved all my adult life."

"You can't do that to me."

"I most certainly can. You don't seem to understand exactly how precarious your position is here, Elizabeth." He walked over to the fireplace and lit a tinder stick from the coals, using it to shed some light into the room by lighting some candles. He was glad to see Elizabeth had had the discretion to not come to him nude. It wouldn't have mattered if she had. He would have thrown her out into the hallway regardless.

"What to do mean, precarious? I ha… haven't done anything wrong." She almost fidgeted, and then stopped herself.

"Oh?" He arched an eyebrow at her. "That little display downstairs with Myrgen? That exhibited an intimacy unbecoming a married woman, especially a queen whose king was just murdered. Adultery, when committed by the queen, is treason, Elizabeth. Be grateful I'm merely exiling you. I could easily have you hanged."

Elizabeth gaped at him, toggling her head as if trying to shake off a small, persistent insect. "How? How *dare* you talk to me like that! I'm still the queen and until you perform the Rite of Sovereignty, I still outrank you. I can have you hung for speaking to me like that!"

Alexander walked over to the door and opened it, intending to throw Elizabeth out bodily if he had to. Nicolai was there, his hand raised to knock on the door. "Oh." Alexander took a step back.

Elizabeth stormed over to Alexander in a full tilt rage.

"And how *dare* you threaten me when your pirate whore is married as well, and to the Captain of your own guard!" She turned to see Nicolai standing there and her rage fled like birds before a wolf. She put her hand to her mouth, her eyes wide. "By the Saints…"

Nicolai looked from Elizabeth to Alexander. There was murder in his eyes, and a little satisfaction as well. "Grymalkin, I presume?"

Alexander turned an angry red and clenched his teeth. His fists were ready in case Nicolai decided to attack, and if he didn't, Alexander was going to break Elizabeth's neck. He had gone all year without revealing their connection and now she had just screamed that in front of the one person who really *didn't* need to hear it.

Elizabeth seemed to sense the intense danger she was in and quickly said, "Nicolai, what did you need?"

Nicolai turned to the queen. "Tanglwyst has been found, in the stables. She's been badly beaten, apparently by Catriona, according to the mumblings I've been able to decipher. Lots of damage that's visible, probably hiding more serious internal injuries. She's bleeding heavily from her waist. I came here to see if I can convince the Prince to stop bedding other people's wives long enough to help her."

Elizabeth stepped into the hall and put on her kindest tone. "Of course he will help, Nicolai." She turned to Alexander. "We'll talk more later."

"No, we won't." He slammed the door in both their faces.

He turned to the room and sighed. *What was wrong with that woman? Creeping into my private chambers, kissing me…* The whole encounter felt unreal, but he found everything about the woman distasteful in this moment. There was only one woman he wanted to be with, to touch like that and Elizabeth was just about as far removed from Catriona as possible and still be considered the same species. He went over to his wardrobe and opened the door. Hanging alone on a peg inside was the shirt he had worn that day. He could still smell her distinctive perfume on it. He thought about putting it back on, but the small amount of blood from his brother's room that had managed to get past all the protections was not enough to send it to the laundry to remove her scent. Working on an actual patient that was beaten might change that. He didn't want to run the risk of having Elizabeth decide to clean it as some kind of gesture.

He picked out a clean shirt and pulled it on over his head. He put slippers on that were wool lined, another gift from his days traveling with Catriona. Gwen had made them to keep his feet warm on the ship. Unlike here, Catriona always seemed to be able to surround herself with wonderful people, and he looked forward to having people like that around him. Court had been full of disloyal sycophants for far too long.

He went over to the door and grabbed his kit. He had taken to just leaving it by the door in these last days, it seemed to be required so often. A deep breath to steel himself for going into that room, and he opened the door. Servants were bustling about in a near frenzy and the palace was loud. He was grateful because it meant the likelihood of anyone hearing the exchange between him and Elizabeth had been localized to just Nicolai. Lucky him.

He closed his door behind him and walked down the hall to the room where Tanglwyst often stayed. As the queen's Favorite, she had been given a room at the palace and she had actually started using it recently, about two months ago. Alexander didn't know why, and didn't care. It probably had something to do with Nicolai and that made him care even less. He seemed hourly to despise the man even more.

He opened the door and the servants around him parted to make room for him by the bed. Nicolai had not been kidding. Tanglwyst was a mass of bruises and swollen flesh and completely unconscious. Leeches had already been applied to drain some of the extra blood from those areas, but the damage was pretty severe. He looked at Tanglwyst's chest and saw an impressive boot print stamped into her skin. He recognized it immediately.

He looked up at Nicolai. "Catriona did this?"

"You know her well, Your Highness."

"Apparently not. Why didn't she kill her?" He looked at Elizabeth. "I mean, according to you people, isn't that what she does?"

Elizabeth snarled at Alexander and waved him off, choosing to storm out of the room at that moment with an air of great disgust. *Good riddance. Her dismissal can't come too soon for me.* Nicolai glared at Alexander and he looked at the guard pointedly, and flicked his hand twice, sending a small wave of air Nicolai's direction so he could sniff it for signs of his wife.

Frankly, there was nothing Nicolai could do about that, either now or in the future. Power did have its privileges.

He focused upon Tanglwyst again and inspected the wounds.

*Chapter Thirty-six:*
*"The integrity of the upright shall guide them, but the*
*perverseness of transgressors shall destroy them."*
*~ Proverbs 11:3*

Dominic and Gwen got to the palace to find quite a bit of activity, despite the late hour. The palace never truly seemed to quiet down on the lower levels but right now was a little different. Valets and servants were rushing about the place like sparrows before a hurricane, and Dominic realized what must be going on. "Catherine must be on her way. We have to work fast."

"You go to Myrgen. I'll talk to Alexander and see if he knew about the Writ." She kissed his cheek and spun off, golden hair cutting a swath around her. Dominic looked around and made his way the other direction.

Gwen wasn't sure she would be allowed access to His Highness at this late hour with all that was going on. She knew she could probably figure out the way to his chambers through the catacombs but she didn't want to try when they were so pressed for time. She wished she knew what Catriona was up to. She would have all the answers. She usually did. But she wasn't here and Gwen felt a little excited over the prospect of figuring it out herself. She strode up the stairs and people gave way before her confidence.

She heard a bunch of people talking in one of the nearby rooms and she caught a glimpse of Alexander as a servant took a basin of bloody water from the room. Alexander looked up from his work and perked up. Gwen thought he looked tired and she could understand why. She glanced in the room but couldn't quite tell who was being treated on the bed. Then Nicolai came over to the door, glared at her and closed it.

*Oh. Must be Tanglwyst. I wonder what happened?* She walked around the corridor a bit, looking at stuff and trying to stay out of the way of the rushing servants. She sincerely hoped Catherine wasn't going to show up while Gwen was waiting. She wasn't certain how to explain her presence if the Queen-Mother asked. The door to Tanglwyst's room opened and Alexander came out carrying his chiurgeon's kit. He closed the door behind him.

"Gwen, it's good to see you. I was just thinking about you."

"You were?"

"Yes. See?" He pointed at the slippers she made and she laughed, a sound which startled some people walking the halls. "It is always a delight to see you."

"Why? Because it usually means I need you to patch up the Captain?" Gwen smiled her crooked little smile and Alexander nodded, a small grin sneaking into his features, like the weight of the day left with her levity and insight.

"Probably. Can I get you something?"

"Actually, I have something to talk to you about. Do you have someplace we can talk?"

"Um, yes, my room is right here. Come." They started off down the hall towards the Royal Family chambers. "It is so good to see you! Where have you been?"

"Here in Patras."

"All winter?"

"Yes. It seemed appropriate, what with…" She nodded towards the room with Nicolai in it.

Alexander nodded. "Did you see her often?"

"All the time. I was her refuge when she wanted to see you."

"I wish I'd known, but then I would have been a constant visitor, hoping to be there when she arrived."

"I wouldn't have minded. You two were good together."

"Thanks. All the time, eh?"

"At least once a week. In the past couple months, it's been more than that. He did something, I don't know what…"

"I do. She told me. I saw her earlier today. He, well, you caught a glimpse of it there in that room."

Gwen nodded. "Ah. Tanglwyst again."

He opened his door and stood back to let her in. He closed the door behind them and set his kit down. "I'm going to have to restock that thing. It's gotten a lot of use lately."

"Let me know if there are any special herbs you need. I have loads."

"You're so helpful. Thank you. Now, what did you need?"

Gwen took a deep breath and frowned. "When was the last time you saw Charles writing any decrees or writs?"

Alexander blinked, surprised at the path of question. "Uh, well," he ran his hand through his hair and scratched the back of his head. "Today, actually. Apparently, he gave Marco several decrees which were supposed to be on the docket for an evening court tonight. As you can image, the court never happened."

"Before that?" Gwen noticed the jilted table and the broken glass in the fireplace. She immediately started picking it up and tossing it in the fireplace, her attention still on Alexander.

"It has been a while." Alexander came around and started to do likewise. "His emotional state and physical condition haven't been very conducive to writing legibly. He could barely sign his name."

"Watch yourself. Those slippers will get glass in them. So today, huh?"

"Why, Gwen? What has she discovered?"

"Actually, it was Dom who discovered it. A Writ of Destruction?"

Alexander blinked, brow furrowing. "Against?"

Gwen glanced down at the last of the visible glass shards, then back at the Prince, eyes wincing. "Nicolai."

Alexander almost dropped the glass pieces, making an even bigger mess. He tossed them into the fireplace and wiped his hands on his pants. "You're sure?"

"Well, *I* don't know for sure. Illiterate. But Dom seemed quite certain he had figured it out."

"Figured it out? So he didn't see the actual Writ?"

"No, just the paper beneath it. It took a little effort to be able to read it." She stood up as well. "Dom said it could implicate Tanglwyst in the murder of the king if she knew about it in advance. So, you didn't know?"

Alexander shook his head. "No. I had no idea. But he's right. Even if she didn't know about it, bringing that information to light could do a lot of damage. Nice to know I just healed her in time for her execution."

"If Charles wasn't capable of doing it until today, then she had nothing to do with it. That's a bit of a relief, actually. Dom kind of depends upon her for a lot of things."

"Well, don't be relieved just yet. She has some bleeding occurring that is having trouble stopping. I'm going to keep an eye on her for the next day or so. If the bleeding stops, I'll say her injuries are extremely superficial."

"What happened?" Gwen glanced at the floor, spying another tiny piece of glass and discarding it in the fire.

"Not certain, but someone had issue with her."

"Well, I think we can both imagine who that might be."

"And I'm sure Nicolai is already at that conclusion. It will be the only time you'll ever hear me say this, Gwen, but I'm glad she's not around right now. So," he glanced at the floor, then back at her, "have you seen her recently?"

"Yes. She could only think of you and how you were faring with all this."

"She said that?"

"No. She didn't have to. You know her, Alex. She would never admit out loud what her heart was telling her. To do so would make it real."

"It's already real for me. I can barely breathe without her, Gwen. She was here just yesterday and I can't stop begging the Saints to return her to me."

A knock at the door snapped their attention and he sighed. "You may want to duck out the back way." He nodded to the prayer nave. "Elizabeth is in a strange mood." He opened the catacomb door for her. "Go straight down those stairs and keep heading that direction. You'll end up by the kitchen." She curtsied quickly and he closed the door behind her.

* * *

Alexander braced himself to deal with the drama of Elizabeth or Nicolai, then opened his door. The servant at the door had a pile of items Alexander had left in Tanglwyst's room in his hands. "Your Highness. These were in the room with your patient. We were uncertain if you needed any of this or if it was simply to go to the laundry."

Alexander glanced at the pile and saw they were simply cloths he had used to clean her wounds. He shook his head. "No, they can go to the laundry. What of the leeches she had on her?" He knew if the cloths were removed, the leeches were probably done as well.

"Ah yes." The servant shifted his weight and pulled a glass jar filled with bloated leeches in pinkish brown water from his belt. "Here you are, Sire."

"Thank you." Alexander took the leeches and looked at them. The servant started to go off to the laundry when Alexander stopped him. "Wait. Where did these come from? Where on the Lady?"

The servant looked at them. "Um, I believe they were on her face and on her belly, Sire."

Alexander looked back at the leeches. The taint in the water indicated the presence of something he didn't want to see and the placement of these leeches meant he was probably right. "Thank you." He went back inside his room and closed the door.

He went over to his kit and pulled out a poultice he often used upon his own wounds. He broke it open and got some water in a glass brandy snifter. He sprinkled some of the poultice contents into the water and waited. The water turned a beautiful shade of sky blue, tinting the water like a cloudless sky in summer. He took a leech out of the jar and put it in the snifter. The creature twisted and twitched, but settled quickly. It did not seem to be completely comfortable however, and this bothered Alexander even more than if the creature had burned like in acid.

Which was what he had expected.

The brownish color in the bottle confused him. It meant the main ingredient of the additive to her blood was green, not blue, which was the color it assumed when attributed to a person. This meant the Cyprian Herb Tanglwyst had been given was unattached to any single person. He didn't know what that meant, but it revealed two very important things: One, that Tanglwyst was being used by someone who knew what this herb was, and two, Catriona had spared her because of this, recognizing she wasn't in her right mind. He doubted Tanglwyst even knew she was being drugged. He couldn't understand why anyone would knowingly devote themselves to a single person through herbal compulsion, and Tanglwyst had never struck him as the type of person who would willingly submit to such a thing. No, this had an insidious feel to it, and that meant one of two people.

And Mother wasn't home yet.

* * *

Catriona entered the catacombs from the kitchen entrance, having secured the horse once again in the woods nearby. She was exhausted and could barely stand. She needed to check on Myrgen first so she went into the tunnel that slipped behind the cells. She listened carefully for the spot in the wall where she could hear movement on the other side and put her ear to the stone. She heard Myrgen's breathing, clear as if she were standing above him. He seemed to be having a dream but she couldn't discern anything about it.

She blinked and caught herself as she started to fall through the wall on top of him. She put her hands out and hit solid stone of the wall. Her heart was thumping as she realized she had fallen asleep during the blink and had started to dream.

She moved away from the wall and tried to decide what to do. She needed to rest, but where? Alexander's room? He would not want to rest. He would want to talk, or more. She tried to think, but her mind was muddy. Then she remembered the cell Alan had been in. It would be empty and Tanglwyst would be in no shape to actually tell anyone about her, even if Alexander healed the woman. She had a few hours at least. She stumbled to the cell, the door to the passage where Alan had been kept opening before her will without having to find the release stone. She opened the door to the cell without dealing with a key, and fell into the bed like she was being dragged there.

*A war was raging around her. Earth and Heaven were battling and their champions were drawing blood at every turn. Drake stood directing the troops to destroy the Holy Empire's men while Catriona called up spires of stone from the earth, destroying and disrupting the opposing army. Across the way, she could see Champion of Heaven in a suit of armor, directing lightning upon the Caratian army, a woman by his side flooding the area with water to drown out the fires escaping the earth. A volley of arrows flew into the air and Catriona followed their arc. She saw they were going to strike Alan, and Drake used his body to cover the boy.*

*Arrows riddled the back of the great man, but none of them got through to Alan. Catriona ran to Drake's side and saw the Champion raise his visor of his holy armor. She saw, even from this great distance, the eyes and face of Alexander.*

"Myrgen! Psst! Myrgen. Wake up."

Myrgen opened his eyes and saw Dominic clutching the bars of his cell. "Dominic? What are you doing here?" He was trying to sort out the dream where he shot a bald man, but the details were already fading. He shook it off and sat up.

"You don't look very good."

"Really?" Myrgen spat out a small chunk of straw that he didn't want to think about because he had too many visions of what could give it that flavor. "I was feeling so much better too." He actually was. The vomiting earlier had gotten rid of the stuff in his stomach that was making him nauseated and he was almost hungry now. "Is there any water or anything out there? My mouth tastes like I've mucked a horse stall with my teeth."

Dominic looked around and grabbed a waterskin from the guards' station. He handed it through to Myrgen, who promptly washed his mouth out with the stuff, spitting into the corner where the vomit was. He rubbed his teeth and his finger came away an odd color. He washed his mouth out again and the color was gone, along with the foulness. He frowned and went over to the pile of vomit. It was a decidedly nasty shade of blue.

Dominic's face belied a well-held bout of nausea as well, but then he seemed to recognize something. Myrgen asked, "What is it?"

Dominic looked at Myrgen and then back at the pile. "Is that bread?"

"Yes. I was in Charles' room. He offered it to me first thing. I guess I now know why." Dominic's expression grew more pensive and Myrgen looked closer. He poked it with a piece of straw he picked up and then sat up a bit. "I made that."

"What? The bread?" Myrgen looked at Dominic.

"No, the poison. It was an experiment to try and get rid of the Giovanni. I was hoping to put some in his food and have it drive him insane. It would have worked well too, except that the effects weren't permanent. They stop within a day of the last dose administered." He looked at Myrgen, who looked back at the gooey pile. "This was being given to the king?"

"Apparently so. It was the only thing I've eaten all day."

Dominic was about to say something else, but they heard someone opening the door at the top and coming down the stairs. Myrgen handed him the water skin and shooed him out of sight. Dominic ducked around the corner of a wall dividing the cells. Myrgen moved to the back of the cell and waited. A tray of food came into view being carried by Elizabeth. She smiled at him in the dim light supplied by the torch Dominic had lit. "Hello."

Myrgen's heart chilled at the sight of her, and he found that strange seeing as she had been the most important thing to him this hour the night before. "Hello. To what do I owe this honor, to be served by the Queen of Mervolingia?"

"I thought you probably had not been fed all day and wanted to remedy that. I got all your favorite things, well, at least that could be acquired at this late hour."

"Thank you. I truly don't know what to say."

Elizabeth set the tray down on the floor, just out of reach. "Well, I can think of something. I need to ask you something. It's very important, Myrgen."

"Then I will do my best to provide it but," he gestured at his cell, "I doubt I'll be able to fetch it myself."

Elizabeth smiled her most disarming smile. "Word has reached the palace that Catherine has heard of Charles' death and is at present en route to Patras. She might arrive tomorrow morning, or possibly earlier. I have to get something. It's the only way to save you." She stepped in and clutched the bars, looking into the shadows at his battered features. "I need the Rite of Sovereignty. Do you know where it is?"

Myrgen blinked, his mouth giving in to gravity. "Elizabeth? What do you plan to do?"

"I plan to seize power of Mervolingia for myself and turn this place into a matriarchy. Charles lies dead and Alexander is awaiting Catherine's arrival before he performs the Rite. Our only chance is to have *me* perform the Rite and then, even Catherine the Great will be unable to deny my power. The Rite gives the Sovereign power over their populace. Alexander plans to use it to put that Catriona woman on the throne instead of me and exile me and he will be able to do it. All subjects of Mervolingia will do as their Sovereign commands. I can't let that happen. *You* can't let that happen. Catriona will execute your sister and me for our part in this. Our only hope is to let me perform it and gain the sovereignty." She dropped to a knee. "Please, Myrgen, tell me where the Rite is kept, for Tanglwyst's sake."

"What about the boy?"

"What boy?"

"Catriona's son. What about him?"

"What about him?"

"Will you make sure he's safe?"

"Oh," she waved at him, like fanning away a bad smell, "of course." She stood again, fluffing her skirt in an irritated gesture. She seemed annoyed that he didn't just give her the information she sought without asking any further questions, but Myrgen was going with his gut at this point, and it said not to trust her.

"Elizabeth. I mean it. I want to make sure he is safe."

"Why? What does it matter to you?"

"What does it matter? He's a *child*, Elizabeth! A child I never wanted involved in this."

She stepped in and he saw her ambition in full view, the torch sharpening her features like a whetstone. "Then tell me where the Rite is kept or I swear to Heaven I will walk into that cell and cut his pathetic little throat."

Myrgen stepped forward. "You wouldn't dare."

"Try me. I have no ties to that whelp, and Catriona will blame you, not me. You want that boy to survive this night, you tell me *precisely* where to find that Rite."

Myrgen leapt for her and she dodged back, expecting his charge. He was still a bit weak and it had showed in his reflexes. He couldn't reach her any more than he could reach the food she brought. "When I get out of here…"

"That will never happen, Myrgen. You'll die here. But if you don't tell me where that Rite is, I'll make sure that child *starves* to death and has to eat that dog you gave him to try and survive, hoping he'll be rescued. That is, provided that animal doesn't eat him first. If he is rescued, he'll be so insane from the ordeal, he'll become a monster, or a husk. It's your choice, Myrgen. The Rite? Or the boy?"

Myrgen thought about what she had said. She seemed quite serious and he didn't dare risk the boy's life. He felt like he was forgetting something, but he couldn't place it. He had read the Rite when it had been entrusted to him, his curiosity winning out against duty. He had since learned something about the Rite, but he couldn't remember what it was. Between the beatings and the lack of food, he couldn't call it up. Finally, he said, "The main library has a large portrait of Charles in it. Behind it is a loose stone. Pull out the stone and the Rite is in there. But it takes hours and you have to be isolated."

"Then I'd better go." She pushed the tray of food within

reach of the bars and ran to the stairs. Myrgen waited until he heard the door to the main floor close before he called out for Dominic.

The young D'Medici came out of the darkness. "By the Saints, Myrgen. What have you done?"

"I've bought time for you to defeat her, but first, I need you to do something for me." He gave Dominic directions on how to get to where Alan had been put. "You must get him out of there. If Elizabeth succeeds, she'll be too busy fighting a civil war to pay attention to a little thing like a child's life. Luckily, I wasn't lying when I said the Rite will take hours. It will be morning before she finishes if she were to start right now. Dom, I need you to go save that child."

"Why me?"

"Because if Catriona is going to become Queen, wouldn't you like to be on her good side? Saving her son will do that. It's not like I can do it from here." *Frankly,* he thought, *I wouldn't if I could. It would be inappropriate to try and curry favor with her after what I've allowed to happen here. I deserve to be here for allowing that child to be in this mess at all. I damned sure don't deserve anyone's partiality.*

Dominic nodded. "I'll be sure to tell her what you did."

"Yes, I'm sure that will matter."

Dominic and Myrgen both looked at the tray of food Elizabeth had brought, then over at the vomit, back at the food, then at each other. Dominic said, "Don't eat that."

"Wouldn't touch it."

Dominic moved quickly up the stairs with the torch, leaving Myrgen to contemplate his situation in the gathering darkness. Elizabeth had shown her true colors, but he couldn't risk the boy's life. The boy. It irritated him that he didn't know the boy's name. Well, perhaps he would learn it in the afterlife. He stepped back away from the cell front and exhaled, the sound echoing off the rocks around him. He thought about what Elizabeth had said and it caused him to shudder. He had no idea what he felt now. Elizabeth even saying something like that stunned him and the thought of her mouth near his to kiss him now made him cringe. How easily she could have killed him, over and over.

He leaned against the back wall and slid down the comforting stone. He still felt a little feverish, but he knew he could probably heal himself now. He closed his eyes and envisioned energy from his legs and torso going into the bruises on his face. The cooling feel of the stone became cold compresses that lessened the swelling. He could feel the bruises fading and the muscles loosening again. He realized it was probably foolish to heal himself when he was going to be executed in the morning, but he wasn't going to spend his last night in physical pain to match the emotional scars.

He exhaled, all the pain and discomfort leaving his body with the breath. Healing made him tired and he closed his eyes and rested.

## Chapter Thirty-seven

*"Then I was with by him, as one brought up with him: and I was daily his delight, rejoicing always before him, rejoicing in the habitable part of his earth; and my delights were with the sins of men."*
*~ Proverbs 8:30-31*

Dominic put the torch in the holder by the stairs, thinking it would be handy for going through the catacombs but worried it would look suspicious carrying a smoking torch under his robes. He ducked into the garden behind the hedge he and Gwen had almost made love behind once and found the release stone Myrgen had mentioned. He looked around and found a candle lantern on a hanging peg and used the flint and steel nearby to light it. All of these things looked like a new addition. There was still dust on the ground from the placement of the peg for the lantern. Dominic was a little surprised he had noticed something like that. He usually wouldn't have.

He walked into the catacombs and soon came to the center crossroads Myrgen had told him about. He heard someone approaching from the north and tucked the lantern under his robe, hiding the light. He watched carefully and saw Gwen enter the crossroad carrying a small votive candle. He brought out the light and came over to her when she stopped. "How did you get here?"

Gwen looked back over her shoulder. "Up that way is the royal family's chambers. There are several branches. I just left Alexander."

"How is he?"

"Bad. He looked exhausted. And Tanglwyst has been found."

"Really? Where?"

"The Stables. Someone beat the devil out of her."

"Well, I doubt that's possible. The devil has a key to the back door of that woman."

Gwen looked at him, a little confused. "Dom?"

"I'll explain on the way." As he walked to the secret passage trigger, he told her about Elizabeth's threat and the impression he got that Tanglwyst would have no problem going along with the whole idea. "She's always been a strong willed woman. Turning Mervolingia into a matriarchy would be just the sort of thing Tanglwyst would support and, if possible, orchestrate."

"By the Saints, Dominic. That would cause a civil war."

"That's what Myrgen said, but Elizabeth is under the impression that the Rite of Sovereignty will make every subject of the Crown do as they are told. It would honestly explain the Saint Michael's Day Massacre. Once Charles commanded that the Emilianites be eradicated, the swath of destruction was hard to stop and swept the entire country."

"I should tell Alexander so he can stop her."

"Wait, Gwen. Catriona's son is down here somewhere."

"What? Alan is here? Where?"

"I'm going to find him now. Myrgen told me to find him while Elizabeth is distracted with the Rite. He said it will take hours to perform, which will give us time to stop her. But first, we have to save the boy. Alan, you said?"

"Yes." She looked around at the wall. "What are we looking for?"

"A stone that opens the door here. I'm not sure which one."

Gwen looked around the wall, then said, "Oh. Okay." She pushed on a section of the wall and a large door-sized chunk of stone popped away from the rest of the wall. Dominic looked at her. "How did you know where to look?"

"I don't know. I just looked and saw it. I guess I'm becoming more perceptive."

Dominic glanced at the open door. "I know what you mean. Come on."

They walked along the corridor until they came to the T junction and Dominic turned left. Gwen looked down the hall to the right and stopped, her votive raised. Dominic noticed her pause but continued down the hall Myrgen had told him about. He found the door and knocked on it. There was no answer. He tried the latch but the door was locked. He looked around and saw some marks in the dirt that he couldn't quite make out. "Come here, would you? I need your light." She turned and came over, dropping to the ground beside her fiancé to see what he was inspecting. "Elizabeth mentioned something about a dog Myrgen gave Alan. I don't hear anything inside this room and a dog would be especially noisy. Do you have any way to tell whether or not he's here?"

She looked over at the door and then at the ground, her votive and Dominic's candle lantern doubling the light in the area. She glanced around, looking up at the door, then back at the ground. She pointed to something. "He's not here. See that?" She moved her finger in the air near the ground. "That's a child's footprint and that one," she traced another print, "that looks like a woman's boot print." She looked up at the door and raised her candle. "And *that* is the final proof." She pulled something from the place where the door and the wall met, where the door had closed on something. "That is one of Catriona's hairs. She's been here. The size of that boot there indicates a large man was with her, probably Drake. They're gone."

"I need to be sure. Myrgen said to be certain the boy was safe. He made me promise."

The door opened and Dominic and Gwen both fell back. Catriona was standing in the doorway. "Don't worry, Dominic. I'll make sure he knows."

* * *

"Catriona! What are you doing here?" Gwen got up and helped Dominic to his feet.

Catriona stepped out of the cell and looked around. "Trying to get some rest before daybreak. I have so much to do and I needed some rest. Do you know the hour?"

Dominic shook his head. "It's still dark though. I just came from the garden. Perhaps midnight."

"How is Myrgen doing? Is he in any danger?"

"Right now? I don't think so, but I don't know."

Gwen said, "Nicolai is with Tanglwyst right now. I don't get the impression he's going to leave her side. Dominic said he was pretty brutal to Myrgen, beating him."

Catriona felt a rush of intense rage at this news, as if Nicolai had threatened one of her charges. She blinked, getting it under control. "Anything else?"

Dominic wiped his hands on his sleeves, casting the dust off them. "Elizabeth came down and threatened him, and Alan. She demanded the Rite of Sovereignty."

"Did he give it to her?"

"Yes. She said she would make sure Alan died if he didn't. That's why I'm here. He insisted I make sure Alan was freed before Elizabeth did something to him. My lady," Dominic's voice got very formal, "I know you and I have not always shared the same mind on certain things, but I want to say in Myrgen's defense that he seems truly to be a decent man…"

Catriona raised her hand, stopping him. "Dominic, don't worry. I already know this. I have every intention of rescuing him. My only request is, when the time comes, if you could look the other way."

Dominic took in a breath. "Yes, certainly."

She stepped back into the cell. "I need a bit more rest but I will take care of this before anything befalls him. Thank you. You two should get some rest as well. I'll need you to keep an eye on things. Dominic? I trust you will be able to handle anything unexpected that comes up."

"Yes, certainly." He bowed, and Catriona saw that he did so without thinking about it, then realized he had just shown her a respect he reserved only for those he felt had earned it. She returned the bow, for the exact same reason. She closed the door and leaned against it, gathering her thoughts. She could hear Dominic clearly on the other side, as if the door were not a barrier at all.

"Gwen, I apologize. Your Mistress is indeed worthy of your loyalty, so much so that I fear I will no longer feel the same about mine."

"Oh Dominic!" The sound of a kiss and then footsteps away.

Catriona smiled and glanced around the room. The light was gone but her eyes adjusted quickly. It was as if the stone wanted her to see what was there. The battle Alan had drawn on the stones caught her attention and it reminded her of the dream she had. *Myrgen saved me. Why would Myrgen be fighting on the side of Caratia in a war against the Holy Empire?*

She thought for a moment, trying to decide exactly what to do. She touched a small obsidian key she had on a necklace. She had gained entry to this room because Alan had been on the other side. As Stâpâna, this key gave her the ability to open any door or gain access to any building where a citizen of Caratia needed her. It was a gift of the Land, emerging from the stone in the pommel of her sword when she rescued a child from some killers Giovanni sent after her. They had kidnapped the child to lure her to the place, and intended to kill them both, but the key had enabled her to get the jump on them. It was after that that she was recognized as the Stâpâna of Caratia, Protector of the Land. The sword was one she had picked up in the capital city of Zara and it had been discovered to be the Protector's Sword. Apparently, the stone in the pommel was not the one the sword master had put in it originally, so it was seen as a proof of the Land's choice.

She took the key necklace off her neck and set it on the ground. The key sank into the ground like the solid earth was merely an illusion, and the only thing stopping it was the leather it was hung on. She nodded and picked the necklace up again. *As you wish. I am your servant.*

She put the necklace into her bodice and opened the door, glancing one last time around the room, then closed the door behind her. She followed the feel of the ground and opened the door to the crossroads. She looked up to the North, to where Alexander was. She wanted to go see him, but she didn't want to abandon Myrgen. Nicolai may be occupied, but he might decide to leave at any moment and finish what he did to Myrgen. She felt she owed Alexander an explanation, and turned towards his room. She climbed the stairs, every step feeling apprehension. She went to the door that led to his prayer room and put her ear to it, her heart pounding in her chest. The Land saw fit to bless her again and she heard him on the other side.

* * *

Alexander rose from the hearth chair. "No, mother. It's too late. In the morning, please. We'll go see him in the morning."

Catherine D'Medici stood and folded her hands in front of her. "Very well, then. Good night, Alexander. I will see you in the morning." She was still disheveled from her trip, but her stoic bearing made it seem unimportant. Alexander could tell she was as exhausted as he was. She was accustomed to traveling by carriage and her arrival this far ahead of schedule and in the dark indicated she had ridden a horse instead. The trip had taken its toll and Alexander's own weariness had just been added to by having to confirm the reports that Charles had been killed that day. She had cried, but not nearly as much as he had expected. It would probably hit them both hard tomorrow, when the Rite of Sovereignty was performed.

He escorted his mother to the door and saw her out, quietly closing the door behind him. He locked it against any other intruders, no longer caring about anyone else. He put his head against the door and exhaled. "Saints, assist me," he prayed, "I need relief. I need help. I need…" He breathed deeply and gave up. Heaven never answered him when he asked for Catriona. Apparently, she was not under that purview. He couldn't remember the religion of the holder of his heart, he just knew it was different. It didn't matter now anyway. He was too tired and she was too far away.

He heard a whisper of stone and then a small draft brought the scent of spice and musk to his senses and he opened his eyes and stood up. The barest of sound behind him and that unmistakable smell and he turned slowly to see her. Catriona stood behind him, and this time, it wasn't Elizabeth trying to seduce him but actually his Catriona. "By the Saints."

"Hello, Alexander." She smiled. "I'm sorry to visit you when you are so tired…"

He didn't let her finish. He took her up and kissed her, his passion freed by his fatigue to let him do what his will would usually override. She almost protested, but he was unstoppable. He picked her up and sat her on the bed, throwing off his robe and kissing her again. They had tonight, but possibly only tonight and he had just gotten his second wind.

"Trust me," he said, eyes sparked, "I'm not that tired."

"I see that."

He kissed her again and she pushed against his chest. "Alexander. I have something to tell you. It's important."

"Is it that you will marry me?"

"No."

"Then it is not as important as kissing you right now." He kissed her again, climbing on to the bed with her and she pushed him back again.

"Alexander, it's about Elizabeth."

"Then it *definitely* isn't as important as kissing you right now."

Catriona took him by the shoulders and used his weight

against him to flip him onto the bed beside her. She then popped up and straddled him. He liked that and smiled. "Listen to me. Elizabeth has gotten the Rite of Sovereignty. She is planning on stealing the command of the people from you."

"But, that's not possible. Only one man knows where the Rite of Sovereignty is kept."

"Unfortunately, he was forced to give her that information to save my son's life. I'm sorry, Alex."

"She threatened Alan's life?"

"Yes."

Alexander dropped his head back onto the bed and closed his eyes. "Saint's Blood. It just never ends. I'm sorry, Catriona. I suspected she might be involved here, but I didn't realize it was like that."

"I don't mean to burden you further, Alexander. What can I do to help?"

"Honestly? Stay here with me a while. Let me get one measure of peace."

Catriona climbed off him and sat beside him. "I can do that."

They moved fully onto the bed and Alexander wrapped his arms around her as she laid her head on his chest. He breathed in the scent of her hair and was asleep before he exhaled.

### Chapter Thirty-eight:
### "Treasure of wickedness profit nothing, but righteousness delivereth from death."
### ~ Proverbs 10:2

Myrgen felt something skitter across his chest and he was on his feet like a cat avoiding a tub of water. The effort made his head spin and spiral designs in black and white confused his senses behind his eyes. He leaned against the wall and shook his head to clear it. As his vision cleared, he realized there was something under his hand. He caressed the stone wall and found the shape seemed to be part of it, as if embedded. He couldn't see it, the torch no longer lighting the room, but it felt like a small smooth key. It was a part of the rock and he couldn't get his fingers on it, but he could feel its shape and it was strangely comforting. He wasn't sure if he was dreaming or not but right then, it didn't matter much to him.

He thought about what he had been through already and wondered if it was close to dawn yet. He expected to be killed about then. Almost as if in answer, he heard the dungeon door open and close, and a set of feet descended the stairs, proceeded by a light. Myrgen glanced at the wall in the gathering light and saw the small key-like shape disappear into the stone like a shadow. He stepped in front of the stone to hide it from the visitor.

Nicolai came into view, looking like he hadn't slept all night. He accidentally kicked the tray of food covered in dead and writhing insects and glanced down at it as a small roll of bread bounced against the cobbles to be stolen by a shadow in the hollows of the cells. He looked back at Myrgen. "Someone doesn't like you."

Myrgen looked at the wall behind him, then stepped closer to the bars. He saw Nicolai's source of information. Two rats were lying dead attached to a piece of fruit between them, like they died mid-struggle over the item. Myrgen was now twice as grateful he hadn't even touched the stuff. Elizabeth hadn't been kidding around. "Well, I never have had a big following. What brings you to the bowels of the cellar, Nicolai. Is it time to kill me now?"

"That's not my decision, or you would be dead already. I just came to tell you Tanglwyst was found last night, by me."

"How convenient. I'm sure she will reward you heartily."

"She was beaten near to death. She survived thanks to the Prince's agility with medicines. Had she actually died, I would have come down here and strangled you myself."

Myrgen looked at Nicolai and noticed how his eyes were darting about and his nostrils were flaring just slightly. He had the tiniest twitch to his eyes as well. *He's lying. Why would he be lying right now?* "So, what do you want from me?"

"Catriona. You found her before, to hire her. I want to know where she is. She's the one responsible for this and she's going to be thrown into that cell right next to yours, awaiting the same fate."

*So, that's it. He wants revenge for Tanglwyst getting hurt. That's what he's lying about. Or she may not be hurt at all. He just wants to kill Catriona and get her out of the way. Hell, the way Alexander was reacting to the boy's kidnapping was more like a father's rage than Nicolai seems capable of producing. Perhaps that is the truths, that Alexander, not Nicolai, was the father of the boy. It would explain the connection between her and the royal family, and Alexander's desire, if Elizabeth could be believed at all, to put Catriona on the throne as Queen.*

Myrgen felt his ire raise at this thought. *She forgave me for involving her child in this mess, and all he can think about is getting his cock wet.* "You worthless slime. As if I would sell out that woman to the likes of you. You have no currency with which to buy such a gift as your wife, and you prove that with every thrust into my sister. Catriona has been kind in the face of sorrow, forgiving in the face of judgment, and merciful when most mothers would have clawed out the eyes of someone who threatened their child and yet she has not only spared *me* but the life of the woman who brought your own *son* into this mess to use as leverage and all you can think about is getting rid of her so you can bed your whore with more impunity than you have been. You're *wife* is a better human being than you deserve, and frankly I admire the woman. I had heard she was a ruthless, vicious killer, capable of the deed we wanted her to do.

"But I was wrong. Catriona is a better person than any of us and had I known her before this incident, I would never have involved her. The rumors about her are lies. She's remarkable, intelligent, and more virtuous than anyone I know, and you had the chance to be with her. You're such an idiot, Nicolai. You want my sister, you can have her. Toss aside the best things in your life for the physical pleasures of a woman who will discard you in a year. And just to be clear, I would gladly spend the rest of my life on bended knee before Catriona than another moment paying homage to a heartless bitch like your queen.

"Now, unless you are here to fulfill some death warrant, I am busy." He turned his back on him, watching the shadows to see if the headstrong guardsman would enter the cell. Myrgen was feeling spry and rejuvenated after that speech and if Nicolai were foolish enough to try something, Myrgen was ready to take that opportunity and escape.

But Nicolai just snarled and walked away. Myrgen leaned against the wall and relaxed, letting the adrenaline drop out of him like water out of a bucket. He had no idea how much vitriol he had acquired after the incident with Elizabeth, but he was no longer a subject of the Crown of Mervolingia. It wasn't like the Rite of Sovereignty would work on him now. He would never bend a knee to that murderess. That decision alone made him a traitor, and he was glad to be one. At least he would die free of the shackles of a will-raping ritual that could cause a country's people to turn on their fellows at the whim of a spoiled brat.

He glanced around the dungeon cell and realized he could see shapes around the room now that his eyes were adjusted to the gloom. Nicolai had apparently been too angry to take the torch from the sconce to leave, which told Myrgen it must be close to daylight, if not already past, or he would have needed the light to navigate. Something seemed to be nibbling on the pile of vomit in the corner and Myrgen ignored it lest he find himself sick again. He could hear a small noise on the other side of the rock on the back wall, where the key stone had been, and he put his ear against it. Suddenly, the wall gave way and opened like it was on a hinge. He stumbled and just about hit the ground but he fell against fragrant breasts. He and the breasts fell against the wall on the other side of the small tunnel and Catriona said, "Oof!"

"Saint's Blood! I'm sorry!" He grabbed the wall and pulled himself off her as she got her footing steadied and pushed him up.

"That's, uh, quite alright. I didn't expect you to be right against the wall like that."

Myrgen looked at the wall, the opening large and obvious. "I didn't know it did that."

"Well, technically, it doesn't. Here, stand next to me." Myrgen did so and Catriona pushed the door back into place in the wall. She put a small black key on the stone and it became a solid wall again.

"Um, excuse me, but may I see that?"

She turned around and held up the small lantern that was their only light now, the key laying in her hand.

"I saw that." He looked at her eyes. "In the cell, just now."

"Yes, I was about to use it when Nicolai came but was actually having a hard time trying to figure out how to get it to work. What you said enabled me to rescue you."

"Oh. Did you…"

Catriona glanced down at her hand and closed it, putting the key back on her neck. She looked at him with the most beautiful eyes he had ever seen. "Yes. Thank you. You were very kind."

Myrgen blinked. "I meant every word." He realized at that moment that he did.

"I know. That's why the key worked." She searched his features, then looked down the hallway, a bit unsettled. Myrgen did likewise, not understanding why this woman, of all people, would be unsettled.

"Your son. I need to take you to your son. We have to get him out of here." He took her hand and started down the hall but she stopped him by not following him.

"Alan is fine. He's safe. I already found him last night."

Myrgen looked at her. "You did? So, Dom didn't…"

She shook her head. "No, he didn't need to. But thank you for sending him."

"I didn't want him involved in this." He worried for a second that might sound like he was trying to shed responsibility for her son being in this mess and it was important for her to know that wasn't what he meant. "I'm not trying to dodge your anger. I'm responsible for not getting him out myself, and for that, I'm sorry. I just…" He took a breath, seeking the truth.

"You did what you needed to, but didn't like that it needed to be done after he was involved."

He searched her dark eyes in the half-light of the lantern. She *knew*. "Yes. *Yes, exactly.*" He felt the urge to hug her for her insight, her ability to see what he wasn't even certain he had the words to say.

"Well," she continued, "we still have things we need to do. I need your help to get Marie and her baby out of Patras."

He looked back at her. "Marie? Charles' mistress?"

She returned his gaze, a bit more businesslike. "Can you think of a better target for Elizabeth to go after if she succeeds at the Rite?"

*She knows about the Rite. Amazing. That rumor* is *true.* He glanced down at the key on her neck and shook his head, returning his eyes to hers. "No, and she won't care about the infant. She'll kill them both. Come, this way will get us to the city. Do you know how to get to Marie's once we are away from here?"

Catriona nodded and the two took off through the catacombs.

\* \* \*

Catriona and Myrgen emerged from the catacombs and dodged through the garden to the edge of the hedges. The sky was pale with predawn and she recognized the importance of hurrying. She didn't know what to do after they got Marie and the baby out of there. Alexander was still in the palace, and if Elizabeth performed the Rite, she might decide to hurt him. She had not gotten a look at the queen after the initial reading in the antechamber so she had no idea of what she was capable. She decided to deal with that question once Marie and the baby were safe. After that, she would have to see what happened. Alexander was strong. If he were injured or imprisoned, she could fix that. A baby being murdered was not something she could fix.

They ran through the streets to the house with the blue door. As they approached, Catriona looked around to make sure they weren't being followed. Myrgen pointed and whispered, "Is that her?"

Marie emerged from the house carrying a bundle and a man came out behind her, carrying a bag. She looked around and they moved quickly through the streets. Myrgen watched them. "Looks as if they had the same idea you did."

Catriona watched them carefully, especially Marie. If Marie were sleeping with another man, Catriona was tempted to turn around and get out of Patras before the taint of betrayal stained her as well. Marie turned and looked down at the bundle in her arms and then over at the man with her. Her movements belied an affection for the man, but something was… she lost it before she could call the visions. "Come on. We have to get closer."

She and Myrgen kept to the graying shadows, following but not getting more than a glimpse. Finally, they entered a building, closing the door behind them. Catriona looked at the place and frowned. *Tristram's! That meant the man with her was Armand!* "Myrgen, that's the Poison maker's house."

"Poison maker's? Do you mean the one who's been poisoning Charles? How?"

"Let's go find out." She went swiftly to the back door and fiddled with the door out of Myrgen's sight.

"Does that key just open any door?"

She looked at him and got the door unlocked, then held up a brass key. "No. I actually have a key." She smiled at his expression as he practically laughed at his own imagination and they slipped into the kitchen area. They moved quietly through the house until Catriona heard the baby in the main room. She looked in and saw no one at first, then a small hand waved around from Tristram's chair. She went into the room and picked up the child, making sure he was okay. She looked up at Myrgen whose smile suddenly turned to shock.

"Catriona!"

A blow to the back of her head stunned her and she fell forward onto the chair, then to the floor. Her hold on the child loosened as she hit the floor but she had the capacity to make sure the child wasn't hurt. Catriona crumpled into a heap, her body cushioning the child from the floor. The baby seemed startled at the sudden drop, but rolled off Catriona's chest and onto the floor. She heard Myrgen run into the room, engaging Armand in a fight as the blackness was pierced by a large light behind her. She turned around and saw the Old Church start to come into focus, but then Father Benjamin ran to the doorway and shouted, *"NO! Go back! You have to stop the baby. You have to stop the baby.* A bright light shot forth from the priest's hands and she felt herself knocked back into her body. She shook her head to try and clear it, and her eyes focused slowly.

She saw a form cross in front of her, moving quickly on all fours and she tried to identify it. Her vision finally came to her in time to see the baby about to pick up a piece of ceramic pitcher that had hit her. Remembering Alan's tendencies at this age to put everything in his mouth, Catriona reached out and grabbed hold of the child's legs, stopping it from quite getting to the area of the pitcher piece he was going after. Unfortunately, she could see several pieces within reach of the child and he was already recognizing the other opportunities available to him.

"…Myr..gen.."

Myrgen punched Armand and sent him out cold to the floor, then turned to see Catriona's struggle. A door opened in the rooms above and Marie screamed from the railing, "Francois!"

Myrgen threw himself at the child, sliding along the smooth wooden planked floor to lay right before him. Francois grabbed onto Myrgen's nose and pulled himself up to a standing position, gaining leverage on his ear. The child looked up at Marie and smiled as Myrgen looked past him to Catriona. "Are you hurt?"

He put an arm around the boy and sat up as his mother came running down the stairs. He lifted the boy up to his mother who grabbed him from this home invader. Myrgen expected a kick to his face.

Marie stepped on some of the ceramic pieces all around them and looked down, assessing the situation. She looked over at Armand who was stirring now and went over to him. Myrgen watched her go, then looked back at Catriona. *"Are you hurt?"*

She rolled onto her stomach and tried to push off the ground. The effort made her dizzy and spots of blood hit the floor in front of her eyes. She looked up at Myrgen. "Apparently so…" she closed her eyes and fell forward, just barely sensing Myrgen catching her in his arms.

\* \* \*

Myrgen looked at Marie. "Do I need to fight you both to get her out of here?"

Armand was getting to his feet, slowly. "Why were you following us?"

"Catriona wanted to come and get Marie and the baby and take them to safety. Elizabeth is right now performing the Rite of Sovereignty. She plans to seize the throne. If she succeeds, Catriona feared for the lives of you and your child, Marie. I can vouch for the fact she is right to be concerned."

Marie looked back at the child squirming in her arms, then back at Armand. They exchanged a look and she nodded and turned to Myrgen. "Bring her upstairs. Armand, get some water and towels, for both of you." She went for the stairs as Myrgen picked Catriona off the floor and carried her up the stairs to the bedroom Marie indicated.

Myrgen checked the wound on his charge's head and found it swollen and bloody from a cut to the scalp. Marie put Francois in a crib in the room and Myrgen looked at her. "Obviously, you frequent this place."

"Yes. Armand is my brother. I often stay here to keep track of the place when he's away on the ship. Keeps me out of the public eye."

"Is that the reason for the packed bag?"

"This time? No."

Armand came in with some towels and a basin of colored water. Myrgen looked skeptical but Marie said, "It's an herbal remedy I created. Something I picked up from Alexander and perfected. I assume you know who I am."

Myrgen nodded to the child who was happily chewing on a small rag doll in the latest fashions from Mande. "And him. He has a strong resemblance to his father." She looked away and he cleared his throat. "I'm sorry about your loss."

She looked back to Myrgen. "Don't be. I think you should know something. It's about Charles, the king…"

"Marie?" Armand stopped his ministrations on Catriona's wound and looked at her, his eyes sharp with an unspoken scolding.

"Armand, they just saved his son. Don't you think he would trust them?"

Myrgen looked back and forth between them. "If it helps, I know for a fact he trusted *her*. She saved his life. She's Catriona."

"Wait, you mean the woman Alexander loves?"

Myrgen felt his heart sink when she said that out loud. "Y, yes." He looked back at his savior. "Yes. Of course he does…"

* * *

Catriona entered Father Benjamin's church for the third

time in as many days and greeted the friar soon thereafter.

"You're certainly taking a lot of spills these days," he said concerned.

"Remember, one of those was intentional."

"Ah yes, but not this one, right?"

"Well, no, but I'm afraid I'm confused. Did you just *block* me from coming here?"

Father Benjamin took a deep breath. "As a matter of fact, yes."

"You can do that?"

"Only under extreme circumstances. It takes a lot of effort to do so. I can also bring you here if you're teetering on the edge. Nevertheless, I have been thinking about your predicament, my child."

"My predicament?"

"With Alexander."

"Yes?"

"Would you rather be free, and alone, or imprisoned with him by your side?"

"What an impossible question. I'd rather, of course, be free with him by my side."

"You had your chance at that and never took it."

Catriona cringed at the comment, saying, "That was harsh."

"It hurt like the truth, didn't it? Answer the question."

"I…I don't know…"

"I only ask this because you have the means to be his bride. You are the Stâpâna of Caratia and the adopted daughter of the Dûce. Even Catherine will acknowledge that claim as being nobility enough to put your blood within reach of the royal lineage and an alliance between the two countries would make both your countries safe from all attackers. With Caratia's endless army and Mervolingia's endless supplies of food and medicinal advancements, your pairing would be the greatest in history. Accept this lineage and be willing to blend it with his, and you two can be together, even produce an heir. Your presence will bring a healing strength back to his bloodline, saving it."

Catriona stood up and walked over to the windows, looking out. She could see Armand tending to her wounds and felt the pings of pain on the back of her head. She could see Marie explaining something and the child of her old friend bouncing a doll against a crib wall. And she could see Myrgen, sitting next to her on the bed and paying very close attention to what Armand was doing while nodding and acknowledging Marie's comments.

"I, I don't know. The Land sent me back to save the one I'm supposed to be with, but Alexander is still in there. Is that what Anika was talking about when she said I needed to save him? Restoring the bloodline? Or was I supposed to get him out of there?"

"Well, you haven't gone to stop Elizabeth. Why not?"

She folded her arms and sighed. "Because if she can seize the power, he could leave Patras with me. But if she succeeds, many will die."

"Time to choose, my dear."

Catriona looked over as the doors to the church opened again. She looked out the window once more and then walked over to the opening and into the darkness.

* * *

"Catriona? Wake up." Myrgen was patting her hand as she opened her eyes. "There you are." He smiled at her and she closed her eyes, furrowing her brow and focusing on the pain in the back of her head.

"Give me a moment, please." She tried to pull energy from the earth but she was too far away. She had healed enough for the bleeding to have stopped though and when she sat up, her head throbbed but was bearable. "Did you tell them our concerns?"

Myrgen nodded, his own concern for her not yet evaporated. "Yes. They understand but they have a request. One of their people is still behind, someone else in jeopardy if they stay. Marie insists on going back."

"Then we have to hurry. It's already dawn." She looked at him, his steel grey eyes poring into her as she recovered from the blow to her head. "Perhaps you should stay here. If you're caught…"

"It will be no different than if you are caught. Trust me. If Elizabeth becomes Sovereign, you're as dead as I am. How's your head?" He reached up and felt it and her blinking stuttered at his touch.

"I'll be better once I get back in the tunnels. I assume that's how we're getting in?"

"Yes." He took his hand away, checking for blood. Finding none, he rubbed his fingers together, then stood. "Then we need to be going. What are we going to do with the baby? He can't come along."

Marie cleared her throat. "I'll stay behind. Armand knows what to do. We'll meet back here and leave right away."

Catriona looked at her. "Do you have safe passage?"

"We will once we get to Rouen. Tristram is waiting. Before that will be the challenge."

"If need be," Myrgen volunteered, "we'll meet here as well and travel together." He looked at Catriona. "It only makes sense."

She nodded and they made their way downstairs. Armand got a small satchel from his laboratory and slung it over his shoulder. Catriona closed her eyes and pulled energy from the ground beneath her feet. There was still a slight barrier, but she got rid of the lingering pain and the lump, nonetheless. A hand on her shoulder opened her eyes. "Are you sure you're okay?" Myrgen's eyes searched hers for signs of internal damage.

She put his hand on the back of her head. "Yes. See? All better."

He felt the back of her head and furrowed his brow in confusion as the damage seemed to be completely gone. She suddenly felt his proximity, the feel of his hand in her hair, and he hesitated taking it away. She felt her breathing become shallow and when she removed his hand, it brushed the back of her neck and her eyes closed as he instinctively found one of her erogenous places.

His eyes sparkled at her response and the barest of knowing smiles snuck into his features. "Yes, I see." He turned to Armand. "You have everything you need?"

Armand nodded and Catriona said, "Then let's go. Our time is already too short."

***Chapter Thirty-nine:***
***"Pride goeth before destruction and a haughty spirit before the fall."***
***~ Proverbs 16:18***

Dominic walked up the stairs, planning on checking on Tanglwyst's condition before he went to the Chancellor's office to prepare for the day. He and Gwen had gotten home late and he had gotten a few hours' sleep before his internal clock told him to get back to the palace. Downstairs, Catriona had looked as exhausted as he and Gwen had felt and he sincerely hoped she had gotten some rest. He met up with Nicolai at the top of the stairs.

"Dominic. Good. This saves me a trip. Tanglwyst is awake. She asked for you."

"How is she?"

"It's the first time she's been awake since I found her. She mumbled something earlier about Catriona doing this, but I don't think she was herself. She also bled a lot earlier, but that, too has stopped. I'm going to get the Prince now."

Dominic nodded and went down the hallway. He knocked on the door to the room Tanglwyst was in and opened it. She sat up in the bed, her face bruised and her arms bandaged but clearly not dead.

Tanglwyst said weakly, "Hello there…"

Dominic sat down on the edge of Tanglwyst's bed and looked over the damage done. *All cosmetic. Why didn't Catriona kill her?*

Tanglwyst smiled at her friend. "Dominic."

"I was told you sent for me?"

"Yes. Dominic, it was Catriona. She's turned against me. What can I do?"

"Why don't you start by telling me *why* she's turned against you."

Tanglwyst averted her eyes for a second and asked, "What do you mean?"

"Well, you and I both know she's very particular about her assignments. If she doesn't agree with the principles behind it, she won't do it. So what did you have her do that was against her principles, and how did you trick her into doing it?"

"Dom, I don't know what you're…"

"Tanglwyst," he interrupted, "you're wearing perfume applied in the last twenty-four hours. You've been missing for over a week. You figure it out."

Tanglwyst's eyes snapped up to his, stunned by the revelation. She looked for a moment like she was going to try and deny it, but then she sighed instead. "When Beth called me to the palace because Charles had beaten her, I was furious. After my own ordeal with my first husband, I have terrible nightmares still about the beatings. I didn't think anyone should be allowed to treat someone like that, not even the king. Charles had done a thousand things to prove he was unfit to rule this kingdom, and Alexander had done as many things to prove he could do it better. So, I talked to Myrgen about what we could do. He got quite a few of the ruthless genes in the family. In fact, when Daddy hired Guillaume to kill my first husband, he got the contact name from Myrgen.

"Myrgen was outraged. He confided in me that he was in love with Elizabeth, and he would gladly make Charles pay for hurting her. He said we needed a contact for an assassin and came back a few days later with Catriona's name from the Underground. When I told him I knew her, he decided to contact her himself, so my hands wouldn't get dirty on this.

"She refused the job. So, I recommended he use *me* as a persuasion lever."

"Whose idea was it to take her son as well? Myrgen's?"

Tanglwyst blinked. "How did you know about that?"

"I have my sources as well, Tanglwyst."

"No, that was mine too. Myrgen actually wanted to go with someone else, but you might say I had plans for Catriona."

Dominic folded his arms. "You mean plans involving Nicolai."

"Dominic, you and I have always been able to talk about even our most vile inner feelings. I set it up for Catriona to be poisoned, killed by the dart which was supposed to put her to sleep, but she avoided being stuck by the dart. I fully expected to have Alan back in Nicolai's arms by the next morning or afternoon."

"I see. So, you used your friendship with Catriona to blackmail her into doing this deed, so you could kill her."

"She's not a friend, Dominic. She was never a friend. She's

a resource. Resources are meant to be used."

Dominic blinked at the callousness of that remark and sat back from her. "Is that what *I* am too, just a resource? Can I expect to be sold out as well?"

"I hardly think you are the appropriate person to be getting self-righteous here, Dominic D'Medici-Giovanni." She sat back a bit as her dart flew home. "Besides, I would never betray you, Dominic. I love you. You know that."

"I thought you loved Nicolai this week."

"That was cruel."

"I learned from the best," he replied, gesturing to Tanglwyst.

"Well, I had to do something after Gwen captured your heart. Nicolai seemed like a good bet."

"Until August, when Catriona walked into the room and they saw each other."

Tanglwyst flinched at the memory. "I was in love with him by that time, Dominic, and he had loved me. He had spent years mourning the death of his wife and by that summer, had finally laid her to rest in order to be with me. I couldn't bear to see him thrown back into the sorrow of those memories, nor make him endure the pain of trying to determine what had happened. Then that thing of yours with the Church interfered this year and they have been in a limbo ever since.

"I wanted to put an end to it, for both of them."

Dominic swallowed heavily, attempting to steel himself for what lay ahead, but knew he was not quite ready. He shook his head and closed his eyes in shame. "What were you going to do about the king, or didn't you care about that anymore?"

"Myrgen could find someone else as easily as he found her. It was a very convenient way to… kill two birds with one stone. But look, she must still have some code against killing me. After all, I'm still alive now, and she could have killed me if she wanted to."

"It hasn't occurred that she didn't kill you because she has a worse punishment in mind?"

"Such as?"

"Do I look like Catriona? I have no idea what she'll do, and neither do you."

"Well, at least I won't be alone, like she will be. Her

actions today have firmly set Nicolai against her. She realized they would. She told me so. He'll kill her if he sees her again, to avenge me." Her head got a righteous toss in at the end

Dominic just shook his head at her utter foolishness. "You idiot. You kidnapped the son of the most dangerous woman I have ever met and you have the audacity to act like she deserved it."

Tanglwyst arched and eyebrow and got out of bed. "I'm still alive, Dominic. That's more than I can say for Charles. He was a bloody mess."

Dominic blinked. Tanglwyst had been unconscious all night, according to Nicolai in the hallway. That level of detail would be known only by someone who was in the room. "Tanglwyst, what have you done?"

"Nothing. It was already done. But I saw the aftermath."

"Did you see who did it?"

"No, but I didn't care. It was done. Frankly, the who is insignificant. I can implicate Catriona at every stage and *this*," she pointed to the damage on her face, "just makes my accusations that much more believable." She walked over to the mirror in the room. "She never should have messed with me, Dom."

* * *

Alexander awoke to a knock at the door and he tumbled out of bed, barely conscious. He unlocked his door and peered out into the hallway. It was Nicolai. "Pardon me, your Highness. Tanglwyst is awake. Did you want to look in on her?" Nicolai's formality didn't hide his true feelings for the Prince and Alexander was beyond caring about the man's emotional state.

"Is she lucid?" He rubbed his head and hair.

"Yes, and thirsty."

"Then get her some wine or water and let her heal. Has her bleeding stopped?"

"Yes. It had stopped by the time I got back."

"Got back?"

"Yes. I went to see Myrgen again."

Alexander blinked slowly. "Why?"

"I wanted to find my wife."

Alexander suddenly remembered his companion from earlier and looked over at his bed, fully expecting to see the subject of their conversation with her beautiful hair splayed across his pillow. But the bed was empty. He turned back to Nicolai.

Nicolai's nostrils flared and he breathed in, eyes enraged. Alexander realized he had just given away the fact that Catriona had been there and he realized he could smell her on himself. If he could, there was no doubt Nicolai could. The guardsman shoved the door open and stepped into the room, looking around. Alexander stepped back, his anger coupling with his desire to protect Catriona. "What are you doing?"

"Trying to catch a traitor to the Crown, *Your Highness.*"

"Are you accusing me of treachery, Nicolai?"

Nicolai looked him full in the face. "Of sleeping with the enemy? Yes." He walked over to the bed and looked around, sniffing.

"GUARDS!" The sound of the Prince's bellow brought a sound of running boot strikes down the hall. The liveried guards arrived just as Nicolai grabbed something off the pillow of the bed. "Throw him out of the palace! Get him away from me now!"

Nicolai held up something small that Alexander couldn't see. "She's been here! Here's the proof!" Nicolai came over and had a long black hair in his hand. "Deny it now."

Alexander leaned in. "You are dismissed, Nicolai Moriarity. Leave my house and don't return. If you *dare* come near me or my family again, I'll have you executed." He nodded to the guards who grabbed their former leader and muscled him out of the room. Alexander slammed the door and ran to the prayer room, looking for Catriona. He needed to make sure she was safe. She wasn't in the room and he opened the secret passage, running through the catacombs to the crossroad. "Catriona! Are you here?"

He stood in the middle of the room, the sound of his cries echoing throughout the underbelly of the palace but no response returned to him, no matter how many times he called her name. She was gone, again. He fell to his knees, fist slamming the ground beneath him, and as he beat the earth for taking her again. His loss demanded the sacrifice of tears, and he gave them.

* * *

Dominic watched Tanglwyst examine the wounds and felt his disgust rise like bile in his throat. Then he heard a call in the hall and opened the door. Guards ran down the hall towards the Prince's open door and Dominic stepped out into the hall. Tanglwyst asked, "What is it?"

"I don't know, but I'm going to find out. Wait here." He closed the door behind him, the physical barrier between them making him feel better already. *To think I almost kissed that viper once.* Guards piled into the Prince's chambers and a struggle was clearly happening. Nicolai was growling and shouting something about proof and the Prince was answering his accusations. The guards dragged the man out of the royal chambers, it taking all of them on this level to keep him under control. As they removed the snarling Latian from the area, Dominic thought about what Tanglwyst had just told him. Alexander needed to know this.

He knocked on the door but didn't hear anything. He opened the door. "Your Highness?" The room was empty and Dominic looked around the hallway, making sure he wasn't observed. He knew the Prince had not passed him so he must have gone through the catacombs. Dominic remembered Catriona's charge to him, to handle anything unexpected, and he felt like this qualified. He ducked into the room and closed the door, locking it against further discovery.

He went into the prayer nave, the only obvious place for an escape route, and pushed the now-familiar trigger stone. *Thank the Saints they seem to use the same craftsman as the ones down below.* He could hear someone shouting in the catacombs, the sound funneling right to him. He looked around for a light, worried the Prince had encountered someone else in the darkness. He found a torch right outside the nave and used a flickering votive to light it quickly. He took the torch and followed the sound of the shouts. They stopped, and Dominic moved faster, not daring to think about what would have stopped him. He saw the man in a heap on the floor, pounding the stone and weeping. Dominic looked around for anyone else, then stepped over and put a hand on his Prince's back.

"Your Highness...?"

"...she's gone... again..." Alexander lifted himself up from the ground by his fists, his hair hanging toward tear-marked flagstones.

"Who? Who's gone again?"

Alexander looked at Dominic. "Catriona."

Dominic took a knee beside him, hand still resting on his

shoulder. "She is trying to save your kingdom, Your Highness. Let her do her work. Come, I have something to tell you, something important. It's about Tanglwyst."

* * *

Elizabeth opened her eyes, the brocade pattern from Charles' doublet indenting her cheek. She had done it. She had completed the Rite of Sovereignty! The power to control the people of Mervolingia was hers to command. She stood up, the pains from her efforts creaking in her bones and muscles. She stumbled a bit from exhaustion and fell to the ground next to the crypt. She laughed, her voice bouncing around the cave-like room like a bat. "Thank the Saints I'm alone, Charles. It wouldn't do for the people to see their Sovereign unsteady on her feet."

She stretched her legs and arms, deciding not to get up just then. She had no idea what time it was, but the scroll on the crypt had indicated several hours' worth of work. Her voice was hoarse from the chanting and her calves ached from the walking. On the other hand, the constant movement had kept her awake all night. When she had reached the end, she had felt a rush of energy enter her and had apparently collapsed across Charles' body. She ran her fingers through her hair and they caught on the snarls there. It took some effort but she managed to finger comb through the mess. She looked around the room and saw a dried corpse in an elaborate, but rotting gown and hat from a few generations ago.

She grabbed the stone slab above her and pulled herself up, eyes on the hat. Her steps were starting to smooth out and she pulled the hat off the corpse. The head came with it, detaching from the rest of the body easily. She pulled the hat off the cranium and looked inside. She spied what she wanted and ripped the securing comb out of the hat, tossing it aside next to the abandoned skull. "You don't mind if I use this, do you? After all, I'm your ruler now. You have to do as I say." She started combing her hair with the silver comb, small bits of ancient skin joining her auburn locks.

She spun around, wielding the comb like a scepter. "You *all* have to do as I say! Bow before me, Mervolingia!" The sound of her shouting caused the disrupted bones of the woman to fall off the shelf she had been on and she crumpled into a dusty heap at

Elizabeth's feet. Elizabeth looked down and nodded to the remains. "Thank you. I'm going to promote you to Chancellor. I understand there's an opening."

She laughed, the sound carrying throughout the crypt.

* * *

Catriona, Myrgen and Armand entered the catacombs at a run, this being the first opening they had seen in twenty minutes. Once inside, they leaned up against the wall to let their eyes adjust. "Myrgen," Catriona whispered, "the Rite of Sovereignty. Have you ever seen it?"

"Performed? No. Charles was already in power when I came here. But I've read through the ritual."

"How long does it take?"

"Saints, hours. There are places where you have to chant something for about an hour, and there's walking around to drive away all spirits that want the power for themselves. It's a long and elaborate process."

"Would Elizabeth need help for it?"

"No, it can be done by one person. In fact, it says it must be done only by the person getting the power. No other souls in the room."

"How long has she had to do it?" She looked at him, the light from their entrance giving them a little to see by. "Enough time?"

"She came by right before I sent Dominic to help Alan escape. That was the middle of the night."

"I saw Dominic about midnight."

"You had already saved your son by the time I talked to him." His head was cocked a little and his voice revealed his embarrassment. He folded his arms across his chest. "I feel now like I should have guessed that would happen."

She blinked and touched his hand. "You wanted Alan safe, Myrgen. He is."

"Alan? That's your son's name?"

"Yes."

"I'm sorry I didn't know. I never meant for him…"

"I know."

He looked down at her hand on his, then up again into her

eyes. A light flared behind them as Armand lit a sulfur stick and used it to secure light from a torch. Catriona looked back at Myrgen. "Where to?"

He looked at Armand and took the torch from him. "The Royal Crypts. That's where they would have taken Charles. This way." They went down the hallway past where the holding cells were and entered the torture chamber. Catriona could see Myrgen was very self-conscious about the room and kept glancing at her to make sure she was not attacking him. She smiled behind his back, amused at his concern. She followed him to a secret door on the other side of the room and it opened up into a hallway. On the one side was a shelf with a skeleton on it, and above that was another. Myrgen looked back at Catriona and Armand. "I think we're in the right place."

Suddenly, a high, eerie laughter bounced down the walls from far away. The sound was incredibly unsettling to Catriona, having seen the dead talk before. She touched the stone of the walls and took a deep breath, gathering her courage from the rock. They moved down the tunnel until they saw a light up ahead. Catriona took the torch and set it back a few feet on the ground. The light was lessened and they proceeded forward slowly. Catriona watched carefully the shadows before her for any changes. They came around a corner and there was Elizabeth, standing over a crumpled skeleton in rotted clothes, talking to it.

"Thank you. I'm going to promote you to Chancellor. I understand there's an opening."

Myrgen and Catriona looked at each other, disturbed at the scene before them. Myrgen looked about ready to move and Catriona stopped him with a hand on his arm. She could feel the approach of something, someone. The ground told her not to move and a moment later, the main door to the crypt opened and Alexander himself came in, followed by Catherine and several guards and retinue. Elizabeth turned to look at them, composing herself as she did so. Catriona moved to the other side of the crypt, blending into the shadows of the rock.

"Elizabeth." Alexander was dressed well and looked good. She was glad she had stayed with him a while last night. It appeared to have helped him immensely although, she could still see the wear in his eyes.

"Ah, Alexander! My Heir Apparent."

Alexander looked around the room at the candles and the scroll on his brother's body. "Elizabeth, what have you done?"

"I've seized the power of the Throne for myself, Alexander. You were foolish to defy me. Now you will pay. I have completed the Rite of Sovereignty. Bow before me!"

Alexander took hold of the Sword of State on his belt and drew it out. The guards behind him followed suit and then, as if compelled to, he put the Sword, tip down, in front of him and took a knee. He bowed his head and all the others did likewise. All but Catherine. She merely bowed her head, a slight smile lighting her eyes. Catriona saw a spark of defiance and destruction in the Queen-Mother and apparently Elizabeth did as well. She stepped over towards the kneeling group and stood before Alexander.

"She defies me, Alexander. Execute the traitor."

"As you command, my Queen." He stood and walked over between his mother and Elizabeth, the Sword of State glittering in the firelight cascading around the room. He looked at his mother and then spun around and with a thrust, embedded the Sword of State in Elizabeth's gut. The look of horror and shock on her face was immense and she dropped to her knees in great pain.

"You are such a fool, Elizabeth. Only one person ever knows the Rite of Sovereignty, and that is the Heir." He walked over to the body of his brother and picked up the scroll she had used. "This one we give to the Chancellor so that the person sets themselves up to be alone, undefended and exhausted by the time we find them. Nothing on this scroll is correct. I don't need to chant for hours, I don't need to be alone, and I don't even need to have the person dead to take his power. He just needs to relent it to me, something that," Alexander's voice grew softer, "for our own reasons, Charles was never willing to do before." He touched his brother's chest. "Go in peace my brother. You are released."

A golden light flowed up Alexander's fingers and into his body, culminating in his eyes. A regal air came around him and Catriona saw him as the leader he had always avoided being. She could see how people would follow this man into battle and give their lives for him. And she felt humbled to be in his presence, almost enough to take a knee before him. He took a breath and let it out, then turned back to the assembled populace. "Gentlemen, get this garbage out of my family burial chamber. Finish executing her and put her body on a pike by the river." He walked over and removed the Sword of State from her belly, not caring about any further damage.

The men around him surged forward to do his bidding and he turned to his mother. She curtsied deeply before her son and straightened up to give him a hug. "You have done well, Alexander. "

"Thank you, Mother."

"You are king now and must act accordingly. Tell me, do you have someone in mind for your queen?"

"I have, Mother."

"So the rumors are true then. Will I like her?"

"I will insist you do so."

Catherine blinked slowly, nodding. "Ah, so you love her, then?"

"Every breath without her is an agony and a thousand lashes with her before me would not be a bee sting."

"Well said. Make sure you tell her that." She turned to leave, "Women like it when you say things like that to them. Now come, escort your mother out of this dreadful place."

*Chapter Forty:*
*"The wicked is snared by the transgression of his lips, but the just shall come out of trouble."*
*~ Proverbs 12:13*

Armand stepped away from Myrgen and Catriona and retrieved the torch from down the hall. She tried not to think about what Alexander had just said, but she couldn't help it. Father Benjamin had told her she could save him, save the whole family and she wanted to help him. She was still holding back, though she knew, if he asked her again in earnest, she would be unable to deny him his wish. She would indeed defy the laws of the Land and marry Alexander. The mere thought frightened her and she didn't know why.

They watched the light flare as the poison maker lifted it, allowing the whole torch to burn again. They followed him into the room and Myrgen took the torch from him to free up his hands. He opened a small jar and put the salve inside on Charles' teeth and lips. He pulled another jar from his pouch and smeared it on his hands. He then handed Catriona a brass goblet and poured some wine into it. He looked around and picked up the hat Elizabeth had foraged and handed that to Myrgen.

"Hold this right here." He positioned him next to Charles' waist, the hat raised to about hip level. Myrgen looked at Catriona who shrugged. Myrgen looked surprised and squinted his eyes at her, then flicked his gaze at Armand. She arched an eyebrow and looked at Armand, then back at Myrgen, who squinted and flicked again. Then she understood. *Ah. He wants me to read him. All right.*

She looked at Armand who was bringing out a vial this time and she called the visions on him. Almost too late, she saw what was happening. "By the Stones!" She grabbed Myrgen's arm and pulled just as the vial hit Charles' lips and the fluid passed over his tongue. Charles sat straight up, gagging and gasping for air. He turned to the side where Myrgen had been holding the hat and vomited, Catriona's intervention saving Myrgen's coat. The expulsion was blue and smelled like rotting bread. Myrgen stepped away, shaking his head and Armand covered a snicker with his sleeve.

Catriona handed Charles the goblet of wine and he drank it

in two gulps. He finished and took a deep breath. "Where am I?"

"In your family crypt, Charles. You're dead."

He looked around. "Really? Then it worked?" He looked at Armand, who nodded. "What about the Sovereignty? Did he take it?"

Catriona's breath caught as she thought about what that would mean and she glanced away. Myrgen noticed and glanced at her but stayed focused on Charles' questions. "Yes. He said he could have done it at any time but for your own reasons, you never did."

Charles flicked his eyes to Catriona, then at the floor. "Yes." He looked back at Myrgen. "What are you doing here? Did Marie involve you too? Because you love Elizabeth?"

Myrgen closed his eyes and shuddered. "Uh, no. I'm… here with her." He nodded to Catriona. "You knew I cared for Elizabeth?"

"Saints, yes, Myrgen. The way you pined after her? Obvious as blue… vomit… Oh Saint's Blood, can we go?" He put his sleeve to his nose. Armand offered his other arm to help Charles down.

Myrgen looked at Catriona. "So, did you know he was still alive?"

"Not until I read Armand, like you asked." She looked at Armand. "This was Marie's doing?"

Armand nodded. "She's quite an accomplished chemist. She found a family recipe from a Mandian cousin that would make him appear to lose his sanity. Then, she was going to administer a final dose with an added ingredient that would simulate death for a day. He was going to come out of it on his own, but when you offered to go get him now, I brought the stuff to bring him out early."

"Dominic D'Medici is your cousin?"

Armand looked at Myrgen. "How did you know he was the creator?"

"He told me. He also said it wasn't lethal."

"It's not, but she decided to give him the other dose, the one that would kill him, because of the attack on the servant, and Elizabeth. The poison wasn't supposed to do that. Marie determined that someone must be adding something to the mix to make him actually go insane."

"Someone else was poisoning you?" Myrgen looked at Catriona. "I'll bet it was Elizabeth. She poisoned the food she brought me last night."

Charles squatted by the bloody mess on the flagstones. "This looks fatal." He looked up at the assembled rescuers. "Who's blood is this?"

Myrgen said, "Elizabeth's. Alexander made his first official act her execution. For treason." He picked up the false ritual and handed it to Charles.

Charles shook his head and stood. "Thank the Saints I'm out of here." He tossed the scroll aside where it landed on the blood trail. The vellum scraped the stones as it skidded to rest against the wall, slurring the blood a bit more.

"Well, not exactly yet," Armand said. "Marie and I don't quite know how to get you to Rouen. Not without being seen."

Myrgen said, "I can get you there without being seen. There's an escape tunnel under here that connects to a dock just out of town. It was my back-up plan if things went foul here. It's a bit rickety and tends to cave in, but when faced with dying on a gallows, well…"

"We don't need to do that. I have made a few preparations myself," Catriona brought up, "Michael is already waiting in Rouen for us. I told him we would have extra passengers."

"Perfect. Shall we then?" Charles walked off with a sprint in his step and Armand ran to catch up to him. Catriona and Myrgen looked at each other and then followed suit.

Myrgen asked "You were expecting other passengers?" Catriona nodded.

"If you didn't know Charles was alive, how did you know you would be bringing him?"

"I didn't." She looked at Myrgen. "I thought I would be bringing you."

He blinked, his brow furrowing at the realization. "Thank you."

They entered the torture chamber after Charles and Armand and met in the center of the room. Charles looked around. "What a horrible place. I had no idea this was down here, and so close to the old church."

Myrgen glanced at Catriona, the guilt he felt at their first meeting evident in his face. She walked over to a canvas sea bag that was stored over by the cage in the center of the room. "First things first, Charles. The grounds are covered in servants, mourners and townspeople who know what you look like. We need to disguise you in order to get you out of here." She pulled out a small hinged and latched box and some dark traveling clothes. She tossed the clothes to her friend. Myrgen came over to inspect the box as she set it on the desk next to a sheaf of darts and a blowgun. Inside was a performer's make-up kit. It contained various pieces of hair and a couple fake noses. She pulled out an eye patch and handed it to Myrgen.

"An eye patch?"

"Best disguise out there. If you can only have one thing to distract from your appearance, make it an eye patch. People focus on the patch and forget everything else about you." She glanced over at Charles to see what stage he was at in dressing and saw he was stripped down to the waist and putting on the black shirt. She turned back to Myrgen and called the visions to her as she asked, "Myrgen, did you know these darts were poisoned?"

"Yes. Well, actually, it wasn't poison, just sleeping agent, but yes, I knew they were dipped."  He smiled. "You were a dangerous woman. I didn't want to take any chances."

"No, I mean did you know they were *poisoned*?"

Myrgen looked at her, confused, then picked up the darts and inspected them in the lantern light. The greenish sheen gave the poison away and he turned to her. "It was supposed to be a sleeping potion."

"Where did you get it?"

Myrgen looked at the darts and then he frowned, disgusted. "Tanglwyst. Saint's Blood, that's why she was pushing so hard to get you to do the job. I never figured it out before." He leaned on the desk with both hands and shook his head. "What a fool I was. She knew just how to distract me from what she was doing."

Catriona sensed with every fiber of her body and found his response to be truthful. She looked down at the desk. "Your sister is a master manipulator. Don't damn yourself because you fell prey to a professional."

"She's my sister. I never expected she would turn her tricks on me."  He threw the darts onto the desk and they skittered and bounced against the pigeon holes at the back.

Catriona watched him, saw he truly was sorry and feeling

Karma pushing him towards balance with all these revelations. She turned her back to the strip show behind her and asked him, "Why did you give my son a puppy?"

Myrgen looked up from the poisoned darts. "I had one as a child. He was my best friend. Thanks to my dog, I was able to get through an awful lot of trials because there was someone who was always there for me. It seemed like a good idea."

Catriona put his hand on his arm. "Thank you."

Myrgen looked down at her hand and then back at her. "Why are you thanking me? I took your son so you would murder your friend."

She detected the lie in his words and shook her head. "No, Myrgen, you didn't. Tanglwyst took my son to get me here so she could bloody your hands killing me. You would just as easily use someone more professional, someone whose loyalty could be purchased with the simplicity of money." Myrgen turned to face her more as she continued to unroll the entire situation in front of him, his amazement at her accuracy evident in his facial responses.

"When you saw you had been manipulated, you dealt with the problem as best you could, showing great kindness and consideration where none was truly expected. Your sister has betrayed us both, as has the woman you love. Yet, even after you were caught, you sent Dominic to fetch my son, to ensure he would be safe. That's why I'm thanking you, and that's why I'm getting you out of here."

"Except you had gotten your son out already."

"Yes. When Dominic came to the cell where Alan had been, I was there, resting. It was the one place I felt no one would disturb me."

Myrgen put his hand to his mouth, then shook his head, spreading his arms wide. "You are every bit as legendary as I've been told you are."

Catriona smiled, glancing at the desk. She felt like blushing, which surprised her. "Thank you."

Charles said, "How do I look?" He turned, the simple clothes comfortable-looking. Catriona noted that they looked right on him now, where before, when she had seen him leaving Marie's in commoner's clothing, she had noticed the regality of his bearing, despite the humble outer appearances. He still could carry himself well, but without the burden of Sovereignty, he would be able to blend in.

"Good. Now, put this on." She handed him the eye patch. Armand helped him fasten it on his face and the look was complete.

Myrgen nodded. "You're right. I can only see an eye patch."

"Now what?" Charles waited, fidgeting in his excitement to begin his new life.

Catriona closed the drawstring on the sea bag and handed it to Charles. "Now, you walk to your lady and child and leave. Armand said you have passage on the *Righteous*."

"Yes. Yes we do."

"Then go out that door, turn right and leave the area by going past the kitchen. You should be able to get away unmolested."

"What about you two?"

Catriona looked at Myrgen, then back at Charles and Armand. "Unfortunately, I only brought the one set of clothes. I wasn't expecting to rescue you as well, Charles."

As Charles started to protest, Myrgen held up a hand. "Don't worry about it. I know how to get us clear of here without being seen. We'll have to cut through the old burnt out church to the west, but we can get out of here. You go, before we're discovered."

Charles came over to Catriona and gave her a hug and a kiss on the cheek. "Thank you, old friend." He turned to Myrgen. "And thank *you,* new friend. Fair winds and following seas, folks." He backed away and turned to Armand, shouldering the sea bag and clapped him on the shoulder and the two men left the area.

Catriona turned to Myrgen. "Through the burnt out church, you said? There's an opening across from where my son was held."

"No, that way is blocked. A bunch of timbers and stones fell right there. There's only room for a small child to squeak through. Here," he grabbed a small lantern on the desk and pulled a set of sulfur sticks from one of the drawers to light it. "We're going to need this. The floor isn't very stable through there and because of all the fire damage, you can't always tell a charred rafter from a pit." The lantern flared to life and he pointed to an iron maiden on the other side of the room. "C'mon. This way."

She followed him and he opened the torture device, pushing a clasp inside the thing. The back swung open and they stepped through to a small, dark tunnel. It turned twice before opening into the rectory of an ancient husk with a few holy symbols still visible in the inadequate light. A slight creaking seemed to call from every corner and the whole place felt dead to her.

Myrgen squinted through the darkness. "You'd better let me lead. I'm not sure if the corridors are intact or not." He took the lantern from her. "Take my hand." She did so and they walked through the ashy corridors of the old chapel. They passed through a larger room and Catriona pointed to a doorway with fallen timbers and stonework.

Catriona said, "That's the doorway across from where Alan was held."

Myrgen lifted the lantern. "Yes. What's that?" He walked over to the doorway where a pile of white cloth lay caught under a bunch of boards. Myrgen picked it up and looked at it closely under the lantern glow. It was stiff and black, but not from the charred boards and ash, and he sniffed it to find out what it was. He handed it to Catriona and she, too, sniffed it. It was blood, and the fabric was a fine silk.

"This is Tanglwyst's. I brought it back from Yndia for her several years ago. I think that's blood on the cuff." He looked out the boards, searching for something. "I don't see any more blood and she wasn't hurt last time I saw her."

Catriona took a deep breath. "I'm afraid she is now."

He looked at her, the question blatant on his face. He looked at the chemise. "Did you do this to her?"

"No. She wasn't wearing that when I got her out of here."

He stood a little taller, as if bracing himself. "Did you kill her?"

Catriona swallowed and she saw him tense in fear of her answer. "No, but I was not kind. I saw what she did and why she did it. She betrayed my trust, and endangered my child. I don't take kindly to that." She was suddenly very scared that he would walk away from her and she closed her eyes in case that happened. She was very ashamed of her actions at that moment, standing here in front of a man who had lost everything he cared about in a single afternoon.

"After what she's done to you, not killing her *was* kind."

Catriona opened her eyes, relieved. Myrgen looked back at the embroidered garment of silk and dumped it into the ground. Myrgen sighed and began walking again, taking Catriona's hand as he passed it. "Do you know much about Tanglwyst's history?" Catriona shook her head when he looked over his shoulder at her. He proceeded on through the broken and charred remains of beams and pews.

"Tanglwyst's first husband was a real spawn of the devil. He used to go to taverns and bring home drinking companions to watch him rape her. Before long, her mind snapped. She began thinking her only worth was between her legs, and became rather unstable in any situation where violence was involved. I knew there were problems when she sought a device made which would stop her from ever being raped again. It was a knife in a special sheath. The knife was small, but would still flay any unwanted... penetration."

"I've heard about that device. I thought it was a falsehood because the mechanics of the knife would do as much damage to her as to him, wouldn't it?"

"Trust me, it's real, and the rumors of its existence are enough of a deterrent in and of themselves, but I'm assured she has the muscle control to work the device properly without hurting herself."

"I'm impressed." Suddenly, Catriona understood why Nicolai was so enamored with Tanglwyst. Nicolai equated sex with love, and someone with that kind of ability would be the purest love he could find.

Myrgen stopped for a moment and then asked, "What did you mean back there, when you said the woman I loved had betrayed us both? I mean, I know what she did to me, but what did she do to you?"

"She was willing to let my son die for her ambition."

"Yes, but, she's never *betrayed* you. You never trusted her in the first place. That was something I did." He started to walk again but Catriona put her hand on his arm.

"Myrgen, I'm sorry. You don't deserve what you've received."

Myrgen exhaled and looked down at his coat. "Yes I do..." He undid the right cuff of his shirt and pulled a small necklace and his sister's favor from his sleeve. He turned the favor over in the lamplight, then dropped it beside the charred remains of a votive candle, wiping the soot from his hand on his breeches. He held up the necklace Anika had given Alan. "Here. You can make sure he gets this back."

"I think I would rather you kept it for a while. It would be more appropriate if *you* gave it back."

He looked at her, worry and skepticism governing his words. "I think you're assuming I'll see him again, and that he'll let me talk to him."

"The way to find balance is to seek out those things that are a weight and relieve them." She nodded to the necklace. "That is your burden to bear. Not mine."

Myrgen looked at the necklace again, then reached up and put it on. "Just until I can return it."

He took Catriona's hand again and they left the room. Catriona found herself strangely touched by Myrgen's pain. He seemed to truly be a decent person, and she wanted to help him get through this somehow. Myrgen continued to lead, picking his way through his thoughts rather like they were picking their way through the wreckage of the church. He shook his head and Catriona caught the gesture. "What is it?"

Myrgen glanced over his shoulder and asked, "How good are you at reading people's thoughts?"

Catriona cocked her head at him. "Why do you ask?"

"Well, because I wanted to see if I could have any secrets from you."

Catriona stopped and Myrgen turned to look at her, still holding her hand. "What are you thinking, Myrgen?"

"Do you know the concept of Karma?"

Catriona nodded. "Quite familiar."

"I have a rather extensive library on the subject, most of it from my time in Yndia teaching a young prince how to speak Mervol. I was just going over the concepts behind it."

"Here? In the husk of an ancient royal Augustinian church?" She smiled. "What acrobatics is your mind performing to have put those two things together?"

Myrgen sighed. "I've been alone often in my life. Much of that was my choice. My sister was taken away to a convent to be educated because we became too close for family comfort, and that dog was the only companion I had. I had a lover here in Patras which produced a son, who was killed in the St. Michael's Day Massacre. His mother committed suicide after we buried him. I never married her. I didn't want to," he coughed a mirthless laugh, "*limit* my opportunities. It was stupid pride which kept me from her side. By the time I was wise enough to propose, she decided I was right and refused me, several times, although she did stay with me. I have managed to live my life without regretting or second guessing my decisions before. Stayed practical, reserved, untouchable. I even managed to hide my secret obsession with Elizabeth, mostly."

He turned to look more fully into her eyes in the flickering candlelight. "But you have turned all that on its head. Since the moment I involved you, my life has gone completely out of my control. One moment, I'm in the arms of a woman I've loved for two years, acting like newlyweds. The next moment, I'm brushing blue vomit off my best coat in the bowels of the palatial prison. I've saved the king I tried to murder and been saved by the assassin I hired to kill him. And all this has opened my eyes in a way nothing less extreme could have possibly done. I find myself capable of seeing and doing things I never could have before."

Catriona smiled at his new-found freedom. "Like what?"

He handed her the lantern, saying "Here, hold this." She took it and suddenly, he seemed to touch a thousand centers of pleasure in a single movement so fluid, she was encompassed in it before she knew it was happening. He placed a hand behind her head, stroking the nape of her neck as he slipped into the unbound beauty of her ebony hair. His other hand went to the small of her back, slipping over uncorsetted flesh, and he kissed her. Yet to say he kissed her is akin to comparing the sun to a candle glow. Her skin tingled, her fingers trembled, her thighs seemed to burst into flame. She could feel every heartbeat, every breath, every ounce of vitae in her being, and, more importantly, she felt him embrace her very soul with his kiss. He pulled her closer, his hand flowing around her to encircle her waist with his arm. The feel of his lips sent shocks through her and she dropped the lantern.

He ended the kiss and looked at her. "Like that."

She blinked. "Oh..."

"You dropped the lantern."

"Did I? I didn't notice…"

Myrgen released her and picked up the lantern, which, remarkably, had dropped straight down and not gone out. "I'll take that as a compliment." He took her hand again and Catriona fought to get herself under control, shaking off the experience for the time being. The two continued on a bit farther until they got to the entryway to the old chapel. It emptied out on the west side of the palace grounds, into the woods. Myrgen looked around quickly, then led Catriona out of the underground passage. Catriona whistled for her horse and it came out of the woods near the kitchen to her a few minutes later. Myrgen looked around. "Only one horse?"

"For now." She opened the saddlebag and pulled out a cloak, which she handed to him.

Myrgen looked her over. "What about you?"

"We can't both wear cloaks and ride the same horse. Too bulky."

"Will you be warm enough?"

Catriona smiled and looked over at Myrgen, amused at his nervousness, especially after what he did to her in the old chapel. "Well, I figured you'd be a gentleman and share your cloak with me."

Myrgen realized how this was sounding and smiled a sultry smile back, arching an eyebrow. "If we share a cloak, what makes you think I'll be a gentleman?"

"Well, I can hope." She looked at the palace as Myrgen mounted the horse and then smiled and mounted the horse in front of Myrgen.

Myrgen noticed her smile. "What?"

"Dominic. He just nodded to me from the window up there."

Myrgen looked up at the windows but saw no one. He looked at her again. "Is he alerting the guard?"

"No. He just wanted to make sure he knew when to look the other way." She kicked the sides of the horse. The two took off toward the woods and spring where she and Michael had parted company, then turned towards the back roads to Rouen.

***Chapter Forty-one:***
***"Hate stirreth up strifes but love covereth all sins."***
*~ Proverbs 10:12*

Nicolai leaned against the shadowy wall and watched Catriona's ship bounce in the small waves of the docks. A storm had sprung up in the last hour and he was lucky to find shelter in a doorway in a slender alley. The wind was threatening to make it a vicious one, delaying all seafaring until it passed. This was probably the last great storm of the pre-season and he felt it fitting that it would wash away the filth of the seas along with the blood he planned to spill.

He heard horses arrive and saw Catriona on a horse with another man with a scarf across his nose and mouth. She talked to a man with an eye patch, who was riding alongside a woman holding a child, an oilcloth protecting both from the outpour of the skies. Catriona was shouting over the storm, directing them somewhere and the man with her said something to her. She listened over her shoulder to him and nodded, dismounting out from under the cloak they were sharing. He moved forward on the saddle and wheeled the horse around to talk to her when he noticed some other riders coming up. He leaned down and tapped her shoulder, then nodded to the new arrivals. She looked over her shoulder at them, then patted the horse, nodding to his comment. He put the hood up on his cloak and nudged the horse down the street, guiding the family to another area of the docks. Catriona stood in the street, stepping forward to impede the pursuit of her escort.

Alexander pulled up rein before her, his horse splashing her in the puddles forming in the street. The other two riders, men Nicolai recognized as Alexander's guards, pulled up at a respectful distance, giving His Majesty a modicum of privacy while still staying within range to protect him. Alexander dismounted and escorted her away from the horses and guards. Nicolai could hear them now, despite having his senses blocked by the weather and dulled from the ale he was sipping from a water skin to keep warm.

"I'm glad I caught you before you set sail." Alexander put his hand on hers.

She looked down at their hands and smiled. "So am I. I was wondering if you would come."

"I can't stay away from you. You know that. After our last night, well," he looked into her eyes again, "I just can't stand aside anymore. I love you. I want you to stay and be my queen."

"Alex..." She let her eyes meet his and Nicolai was disgusted to see the emotion they shared in that look. She hadn't looked at him like that since she disappeared and he couldn't tolerate it anymore.

He stepped out of the shadows, shoving the cork back into his water skin. "Don't you think it's time you found an *unmarried* woman to seduce, *Your Majesty?*"

The two looked up, startled. Catriona recovered first. "Nicolai. What are you doing here?"

"I just wanted to see my wife off." His balance was not completely cooperating and he felt his speech slurring just a bit, but he knew he could kill her. He would too, for what she had done to his Tanglwyst.

The guards saw the threat and called out, "Your Majesty!" They started to dismount and Nicolai took his cue as time to attack. He drew his blades and ran at Catriona. She dodged the blades and Alexander said, "Get to the ship!" She was unarmed, her blades undoubtedly in her cabin. If he could prevent her from getting to them, she was his. Nicolai circled around her, putting himself between her and the ship. The guards ran up and assembled next to the king. He said, "Protect her."

The guards placed themselves between Nicolai and his quarry but he was unconcerned. He had taught these whelps and had absolutely no fear he could defeat them both, drunk of his ass and half-asleep in a thunderstorm. They charged him and he disarmed the first one with a slice to the upper arm, then a back slash to his chest. He was far quicker when he wanted something than they were scared. The other guard engaged him and got off a couple passes when Alexander decided to join, drawing his own sword. Catriona shouted, "No!"

"Get back, Catriona," Alexander commanded, his focus on Nicolai. She looked around and a call from her crewmen caught her attention. She tried to dodge past Nicolai and Alexander but he kept her in place, pinning her behind her defender.

Alexander got a very determined look on his face. "You can't win here, Nicolai. Walk away. If you attack her, I'll kill you myself."

"You don't have the stones to take a life, Alexander. All you do is save them."

"You're wrong, Nicolai. I'm quite capable of taking a life. Even one as pathetic as yours."

"Pathetic? *Pathetic,* am I?" Nicolai swung his arms wide. "I'm the one who actually married her. I'm the one she loved for all those years. I understand she couldn't even be with you because of me. And I wasn't even *alive* to her. You couldn't even compete with a *dead man*, Alexander!"

"I think I can now." He lunged at Nicolai and the guard did likewise. Nicolai blocked both attacks and took out the guard with a stomach wound. Alexander got a slash on his shoulder but his doublet took the brunt of it. Alexander barely dodged the swipe that came at his chest, and he and Nicolai threw a few passes at each other, both trying not to circle too much. Nicolai saw Catriona casting about, trying to figure out how to get past him and he edged them both over so that they were trapped with no place to go. Alexander glanced around and saw something over Nicolai's shoulder and Nicolai took the chance and stabbed for him. It was enough and he cut Alexander's leg.

The king crumpled before Nicolai and he raised his sword to finish the man off when Nicolai was slammed from the side and knocked to the ground. He looked up and saw Myrgen on the horse Catriona had rode in on standing between him and Alexander, the scarf pulled down from his face. A streak of black flashed across his vision and he saw Catriona running for the ship, calling for her swords through the din of the rain on cobblestones and the occasional clap of thunder. Nicolai kicked up to his feet, narrowly escaping Myrgen's attempt to have the horse step on him. Myrgen dismounted and dropped next to the king but Alexander yelled, "Protect her, damn it!"

Nicolai ran after her but Myrgen slapped the horse's rump and it charged right before Nicolai. He dodged and over estimated the amount of space he had and slipped on the wet planks. He fell into the water off the edge of the dock.

Underwater, he sheathed his swords quickly while he oriented himself, then looked around under the filthy water. If he tried to come back up right there, Alexander would surely run him through when he broke the surface. He knew what he had to do.

He swam underwater until he saw the belly of the *Enigma.*

He moved to the side away from the docks and emerged quietly from the muck. There was a starboard ladder here for manning the dinghies and he grabbed it and started climbing. The crew's attention would be on the injured king and he could catch her by surprise. Maybe he would wait in her cabin and take her one last time before he killed her. He crested the deck and looked carefully at the ship's population. The whole crew seemed to be off the ship, scouring the area for him and failing to find him in the torrential rain. The weather had churned the sand and trash from the docks and harbor, making the water opaque and even their most sharp-eyed crewman could not see through it. Catriona stood at the top of the gangplank, swords drawn and watchful, drops of sky water bouncing off her shoulders and head, precipitation running off her long coat's hem and cuffs. He climbed onto the ship and quietly drew his steel. This was going to be easier than he thought.

He stepped up behind her and thrust his sword at her back. A swirl of blackness and his blow was blocked, his dagger in his off hand flying overboard onto the dock, calling the crew's attention. He looked down at his hand, surprised she was able to stop him. She looked him in the eye, circling around him, her weapons hanging relaxed at her side. "Nicolai, don't be a fool. You can't beat me, not on my own ship. I knew the second you touched her. Go back to Tanglwyst. Take the gift I have given you and go."

"Given me? I've had to take everything back that you took from me. You beat her, you bitch. You'll pay for that."

"And what about what she did to our son?"

"*Your son!* I have no way of knowing whether that child is even mine. You could have been whoring around for years before you actually got pregnant. That spawn is as likely to belong to Giovanni as to me!" He lunged at her and she knocked his blade aside. Her visage became cold and cruel, the evil that dwelled inside her performing magic and witchery finally coming to bear as a pale glow around her eyes. The adrenaline pumping through him was clearing his head of the effects of the ale, but he didn't feel any more stable looking into those eyes.

There was a flash of steel in a lightening strike offshore and he felt a slap on his right cheek, sending his head spinning. He stumbled back and suddenly, his left sleeve fell from his shoulder. He looked and blood was seeping down from the wound she had just placed there. He looked back at her and with a swish, the point of her sword was an inch from his eye. She held the blade steady there and he realized she was right. She could take him apart. The deck felt muddy to him, like the ship itself was slowing him down, putting weights on his ankles. His breathing came harder and he started to feel dizzy. He raised his hands in defeat and dropped his sword.

She circled him around and backed him towards the gangplank. "Leave, Nicolai. Don't seek me out and don't bother me again. Just take Tanglwyst and go. I'll leave here and we'll be dead to each other again."

Nicolai didn't understand. He looked at her. "What about him?" He nodded towards Alexander, who was being helped to his feet by Myrgen and Octavius, her First Mate.

"Don't you worry about him. I'll deal with that. Just go."

He looked around and then nodded. "I see. If you marry him, you'll never sail again. You won't be able to. If you're his subject, then he can command you to stay. And you never have been one to do as you're told." He looked at her and realized just how much he had kept her when they were together. He remembered her as a young woman, alive and fluid like the sea. She took to life on the ship like it was her natural calling. She could breathe life into dead sails, even back then. The glow in her eyes faded and the weights on his ankles disappeared. Her connection to this ship was more than just as a Captain. To take her from this would mean her death, and even then, were she to be put to rest at sea, the sea would probably revive her and give her back. For all he knew, this had already happened.

She was right again. She was no threat to him and Tanglwyst. He just needed to figure out where they would live, but she was indeed dead to him now. And him to her. He looked at her and nodded, tightening his lips against saying anything else. She saw his change and relaxed her grip on the sword. He thought he saw a glimmer of shine in her eyes, the beginnings of tears and he knew she did still love him, at least a little. He realized he was feeling them too and decided to leave before his own tears revealed that last vestige of emotional memory. At least they both could hide them in the rain. "Good bye, Catriona."

\* \* \*

Catriona watched him leave her ship and her life. Her swords lowered slowly to rest forgotten by her side. He had pegged it precisely. She couldn't marry Alexander, not now, not ever. She would lose her freedom, her ship, her crew, her life if she left the sea and she was far too selfish to do that. The tears she was keeping at bay betrayed her loss and she closed her eyes against the pain of her heart breaking. She was not a subject of Mervolingia, but when Alexander had taken the Power of Sovereignty, even she had been tempted to bend her knee to him. She doubted he would ever take advantage of that power with her, but just for him to have it was too much to bear.

She sheathed her blades as the rain started to let up and stepped off the ship to try and help Alexander on board. He had a physician's kit here from his last visit and she knew he would heal quickly if he got some rest. He always had. The crew saw the mercy she had shown Nicolai and parted to let him go. Every step felt painful as she realized she was going to have to break Alexander's heart and she had no idea how to do it. One night in his arms would break her will and she would be saying yes before she could stop herself. A lifetime of imprisonment, away from her home and her ship. She just couldn't do it.

She looked at Nicolai and felt something was wrong. She couldn't just leave it like this. He had been too important. She took in a breath and shouted, "Nicolai!"

He turned and looked at her, stopping in the street.

She ran down the gangplank, letting her heart guide her to do the right thing. He was still going to be gone, but she wanted to actually say goodbye. As she neared him, she caught a movement out of the shadows near one of the buildings bearing witness to the battle. The shadow was tall and bald, dark eyes piercing the drizzling rain. He puffed and her eyes widened in horror as she watched the dart fly through the air to embed itself in Nicolai's neck. His hand went to his neck and he pulled it from his flesh and looked at it before his eyes rolled up into his head. He fell to the ground.

"Nicolai!" Her scream called the attention of every one in the area as she ran towards him. Suddenly, the ground beneath her feet turned to sand and she tripped, falling to the ground a few feet away from his body.

His mouth started foaming blood and his body convulsed.

She screamed something, getting to her knees, and then her crew was on her as she reached out to him. "Captain, no!" Octavius grabbed her waist from behind. "He's been poisoned! If you touch him, you'll die too."

"No! I can save him! I can save him!" She pulled at Octavius' arms but he was strong and refused to let her go and he was joined on all sides by several other crewmen. She raged against them all, clawing and screaming at them to let her go as she watched Nicolai twitch violently, like he was being pulled behind a great horse of uneven terrain. Bones snapped from the spasms, then became still. Alexander limped in a run over to her, and knelt before her, hands on her shoulders. "Catriona! Stop! He's gone. He's gone."

Her face was contorted in anguish and she went limp and dropped to the ground at Alexander's feet, her crew easing her down. He looked up at the crew. "Did anyone see who did this?" He looked around at each man but they all shook their heads, being too caught up in the scene to pay attention to the other audience members.

She put her hands on her face and shook her head. Alexander took her in his arms and she cried into his shoulder, her body wracking with pain. She pounded on his chest, looking over at her husband's body. The dart was still in his hand and the blood from his body was starting to stain the stones of the street. Alexander turned and looked at the body, then looked up at the crewmen standing around them.

"We need to get her on board. Will you see to it, Octavius?"

Octavius nodded. "Of course. Come on, Captain."

Catriona was too numb to protest.

* * *

Myrgen stepped over to the processional but stopped when Alexander called to him. "We need to burn the body."

Myrgen looked at Nicolai's broken form lying in the mud. "Why?"

"The body's been poisoned. If it comes in contact with the water or soil, or if someone touches his blood, it could claim them too. How many others need to die?" He looked around at the alleyways bordering the street. "I'm going to see if I can find some trace of the monster that did this."

Myrgen nodded. "Be careful. That dart was probably meant for you."

"Then let's hope his Patron Saint is ready to claim him. I'll bring the entire power of my position to bear to destroy him for the pain he has caused her."

Myrgen went to one of Catriona's crewmembers. "Excuse me, can you help me find a blanket to wrap the body? We need to get it off the street."

"Aye." The rugged sea dog climbed the gangplank with practiced ease, to even jostling the captain and her crew as he passed them. He returned moments later with a wool blanket. "Thayse shood 'andle ait."

Myrgen nodded thanks to whatever the man had said and walked over to the body. A dog had snuck up to the body and was licking the foam from Nicolai's face as they turned. Myrgen kicked at the dog but it was too late. The dog fell to fits, bones cracking as it seized and twitched. In a few seconds, it too was a miserable heap of flesh.

"*Bloody Saints and Martyrs.* No wonder he told me to burn it."

The sea dog put his hand on Myrgen. "Ye cain't bairn ait, lad. Thet main wus Laitayen."

Myrgen's brow furrowed. "What? I don't understand…"

The sea dog rolled his eyes and shook his head. "Thet main." He pointed to the body. "Hey wus Laitayen. Hey cain't haive hais baidy demmejed. Hail wailk th' Airth in Laimbow."

"What? Did you say 'limbo'?"

"Aye, a ghaist."

"Ghost?"

"Aye."

Myrgen looked at the body. "You mean, if we burn the body, he'll become a ghost?"

"Aye."

Myrgen looked at the darkened sky which was threatening to down pour again. The way the dog went down, he was afraid to allow the rain to put any of the body's waste into the water or ground. He looked at his companion. "Sir, I'm…"

"Thessius."

"Huh?"

"Meh naime ais Thessius."

"Right. I'm sorry, Thessius, but you saw what happened to that dog just now. If that gets into the water, or a child touches the ground where his body bled or anything, well, I think you see what I mean."

Thessius looked at the dog, then at the windows around him, aglow with candlelight as people were putting their families to bed for the night. Few would venture forth with a severe storm coming through. He looked back at Myrgen and nodded.

Myrgen looked at his hands for any cuts or scrapes, then remembered the wounds from his captivity. He knew they weren't all healed. He looked around but saw nothing to lift and roll the bodies. He put the blanket down on the street and used his boot to roll Nicolai's body onto it. Thessius went over and did likewise with the dog, carefully dragging it with his toe. Once on the blanket, Myrgen and Thessius picked up the edges and hauled it out of town. Myrgen had noticed a sheltered fire pit just outside of town, probably from a nomadic merchant caravan which had left that morning. He and Thessius carried the bodies to that pit, then Myrgen fetched some wood from a pile covered by a oil cloth tarp. He knew from Tanglwyst's dealings that these caravans would get to the city's edge, then send in the merchants while the animals and supply wagons waited outside town. They would use the wood in places like this, then chop wood for the next caravan so they wouldn't have to wait to start a fire. It was this custom which served them now.

Myrgen covered the woodpile after he got a few logs, then brought them over to the pit. Although the wood and fire pit were dry, the blanket and the bodies were soaked and he doubted they could get a light. He looked around but saw nothing to help him. "Hey, Thessius, what are the chances you have some lamp oil on you?"

Thessius cocked an eyebrow and shook his head. "Aye ken gait saime froom th' shaip."

Myrgen nodded. "I see." He had no idea what the man had said but it sounded like an offer of some kind and he hoped his reply was at least somewhat on target.

Thessius nodded and ran back into town. Myrgen waited and watched to make sure nothing disturbed the bodies, making more.

* * *

Duncan McVryce watched the scene from the doorway where he had hidden after sending out the dart. For a man over six feet tall, he was able to hide quite well. The medallion on his neck allowed him to disappear, taking him instantly to a few safe destinations to which it was keyed. It produced a flash of light when the effect was accomplished so he made sure to do so out of sight if possible. When one did the sort of work Duncan did, for the people he did, one needed to know how to be discrete, for the jobs as well as the follow-up. He had watched the King closely from the moment he arrived in Rouen.

The king was coming his way and he stepped out of the shadows long enough for the man to see him and direct him to a different alleyway. A moment later, he stepped out of a shadow in a nearby alley with no witnesses and the king came around the corner.

Alexander reached into his doublet and produced a velvet bag heavy with coin. He tossed it to Duncan who recognized the distinctive sound of gold, not silver, in the pouch. "Well done. I am in your debt."

Duncan held up the bag. "I'm pretty sure this should cover it." He put the bag in his belt pouch. "I'm glad you were willing to settle your brother's debt." He produced the Writ of Destruction.

Alexander looked at it as Duncan pulled a sulfur stick from the pouch and struck it, catching it aflame. He put the flame to the paper, destroying the Writ. "That wasn't my brother who wrote that."

Duncan arched an eyebrow. "You work fast."

"Luckily, so do you." He looked towards the edge of town where he could see for just a moment Myrgen and Thessius dragging the bodies to the campsite out there.

"I wasn't certain you still wanted the Writ carried out, Your Majesty. You gestured for me to stay my hand when he was on the ship."

"Luckily you likewise saw my gesture for you to go ahead with your task. I didn't need him interfering in the future." Alexander looked back at Duncan. "I was worried for a moment you didn't."

"I do my King's will, regardless of the reason." Duncan tiled his head and gestured to the edge of town. "So, tell me, Nicolai was Latian, wasn't he? Don't they believe they'll walk the earth forever if their body is damaged after death?"

"Oh yes," Alexander said, a dark smile crossing his features. "With any luck, he'll be trapped forever, watching me make love to his wife like he never could." He looked at the street and started to leave.

"Aren't you worried she'll know it was you? They say her powers of observation are legendary."

Alexander looked back at him. "No. She'll never see through me. However, that does remind me. I may have more work for you should one particular pest decide to be stupid and let me know he has information about this deed. I'll let you know if that becomes apparent" He stepped out of the alley as Duncan stepped further in and disappeared into the stormy night.

---

*"The highway of the upright is to depart from evil, that he keepeth his way preserveth his soul."*
*~ Proverbs 16:17*

If you have enjoyed *Thine Enemy's Eyes*, don't miss the next exciting chapter in the Souls of the Saintlands series, *An Unpolished Gem*.

Coming soon from the mind of Tonya Adolfson. Turn the page for an excerpt!

# *An Unpolished Gem*

*A gem cannot be polished without friction, nor a man perfected without trials.*
*~Chinese Proverb*

## Chapter One:
### *Fail to steal the chicken while it ate up your bait grain.*
### *~Chinese Saying*

"Forgive me, Father, for I have sinned. I killed a man today."

The Archbishop Alonzo de Patrone acknowledged the man on one knee before him, his covered head bowed in respect, and smiled. Alonzo had been listening to confessions personally since he had been given the Archbishopric of Patras ten years ago and was the secret leader of the Patrasian Underground, the network through which unsavory types got their assignments. As the confessor of every thief, cutthroat and con artist in the capital city, he was kept well-informed of who was the best candidate for which assignment. The man before him was one of his favorites, evidenced by the fact that he was allowed a face to face confession instead of the usual screened box ones everyone else received.

"Then Writ has been carried out?"

"Yes, Your Excellency."

"Good. There's someone who wishes to speak to you then. Rise, my son."

Alonzo rose from his receiving chair, a beautiful carved creature with a high back and wide seat. The Archbishop had gotten large before he took this post, needing this heavy oak chair to support his massive weight. However, the bishops underneath him had felt he needed exercise to keep him sharp and around for a while, so they had started him on a regimen of diet and activity. At first, he had protested of course, but then he started feeling the effects in increased stamina, and now, he was far more fit than he had been even in his youth. The only drawback to this was the excess flesh from his over three hundred pound body, which kept a bit of bulk to his body in sagging bags now that he was half that weight. His furniture had never been replaced, at his request, to remind him of his change in life.

The loose folds of his cassock hid this bulk nicely and the mitre on his head added height to counter the weight. The white and red he wore that day was complemented by gold filigree embroidery in ancient crosses all over the fabric. Alonzo had decided to grow a beard to cover the excess flesh of his chins and after the weight was gone, had decided he was too used to the look to get rid of it now. He worried he was slowly working his way through the entire list of deadly sins, with Pride, Sloth and Gluttony already covered.

Alonzo stepped before a large gold mirror that hung over a basin of matching design set into a mahogany cabinet. He took an ewer from the cabinet top and blessed the water before pouring it into the basin. As he did so, the mirror's surface wavered like the surface of the water in the basin and when he stopped pouring, it took a moment for the surface to settle into a flat reflection again, but when it had, it showed not the Archbishop's reflection, but that of a small but venerable man.

"Yes, Alonzo. What news have you?"

"I have the one I spoke of, Your Holiness. Duncan McVryce."

The Pope nodded and Bishop Alonzo stepped aside to permit the other man to be seen. Duncan pushed back his hood and allowed himself to be seen by the dignified man who was Heaven's Representative on Earth. Duncan was very tall, his head shaved completely bald with a black patch of hair framing his mouth. Hazel eyes were constantly shifting colors, like shadows were chasing the bright points away from the light. He bowed his head in deference, his voice crisp and hiding a cheerful lilt behind a somber expression. "I understand you asked for me, Your Holiness."

"Yes. Bishop Alonzo has stated you might be interested in a particular assignment, one that involves great danger. I need you to rescue a lady in distress."

"I'm much better at putting ladies *in* distress, Your Holiness."

"Well, I see. However, Bishop Alonzo insisted you would be more inclined to this task than the other task I needed accomplished."

"Perhaps if you offered me both, I could decide for myself."

"Very well. The first task is to stop the King of Mervolingia from getting engaged to a Catriona Moriarity. It should be fairly simple. I understand the woman is married."

"Moriarity? I'm afraid that man is dead. Killed earlier today in a street fight with the King."

"Oh. I see. Your sovereign is quite insistent about securing this woman."

"It appears so. What is the other job?"

"To rescue the Honorable Lady Tanglwyst de Holloway and get her safely here to the Papal City where she will be under my protection."

Duncan grew still. "You were right, Your Holiness. I shall indeed take the second job and make it my priority."

"Good. It is mine as well. The other task can be handled later, possibly by someone else. This one, I was assured, was best left to your abilities."

"It will not be a problem. Where is she being held?"

"Under house arrest, at her Patras estate."

"Thank you, Your Holiness. It will be done according to Heaven's Will."

"Saints and angels protect you, my son."

Duncan stepped away from the mirror and it went back to reflecting the Archbishop's visage. "Will this be a problem for you, my son?"

Duncan shook his head. "I serve Heaven first, then the Crown of Mervolingia, according to the Oath of Fealty I swore. Every citizen knows this is the case."

Alonzo nodded. "I'm satisfied this will work out according to Heaven's will then." He put his hand upon Duncan's shoulder and glanced at the centuries old amulet on his neck. It was one of only three remaining from a holy war that resulted in the purging of fae and arcane practice from the Saintlands. "You are in Heaven's hands."

\* \* \*

Tanglwyst sat in her study, overlooking the alleyway where her husband was murdered, twirling her long, auburn hair. Her injuries from the catacombs are gone now, thanks to the healing herbs the Prince gave her, but the brutal loss of her best friend and Queen, Elizabeth, was overwhelming. For all his kindness, Alexander apparently had a vicious side to him as well. He had stabbed her through the stomach and then had her dragged away to be impaled and hung to finish dying outside the city. Tanglwyst had seen a peasant girl wearing the Queen's gown walk past her window an hour ago, the blood and rips barely washed away, the final indignity for Tanglwyst's best friend. *By the Saints, I hope there are no necrophiliacs in Patras. That would be Alexander's ultimate victory.* She found her ability to cry no longer accompanied her, and now she simply sat and watched the world mock her in the streets with its lively step and music of the marketplace.

She shifted on the window seat, the stained glass figures of the window casting blue and orange shimmers on the small wrinkles near her eyes. The bruises on her face and body from the fight with Catriona Moriarity had faded within the day and she faced her imprisonment the way she faced all her other challenges: With elegance and opulence. She was dressed in a long robe of Mandian design, the brocade several shades of green to complement her envy colored eyes. Her hair was unbound, a luxury she reveled in since she wasn't allowed out of the house. Usually, her hair was bound in several different braids, some hers, some from a young woman down on her luck who sold her hair for just such an occasion. Small shoes and stockings kept her feet comfortable and she had almost neglected the fire in the fireplace chasing away what discomfort did get in. She wondered where Nicolai was and why he had not yet come to rescue her.

She was under house arrest until the new King returned, and Elizabeth's guilt in the murder of Charles, and Myrgen's inexplicable escape from prison left only her with whom to be dealt. The wait was as bad as the news of Elizabeth's death. It had only been by intervention of her grandfather Pope Gregory that she was not swinging from a crow's cage at that moment. Alexander's disappearance after Myrgen's escape was the final stroke of luck but she didn't expect to survive his return. Moreover, she doubted Myrgen would survive his absence. She let out a sigh that threatened to call the tears back after all.

A small sound at the door drew her attention and she slowly turned her mournful gaze at whatever servant was bringing her whatever meal. She blinked and straightened when she saw the tall, bald man standing in the doorway, feet spread and gloved hands balled into fists. His forearms were on the doorjamb and his head lowered, but he raised his eyes to meet hers.

"Tangl."

Tanglwyst stood. "Duncan?" She saw the blood dripping from his gloves and the handle of his rapier.

"I think it would be wise for us to go now." His tone of voice left no discussion points available.

Tanglwyst stood up as Duncan looked over his shoulder to make sure no one had discovered the bodies. She rushed into her bedroom and untied her robe.

"Darlin' I don't think now's the time for that." She looked up and saw Duncan glancing about the room he had frequented so often in the past few months.

Tanglwyst tossed her robe onto the floor and pulled on a shirt over her substantial uncorsetted chest. "We're going to be running, yes?"

Duncan glanced over his shoulder, then back to the better view. "Oh, quite a bit."

"I can't do that dressed like a lady."

Duncan pursed his lips and nodded, sheathing his sword and stepping into the room. "Good point." He tilted his head and she turned her back to him and pulled on riding breeches over her rear. He always loved it when she did that, and this was no different. She smiled to herself, reassured again of her attractiveness. She flipped her hair out of her shirt and pulled a doublet from the wardrobe, tossing it onto the bed. She pulled some high boots out of a chest and he blatantly admired her breasts as she bounced into them. By the time she was clothed and ready to leave, she had Duncan more than ready to make her start the process again.

"Come, I have money in a chest here."

Duncan said, "I wouldn't mind exploring that chest."

Tanglwyst smiled at him and kissed him on her way by. "You get me out of here, and I have every intention of letting you do just that."

"Your horse awaits, my lady."

* * *

Tanglwyst grabbed the chest with the money in it and handed it to Duncan, who recovered his senses and started towards the stairs and the numerous exits the main floor offered. As they got to the bottom of the stairs, the front door opened and two more guards from the grounds entered the room. They saw the bloody bodies on the floor and drew steel on Duncan. Duncan handed the chest to Tanglwyst and drew steel as well, putting himself between the guards and his lady. "Gentlemen, your comrades have already fallen before my blade. Let us be on our way, and you'll live to tell the tale."

The men at the door charged Duncan and he drew a breath and took them on. A parry with the right sword pushed the second attacker away while his main gauche stopped the first guard's blade from finding purchase in his flesh. Duncan shoved them into each other, pushing them back a bit. The opening allowed him to move to a better footing, and caused them to circle to the unsteady footing of their fellow guardsmen's blood pool. He feigned a move and as hoped, one of the men slipped a tiny bit. Duncan plunged his sword through the guard instantly, spraying the other guard with his partner's vitae.

The other guard shook his head and dodged to the side as Duncan spun his partner off his sword. The other guard saw Duncan's mistake at the same time Duncan did, and he, too, took the opportunity. He grabbed Tanglwyst and threw her before him, his sword at her throat.

Duncan saw the blood drip from the guard's chin, his sleeve sullying the woman Duncan loved. Tanglwyst' eyes watched Duncan carefully, and Duncan saw she was not scared. He squinted, his breath low and silent. The guard was breathing heavier, and he seemed to be waiting for Duncan to make his move. Tanglwyst's rescuer watched the man, waiting for the right moment. The guard blinked, his hand on her upper arm and his breathing slowed as he relaxed a bit. Duncan could smell her pheromones exuding from her and the guard was right beside her ear. The guard glanced for a second at the lady's ample bosom and Tanglwyst closed her eyes, and fainted.

Her body suddenly slack, the guard looked down at her, then up just as Duncan's sword pierced him through the eye. He pushed the dead man off his sword and knelt beside the lady. "Angel," he said, his voice a whisper.

Tanglwyst's eyes opened and she winked at her rescuer. "Nice move."

He lifted her to her feet and said, "Were it not dangerous to do so, I would make love to you right now."

"Isn't that precisely why you want to?" She looked out the front door and then toward the kitchen. "Are their horses in back?"

"Yes, in the stables."

"They're using *my* stables for their horses while I'm under house arrest? Bastards." She ran towards the back door and let Duncan take the lead. She grabbed two keys and some papers out of a drawer in the dining room and tucked them into her doublet. Duncan peered out into the garden and saw four more guards by the stables.

He swore. "There's four of them out there. One of them is a lieutenant. I've run across him before."

"How did you do?"

"Well, we're both still alive. I doubt that will happen a second time." He looked back at the front door.

"He's that good?"

"Yes, and there's no wagonload of chickens." He looked at her as she stared at him, eyebrows raised. "Long story. Come on."

The couple crept to the front door again and looked outside. They didn't see anyone in the street in uniform, but it was only a matter of time before the guards on break in the back would be walking the perimeter again. Tanglwyst nodded to the alleyway and took off running. Duncan closed the door behind them and followed. He stopped in the shadows of the alley and watched to see if anyone had noticed their exit yet.

He seemed to find himself in this alley a lot. It was the same alley where he first met this lady, and first realized he loved her. It was the alley where he had held her to keep her from running while his other partners slit her monstrous husband's throat. It was the alley where he had watched her entire mansion being built, where he took his breaks from posing as a worker putting in the carpentry. He planted the roses in her garden out back, each one hand picked by him to complement her hazel eyes and auburn hair.

This was the alley where Guillaume de la Rapier stumbled, cut by his own hands as a ruse to find himself in the lady's bed, under her care. Duncan had watched it all from this alley. He turned to look at Tanglwyst, checking her for damage, then checking himself.

"Where are we going?" She was worried, but excited. Her voice revealed everything to him.

"I don't know yet. I just need to get you out of Patras before the King returns."

Her eyes grew wide. "Am I to be... like Elizabeth?"

He reached over and caught her head in his hand, fingers slipping quickly into her hair. "Not if I can help it, my love." He kissed her, the first of thousands of kisses he planned to give her.

The sound of shouts interrupted them and he took her hand. "This way." They ran through the alleys dodging the shouts of the following guards. Suddenly, Duncan turned a corner and he saw the jande d'arm at the end, entering the alley. They saw the pair and pointed, and Duncan retreated, putting himself between the guards and Tanglwyst. They turned the corner retreating and there, blocking their escape, was Lt. Gomez de Santander drawing his sword and grinning.

"Ah, Duncan McVryce. And with a suspected traitor as well, one trying to escape. And not a chicken in sight."

"I can see one." Duncan's voice was cruel and sharp as his blades, and twice as bloody. He put Tanglwyst behind him, clearly seeing the lieutenant as the real threat but she tapped him on the shoulder.

"Duncan, there are five behind us. What do you want to do?"

Duncan watched four more guards join Gomez at this end of the alley and swallowed. He had one choice to get her out of this alive. He knew he was willing to sacrifice himself for her, but he couldn't warn her, not if he wanted the maneuver to succeed. *Forgive me, my Angel. I have no other way.*

He grabbed Tanglwyst and held her close to him as Gomez seemed to sense something was up. "I love you," he whispered and she looked at him, fright intensifying her eyes so they practically glowed. With a gasp from the woman he loved and a shout from the man he hated, Duncan closed his eyes, fell backwards into the shadow of the building and, in a flash of light and the faint scent of lemons, they were gone.

# About the Author

Tonya Adolfson has been a member of the Society for Creative Anachronism for 22 years and has met thousands of people with very interesting personas. Many of these people have made it into these books and she is grateful to them for enriching her life.

Tonya lives in Boise, Idaho with her husband, two children, two housemates, four cats and two dogs and yet, strangely, the house is actually pretty clean.